The Boy Killer and the Woman Who Talked to a Raven

An Ellen Parker Novel

The Boy Killer and the Woman Who Talked to a Raven

An Ellen Parker Novel

Steven M. Silver

Dedication

Pete Rogers

Acknowledgments and Guidance

There are several electronic devices, software, and techniques referred to in this novel. While there are real-world equivalents, I deliberately did not name actual equipment nor did I describe in useable detail the procedures used. However, having said that, the array of devices and software usable for voice changing is quite large and, in the case of software, both free and adaptable for multiple platforms and is easily found with even a rudimentary search.

Once again, editing assistance came from Thub and Colonel Khayman. Cover by Eric Strehl.

For those interested in a little additional reading on ravens, I would recommend the following:

Heinrich, B. (2009). *Mind of the raven: Investigations and adventures with wolf birds*. HarperCollins: New York City.

Savage, C. (2018, rev. ed.). *Bird brains: The intelligence of crows, ravens, magpies, and jays.* Greystone Books: Vancouver.

Heinrich, B. and Marzluff, J. (1992). Age and mouth color in common ravens. *The Condor, 94:* 549-550.

Pika, S., Sima, M.J., Blum, C.R., Herrmann, E. and Mundry, R. (2020, December 10). Ravens parallel great apes in physical and social cognitive skills. *Scientific Reports*, *10,* 20617. https://doi.org/10.1038/s41598-020-77060-8.

Table of Contents

Chester County, Pennsylvania
Summer, 2018

Chapter 1: Nobody knows

The grave lay ready for several days.

Its small size might have led anyone who saw it to think it was something else; the oblong hole could be for trash or part of a blind for a Pennsylvania hunter, both projects abandoned uncompleted. But no one came across it. The dark woods had few visitors other than wandering deer and even they, tails flashing signals to one another, stayed away, moving off their usual path to avoid the disturbed ground.

One gray morning it was filled, tamped down by the back of a shovel. No one had watched it in the night's darkest hours and no one saw what was laid almost gently in it.

That was not the end of it. Even if no one ever came to the woods again, things would not have ended. Tragedy does not ripple outward. Human hearts are more than the surface of a pond. Tragedy ripped, tore across space as fears of what might have happened spread.

A child was missing and people came to search. Police in gray and black and blue, volunteers in jeans and wool, farmers in coveralls, search dogs and their handlers, and the family of the child, clutching one another like a kind of prayer, they all came. As they always do.

They did not find the grave. It was deep in the trees and brush, a wooded lot bordered on two sides by a farm up for sale going on half a year, on another by a county road only lightly used, and on the final by a Baptist church's parking lot.

But the killer left a sign because, without it, the lesson would have ended too soon.

Two men walked out of the church's side door into the parking lot. In addition to their cars, two others were parked as far from the entrance as possible. From time to time, church members left their cars because of malfunctions or various other reasons. There always seemed to be one or two cars waiting for their owners to take them away.

The Elder saw across the parking lot a flicker of red on the edge of the woods, just on the other side of an old dirt track dividing the pavement from the trees.

"Bob," he said to the man who had come out of the church building with him, "what is that thing?"

The other man, White, somewhere in his Thirties, lawyer, looked, squinting in the sun. He frowned.

"Looks like surveyor tape or something."

"Someone getting ready to sell that parcel?" The Elder, White, middle aged, shook his head as if disappointed. "I hadn't heard it was on the market." He liked the view of the trees.

"Don't think it is," Bob said, walking away, his voice very serious. Unlike the Elder, he kept up on the local county news and the red ribbon – it wasn't surveyor's tape – reminded him of something he had read. The Elder, surprised at Bob's sudden long, quick strides, followed.

Bob crossed the parking lot and walked onto the track, ignoring a small splash as he stepped into a puddle left from yesterday's rain. He stopped and crouched, close to the ribbon. He did not touch it, just looked at it. He glanced over his shoulder.

"I don't think you should come any closer," he said as he stood.

"Bob?"

"There's a child missing," Bob walked back onto the pavement. His words pressed against one another, the push of a desperate hope that what was thought was not real. "Remember three, four months, that other child, the one near…"

"I remember." The Elder stopped, his eyes widening. "They found a ribbon. A red ribbon." Bob said nothing, as if saving his words, maybe as if afraid to say the words, and took his cell phone from his pocket.

The 911 call was routed to the county sheriff's service and the sheriff took the call. She patiently heard Bob out and then calmly ordered a county deputy sheriff to the scene to confirm Bob's report and secure the area. Then she made a call to the FBI agent in charge of the joint task force working on what was already called the red ribbon murders.

The deputy arrived within minutes that seemed to be measured in hours. He parked directly behind the church. He introduced himself as Chester County Sheriff Deputy Michael Bridger and talked briefly to the Elder and Bob, asked them to stay back, and then walked to the ribbon.

As he approached, he saw tire tracks on the old road and carefully avoided stepping on them. He crouched at the ribbon. It wasn't the kind of ribbon used by surveyors. It was thinner, the kind of ribbon that might be used for gift wrapping, so red it almost glowed in the shadow of the trees. He looked up and saw crushed weeds, a trail left by someone who had gone into those trees. He had followed trails in woods and knew how to read the foliage. Bent stems had not had enough time to straighten themselves out. He guessed that the trail might have been made sometime in the night.

"Shit," he said in a voice surprisingly deep but kept low. He thought there might be something in the trees that would not be happy to know an armed law man was coming.

The deputy spoke into the microphone clipped to the front of his shirt and drew his pistol. Then he stepped into the dark of the trees and followed the trail of whoever had gone before.

Bridger was deep in the wood lot when he saw the grave and stopped. He knew what it was. He carefully spoke into his microphone again, forcing his eyes to move around. There was little chance anyone was in the woods with him but it felt like someone, some thing, was, something that did not belong, something darker than the trees' shadows.

"Can you tell how long...?"

The question pressed down on him. He looked at the grave, trying to estimate how long it had been a grave.

"It's fresh," he said. He looked at the sharp edges of the outline made by a shovel that had pressed down on the loose earth. "Maybe early this morning, maybe just a few hours old."

"Deputy Bridger, we have people on the way. Is there a chance...?"

Bridger didn't answer. He holstered his pistol and stepped to the grave. He dropped to his knees and tried to move the earth with his bare hands. He dug as fast as he could, not pausing as his skin turned raw and fingernails tore. He did not stop when he touched the sheet. Horror and fury drove him to grasp the sheet – he felt small shoulders within it – and pull the bundle free of the remaining earth.

He did not try to unwrap the child. Instead, he used what felt like massive strength to rip the sheet from child's face.

Then he saw all there was to see. But he did not stop and tried to resuscitate the cool body, even knowing there was nothing else he could do.

The other officers found him curled against a tree, tears cutting paths through the dirt on his face, his furious strength gone, drained away. The child lay beside him.

3

People came. The Elder kneeled on the pavement beside his church and prayed. Bob joined him when the paramedics, supervised by the county medical examiner, came out with the boy's body.

They stood as the ambulance and the examiner's vehicle left together with lights flashing but sirens silent.

"How could anyone do such a thing?" The Elder's voice was cracked by despair.

"Nobody knows," Bob said. He rubbed his face as if trying to awaken. "God does, I am sure, but, here on Earth, nobody knows."

The red ribbon and the branch it embraced were removed. The path into the woods was photographed, as were the grave and tire tracks. A skilled technician used dental stone and made several casts of the tracks. A search of the area was organized and people slowly walked a pattern, stopping the line every time they found something. Then they did the search line again coming from a right angle to the first. Everything they found was bagged. Yellow tape spread across the brush and trees. It was a long day.

The news people came but were kept out of the woods and off the parking lot. One was a woman; her short, shaggy hair identified her as not one of the television reporters. Though she had a cell phone pressed to the side of her head, her eyes never left the woods, never stopped looking for something.

"I'm here," she said. Her name was Ellen Parker and she worked for the online branch of The Philadelphia Inquirer. She was slim, though her body showed muscles from daily runs and regular training sessions in self-defense; her old blazer hid a pistol holstered over her jean's right rear pocket. A spare, fully loaded clip rested in her front left pocket.

Thus far, Ellen Parker had led an eventful life.

Her eyes, still scanning the trees and the dark shadows among them, were narrowed, something accented by high cheekbones; her White woman's face could look as hard as a determined southern Ohio farmer, people she was descended from. "Bobby's on camera," she said. "They haven't said much more than the prelim I sent in."

She paused, listening, and watched a small group of blue windbreaker-wearing agents form around a taller Black agent, clearly their leader. From FBI press briefings, Ellen recognized the tall man.

"The task force is keeping low profile. I see Special Agent Thomas Brown with a small group. The FBI has... Hold on."

She lowered her phone as people emerged from the woods. Several carried dark blue duffle bags and at least one had a large suitcase. Their leader, a middle-aged woman whose ponytailed blond hair flowed past the collar of her FBI windbreaker, walked over to Agent Brown and spoke to him and the small group. He asked several questions. Several with him wrote in the little notepads that police everywhere seemed to carry. She responded to his questions, her hands making motions in the air in front of her like a pilot. She half turned and drew a line connecting two invisible points somewhere among the trees. Brown nodded and seemed to thank her. She nodded back, picked up her bag, and joined her group.

"Looks like the forensics leader just briefed Brown. No one seems excited but that doesn't say anything about anything. They're cops. They could have found the perp, gold, or a great place to eat, and those people wouldn't give anything away. Yeah, cops. They'll probably have something this afternoon. You want me to catch it or come in...?" She waited and her eyes moved back to studying the silent trees. She nodded, listening to the voice in her ear. "All right, be there in a little less than an hour."

Ellen put her phone away, glanced one more time at the woods, and talked for a moment with Bobby the photographer. Then she walked to her car. Living in Chester County meant she sometimes was tagged to get on the scene of something rather than catching the commuter train into Philly. With her schedule turned upside down, she would catch the next train and the assigned reporter would attend the briefing whenever it went down.

She walked past the television crews, each set up to have their reporter in front of the woods, though still distant from them. Ellen nodded to a few people she recognized from other stories, other tragedies, and tried to avoid eye contact with the on-camera reporters. They broadcast their reports but they had little to say.

They did note that this was the county's third missing child found dead in the past five months.

Someone saw the broadcast and nodded at the mention of the red ribbon. Why the other red ribbons, the other signals, had not been seen was a puzzle. Only three? It felt like proper credit was not being made. A long sigh provided little counter-point to what seemed like aimless chatter on the news program.

The other two children should have been reported, there should have been a search, the other red ribbons should have led everyone to the graves, there should have been recognition of the work. It was important work, not meant to be hidden, but to teach. Filling the graves was not just a series of acts, not just tiny works of art. Yes, all artists wanted recognition. But teachers wanted certain lessons learned.

That was much more important.

Chapter 2: James Hardy's dog

Two days after the dead boy was found, on a Saturday morning, James Hardy killed his dog.

The dog's death was an accident, a word he used to describe many of the events of his life. James lay in bed, exhausted from work but unable to sleep, and his dog jumped up onto the foot of the bed. James' wife stirred in the darkness but did not awaken. The dog, perhaps sensing his master's wakefulness, took several small steps towards the head of the bed.

James sat up, meaning to guide the dog to curling up near his legs. The dog suddenly nipped James' nose; it was not a bite, no blood was drawn, though it carried a sting. James swung his hand, clenched in a fist, and struck the dog just behind its jaw. The dog flinched and dropped.

It was dead. He felt its side and could find no heartbeat, no movement, no breathing.

James sat in the dark, his hand slowly stroking the dog's side – he could think of nothing else to do – while the smell of urine slowly filled the bedroom.

He was still stroking the dog when the alarm sounded. His wife, Carol, awoke and did not understand what had happened until she walked back into the bedroom, a bath towel in her hands. She reached for the light and froze in place as she saw James and the dog.

"He's dead," James said, his normally quiet voice almost a whisper. "I did it. I didn't mean to. I didn't. I just…" No other words came and he slowly slid his hand back and forth on the dog's still ribs. His wife, standing still, said something as she clenched the towel as if was something she needed to strangle, but James did not understand her and did not ask her to repeat it.

Movement returned to both of them, as it had to. It was Saturday and she had a social worker shift at a local hospital. Since James did not have to go to work, he was free – a word that seemed very inappropriate to him.

"Trapped" seemed more exact and if he had thought about it for a moment, might have said it described him for some time. The moment disappeared as he pulled his attention away. He was, then, free.

He was free to bury the dog and so he did.

He wrapped the animal in an old sheet and carried it in his arms to a place in the yard, next to his wife's flower garden. James carefully cut the sod and lifted it free. Then he dug the grave.

He dug without stopping, the digging an activity meaning something in itself, though it did little more than occupy his focus. James stopped when he could just barely step out of the pit. Then he carefully lowered the dog into the grave. He stood over it, searching for words, for thoughts. None came, but memories did, and each seemed to carry a cold pain settling inside him.

James slowly shoveled dirt back over the shroud, holding some back so the sod lay almost flat when he put it back. When he was done, the pain moved to his throat with a claw-like grip. For several heartbeats, he felt an urge to cry.

But he did not.

He threw the bedspread and blanket out, the small, circular stain the last thing the dog left behind. Surprisingly, the sheets were clean and the thought occurred to him that the old dog had tried to make things easier for him. He stood beside the garbage cans and gripped a lid with both hands so hard the plastic twisted. Then he put the lid back on and walked back into the house without looking towards the garden and never noticed that he had not thought of the dog's name while burying him.

James sat in the living room all morning without turning on any lights. It was not until noon he noticed how dirty he was. Mechanically he went up the stairs, stripped, and stood under the shower.

It was as if all his strength had gone into digging the dog's grave and now, he had none, not enough to push back against the steady stream of the shower. Each drop seemed to possess more life than he felt. He stood like that for several minutes.

Then he moved automatically, as if a thrown switch started processes not entirely under his control. Still, his hands had difficulty with the washcloth; there seemed to be something puzzle-like about it, making using it efficiently a small challenge. Twice he dropped the bar of soap. The second time he stared at it for a moment before reaching down for it.

He dressed and did not notice how quickly he left the bedroom. When he returned to the living room, he turned the television on. College sports were on but he had no interest and little ability to understand the games. He keyed the channel selector idly, finally stopping at some discussion show. The words went past him as the people argued about something. He didn't care and their words flowed into a stream of static that emptied into a sea for which he was indifferent.

James was still in his chair when Carol returned. She brought with her some take-out from their favorite Italian restaurant, a tradition when she worked Saturdays. He looked up as she walked in and realized he had not eaten all day. He got up and made a small wave.

"We can eat in the living room," she said as he approached. "If there's something you were in the middle of."

"No, not really." He brought out plates and silverware and arranged them on their small kitchen table. She ladled things out of the white containers as he sat down. She brought a couple of glasses of water and carefully placed them next to the plates. She paused, looking at James, and then sat down.

"How was your day?" He asked, his eyes on his food, pulled down perhaps by gravity.

"Fine, fine," she said. "Yours?" She pressed her lips together after she said it, almost wincing. He shrugged, saying nothing for a moment.

"It was all right." James resumed chewing food he could not taste, his eyes still down, and Carol just stared.

Chapter 3: Leaving

On Monday, Carol's day off, she moved out. She left in the morning while James was at work but returned with her brother and a friend of his in the afternoon to remove most of her possessions.

When James got home, he saw her car and her brother's pickup truck, all their doors open. He parked to one side so he did not block the exit. He knew what she was doing.

James had seen her drifting away from him for months, maybe years – he could not remember a time when she was not but knew things had not always been this way.

He wondered what way was different from "this way"? He could not answer his question.

There were times over the past decade when he tried to explain what was happening to him but, since he didn't understand it himself, his attempts foundered and did little more than confuse her and frustrate him.

He knew she tried to help, tried to supply the words he sought, but James reacted with anger. He said it was because she was treating him like one of her patients, like a child, like whatever, but it wasn't true, and he knew it.

The anger was what he turned to, a way of getting away from the shame of not being able to talk about what was happening.

No, the anger was about what was happening and his helplessness. The thought bobbed into his awareness and then vanished, pulled deeper like something caught in a dark undertow.

It was if he could live with anger but almost no other emotion. When the anger seemed to be verging on getting out of control, he would try to feel nothing at all, submerge everything. It was a balancing act but it was, James thought, the best way for him to live.

Of course, his emotional tightrope left his wife with nothing useful, nothing attractive, nothing supportive, nothing of value.

Carol came back with her brother on Saturday.

"This isn't a trial," she said to James across the kitchen table. "I don't see any point in a trial separation." She waited for his response. Her brother stood in the living room.

"I understand," James said. He started to add something but stopped.

"This isn't about the dog."

He raised his eyebrows but said nothing.

"All right, yes," she said, "some of it is, but things haven't been right for a while. A long time. Your job... We've talked about it, I've talked about it. Talking hasn't gotten us anywhere."

"I know."

"Listen," and her concern was evident, "you need to get some help. You need to have someone you can... I was going to say talk with." She shook her head slightly, made a small smile that vanished quickly enough to make its existence doubtful. "I think you're right, talking alone won't change things. But you need someone who can help you make things better for you. Do things differently. Get out of that job before..." Carol took a breath slowly. "Before it drives you crazy."

"I'll be all right." He was calm, as if everything she said he had considered and resolved before she spoke.

"I don't want anything. Let's make it clean."

"Whatever you want." His stomach heaved but she could not tell; he was very good at appearing calm.

"You need to talk with Johnson."

"Our lawyer."

"Yes." Carol took a breath. "I called him this morning. He said if we didn't contest anything, it would be pretty easy."

"Easy." He nodded.

"Yes. The house..." She looked around, nodding. "This was your parents', it's yours. I'll take the Honda."

"It's yours. You paid for it."

"Yes. You keep the checking account. You've done most of the bookkeeping. Bills and all that. What about the savings account?"

"Fifty-fifty."

"All right. How do we do it?"

"I can send you a check." He paused. "Do you want the amount in the account, some kind of bank statement?"

"A check will be fine. I'll take your word for it. No paperwork – I get enough of that at work." She tried a smile.

11

"Well, Johnson will probably have some guidelines or something. Suggestions. Things we need to do, insurance, things like that."

"Sure, he will. He'll be looking for your call."

"All right."

Her brother, his name was Michael, turned as they entered the living room; with most of the packing and moving done, his friend remained in the truck. She went to get a few last things.

Michael looked at James.

"Sorry things turned out this way," he said.

"My fault," James said. "She's a good person. She deserves better."

The brother paused and stared at James' impassive face.

"That's very…" He cocked his head. "I don't know if I would react like that."

James shrugged.

"Listen, man," Michael said, "I hope everything works out for you." He seemed sincere.

"Thanks," James said, nodding slightly, as if he had just been given directions some place rather than a part of his life, what at one time was the most important part, was ending, taken away like luggage.

Later, as the brother wiggled the last bag into the back seat of her car, Michael looked over at his sister sitting behind the wheel. She was looking at the house, though James had gone in and could not be seen.

"He seems to be taking it well," he said.

"What do you mean?" She started the car

"He's pretty calm." Michael closed the door.

"He's not," Carol said. She shook her head. "He's not at all."

Standing beside a living room window, James watched the car and truck drive away down the empty street. Then he turned and walked deeper into the house. He still had the rest of the weekend before he had to go to work.

And work…

Chapter 4: The woman

She looked down into the palm of her left hand as if divining meaning, though she studied a cut oozing blood. She squinted at the wound.

"I'm an idiot," the Black woman said, using a voice clear and precise, like what you hope to hear from your surgeon when talking about very sharp steel and maybe a laser going into your body to fight something so scary you can't say its name but you hope the doctor can. If you told her it was a voice of competence and strength, she would have looked at you as if not quite sure of your sanity but quite sure you really did not know her.

She lowered the Trow and Holden stone hammer in her other hand onto a well-lit work table and then fished a handkerchief from her jeans' pocket. She pressed it onto the wound and closed her hand.

For a moment, she did nothing, her dark brown eyes staying on her clenched hand. Her long hair, black-brown featuring a style that might have been named "long enough to get in the way," was held in place by a blue bandana threatening to give up its task and slide down over her eyes. She grimaced as she saw red slowly stain the handkerchief.

"All right," she said as if conceding a point no one made.

She opened the door of the barn facing her house and glanced at the side porch roof. A large, black bird looked at her from its perch, first using its right eye and then its left and then both, as if doubting what it saw. The raven opened its beak but she interrupted before it could scold her clumsiness.

"Not a damned word," she said. She sighed. "And, yes, I know the studio first aid kit is empty. I'll put it on the shopping list." Her long legs moved with an almost gliding grace and she went into the house, letting the screen door slap behind her.

The first aid kit in the barn might have been mostly empty but the shelves in the house's bathroom cabinet were well stocked. She worked on her hand with a careful efficiency suggesting experience; part of the trade of a sculptor in stone and metal was a close familiarity with the vagaries of tools, both powered and hand operated, and the cost of inattention. She finished and put the medical supplies back in the bathroom cabinet.

She took the loose bandana off and looked at her reflection in the cabinet mirror.

"Woman," Morrigan Kildeere said to herself in a tone touched with anger, "that was dumb." She said nothing else as she looked into her eyes. They revealed nothing, perhaps the result of years of practice. She grimaced and shook her head. She ran cold water for a moment and used her unbandaged hand to wipe down her face and then serve as a cup as she took a long drink.

Kildeere dried her hand and face, looked at the mirror again and again shook her head. She pushed her hair back and re-tied the bandana tightly, ignoring the irritation it caused her hand. The tight bandana seemed to emphasize her cheekbones. She stepped into the hall, her ankle-high, steel toed leather boots making her footsteps heavier than her usual walk. As she approached the front door – the mail was due and she would check it before returning to her studio in the barn – she heard a heavy car pull onto the gravel shoulder of the road in front of her house. It was not the light mail truck and she paused as she moved her head to one side so she could look out a window.

Sergeant Chernov looked at the house as the police SUV slowed to a halt. She smiled slightly as she opened her door and dropped her clipboard on the seat.

"Lots of metal," she said to the driver, a slim man noticeably older than her and who wore corporal's stripes. "Someone's an artist."

Metal sculpture, most pieces only a few feet tall, rested on cinder blocks and flat stone slabs in a haphazard pattern. Among them slightly larger stone sculptures of abstract designs favoring curves and loops rested on the grass. Most of the metal was dark brown while the stone pieces varied in color.

"Knows how to use a welding torch," the corporal allowed. He looked toward the small barn next to the house. "But what the hell is that thing?"

Chernov turned her head and her eyes narrowed. The corporal was referring to a tower, a little less than a story and a half tall, but looking taller. It was made of metal rods of varying thickness that, vine-like, twisted around one another. No, not vine-like. No plant in nature was like the tower. The spacing of the rods – rebar? – was irregular as if the parts were angry with one another, refusing to cooperate, though all seemed to go to the same place. Paint, reds, blacks, a deep purple, was smeared without regard to pattern and she felt if you could just find the right place to stand the colors would suddenly reveal a picture. And it would not be of anything pleasant.

The house front door opened and a woman stepped onto the porch. She came no further and waited with her head slightly cocked to one side.

"I'm Sergeant Chernov," Chernov said, walking to the gate. "Elizabeth Chernov, New Joyton Police." She nodded at the man, who had unfolded himself from the car and had braced himself with one elbow on the top of the door and the other against the frame, casual, but someone with sharp eyes and the kind of alertness that might set off a cop's internal alarm system would notice he stood so nothing would block his right hand's rapid descent to the holstered Glock semi-automatic pistol on his hip. He had no reason to be on guard but he was whenever meeting a citizen he didn't know because, as his favorite male singer put it, Ain't that America, for you and me?

"This is Corporal Michael Janowski," Chernov said. She placed her hands on top of the gate, lightly, but made no attempt to open it.

"I'm Morrigan Kildeere," the woman said. She wore faded jeans and, over a gray t-shirt with a couple of small, burned holes, a flannel shirt with sleeves rolled up to her elbows revealing strong forearms and hands, an impression confirmed by shoulders putting tension on the shirt. Strong, then, Chernov thought. Taller than average, dark hair pulled back by a bandana knotted behind her head. A face kept still, perhaps guarded, though Chernov could not see anything that would have Kildeere on her guard. Still, a small alarm bell in her cop's sensors tentatively rang in the background of her attention. Eyebrows not plucked since high school arced over eyes sharply focused on anything she looked at. Her eyes…

Chernov knew soldiers and some cops with those eyes.

Kildeere walked toward them and something black swept from behind her, passing over her, uttering short, almost barking high notes that were so clear as to be near musical, and Chernov swore it turned its head and looked at her as it passed Kildeere, banked, and disappeared behind the house.

"Big damned crow," Janowski said.

"Raven," Chernov said.

"Right," Kildeere said, almost smiling as she reached the gate. "You know the difference." It wasn't a question.

"Bird watcher. I guess it thinks we are intruders."

"You might be." This time the smile emerged. "What can I do for you, sergeant?"

"We're canvasing the area. Looking to see if anyone has seen anything unusual."

"I get to define what's 'unusual,' I take it."

"The thinking is, people living in the country get used to things being a certain way and might pick up on something that would help."

"This is about that boy they found." The smile was gone.

"Yes, ma'am, but I…"

"You can't tell me shit, I know," Kildeere raised a bandaged hand as if waving away any excuse as unnecessary. "Heard they found him next to the church up there. Mile and a half, straight line, and there was never a Pennsylvania county civil engineer who could make a straight line, so a little over two miles driving distance."

"That's about right."

"Not much traffic through here," Kildeere said. "You probably know but to your right, the road goes east to a big housing development. To your left, west, it goes into State Route Ten, which passes for a main travelled road around here. Not much traffic of any kind between Route Ten and the development since all those people head towards Philadelphia. Almost directly behind you, bordering that wooded lot I own, yes, the one with all the Posted signs, that road goes south and connects with half a dozen cow paths converted to pavement before finding Maryland. I'm guessing you have reason to think someone came up or went down that road before turning almost in front of me and going to Route Ten."

"*Might* have come up or went down…" Chernov paused, considering. Then she added, "Might have come up from the south. If from the south, likely would have used Ten to get to where we found the boy. But there's a chance someone could have come north and went over to Ten on your road."

"Wish someone *had*. I'm here at home most of the time working in my studio. I would notice someone coming up to the intersection."

"Even in the very early hours?"

"Even in." She motioned with her head towards the small barn beside the house. "That's my studio."

"Studio?" Janowski asked, squinting towards the barn. "You a painter?"

"No," Chernov said.

"Score two for the sergeant. No. Sculptor in metal and stone. Mostly stone nowadays."

"You made that thing?" Janowski asked and Kildeere saw where he was looking.

"I made almost everything in the yard. A few things were gifts from other artists. But 'that thing,' yes, I made it."

"What the hell is it?"

"Close enough." She looked at Chernov. "Any other questions, sergeant?"

"No," Chernov said. She took a card out of her shirt pocket and reached it across the gate. "That's me and how to get in touch if someone, even in the very early, catches your eye."

Kildeere looked at the card, studying it closely, and then looked up at Chernov. She nodded. "All right," she said. She turned and walked away. The two police officers watched her disappear into the house.

"You know," Janowski said, his voice low, "I'm beginning to think…"

"…There's something in the water of Chester County," Chernov said, completing the old joke. She smiled slightly and a few minutes later she and Janowski were on their way to the next house sitting by a country backroad that an FBI person, or computer, figured might have something of interest to relate.

Not so interesting the Fee-Bees are out here doing the leg work.

Morrigan stood in her living room, rolling the sergeant's card in her bandaged hand so smoothly a professional card dealer might have been jealous but her eyes were closed.

"Damn it," she said. It was the fourth time said since she had entered her house. "Damn it." Fifth.

Chapter 5: Newt and Billy

Ellen Parker stared at the copy and shook her head. An older editor had told her that new reporters' writing skills "sucked frog slime" and she thought what she was reading had more than one frog jumping on it. She shook her head and looked up.

The young man stood beside her desk on the crowded floor and shifted his weight from foot to foot. He was an intern and in the mythos of the news profession such a creature was touted as not smart enough to be an anchor in the Delaware River. Ellen thought most of that mythology was started by the same older editor she had learned from and she worked to keep such things from influencing how she dealt with interns – she still remembered being one – but there were days…

"William, it is called a 'spell checker,'" she said slowly.

"Yes, ma'am." He was trying to make his young White face appear interested and competent; all he got was confusion touched by fear. Ellen thought he needed practice to become a convincing liar, something that could be important if he was ever to be a journalist.

"Don't call her 'ma'am,'" a tall Black man with a gray-touched beard said as he hurried past, his eyes on the top page of a sheaf. "She has access to firearms."

The intern was startled enough his eyebrows disappeared for a moment under his bangs, reminding Ellen of a pair of caterpillars fleeing for their lives.

"Use it and the grammar checker." She shook her head and looked back at him. "Have you read our guidelines?"

"Yes."

"Really?" Now her eyebrows were up. He really was a poor liar.

"No." William looked away from her stare. "I started them and then I got busy."

"Read them. Study them. Carve them onto your heart. With a spoon." She leaned back in her chair. "Look, the information you were given is just for practice, right. It's an exercise. But what you have are the equivalent of a reporter's notes. They're taken from a real accident. Getting this right will teach you some things. But I'm not going to ask you a bunch of questions or tell you what to do until you have read the guidelines. Then we'll see what we need to teach you. Is that reasonable?"

"I guess so. Yes, it is." William nodded. "Yeah, I screwed up and tried to wing it."

"That's good, that you can say that. Look, you had classes on writing, writing for news. The principles are good but every outfit, like Philly dot com and the Inquirer, have their own style sheets and guidelines of how to organize your presentation. Rely heavily on that until you have it cold and then you'll naturally start to bring in your own style. As for spelling and grammar…" She shook her head. "Back to the Drexel bookstore and get a copy of Steve Pinker, *Sense of Style*."

"I have one, it was required."

"I'm guessing you didn't bother to read it." She jabbed a thumb at her screen. "That says you didn't."

"I thought he was mostly a psychologist."

"What, you thought you'd catch the Netflix version when it came out?" Ellen shook her head slowly. Interns. "What did you learn from this?"

"I guess I need to do some more learning."

"Congratulations." She pulled open a drawer, rummaged for a moment, and then pulled out a worn paperback copy of *Sense of Style* and tossed it to William. "Read this until you can get your copy." She nodded at the screen. "Then try again."

"Yes, ma'am. I mean, yes, Ms. Parker."

"Ellen will do."

"OK." He tried a smile. "And I'm Billy."

"I know who you are," she said, "but I'm calling you 'William' until you can write an acceptable piece of copy."

He made an exaggerated grimace.

"Only my Mom calls me 'William.'" He had a sense of humor. That could also help him be a journalist.

"A wise woman. Get to work."

Billy, aka William, grinned and walked away. The Black man came back. Ellen nodded.

"Hey, Peter."

"Morning, Ellen," he said. "I read it. It's terrible."

"True."

"He's so poor a writer…"

"We'll have to make him an editor," Ellen said, finishing an old newsroom joke.

"What did you call him?"

"William."

"He probably won't sue for workplace harassment for that." He smiled. "Do you remember what I called you?"

"'Newt.' Took me a while to figure out you were a James Cameron fan." Ellen paused. "I called you 'Sir Senior Editor,' as I recall. At least to your back."

"You should have sued. You could be rich now."

"Maybe later. He just needs practice."

"Hope never perishes. I deserved the title, by the way." He glanced at a piece of paper in his hand. "Onto other subjects. What did the VA Medical Center say about your idea?"

"The Public Information Officer gave it a green light. I'll talk to the art therapist and I already talked to the team leader."

"Pictures?"

"PIO says it is up to the individual vets whether or not their art work is used and there can be no violation of anyone's confidentiality. Signed releases, copies to everyone. The team leader said it would not be a problem. If we identify some pictures we can use, he said they can get them put on a thumb drive for me."

"That would be great. We have a review of George Bush's art book in the pipeline. Be a nice hook."

"Can I tap the reviewer for some comments?"

"Sure, once you have some images." He took out a pen and grabbed a notecard from Ellen's desk. He wrote quickly. "That's his name and email. I don't think you've met, so give him a call."

"Will do."

Peter left, disappearing into the islands of desks across the floor, while Ellen leaned back and stretched. William would probably work out, most interns did. She had. But it was true the quality of writing skills among college students and recent graduates was lower than in the past.

Not that she had much of a "past" with Philly dot com. The hub of Philadelphia's newspapers as well as the online site, she had been an intern back in 2003 and loved every minute of it. Now she was a full-fledged journalist with an intern of her own to bring along and it all seemed like it had happened so quickly.

There were days, though, when the things that had happened between her internship and now, things that had resulted in violence and death, stretched time out and turned it into a mountain range – hard and immobile. The good news was, and she smiled as she realized it, the mountain range was now something that she could appreciate the view it offered and did not block her movement.

Maybe not a mountain range, maybe just low foothills.

Grinning, Ellen returned to work.

As she did, James Hardy looked at guns. He was not sure why, which was almost true.

Even as he directed his computer from site to site, article to article, his mind formed pictures. He saw himself with each gun. Rifle, pistol, shotgun, each changed, but he always saw himself.

What was unclear was what he was doing or where he was. He just saw himself holding the weapon, like some of the models used on the sites. Bland, placid, just standing around, with a gun the only thing different from his usual self-image.

His picture of himself – White, medium build, youthful oval face with hair cut professional-short – never included a scale, but he pictured himself shorter than he was, as if there was less of him than the reality.

His searching naturally came across articles by gun advocates arguing for the Second Amendment or other political matters. He ignored them. But he paused with several focusing on self and home defense. Oddly, after reading them, he would hurriedly move on to another site. Defense… Something needed defending.

He did.

This was an idea he glimpsed like a dark cloud on the horizon and then quickly averted his attention. That idea was why he was looking at guns but he was not ready to pursue the cloud and see what it hid.

Not yet.

Chapter 6: Fake news

At two in the afternoon, the Pennsylvania sun shone down through a cloudless sky, bright enough its light was like something intruding. It was magnified by bouncing back and forth off the two- and three-story buildings of one of the blurred together communities feeding Philadelphia. Even so, the sun had competition from the strobing lights of the emergency vehicles. There were a lot of vehicles; FBI, Chester County Sheriff Service, Pennsylvania State Police, three or four – no one had organized a list yet but they would – local police departments, and, on the medical side, ambulances from three   that list was done – communities, and two SUVs from two different hospitals following county protocol for head or heart injuries.

There was only one head injury but there wasn't much for the hospital emergency response crews to do as the injury had taken away most of the individual's skull. The initial form they filled out would state, under "Nature of Injuries," the laconic entry of, "Head, GSW, TnT". The shotgun's Gunshot Wound effect indeed had been "Through and Through," which explained the mostly gone head and the ugly debris field extending in a fan from slightly more than a yard behind the young body on the sidewalk to the brick wall twenty feet away.

Near but separate from the body, a small pool of blood, now congealing, had dripped off the edge of the sidewalk into the gutter. Like the dead man and other objects, small, numbered yellow markers served to tell a story of interest mostly to law enforcement. The still-living person the small pool of blood once belonged to was gone, taken into one of the ambulances and soon would leave. Emergency vehicles already were making a lane for its departure.

Special Agent Karen Deevers of the Philadelphia FBI Field Office stood next to a young Agent whose breathing was so regular it was clear he was working hard to keep it under control. She said nothing but stood a little closer than she ordinarily might to a male Agent. She knew something about the psychological consequences of a shooting, so she stayed close to the younger man.

Deevers appeared taller than she was; on the job, she tended to hold herself with almost military erectness. A White woman of average height, her oval face seemed to default to an expression of interest in whatever her eyes saw, eyes not dimmed by the lines in her face. Now she deliberately looked relaxed, silently communicating with the young Agent. Her hand passed over her blond and silver hair.

She looked around; other Agents and the police were keeping a distance, giving her time with the young man, and one of the other Agents caught her eye for a second, nodded, and then returned to his conversation with a Philadelphia police officer.

"Hey, Karen," someone said. She recognized the voice of the Agent in Charge and noted his use of her first name, something he did not do in public. Ordinarily.

"Hey, Michael," she said, turning. She understood the circumstances for the young Agent were nothing like ordinary and, maybe, might never be again. So, a little informality, a small chance to catch psychological breath.

"Agent Fellows," Michael said to the young man. Title, reminding him what he was a part of. Some stabilizing. Michael smiled, an expression he seldom used in public. "Got briefed by your team leader. They have it on video." He glanced towards the sidewalk and then looked at the young Agent. His voice was calm. "Protocol is in effect, of course."

Of course. Deevers nodded. Putting two bullets into the legs of a man who just killed someone with a shotgun caused investigative protocols to kick in. Agent Fellows would find the process irritating, everyone did; she had, twice, but it was a structure one might cling to. Step A led to Step B to Step Z. Eventually, it ended and along the way one might get a sense of progress, of getting to some kind of resolution about witnessing death or even causing it. One might.

"I never saw it coming, sir," Fellows said, shaking his head. "We'd been following him all morning, didn't know someone else was looking for him." He stopped shaking his head. "No idea. No idea someone wanted him dead."

"I understand. OK, let's have you go with your team leader. She'll get the ball rolling, all right?"

"Yes, sir."

A woman in dark clothing appeared, nodded to Deevers and the Agent in Charge and, lightly touching the young man's elbow, steered him away. They watched him for a moment before the AIC turned to Deevers.

"Thanks for stepping in, Agent Deevers."

"Not a problem, sir. Four blocks away when I got the call. Probably would have heard it happen if I had my window down."

"This looks like a clean one."

"Hope so, sir."

"He waited to fire. Suspect was allowed to turn most of the way around and started to chamber a fresh round before Fellows fired. Two shots, both low, not center of mass."

Deevers nodded. It didn't mean Fellows fired low in an effort not to kill the killer. They taught Agents to aim at the center of their target's body mass because in the stress of combat target range accuracy might deteriorate. She was glad none of the rounds had missed, though the brick wall likely would have caught them – there was always the chance of the unexpected, a round ricocheting somewhere, into someone, and nightmares would follow.

"How did the panel go?" The Agent in Charge still studied the scene, trying to find meaning in what had been and what was left.

"Well attended for a university presentation," Deevers said. Her eyes were doing the same. "Lots of questions about Mueller and Comey."

"Of course. Are we going to be fired because of some gaffe of yours?" He smiled.

"I don't think so, sir. It seemed like everyone was expecting my 'no comments'."

"Given both were our boss at one time or another, they were probably expecting some sort of endorsement." He shook his head and turned to her. "Other things. I want you to lend a hand with our people on the 'red ribbon' task force. Can you put your other things on a back burner for a while?"

"Yes, sir. My position?" Her expression carefully was neutral.

"Advisor, bottle washer, not in charge. I want Agent Brown to get some experience working a coordinated task force, so he's still the boss. For the past several months, he's gotten nothing but praise from our colleagues and that matches my impression of his work. I want to give him more people, more resources, but, like everyone, we're shorthanded. You're a resource consultant. If we have to pull you out to get back to work here it won't upset things there."

"Sir, does Brown know I'm coming?"

"He will in the next few minutes. Wanted to see if you were up for it. Pretty senior to be looking over someone's shoulder, might be a little awkward."

"I'm a master of tact, sir."

"God, I hope not." He smiled. "You've worked with Brown, he's good people, up and comer and all that. He's been on a couple of task forces but hasn't had lead until now."

She nodded. She had seen some of Brown's work and agreed.

"State, county, locals. You're known to them. That will help."

Known to them.

Back in 2013, outside of a Chester County pizza shop, Deevers, while taking a round herself, shot two very bad guys trying to kill a woman cop and a child. As far as the locals were concerned, the FBI agent could walk on water and never sink below her ankles.

"Press is around," he went on. "We haven't had any significant leaks, but they are pushing hard."

Deevers nodded again.

"Brown will bring you up to speed." He leaned forward slightly as his voice dropped. "There are a couple of things the task force is sitting on. Your profiling background may be very useful in helping to interpret the wisdom from Quantico."

"Yes, sir."

"Speaking of the press…" He grimaced as he looked past Deevers. "Your friend Ellen Parker is here." He emphasized the word "friend" as if it was a title of dubious worth.

"Has she been a problem, sir?" Deevers' voice was carefully neutral but he raised his eyebrows.

"If she was, I would have told you." He paused. "No, she plays fair. And I know I don't have to caution you about letting anything slip." He paused again and looked into her eyes calmly. "I don't."

"Thank you, sir," Deevers said. He nodded and walked away, taking out his phone and calling someone. She turned and saw Parker standing beyond the yellow tape. They made eye contact but the other woman carefully gave no sign of recognition beyond a very slight nod.

Deevers walked to her car and arrived as her phone buzzed.

"Deevers," she said into it as she slid into the driver's seat.

"Brown. Can you talk?" That was quick.

"Yes."

25

"I was just told you'll be working with us. Glad to have you. Boss said you were near Paoli. Can you come out to our office?"

"I know where you are. Can do. Should be a little less than an hour."

"Great. I'll give you the briefing, keys, all that."

"Fine. Talk to you then."

"Bye."

Probably Brown was not thrilled about having a very senior Agent assigned to him but Deevers thought he was professional enough to go with the flow and smart enough to make use of her. After all, she had been a member of Behavioral Analysis Unit 4 of the FBI's National Center for the Analysis of Violent Crime almost from its founding in the late Nineties and had delivered her share of the "wisdom" Michael referred to.

She smiled as she drove away; on the other hand, careful student of human behavior though she was, she might be totally wrong about Brown.

Ellen Parker watched Deevers leave and wondered why her friend was in the neighborhood. In response to her question and waved Reporter identification, one of the officers had said a bad guy had shot a bad guy and then been shot by an FBI guy following the first guy and he didn't know shit about what was going on and she'd have to stay behind the yellow tape and then ignored her.

She didn't take it personally; some of her best friends were cops.

Ellen got the statement from the senior detective – it wasn't very different from that of the cop behind the yellow tape, though it took longer to say and the language was cleaned up. She noticed he simply referred to "the actions of an FBI agent" without explaining why he was involved, which seemed odd, and questions about the subject had been gently deflected and then ignored. The FBI was seldom slow to toot its own horn when the opportunity arose. She guessed Deevers' people still were working on how much to tell the locals about what they were doing following the one man and shooting the other.

The spring sun slipped behind the buildings around Philadelphia's center as Ellen returned to her desk at the headquarters, if that was the proper description, of The Philadelphia Inquirer. Her fingers entered what she had on the shooting and she added the small bit about a lack of information about why an FBI Agent happened to be on the scene.

She paused, re-read the report, and then sent it in. It would appear, after the duty editor reviewed it, on both the Inquirer's website and the print edition. For several years, she had helped to run the website which had meant editing, a task she had not enjoyed. Now she worked at reporting and in her years at the paper had resulted in three nominations for Pulitzer prizes. She liked the recognition but she also liked that the nominations resulted in more attention to her reports. That was the exciting part for her – telling a story that got things changed.

It was after her work shift but that was the nature of journalism. She started to shut down her computer when a thin woman motioned from inside her glassed-in office across the desks covering most of the floor and the irregular stream of people making their way to the elevator. The woman used her hand to summon Ellen and then sat down, dropping out of sight, not bothering to see if Ellen would comply. Of course, she would; one did not ignore a senior editor.

Ellen picked up her bag, made sure her cell phone was in it, and shrugged her shoulders into her jacket as she made her way to the editor. She didn't bother to wonder why the editor didn't use email or phone her. Rumors suggested she didn't know how to use such modern devices but Ellen thought such thoughts were well off-target. The editor, Sidney Hallen, was very sharp. But she had a style Ellen guessed reflected her college years of national-level sports but did not quite include hitting her reporters' heads with her lacrosse racket.

Hallen motioned to a chair as Ellen opened the glass door.

"Hey, know you're headed home, just want to get…" Her desk phone rang. She grimaced and picked it up.

"Hallen." She listed and frowned. "All right, I'll put her on." She handed the phone to Ellen. "Call, someone asking for you, they said he was pretty emphatic." Ellen nodded and put the receiver to her ear, expecting to hear from someone complaining about some story or other.

"Ellen Parker."

"Hard woman to find. But good, good. Won't take much of your time." There was a tinny quality to the voice, as if it was heard through a metal barrel, a quality that made it hard to tell if it was a man or woman talking. "You all have been covering those children, those boys. You said there are three. That's not right. There are five. I don't know why they haven't been found. Hibernia Park, Park Road where it goes over the creek. There's a red ribbon right there, I don't know how it's been missed. Go downstream a hundred feet. Pile of rocks. Another one, Ray Mar and Watermark Roads. From the intersection, Ray Mar north maybe five hundred feet, left side, ribbon. Go into the woods, maybe twenty feet. Good bye."

"Oh, no," Ellen said even as her hands snatched at a notepad and pen from Hallen's desk. She wrote as if being timed by a demon.

"Call was recorded," Hallen said quietly.

"Can't take the chance it's broken," Ellen said, finishing the note. She handed the receiver back to Hallen. "Claimed to have knowledge of two more boys not found. Gave their locations."

Hallen punched a button on her phone. It opened a line to the Philadelphia Police Department.

"This is Sidney Hallen, Philadelphia Inquirer. We've just had a call from someone purporting to have knowledge of the murders of those boys. Please connect me with the police officer in charge of the investigation." She put her hand over the mouthpiece and looked at Ellen. "This may take a bit. You know the drill. See if we have it."

Ellen nodded, slid the notepad to Hallen, and stepped out of the office. She picked up a phone at the first desk she came to. The occupant, a paper cup of coffee half way to his lips, raised his eyebrows but said nothing.

"Hi, Ellen Parker. Editor Hallen just received a call, ended about thirty seconds ago. We need it extracted and held. Yes, I can wait." She nodded at the reporter, resisted the temptation to look at her watch, and then listened closely. "Good, excellent. Freeze and hold it. No one touches it without Editor Hallen's permission, tight protocols, right? Police are coming for it." She listened. "Okay, yes, play it." Her eyes slowly closed as she heard the recording. "All right, that's it, thank you." She handed the receiver to the reporter who took it without any questions.

"We have it," Ellen said, walking into Hallen's office. She felt like someone had her by the throat. Hallen nodded, her grip on the phone tight enough her knuckles were white.

"It was for Ellen Parker," Hallen said, looking at Ellen. "We have it on audio recording. Yes, she'll be available for any questions you have." She covered the mouthpiece. "FBI Agent named Brown, running the task force. He's getting the paperwork together to get a copy of our recording and wants to have someone talk to you about it."

"All right. He say when it might be?"

"Coming over with some of his people right now. Okay?"

"Yes." Ellen felt her heart beat and then settle. If there was any chance to catch the monster... She didn't notice her eyes narrowing as they had when they studied the dark of a wooded lot.

Running against the outbound flow of commuter traffic and probably using every emergency vehicle light they had, the task force team of four arrived in forty minutes. Agent Thomas Brown led the group and had his identification out as he stepped off the elevator. Behind him were two people Ellen did not know, both carrying brief cases, and Karen Deevers.

As Brown entered Hallen's office, he showed his identification to Hallen who pointed at a short, older White man who barely glanced at the identification but spent almost a half-minute reading a document he took out of an envelope Deevers handed him.

"All in order," he said and nodded to a young man whose tie gave him some formality that was largely erased by his rolled-up sleeves. "Give it to them."

"True copy," the young man said, handing over a thumb drive. "We've got the original on media stored separately from the ongoing recording." He glanced at the bald man and then back at Brown. "We figure you'll want to make your own copy but wanted you to have that right away. I can take whoever is going to make the copy down to…"

One of the agents held up his hand and the young man stood. He looked again at the bald man who nodded a last time and the young man led the agent away.

"We have questions," Brown said, "but let's hear this thing first." He handed the drive to the fourth agent who took a small device out of his brief case and plugged it in.

The voice on the phone spoke again with surprising fidelity, though the tinny quality was still present.

"Hard woman to find. But good, good…"

Ellen strained as she listened, trying to match the voice, but it seemed false, almost mechanical, without any accent she could identify, and did not resemble anyone she knew. The cadence was unremarkable. Seemed to be male, but the alteration might be disguising a woman. Word selection… You all… Country? Black? She sometimes used the phrase herself, her Ohio upbringing coming to the surface. Maybe it was something.

Brown looked at the agent, who slightly shook his head.

"Modified," and Brown nodded. He turned to Ellen.

"Based on the earlier call, we have people going to the two possible sites. My first question is obvious: Did you recognize the speaker?"

"No," Ellen said. "The voice was not familiar to me, nor was the cadence, tone, or word choice. I've been trying to match it with people I have talked to but can't come up with anyone. Hard to tell, but I think it was a man." She shook her head. "No obvious accent, which is a little odd."

"You just answered a couple of my next questions," Brown said. "As a reporter, I would assume you'd have a good ear for people and their speech patterns. Have you received any contacts from someone asking about these crimes or tossing out conjecture?"

"No. I do sometimes get email and letters, mostly email, about articles I've written, but most of our coverage hasn't been over my byline. I don't know about the other reporters who have been more involved in this case."

"If I can add to this," Hallen said, paused, and then continued. "Only one article had Ellen's byline. I contacted our primary on this story, John Joyce, while we were waiting for your arrival. He said he's gotten some email about it, mostly condolences and similar expressions, and is on his way in. We've checked and such commentary email is regarded as proprietary to the paper but we're waiving that right. He'll print out whatever he has in terms of the comments. If you need the meta-data, we will need an order for that." She glanced at the bald-headed man who nodded.

"We appreciate your cooperation," Brown said with a voice devoid of irony.

"There he is," Hallen said, standing. She waved at a figure in jogging clothes and motioned him into her office. As he entered, she sat down. "John Joyce, Agent Thomas Brown. John, they need the list of emails we discussed. Any comments at all on the crimes."

Joyce grimaced slightly and looked at the bald man who raised his eyebrows.

"Email content only," the lawyer said. "Do you have any letters?"

"No, just emails." He looked at Brown. "I can print you out a hard copy of everything."

"Great," Brown said. "How long will it take to sort it out?"

"It already is, so to speak. All my email is arranged by subject. It's also cross-referenced to sender, dates, pretty much everything. It's done automatically as I read it."

"All right, Agent Lopez will go with you and pick up the hard copy." He glanced at the agent with the briefcase, who nodded and left with Joyce, leaving his briefcase and playback device.

"A couple more questions, Ms. Parker. We were contacted by Ms. Hallen. Was the sequence, he called you, you picked it up, and then you notified your superior?"

"No, I was leaving for the day. Ms. Hallen called me into her office to discuss something. I hadn't checked out so the call bounced back from my desk phone to our switchboard. The person on duty thought I might be in with my editor since we all tend to swing past her before leaving, and tried her office. If I had checked out, I could have taken the call on my phone. Same with email."

"Again, if I might add something," Hallen said. "Only calls to our staff are recorded, which means our switchboard calls are not. I've asked the operator to stand by for any questions you might have. She's in the break room over in the corner of the floor, other side of the elevators."

"Thank you, good thinking," Brown said. He looked at Deevers and raised his eyebrows. She nodded and left. He turned back to Ellen, frowning slightly.

"The call was for you. On our way here I read that article with your byline. You did refer to the third child. You used the phrase, 'The third death.' He wanted to correct you."

"And Joyce didn't write that article," Ellen said.

"No, he didn't. On the other hand, in his earlier articles, because of his interviews with law enforcement people who have worked on serial crimes, he suggested there were more. He said, 'might be more.' Maybe you were too definitive, so he wanted to talk to you."

"It's more than that," Ellen said. "Isn't it? He wasn't just about correcting a reporter. He wants recognition. Probably needs it."

"I can't get into what we think he's about," Brown said, shaking his head slightly.

"Understood," Ellen said, recognizing from Brown's tone that he wasn't going to get into describing what the killer's motivation might be about. She folded her arms and thought for a moment. "I notice we're all referring to him as a 'him,' a male. Is that the FBI profile?"

"Not enough data to be sure," Brown said. "I'm trying to remain nonspecific about it." His lips twitched and Ellen wondered if he was sending a message she could interpret. It probably was a man, all the profile studies pointed at that being the odds-on favorite, but there were just enough cases of identified female serial murderers to make an FBI Agent conservative. She decided to press on.

"His voice was a little strange. I don't mean the accent. It was like it was on some kind of playback."

Brown said nothing, but slightly raised his eyebrows.

Ellen said nothing more but raised her own eyebrows. All right, that's FBI for thank you for calling us and your reward is, we're going to slightly confirm your idea but will disavow you if you put it into print.

The other agents returned, all providing Brown with quiet nods. Ellen suspected they learned how to nod FBI-style during their training at Quantico. When everyone was back, Brown shook hands with Ellen and Hallen, thanking them for their cooperation and assistance – he used both words – but paused in the doorway as his team left.

"Ms. Parker," he said slowly, "he may call back. Specifically, for you."

"I understand."

"That's not a good thing if it happens." He looked at Hallen and then back at Ellen. "These situations, they can turn sour pretty quickly."

"I understand."

"I know you do. I just want to say this is one of those situations where you want to stay careful."

"I understand."

Brown smiled and nodded, possibly at her repetition. Then he was gone.

Hallen stood slowly, watching through her glass walls as the team made its way to the elevators and then vanished.

"He said he knew you understood this kind of situation. I took that to mean he knows about your history."

"You're probably right," Ellen said. She gathered up her bag and jacket. "He probably makes a point of knowing the background of everyone he talks to."

"Probably bored out of his mind reading up on me but you…"

"It's all old stuff." She shrugged her way into her jacket.

"Really." It wasn't a question. "He's right about being careful."

"He's a child killer," Ellen said, her eyes sharp. "He doesn't come after adults."

"That we know of." Hallen took a breath. "Let me say that again. That we know of. He's not some disorganized schizophrenic, raving out of control, baying at the moon. He is methodical. He prepares. He's taken children, yes, but no one has spotted him. He is controlled. And he enjoys doing terrible things. He's not some shooter looking to die. He plans. Yes, he's killing boys. But remember. That's all we are aware of. Maybe he likes killing young women, too, but we just haven't noticed." She shook her head. "Listen to us, we're all saying 'he,' and it probably is, but it might be…" Hallen grimaced. "We don't know anything except there's a monster out there. Be damned careful."

Ellen said nothing for a moment and seemed to be staring at her hands. Finally, she raised her head.

"You're right," she said. "I know. I *really* know." She took a breath. "I don't want to encounter another freak in my life." She smiled at Hallen. "Really."

"Good to know," the editor smiled back and didn't say she thought she heard a lie somewhere in Ellen's words, almost hidden from sight. Awareness of other peoples' lies was also a journalist's skill. "Go home."

"To hear is to obey," and then she was gone.

Hallen sat down and leaned back in her chair, staring through her glass wall at the slim figure that was soon out of sight and wondered about hidden words.

Chapter 7: The dancing elephant

James sat at the oval conference table with the other line supervisors, a notepad of yellow paper in front of him, and looked at the presenter who stood facing the small group with the tight, satisfied smile of a schoolyard bully.

"We don't want anyone to work harder," he said, the smile fading. "We want you to work smarter." He said it like it was biblical and he was a true believer. "But people get used to doing things a certain way. That is what we want to change."

He stopped and smiled as if remembering to do it and James thought he was waiting for one of the line supervisors to ask how to cause change. But no one did, mostly, James thought, because their supervisor, the division manager, was sitting next to the presenter, his arms folded, not taking notes, and looking at James and the others as if they were people he wanted to sell a used car.

"In a circus," the presenter said, "you have an elephant, all its life it's chained to a stake. Now you want the elephant to do something different, you want it to dance. But when you take the chain off its leg, guess what, nothing happens. It doesn't move. There's nothing holding it back but it isn't going to move beyond the distance the chain would allow even though it is not attached. Its conditioning holds it back. So how do we get the elephant to dance, especially if we don't want to take a long time to re-condition it?" Again, he waited, again there was silence.

"How? You set the circus tent on fire," the presenter said, his tight smile stretching further. "Now our elephant will discover that the chain is no longer attached."

The presenter turned to a flip pad and swept the cover up and behind the pad. Now revealed was a picture of a circus tent on fire. Cartoon people and elephants fled.

"You see?" He flipped the page.

"Now," he said, "we're not going to burn down the building. Tough way to run a business." He paused, making room for laughter but there was none. "But we want people to think the building is on fire. How do we do that? No flames, but we are going to apply some heat." He looked at the group as if again expecting some laughter at his joke but there was only silence. He looked back at the pad. On it was the phrase, Desperation = Tent On Fire.

"When people are desperate," he said, "they are willing to try new things. So, we want to find ways of making them desperate. For example, we let everyone know we're going to do some outsourcing, maybe do some downsizing, because our budget is too big. What do you think is going to happen?" Not hearing any response, he pointed at a line supervisor. "What would your people do? Do you think they'd be open to changing how they work?"

"Oh, sure they would," the middle-aged Black woman said sardonically, shaking her head. Her name was Mrs. North; no 'Ms.,' Mrs., and James had never heard anyone refer to her first name, though everyone agreed she had joined the company back "…When Jesus Christ applied for medical assistance," among other somewhat more believable stories. He had never seen her husband but people said he was in corporate finance law somewhere and she kept on working because she had nothing else to do. James doubted the story was true but whatever stories about her he ever heard all agreed she knew everything about everything.

"They've been going," Mrs. North said, "through all those changed accounting procedures we've tried in the past couple of years and finally settled on the latest requirements. They're going to be reluctant to do something different."

James shook his head slightly. Other stories about her said she had been with the company since it was a start-up in someone's garage, worked in housekeeping before it was contracted out and climbed her way up via night classes in business administration. He wasn't sure if that story was truer than the one about Christ's application, but they trotted her out every time someone in the media wanted to do a story on diversity. Still, if she kept pushing the limits, management would squash her like a bothersome insect.

"Exactly," the presenter said. "People like to stay with what they know. They are chained to holding their position."

"Well," Mrs. North said, "there's already been all this change…"

"Where they are now is, they think they are chained," the presenter cut in. "Doesn't matter where they were or how things were." He turned back to his pad and didn't see the woman look around at the other supervisors, her astonished look quickly erased.

He flipped the page and revealed a black and white photograph of a burning circus tent – it looked real, maybe from the Fifties. There wasn't an elephant in the picture, just people running, terrified.

"That's what we're going to do," the presenter said. "We're going to find a way to set the tent on fire." He looked at the man sitting next to him. "And the specifics of how to set that fire will be up to your managers." He stepped back as the man with folded arms unfolded and stood.

"As you know, for the past several months we've had everyone coding their activities so we know how much of what kind of work people are doing. Business on the phone, entering data, sending email, all of it. We've identified some people as outliers in terms of their activity and I'll be sending each of you a list of people and their work units, along with the average for your section and averages for assignment areas and for the company as a whole. That way you can do some comparisons and have some hard data for your evals."

"Excuse me," Mrs. North said slowly, her eyes hard as ice. "We were told that the coding wasn't going to be used to evaluate anyone, just identify what all our people were working on and establish baselines."

"Of course it was going to be used for evaluation," he said, raising an eyebrow and smiling politely as if at an obvious joke. "You can tell them now that's how it is. That's part of setting the tent on fire."

He then launched into a presentation about the compilation of data and the whole system of scoring, something they had sat through several times before. Finally, he stopped and looked around. "Questions?"

There were none. The meeting had been labeled an "in-service" and James was sure that it was so the person who called it could code an education activity on their personal weekly report. Forms evaluating the in-service were passed out for everyone to fill out. James put on his name and then scored all the questions as fives, the maximum. He knew that to score an in-service low was to be invited into the supervising manager's office for a chat.

He dropped his form off into a cardboard box everyone suspected often went directly to recycling and left the room with the stream of other supervisors.

"Same old, same old," another supervisor said, his voice low. Before James could respond the man turned down the hall.

James went into his office and checked his email. There was a message posted by the manager to everyone, telling them the supervisors had everyone's coded data and would schedule meetings with everyone in their groups.

A second message was the compiled data of all of James' supervisees. Several people were outlined in red as "outliers." It ended with a notation, "Report action taken." No suggestions as to what the appropriate action would be. James understood the intent was to limit peoples' responses, particularly their angry responses, to their immediate supervisors. This use of management insulation was common and he had seen supervisors who had taken action left with angry, miserable teams. The managers then would find a way to give the supervisor a hard time while letting the team know the action wasn't their idea.

A third message was to him from the manager. It was a form message used for supervisors with his average coded activities shown. He was higher than the other supervisors in some categories, lower in others. At the bottom the manager had added a note.

"James. See me next Monday, 1:15 PM to go over your numbers."

That was all. There never was anything else for these kinds of messages. The line supervisor would be summoned to a meeting sometime in the future with no idea if things were good or bad. James believed the time lag was deliberate, so he would have to stew until the meeting. Of course, they never had a meeting for anything good except giving out years of service pins, so there wasn't much of a surprise in that regard.

The anger roiled through him but James fought it back down. It was always like this, nothing new, and they would expect he would pass it down the chain of command. He tried to protect the people he worked with but most of the time, more in the past few years, he felt helpless.

James slowly tapped out an email to his people, reviewed the meeting, and told them he had the data. He sent that message and then sent each person's data to them. He set up appointments with everyone on his team, not just the outliers. He didn't want people to feel coming to his office was a stressful thing but knew it was.

Stress… Everyone was under stress. James didn't think it had to be done this way. Just let people know what was going on, what the profits were, maybe even try to get ideas from them on how to improve the bottom line, and the company would do better. But someone in management, someone near the top, had decided that beating up the people who did the work was the way to go. Maybe got the idea from a consultant, like the one who provided the in-service.

The result was turnover. That meant they had to keep training new people. That was inefficient but no one asked James.

It meant other things. James knew of several employees in rehab. Drugs were a no-no but several supervisors drank, something that seemed to be part of their job description, drinking with other supervisors.

And he knew several people whose marriages had crashed... James paused.

Your marriage crashed. You know the job messed with you. That's why you failed her. She did everything she could but you didn't hold up your end. You didn't have enough to take care of her – they drained you dry.

It was not the first time he had the thought. It wasn't the twentieth time. But he pulled his mind away because thinking about what the job had done to him filled him with anger he couldn't do anything about.

He couldn't?

The questions was new and it stayed with him.

Chapter 8: Hunters

Thomas Brown lightly tapped a small pile of papers neatly together on his small podium as his eyes looked at the various law enforcement officers sitting quietly at their tables, watching him with no expressions, small notepads open, waiting for something else. While they came from various jurisdictions, the men and women of the task force had the same ability to make their faces expressionless, though that blank stare, taking everything in, giving nothing away, patiently waiting for whatever came next, was the signature expression of cops. Professional criminals had no difficulty recognizing it.

There were odds and ends of furniture, most of it broken, in the basement and on the first floor of the two-story building but the team members sat behind identical brown tables with folding legs. Yellow stencils on the table undersides proclaimed the property of the Chester County Sheriff's Service. So were the metal folding chairs.

The building housing the team was old, maybe built in the Thirties of the previous century. Brickwork and broad, concrete steps up to the multiple doors of the first floor, made it look like the place had been a bank once upon a time, but it hadn't. No abandoned vault rested on the first floor, no tellers' cages, and the name was simply "The Williams Building," carved into stone stretched beneath the roof. Nonetheless, many of the locals, and Brown thought they should have known better, insisted on calling the two-story lump "The Bank Building." He had no idea why. Maybe there had been an ATM parked against the back wall.

They were lucky to have it. Coatesville, a town whose primary industry of making and processing steel had been fading for decades, had more than a few abandoned buildings. Attempting a revival, they cleared the problem of unoccupied buildings by demolishing them. The Williams Building was tagged to become easily hauled away rubble when the FBI came calling, looking for space for a task force. Updating plumbing, electrical, and internet connections, and getting a couple of the bathrooms functioning, probably invested more into the hulk since the building was foreclosed a decade and a half ago. Maybe after the cops left someone would buy it now.

Brown tended to use the generic term *Cops* when thinking of the members of the task force and it wasn't from the arrogant heights of the Federal Bureau of Investigation. He regarded himself as a cop, a reflection of several years of service as a uniformed officer in Cleveland.

Cops were human, they could get bored. But these people, he understood, were cops and they were hunting a child killer. They might be bored by his briefings but they would stubbornly go over the same information a dozen different times, trying to find the one little thing leading them to the killer. Yes, they were human, and that meant they could be very, very tenacious.

"He knows the area. He may be a local. He's mobile. He owns a car. He's not as bright as he thinks he is because he called a newspaper. He used a voice disguiser and we have people working on figuring out which one." He rubbed his chin. "I've already covered those things but want to draw your attention to the boys." He tapped his laptop's keyboard and the screen behind him lit up with a projected spreadsheet.

"Let me start by reminding you this is a work in progress. Any references I make, especially to the two new cases, take with a large grain of salt because we are still digging." He looked around. "And we're talking about boys, victims, not just pieces of evidence. Michael Jones, Philip Lang, Joseph Carbano, Peter Davidson, and Bruce Vickers." He paused as if needing to take another breath.

"What we have now are one Black and four White victims. One of the Whites was third generation Hispanic. Ages nine through twelve. They all live east of State Route Ten and south of the turnpike, all in Chester County. The first three we were aware of were Catholic. These last two were Protestant, one," he paused to look at the screen, "Lutheran, one Presbyterian." He looked back at the group. "We thought we had something going with religion but there it is." He turned back.

"Mix of family attributes, generally middle class. None of the fathers or mothers work for the same or rival employers. None has a police record. Two of the Catholics went to the same grade school, Saint Barnabas; none of the others are in the same school. The third Catholic family used to go to Barnabas for services but moved into another parish. Yes, we thought that might be something, but that idea has slid to the back burner, I'm afraid. A couple of boys spent a lot of time on social media but the others less so. We've been all over their phones and computers. Zip communications to third parties so far but we are still looking. Several computer games are common among all five, including some very large and popular multi-player ones. Checks on log-in and log-out times shows some overlaps but that may not mean much as all the games are fairly popular, some are not common among the five, and the times seem to reflect obvious schedules, like after school, weekends, and so on, but we have people going through the game company records to see if there are other people they might have all played with. So far, no such pattern." Brown paused to take a sip of water.

"After school activities, two are in local soccer league but different teams, two played in Little League." Brown paused and pressed his lips together tightly. *Were in soccer...* He glanced up and saw several in the group had caught it. He shook his head and then continued. "Three were active in their churches, bible study, catechism, one, the next to oldest, an altar boy at St. Barnabas, and all attend services with their families."

"Differing numbers of siblings, from zero to four, and no connections found between siblings." He looked up. "As I said, all of this is still in development," he said, gesturing at the screen. "A lot of you have contributed to it and there are more things we're getting into, especially now that we have two more. And that takes me to the next thing." He forced a smile. "Assignments." There were mock groans.

"I know some of you are still working on earlier assignments and your team leaders aren't trying to crush anyone with workload." He grinned and let the few laughs spring up and fade. "We divided things up during our team leaders meeting and hopefully we've got something for everyone." That got another set of groans and he made a gentle wave in dismissal as Brown gathered up his laptop and papers.

The laughter and groans were good news. Morale was still solid. He caught Karen Deever's eye and head-motioned towards his office, a small room formerly used by a secretary to the president of whatever business had occupied the building's second floor. The president's office, if that was what it had been, was now the team's conference room.

He dropped into his chair a little harder than he intended. He needed some sleep but it was getting harder to sleep nights. He watched Deevers close the door and then take one of the other chairs.

Deevers was older than Brown – silver strands swirled through her tangled, short blond hair – but she wore her age lightly. Short, her tight body showed she exercised. But the mind of the White woman was what Brown valued most. Deevers had been in the FBI's Behavioral Science unit, which was impressive, and had showed a coolness under fire, twice, even more impressive to other cops. Her role on the task force was a cross between a spy and a consigliere; she had, he knew, a direct pipeline to the Agent in Charge, which didn't worry Brown much, and experience tracking very serious killers.

"What do they think of your idea?" Brown asked as Deevers dropped a small purse with entirely too many keys attached onto the floor. She pushed her hair back without serious intent and raised her eyebrows.

"They think we're," she emphasized the *we're* very lightly, just enough to be noticed, "on the right track." She paused as Brown pulled open a drawer from his dinosaur of a desk, something left behind when the unnamed business evacuated because, he thought, it weighed more than the building it crouched in and was immoveable. He brought out a worn map of Chester County and spread it out. His fingertip traced an orange highlighted oval occupying the southern half of the county and ignored an older and larger yellow oval.

"Makes sense," Brown said, perhaps reassuring himself. He looked up. "I *want* it to make sense."

"Pattern analysis agrees with you," she said. "Yes, our target has made the same error that most people do when trying to do things randomly; he's avoided clusters, tried to make all of the burials equidistant. But, and the last two corroborate this, he's used sites requiring familiarity with the ground, not just a casual appraisal. He's local, not a visitor coming up from Maryland or over from Harrisburg. He lives here, at least long enough to get to know the land."

"The pattern suggests he likely lives in the southern part of the county." He nodded.

"Probably," Deevers said. "Keep that in mind. It's all about probabilities. Male, White, lives alone, adult, lives in Chester County, most likely in the southern half, all of that is a series of probabilistic statements. It's not like the autopsy results, hard data."

"I'll try to get confirmation from the son of a bitch when we get him." He smiled without humor. "Did those Quantico geniuses have anything else for us?"

"They did." Her lips tightened. "It's theory, but I think they have something. These boys are not his first kills."

"No shit," Brown said. He shook his head. "We already thought of that. He's too thorough. He's obviously practiced this, maybe a lot. But there is no history of any serial child murders in the area."

"No, there are not," Deevers said emphatically. "But that's actually good news, probably good news. We think he's local, at least to the extent of living here for more than a few months. What Quantico thinks is he was killing somewhere else and…"

"And left there, came here and started up here," Brown said. "Which means somewhere else…"

"There is a pattern of kills using his methodology."

"Tell me they ran this through the computer."

"Yes. They are sending a report to you by email with the details, started putting it together as we ended our conference call, but they have a lead."

Brown turned to the dinosaur and tapped the keys on his laptop. He shook his head.

"Nothing yet," he said. He turned back to Deevers. "What's their idea?"

"They did a preliminary and found a pattern that ends about five months before the first of ours occurred. It's not boys or children, it's women, prostitutes usually."

"And the odds become higher it's a man. What's the methodology?"

"The things in common range from the general to the very specific. The general items are abduction, wrapping in plastic, living burial, suffocation. The two very similar are the use of an animal tranquilizer by injection and no evidence of sexual activity, at least not involving the victims."

"Meaning the sexual component, if there is an overt one, might be deferred or, if onsite, masturbation into a condom."

"There's some debate about if there is an overt sexual component. They are working to get us the details. Crimes took place over a period of thirty months in the Atlantic City area."

"All right, women who might not be noticed if they go missing. Common enough target for killers." Brown nodded, considering the possibility. "Atlantic City, prostitutes around the casinos, targets. He stops, why? Maybe he has to leave, personal business, maybe he has a brush or two with the law. Why come here? Unknown, but he came here for a reason, not random chance. Why switch to boys?" He fell silent.

"He needs to kill," Deevers said. "There was a pause while he got to know the area, maybe, or figure out who his new targets would be. But he still has the need. We'll know the time of the last New Jersey killing when we get the report. They're digging to make sure their list is complete as it can be." She frowned. "A reason for changing targets might be there are not enough prostitutes in the area, or they aren't vulnerable enough to get at. Or…" Her voice trailed off and her eyes narrowed as she thought.

"'Or' what?'

"Or he found a purpose, more than the hunt and the thrill of death. A different, maybe a bigger, meaning."

"Moving to Chester County is not exactly a metaphor for taking the road to Damascus."

"I don't think our guy heard the voice of Jesus, no, but maybe something here happened that altered his path from women to boys."

"Interesting idea." Brown tapped his leg. "Interesting…"

"It may have something to do with why he called the paper."

"Going public, get recognition of the righteousness of his cause?"

"Or of his dedication to it. He wanted full credit."

"Wants to be seen as accomplishing something." Brown nodded.

"Not necessarily our acknowledgement."

"God, Satan, Jesus?"

"Powerful figures, currying favor with them. Maybe." Deevers thought for a moment. "Maybe showing he, too, has power, putting himself on a plane with religious figures. But he might think they would know all, see all."

"So, he doesn't have to get column inches to get a pat on the back."

"Or run the risks about making this public." Deevers paused. "Maybe there is someone closer to Earth that he wants recognizing his effort."

"That serial murderer your Ellen got involved with, he wanted his mother to know what he was doing. Trying to dump guilt on her."

"Yes, that kind of thing. Maybe a competition, 'I can kill more than you.' Or something we haven't found yet."

"I love that optimistic 'yet.'"

The drone was cheap, which is why it belonged to a ten-year old boy named Jackie Flinthill. Its receiver lost contact with the small hand-held base unit Jackie used and disappeared behind the white, two-story houses making up the development.

Jackie, a White boy small for ten years, did not panic; the drone had done the same thing in the past. He knew it was supposed to set itself down if it lost contact with its base unit but at random times would not. He drew an imaginary line in the gray, cloudy sky heading west and, pushing the base unit into his backpack, he followed the line as closely as possible on the development's streets.

Quickly there was only one road to follow. Up ahead in the shadowless light of a cold Pennsylvania spring, he could see farmland gently rolling away into the distance. On the right, less than a half mile ahead, was a house inhabited by a crazy woman or a witch, or maybe somebody who was both, depending on which elementary school myth you believed, and across from it was a large patch of woods.

Jackie wasn't sure he believed either version but he slowed down as he pedaled and not just to make sure he was getting a good look at the fields on either side. He saw only corn stubble and had the thought that maybe the drone had hit the witch, like what happened in some fairy tales, and she was now green ooze or something in her front yard.

He saw the house several times before, though from the relative security of his family's car on their way to Route 10. There were things in the front yard that his mother insisted was art even though they didn't look like any of the pictures the school's sole remaining art teacher showed his class. And there was a pretty neat looking barn next to it. Jackie liked the barn and thought, when he grew up, he was going to get one with his house.

Jackie stopped his bike at the top of the T-intersection with the house right in front of him. Across the road the woods spread south and west, coming to an abrupt halt when encountering tillable fields. He wanted to go search the woods – he thought his line in the sky tended more to the other side of the road. And he had never heard that the trees hid any witches or crazy people. But the woman who lived in the house and, everyone said, owned the woods across the road, was a witch or crazy. Maybe both.

But he wanted his drone back. It was his, yes, but he was encountering, in bits and pieces of experience, a sense of responsibility. He had to take care of it and, if a crazy witch owned the woods he thought it might be in, then he was going to ask her permission to go there and look. So, in spite of what felt like a clenched fist in the middle of his chest, Jackie leaned his bike gently against the low chain link fence of the witch's, or the crazy woman's, front yard. He walked slowly down the length of the fence, looking carefully into the yard, trying to see if the blue and white of his drone showed up among the carved stone and shaped metal. He paused, looking at a block of dull red stone that curved and had an oval hole in it that seemed to invite putting a hand in it.

The witch – Jackie decided she did not look like he thought someone crazy would look – stood on her front porch, a large plastic mug in her hand, watching him. For a witch, she was not traditional. First off, weren't all witches White? He had never seen a Black witch. Green, sure, but not Black. And there were no black robes, no claw-like fingernails, no cat with glowing eyes.

Jackie thought maybe it was just that her disguise was perfect. Beat-up jeans, an open, long-sleeve, plaid flannel shirt revealing a faded black t-shirt with a red Honda motorcycle logo on it, and brown leather boots with weird purple laces. She leaned against a porch post, a leg crossed, and sipped at whatever was in her mug. The mug had dancing cows on it.

At least there was no cat, Jackie thought as the lump in his chest seemed to press against his sternum.

"Good afternoon," the possibly not crazy woman said. She took another sip.

"Sure." Jackie hesitated and then asked, "Have you seen my drone? It's blue and white, mostly white." The last part came out quickly.

"No." She seemed to study his face for a moment. "I've been working, haven't been outside very much. Was it headed here?"

Jackie turned and motioned over the trees.

"I think it was coming in this direction but it wasn't very high and I couldn't see it because of the houses."

"That's a bit of a trip, all the way from where I think you live. Back in the development?"

He nodded.

"Any chance it veered off and is in some field closer to your home?" She looked into her mug.

Jackie shook his head emphatically but he really wasn't sure.

"My name is Jackie," he said. He had remembered it was polite to introduce yourself.

"Is it? You look more like a 'John.'"

"That's my name, too. It's my father's name. Everyone calls me Jackie so they can tell us apart."

"Do they confuse you for your father a lot?" She smiled and he understood she was just joking but it felt like she was teasing and he started to say something back, maybe something not very polite.

Then he saw the raven.

Somehow, it was behind the woman, hidden, and only now revealed himself and he clamped his lips tight, holding back a boy's not very polite response.

The bird seemed big and in one instant was a completely flat black allowing no definition and, in the next instance, highlights appeared, sliding on its head and neck on down to its wings, so naturally it was as if it was not reflected light he saw but something glowing from within the bird, something powerful and dangerous.

It was the kind of creature that a witch, or a mad woman, would have.

He wanted to run away, drone or no drone, and did not wish to take the time to mount his bike, but he did not. He did not run even when the black bird he mistook for a crow or a demon, gently pecked at the woman's leg and then turned its head towards him. It saw him, yes, but as it cocked its head like birds do, letting each eye gaze at him, he realized it was studying him, memorizing him, a thought corroborated when it turned its head and looked down its beak at him, using both eyes.

From somewhere a piece of information surfaced about eyes. Side of the head, useful for seeing anything coming, the shape of cows and deer and other prey animals. Both eyes looking forward, great for judging distances to things, eyes like humans, T-rex, and tigers. Hunters. Eyes looking at him.

The bird called, seemed to *talk*, at him with a gurgling caw, its open mouth exposing a blue-black that might have been a tunnel to forever to the eyes of a ten-year old boy.

Jackie remained still. He wasn't going to run and he wasn't going to cry, not even when the fear made his eyes water and he could hear his heart beat.

"He's a raven," the woman said. She took a sip. "He thinks you might have brought him a treat."

"A raven?"

"A raven. Don't call him a 'crow'. He'll feel offended and get all depressed."

"Really?" The idea seemed preposterous enough to make his fear pause.

"No, well, probably not." Another sip. "Come to think of it, I don't believe I have ever seen him depressed."

"What does he eat?" Jackie almost dreaded the answer.

"Almost anything. For treats, he likes boiled eggs."

"He lives here?" He asked his question, trying to be casual, as if his heart was only slowly slowing down from pounding so fast

"Visits. He came by in the fall, seemed to have a strained wing, I let him shelter in the barn and he repays me by laughing at my work. I think he lives in the woods." She nodded toward the trees across the road.

47

Jackie fell silent, watching the raven watching him. He looked at the woman; though she appeared strong, she didn't really look very witchy, even with what might be a familiar leaning against her calf. At least it wasn't a cat.

"What's his name?" he asked.

"He never told me." She took another sip. "I never asked."

"You talk to him?"

"Sure. I think he listens. They say ravens can learn to mimic human speech. That would make him bilingual, since he already knows raven."

"He has a language? There's a crow, I mean, a raven language?"

"No one knows. The bird scientists think there might be. They think they talk to wolves. I think he talks to me but I don't know what the hell he's saying."

"But you said he understands you."

"That just makes him smarter than me."

She took a final sip and turned the mug upside down and shook a few drops loose.

"Well," she said, "I've got to go back to work. See you later." She turned and walked off the porch and disappeared into the barn. The raven watched her go then looked back at Jackie for a moment. With a few powerful strokes, he was suddenly flying and passed over Jackie. The bird went among the trees and Jackie lost sight of him.

The boy stood by the fence for a moment and then slowly walked back to his bicycle. Thoughts about many things moved through his mind but the missing drone slipped from sight until he was half way home.

Chapter 9: Contact with firearms

Charles Dwyer was a big man, not just in terms of his size. Black, the former Pennsylvania State Trooper carried a bit more weight than was best, covered his bald head with a ball cap displaying the American flag, wore yellow prescription glasses, a safety vest with faded reflective stripes and pistol competition patches from various years, faded jeans, and high top, well-polished shoes catching the late afternoon sun. His pistol, a Ruger nine-millimeter semi-automatic, its slide locked to the rear and its clip beside it, lay on a pedestal to one side, along with a good quality but well used pair of sound suppressing ear protectors. He looked at a young woman standing away from the firing line, apparently waiting on him, and scratched his nose.

The woman was Ellen Parker. She wore blue jeans and an old t-shirt from Hawk Mountain. A Galco leather holster carrying a Glock .40-caliber pistol in a canted forward position rode on her waist, held by the jean's belt. On her head was a red ball cap with a Phillies emblem and yellow lensed, wrap-around safety glasses rested on the brim; a pair of electronic ear protectors obviously newer than Dwyer's, dangled from one hand.

Ellen's eyes moved quickly, looking at everything and sparkled with intelligence and humor. Her face was a little thin and she would never be called pretty. But her eyes and high cheekbones were attractive, what in a few decades might result in her being called "handsome."

"I think," Dwyer said slowly as he eyed Ellen's new baseball cap, "I have failed you as an instructor if you have sold your heart to the Phillies." He had the kind of voice that could lend itself easily to the bass line in a gospel choir, though Ellen had heard him only hum what she thought was country music.

"You know I work in Philadelphia," Ellen said, grinning. "It's kind of a job requirement."

"Have they won a game yet this year?" His voice carried the resignation to fate of a long-time sports fan. Dwyer shook his head and reached over to the pedestal and picked up a small, spiral-bound notebook. He flipped it open and, as he studied it, continued.

"Have you got your practice sessions in since our last class?"

"Both of them," Ellen said.

"Weak hand?"

"Yes." She shook her head. "It's coming along but slowly." Her voice, when she was thinking deeply, sometimes displayed a southern Ohio twang.

"That's all right. I just want you able to punch holes with your left hand every time you pull the trigger in anyone you can see out to twenty-five feet. You're getting there." He looked left and right, checking the pistol range; he and Ellen were still the only people using it. "All right, let me see your weak hand."

Dwyer stepped back from the firing line and Ellen walked forward, placing her wrap-arounds over her eyes and putting on her ear protectors. A paper target of an abstract human silhouette was stapled to a fiberboard wall and looked to Ellen as if it was further away than it was.

Dwyer stood behind her, looking left and right, gave the command for Ellen to draw and transfer her pistol to her left hand.

"Ready on the left," Dwyer said in a quiet voice as he looked again to the left. His head swiveled, checking the area. "Ready on the right. All ready on the firing line. All five rounds, commence firing."

Ellen raised the pistol without supporting it with her right hand; Dwyer, in teaching her to use her left hand, wanted her to assume her right arm was not available.

The gun fired almost immediately. Ellen worked to bring it back to the target and get off the next round. She fired in a regular rhythm, methodical, her entire focus on bringing the sights onto the black of the silhouette. In a few seconds all five rounds were gone. Ellen cleared the weapon and dropped the clip, putting both on the pedestal.

"Face me," Dwyer said and Ellen turned around, her back to the target. "Where did your bullets go?" It was a quiz Dwyer used frequently.

"Three in center mass," Ellen said, remembering where the pistol's sights had been as each round fired. "One is high center, maybe in the head, and one low right."

Dwyer smiled. "Let's see." He looked left and right; the other half dozen positions on the outdoor pistol range were still unoccupied. "Range is safe. Recover your target."

Ellen walked to the target and freed it from its staples. She walked back, grinning as she approached Dwyer. He took it and held it up.

"Do you remember your first weak hand?" he said as he studied the holes in the paper. Ellen nodded. "Okay, three center mass. You called it. Two in the circle, probably quickly or immediately fatal. This one is a little high. Fatal, but it will take a little time. One low, a little to one side. Gut shot. Not necessarily fatal with medical intervention. This high one, it's in his face. He's down, probably dead. These are all hollow points?"

"Yes."

"Practice with what you intend to shoot," Dwyer said, nodding, "and that forty will put full jacket rounds through a house's walls. Always better to use hollow points so you don't hit your neighbors. And better cavitation in your target." He folded the target into a smaller rectangle and gave it to Ellen. He picked up his notebook and made an entry.

"All right," he said. "I had you do the weak hand without any warm-up because that's real world, right?"

"Right."

"In your practice, I want you to work on picking up the speed. Right now, you're like… Bang. Bang. Bang." He waited for Ellen's nod. "What you want to do is work towards the same rhythm that you have with your strong hand in a Weaver stance. More of a… BangBangBang.' Again, she nodded. "Key is controlling the recoil, knowing the recoil is coming, and pushing back into it. It will help if you can stay focused on the sights even if they are jerked out of your line of sight on the target. If you can do that, you don't have to reacquire them. Saves a quarter of a second or so."

"I get it," Ellen said. "I think I do that with my right hand but the left still feels a little weird. I'm still shooting with it like I was a beginner."

"Probably right, but you are coming along. Don't let yourself get frustrated. Stay motivated."

"Believe me, I am."

"I believe you," Dwyer said, smiling. "Now, go ahead and put up a new target. Load three clips, five rounds each. Load two more clips one round each. We're going to do a couple of fast draws, strong hand. For the first fast draw, load a one round clip. After expending it, reload a clip of five. We'll pause, critique, and do the same thing again. Then load the last five round clip and shoot it out with your left hand. Then we'll pause and talk about how that went. We're going to work on weak hand reloading without using your strong hand but not today. Questions?"

Ellen had none and she set to work. Later, she and Dwyer sat in the clubhouse's small lunchroom. She had a rectangular cloth bag at her feet holding her spare clips, boxes of ammunition, and her ear protectors. The Glock was in its holster on her hip, partially hid by a plaid-pattern long-sleeved shirt.

Dwyer had coffee from an urn that reputedly was never turned off; the mug had the logo of a Pennsylvania State Trooper. All the people working for the shooting club as instructors had a personal mug hanging from pegs near the urn. Ellen made use of the soda machine for a diet drink.

"You're coming along," he said leaning back.

"Ohio farm girl," she said. "My Grandpa Tom was the family shooter and he showed me a little."

"I remember you saying that. Farmers, some of them are pretty good."

"Some girlfriends, military, did a little instruction. Pretty practical stuff."

"Those women in the stories you wrote?"

"Yes."

"They seemed to know what they were about, judging from what you said in those articles. And," he said, "judging from what you already knew when we started."

"They are pretty decent shots."

"An FBI agent, a Marine, and a former Army MP, yeah, I would guess one or the other of that crew would know one end of a pistol from another." He grinned.

"I'll tell them you said that. They'll be pleased."

"They should be," Dwyer said, still grinning. "Am I not the center of the shooting universe?"

"Maybe, but I thought I was."

"So, my question is," Dwyer said, the smile gone, "how are you handling all this gun business?"

"What do you mean?"

"You know what I mean, Ellen. What that mad dog did to you, what you had to do to that county deputy, and that business in Coalville last year. I still have Trooper friends and I know what happened in all that. You wrote about it, which I think took some spine, and I'm not a shrink. But we're popping off more than a few caps out here. I don't want it to be messing you up." He shook his head slowly. "You have a carry permit, yeah, but discovering you don't have all it worked out while there's a Glock at your fingertips is not a good idea."

"Have you seen anything like that in me?"

"Not at all, but I'm not a shrink, remember. A lot gets by me. But you're more than just another student, all right? So how are you doing?"

"I'm doing fine, Charles," Ellen said. "Some of those things really tore me up. My girlfriends pushed me, dragged me, to someone who could help, and she did." She cocked her head slightly and smiled. "Do you do psych evals on everyone who comes here to practice shooting?"

Dwyer laughed.

"My buddy Obama, now that he's retired, probably thinks we should but, yeah, nowadays we all kind of keep our eyes open. I'm not terribly worried about the people who come in wanting to learn how to shoot and be safe, not worried about people who want to learn some advanced stuff; I worry about the ones who buy a gun and figure Hollywood already has taught them all they need to know."

"I always wanted to be John Wick when I grew up."

"Dear lord," Dwyer said and laughed again. "People don't realize Mr. Reeves did a lot of work getting ready for that movie and I've seen people who think they can do all that because gun equals magic." His expression settled into one balancing seriousness and concern. "But getting back to you, anything we do makes you feel uncomfortable, speak up. We'll work it out."

"I will." Ellen took a sip and cocked her head again. "You said the same thing when I first contacted you."

"Journalist, mind like a steel trap. Never forgets anything." His smile returned.

"I appreciated it. Still do."

"No offense taken?"

"Nope."

"Good. Can I get you to join the NRA?"

"No." Ellen smiled; joining the NRA was a running joke between the two. "Before I forget," she half stood, shoving her hand into her jeans pocket, "I have that recipe I promised your wife."

"The brownie one?"

"The very same." She sat back down and handed a folded page of light green paper. "The ones I brought to dinner last week. And thanks again for the invitation."

"Wife's idea – it's not really dinner if we don't have at least two dozen people at the table." He unfolded the paper and read the recipe. "Another thing my doctor won't let me eat, I think." He looked up and winked. "If he ever learns about it."

"Your wife said she'd let you stand downwind of these and sniff to your heart's content."

"She's a demon. Try not to marry a Black woman, Ellen. They tend towards cruelty."

"Oh, I've got to tell her you said that. You said she had a familiarity with firearms. Should be fun to watch."

"I already told her. How do you think I got this heart condition?"

"Too many donuts?"

"I'm beginning to believe all women share that tendency." He looked at the wall clock. "Hey, I've got to run," he said as he stood and drank the last of his coffee. "Any questions on your homework?"

"No. Same time next week?"

"Good question," Dwyer said as he rinsed out his cup. "Next Saturday is my daughter's birthday, we may be doing a surprise party. I'll email you if there's a conflict." He hung his cup and turned to Ellen.

"My congratulations. How old is she?"

"Twenty-three. I can't believe it."

"I remember being twenty-three."

"I don't – too many centuries ago."

He laughed at his joke, waved, and walked out of the room.

Ellen looked at her soda bottle, not really seeing it, remembering past events. Finally, she shook her head, smiled, and tossed the empty bottle into a recycling bin.

Charles Dwyer was a good instructor, she thought, and a good man. He knew about her history because he had asked if she had any contact with firearms in the past.

Well, I shot a man and was shot by another and was almost shot by a pair of very bad men. Yes, I've had a little contact with firearms. She smiled but it didn't reach her eyes.

And when I was a child, I think, I know, my Grandpa Tom hunted down and, with the help of one of my uncles, wiped out the bastards who killed my cousin Eileen. Yes, a little contact…

Chapter 10: Guidance

Ellen Parker looked up from her computer screen as two reporters, their heads close together, passed her desk. She did not hear much of what they said to each other, their voices low, but she knew what they covered. Her eyes met an older reporter's as he leaned back in his chair. He smiled sadly and his finger traced a downward spiral. Then he turned back to his computer screen.

His motion was a joke, a reference not to a tornado but the circular movement of water in a flushed toilet. Ellen glanced down the aisle but the two reporters were at their desks, hidden by cubicles dividing up the floor. The two covered, in addition to other assignments, the government of the United States and the spiral was, appropriately enough for the employees of a major newspaper, an editorial comment on how things were going in the 21st Century.

She grimaced slightly and wondered, not for the first time, what her grandfather would have thought. Ellen smiled; John Wesley Parker probably would have campaigned for Eisenhower to come back and straighten a few people out. Her desk phone rang.

"Parker," she said, her eyes on her monitor, her mind still on her grandfather, passed on years before.

"I hope I am not intruding," the voice said and Ellen focused suddenly with an almost physical jerk, as if hearing a low, rapid rattle near her foot while in the woods. The voice sounded different from his first call. Definitely more of a "his," but also more of an echo.

"No, not at all."

"I assume they are listening. You would have talked to the police. Of course. I wanted you to." He paused, waiting.

"Why?"

"They probably told you what they thought about me and what I was doing. They are probably wrong. Since you cooperated, I wanted to help you. I read your stories, you know. I didn't know you had been nominated for Pulitzers. That is very impressive."

"Thank you."

"You're welcome. They can't catch me through my call. That 30 second thing in the movies is just a plot device. In real life, and that's what this is, they can track a call almost immediately. But I won't be here by the time someone comes. Anyway, I want to let you know that this is not some kind of random, disorganized perpetrator thing. I am not psychotic. I am not trying to be captured. I have important work to do, protecting something bigger than myself."

"Bigger? I don't understand."

"No, well, you don't have to. But other people will. Maybe they already do. All right, that's enough. I'll be talking to you."

Then he was gone.

Ellen's fingers quickly danced on the phone's buttons as she notified everyone on the short list taped to the bottom of her monitor. The FBI was supposed to be listening in but she did not want to depend on luck.

Everyone responded as if they had practiced and did it so smoothly most of the other reporters and staff did not notice the gathering in Hallen's office. The FBI was represented by a thin, white technician, with the easy smile of someone who knew what he was doing, and he set up his laptop on Hallen's desk so Brown and Deevers were present. Smile still present, he gave Ellen and Hallen a thumb's up as Ellen realized she didn't know his name. She was about to ask when Brown spoke.

"We have the contact; Barry streamed it to us. Nice work."

"Thanks," the technician now known as "Barry" said. Still smiling, he deliberately sat against one of the glass walls, as if not wishing to distract the others.

"He said we couldn't trace his call. He's right about the old 30 second thing being a plot device." Brown smiled. "As you know, land line, cell phone, all calls are immediately traced."

"Since the '80's, right?" Hallen asked.

"Yes, part of the establishing of 911 service. What he does is buy a pre-paid SIM card for a phone and then gets a cheap, unlocked phone. Basic phone, no frills, no plan. Makes the call, it is registered, but only by number, not name. Then he throws it away. Obviously, he does not make the call from his living room. We'll go to where he was anyway, just in case he's that stupid."

"What about his voice? It is 'his' voice, right, not 'hers'?"

"Could be a 'her.' But let's say 'he' because that's what he sounds like. He's using a commercially available voice changer," Brown said. "Certain harmonics and other indicators allowed our technical people to identify the software he's using."

"Good news?" asked Hallen.

"Not as much as you might think." The resignation in his voice suggested he had hoped it was. "There are several variations of the software available. Apparently, some of these producers have borrowed code from open-source applications and, in any case, have made their products free to the public. The particular package we've identified is from an outfit that makes voice changers for phones and computers."

"Computers?"

"For game players wanting to change their voices, often so they can troll other players. Anyway, we are working on reversing the change to see if we can get his real voice. This sample may help. Beyond that, it is clear he has singled you out, Ms. Parker, and plans to continue talking to you." He paused and glanced to one side as if he could see into the split screen display of the laptop. Deevers nodded.

"This is not all good news," Deevers said. "While we are glad to have contact with the perpetrator, it is important to understand this puts Ellen at risk, particularly as we close in on him. If he has to take evasive steps, if he feels pursued, he may blame you and then act on it."

"I understand," Ellen said. "It's all right."

"No, it's not," Deevers said, shaking her head. "Yes, I know you've had more than your share of dangerous situations to deal with. Nonetheless, we don't know how he will react as the pressure on him goes up. He's not a fool; he's methodical. We think that makes him particularly dangerous. And he's not in it for the money, not like the other one you encountered."

"I do understand, really."

"Ms. Parker," Brown said slowly, "we think the situation may be serious enough to warrant providing you with security. We are working with local police both in Philadelphia and near your home and…"

"That won't be necessary," Ellen said. "I have a friend, a professional security person…"

"You mean Blasingame," Deevers said. Her face was neutral. She paused, waiting for Ellen's response. Finally, she said, "All right, Ellen. If he's available. If not, promise me you'll get in touch with me. I'm sure JJ could put you in one of his spare apartments."

"Karen, Agent Deevers, yes, I will."

Brown, frowning, said nothing for a moment. Finally, he asked, "JJ?"

"My husband," Deevers said. She smiled slightly. "Like Ellen, he's from Ohio. Back when he was a deputy sheriff, he got to know some of Ellen's family." She added nothing.

Brown's glance at Ellen found a face expressionless. He nodded as someone came into the office and handed him a piece of paper.

"Preliminary on the voice changer." He looked up. "Not a lot I can share at this point because we don't have a lot. But they have a couple of analytical leads they are hopeful about. I know you want to know what we have but that would be very premature. My promise to share, once we can, is still in place. We are grateful for your cooperation thus far. We really are and I will not forget it." He looked again to one side. "Agent Deevers?"

"Here's a summary of his profile. This is not to go outside your office, not yet." She waited until Hallen nodded. "We think he started in New Jersey and focused on women there. We think he's male, mid-thirties to early forties, well educated, probably White. Observant, plans ahead. Strong impulse control, though he has very powerful emotional needs. Above average familiarity with computers. He may have an independent income or works in a profession where he does not have to put in regular hours. He probably lives alone and has no long-term relationships because of a lack of interest. Buys sex. May be deeply religious but does not regularly participate in services and similar activities; may have contempt for established religions. We think he can be charming as he has shown an ability to get close to his targets. When he drops his controls, he is violent in the extreme."

"That business about 'protecting something bigger than myself,' how does that piece fit in?" Ellen asked.

"It's his justification for murder," Deevers said. "When we catch him, he will tell us he never got off on it, never masturbated near his victims' graves, never enjoyed it. He'll say it was something that had to be done to protect someone or something." She paused and looked to one side and then back. "When he moved from New Jersey, he left his hunting grounds, places he was familiar with, with a high proportion of vulnerable women. He moved to Chester County with far fewer prostitutes in the open and easily accessible. He had to change targets to meet his need. That meant a change in justification. We do not know how boys became targets but this is not about something that happened to him involving other boys."

"He's on a mission from God."

"Something like that and it may be that. But don't let that idea trap you; it is something that he, emphasis on the 'he,' has decided is a good reason. It may not make any sense to any rational person." She shook her head slightly. "Remember, it is just an excuse for his behavior. Its value may be that, if we can figure it out, we might be able to narrow our search."

Ellen nodded.

"There we are," Brown said. "Again, thank you for your cooperation. Hopefully, this call has moved us a step closer to catching this person. We'll be in touch."

Brown leaned away from the computer screen and closed the lens cover of the clip-on camera on its top. He looked over at Karen Deevers doing the same thing at her desk.

"That reporter…"

"Ellen Parker," Deevers said, turning to him. "You read the reports we have on her?"

"Yes, thanks. You've crossed paths with her. What's she like, is she reliable, or should I be reserving seats on the shuttle to DC for us to answer embarrassing questions?"

Deevers smiled and shook her head.

"She's reliable."

"She's been through a lot." Brown waved his hand towards his desk. "That thing with the county deputy and then you and Sergeant Chernov…"

"She was nearly killed, both times."

"Then that thing in Coalville." He paused. "Wasn't…? You asked her about someone named 'Blasingame.' There was a short note about him in there."

"I think he had a bigger hand in what happened there than anyone admitted at the time."

"She and that girl were almost killed. Yes, now I remember, later on she and Blasingame and that vet, Rydell, found Douglas' little girl. Douglas is the guy our DEA comrades would most like to take down." He smiled slightly. "And you came to their rescue and Blasingame somehow catches the kidnapper. A lot of paths crossing one another. What do I need to know about Ellen Parker?"

"She's a friend of mine." Brown nodded at Deever's emphasis. "Reliable, yes, she is brave enough."

"I got that. What isn't in the reports?"

"She takes care of her own. I had knowledge of her family 'way back when she was just a kid in Ohio. Her grandfather was one of those very solid men, farmer, and she seemed to take after him even as a child. An approach to life that was, do the right thing and the devil be hanged." She paused. "A bunch of us, all friends of hers, meet from time to time to have dinner, all members of the 'Shot to Hell Club.'"

"Ellen's idea, I'm guessing."

"Yes. Her, me, Sergeant Chernov, some women vets, friends of hers, pretty informal. And she can keep her mouth shut."

"Good enough. Didn't mean to pry."

"No problem."

"And Blasingame? What isn't in the reports pertaining to him?"

"He's a restorer, working with architects specializing in older homes, looking for original hardware, that kind of thing. That's what he was doing in Coalville. But there are two other threads. First, a few years ago he was in Albany – he was there working with relatives in the restoration business. We're not real clear on how it came about, but Blasingame went also to work for a man named Fredericks. He is someone we know a lot about. Runs things, long history in organized crime. Blasingame was a security specialist for him."

"What does that mean?"

"Good question. Blasingame supplied some overwatch for Frederick's son and kept him from a couple of assassins a rival sent. That was a public thing. What wasn't public was what else he did. Our sources suggest he was, at the least, some kind of investigator, scout, for Fredericks, taking a look at dangerous rivals in what came close to being a full-blown gang war."

"And at the most?"

"Some people thought he might have been some kind of hitter as well but that's a lot less sure." Deevers shrugged. "Sources thought he was in Coalville to take care of some people but that doesn't seem to be how things played out."

"Right, those two who were doing housecleaning and then killed each other while trying to steal something. You said there's another thread?"

"Yes. He was a civilian employee of DOD in the sandbox."

"Doing what?"

"Officially, the Department of Defense used him as an interpreter. Apparently, he's got some fantastic talent as a linguist. Iraq, Afghanistan. Unofficially, he worked with operational teams and was trained extensively in staying alive in unfriendly neighborhoods."

"I recall those neighborhoods. He was a spook?"

"Yes. After the Coalville business, we were contacted by a representative of the Defense Intelligence Agency."

"Why the contact?"

"He wanted to assure us Blasingame was on the side of the angels, and I'm quoting, 'If you include non-pacifists like Michael.'"

"No shit," Brown said softly.

"He claimed they had an eye on Blasingame, hoping he would come back and work for them as an instructor. Blasingame had been some kind of team leader. He did say Blasingame had been injured overseas, something about someone dropping a building on him, and, because of his physical injuries, they wouldn't let him back into the field again. Blasingame wasn't interested in that arrangement."

"DIA does a lot of operational work gathering and analyzing military intelligence. Heavy duty operators. They can tap SEALs, Delta, whatever they need. Very heavy stuff. If he was one of their team leaders, he was a lot more than a translator." He frowned. "Am I reading between too many lines? Did he, does he, have a relationship with Parker?"

"They met in Coalville," Deevers said. "And the two of them worked together on the rescue of Douglas' daughter. Their dating, if I can use that term, seems to be restricted to breakfasts. They joke about it. But I don't know how close they are."

"Not asking you to betray a trust or anything. Just trying to figure out who all the players are. It sounds like we can depend on Parker to keep her act together and Blasingame, I guess, is well qualified to watch her back while we resolve this situation."

Deevers nodded but added nothing. She did not mention her suspicions of Blasingame as working much more dangerously for Fredericks in Albany; some of the rivals Blasingame "scouted" became very dead and she wondered if he had left his skills somewhere in the Middle East or had brought them home with him.

The in-service training was going faster than James anticipated. It was as if the presenters, a couple of people he had never heard of, knew no one was terribly interested in what they had to say. While pretending they were enthusiastic, they were short with the few people in the audience who also pretended they were enthusiastic about asking questions.

James was careful to look attentive. He had a notepad and occasionally jotted a short note. They were random and made little sense outside the context of the in-service:

Bottom-up ideas!
Drill down!
The box blinds your view!
Data driven!

He had half a page of phrases when the training shifted gears. The senior division supervisor got up and led everyone in sending the presenters off with a quick round of applause. Then he turned to the crowd, all hoping to be dismissed so they could return to their jobs and capture more work units.

"All right," he said, his voice catching a squeal as the PA system objected to him for a few seconds. He glanced to one side and the woman from IT who was at the control box held up a hand, adjusted a dial on the black box, and then pointed at the supervisor.

"All right," he said again, this time his voice lower, but it was fine. He nodded at the IT woman as if bestowing a blessing, and turned to the group.

"This has been a great training," he said, a sentiment somewhat weakened by management's referral to every training as "great." "Now, what we're going to do is a quick group exercise." There was complete silence – in the past, people had groaned at such announcements but everyone had learned not to do that. "On your chairs is your group assignment card. Go to the table with your number on it. Have a good time!"

James had been through this before and had picked up his card. Several people had not and seemed to find it amusing to reach beneath their butts without standing. His card had the number seven on it and James had already spotted the circular table with a small placard on it. He got up and walked over.

The "group monitor" was already there. On the job, he was an "assistant supervisor," a position for he was paid no more than anyone else, but indicated he was trying to move higher into management. Most of the assistant supervisors were volunteers, did no supervision, and could be relied on to scurry to their handlers with any information they had working to the detriment to another employee. Like most of them, James thought the man – a White man named Joseph who seemed to be putting on a few more pounds every time James saw him – had no idea, and probably didn't care, how despised he was by his co-workers.

An attendance sheet was passed around. James carefully printed his name and then signed. One did not want to appear to have left a training early. Joseph carefully examined the sheet, comparing it with the nametags everyone wore. Then he took a minute to read a page of directions, something he must have done before but wanting to emphasize his specialness to the others.

"The ground rules are," Joseph said slowly, reading from his directions, "this is completely confidential. Nothing said in group is to be attributed to anyone if discussed outside of group. So be as honest as you can."

Everyone nodded. The same thing was done before whatever participatory exercise was put into the training. No one believed it.

"All right," Joseph said, in unconscious, or perhaps conscious, imitation of the senior division supervisor, "let's get started. We're going to start with going around the circle and I'd like everyone to say what it is they like most about their jobs." He turned to his right. "Carolyn, you can start."

"What I like *most*?" She looked up into the air and shook her head. "That's a bit of a challenge. I think I'd have to say it's being part of a dynamic team."

Joseph wrote something down, nodding. "Dynamic team" had been a repeated phrase used in the last training but, if he remembered, he said nothing.

"Okay, Tony, what do you have?"

"Probably," a thin Hispanic male said, his brow furrowed as if thinking hard, "I like most the importance of the work." He looked at Joseph and his expression relaxed as he took off his glasses. "I mean, it has to be great to work on something that means something, you know?"

Joseph nodded, writing quickly. Without looking up, he pointed at James.

"Your turn."

"I'd like to pass for the moment," James said. His mind had gone blank, as if part of him had left the conference room and was running down the hall. Joseph stared at him.

"I need a second," he added, "to make up my mind." He took a breath. "That business of 'the most' has gotten me a bit scrambled." James paused and took another breath. "There are so many things I could say, you know? Come back to me."

Joseph seemed perplexed but then he smiled. He wrote a short note and nodded to the next person in the circle.

An email was waiting for James when he got back to his desk. It was a summons to see his supervisor immediately. James glanced at the clock. This would probably cost him his lunch time but there was nothing to be done about it.

There was never anything to be done about it.

Nonetheless, he grabbed his lunch – a sliced cheese sandwich and an apple – and carried it with him to the supervisor's office. He was motioned to a chair.

"You don't have anything that you enjoy doing here?"

So much for the confidentiality bullshit.

"That's not what I said."

"You didn't say anything."

"He didn't come back to me. I asked him to. But he didn't seem to be listening."

Dump a little shit back on Joseph.

"What do you mean?"

"I told him I was having trouble choosing among several things, figuring out which one I liked most. Just needed a minute."

"And did you?"

"Yes, I did, but he never came back to me."

"What was it, what did you like most?

"It was, I liked being part of a team doing important things with leaders who look out for their people." James said it as calmly as he could. "What had gotten me confused is that some of the other people had come up with some of my ideas before I said anything and Joseph didn't explain if we had to come up with something totally new or entirely ours or what." He shook his head. "The group wasn't as well run as the one I was in last month." He held up a hand. "That's just my opinion and may be biased by my confusion during the exercise."

The supervisor stared silently at James for a moment and then glanced down at a sheet of paper on his desk.

I read the management books you keep on your shelves – are you remembering the chapter with the rule, 'Own the error to take leadership authority'?

"All right," the supervisor said. He looked at James. "Try to be a little faster off the mark next time, James. Don't sacrifice clarity for speed, though."

"Right, makes sense," James said and left the office.

He stepped into the small lunchroom and fed quarters into the soft drink machine. The sodas were more expensive than the local Wawa store but James knew the machine intake in each lunchroom was tabulated and compared – James had no idea what metric it addressed and might have only been something for senior management to do when they weren't jerking each other off but he made a point of buying something from the machine at every lunch.

James sat down at one of the tables and slowly unfolded his sandwiches from their wrappers – concentrating doing things precisely, he had found, helped to keep his emotions subdued. And every meeting with his supervisor usually meant he needed whatever help there was.

Someone sliding a chair out from under his table surprised him. Since he was a line supervisor, most of the members of his team avoided him, his superiors did not eat in the small lunchrooms, and other line supervisors isolated themselves from one another, always uncertain who might hurry to management with something they heard. James looked up.

"Join you?" The speaker was a tall, thin African American he knew as Terrence Something. A few years ago, they had worked on a project together and it turned out they had a mutual friend, Bill Monahue. Terrence, James remembered, had a sense of humor which made the project go by a little easier.

"Hey, sure," James said, waving towards the chair Terrence held. Terrence sat down and glanced around. "What's up with you? Been awhile."

"They don't like us to eat lunch off our floor," Terrence said, shrugging. "But I just heard Bill Monahue walked."

"Quit? I thought he was in a good position at regional." Monahue was easily the brightest person James knew at work.

"He sent me an email. By the way, he says his email address for you bounces and he didn't want to send anything here."

"Glad he didn't. Be shit to pay. What did he say?"

"He says he's given up on the whole thing, thinks it ought to be 'torn up and shut down,' his phrase, so he's out. Took a job with CRS. Says it's a big cut in pay but the benefits are pretty good, it's close to where his daughter is going to school, and he likes the people." Terrence shrugged. "Anyway, here's his email addy." He slid a small piece of paper over. "Drop him a line some time."

"Great, thanks." James pocketed the paper without looking at it. "How are things with you?"

"'SSDD,' you know." Terrence stood. "I better get back before one of the weevils notice that I'm gone." He held out his hand and James took it. "Heard some nice things about your team, man. People saying you look out for them." He shrugged as he let go of James' hand. "Not a lot of line supers doing that anymore."

"I just try, don't think I'm doing much good." James shook his head. "Maybe Bill has the right idea."

"He probably does, he's pretty smart, but my kids are in school so I'm not going anywhere for a while." He paused. "Heard things got rough for you. Sorry about that."

"Thanks. No, knew it was coming for a while. The job, you know? Didn't leave me much to take home."

"I know what you're saying." He took a quick look around and then nodded at James. "One of these days, all these fuckers will find themselves shit-paid managers in hell. Take care, man." Then Terence was gone.

James looked around. No one seemed to be watching Terence's departure. Maybe there weren't any "weevils" – the nickname he and Terence had used for the weasels who could be counted on to run to management – around. Or maybe there were. Who the hell knew?

SSDD. "Same shit, different day." That had been the phrase they used to dismiss management harassment while they worked on the project. James thought Terence was in the pipeline to become a supervisor but it looked like he was frozen in place. Bright guy, they'd be idiots not to put him in charge of something.

Or maybe they had him in a position where they could use his brightness without moving him up the pay scale. They did that. Sooner or later, though, whoever they were screwing would figure it out and get out. But Terence couldn't. Sounded like he was trapped, taking care of his family.

Another thing I never did.

James chewed without tasting his sandwich and tried not to think about things that never were.

Chapter 11: Information

The evenings were bad. James tried to occupy himself. Vacuuming, even where it wasn't needed, things like that. Television wasn't much of a distraction. Most of what it had was stupid, though he didn't do much investigating.

The house, in his family for three generations, offered little as a distraction. Without realizing it, he withdrew from parts of it. He took his meals in the kitchen, sometimes in the living room while watching the television; the dining room was just something he passed through to get somewhere else. The front porch was never visited nor the back deck, though in past years he often used both until well after sunset.

The house seemed empty, though its rooms still held their furniture. Color had drained away. Everything was a muted dullness with little to catch his eye. Nothing seemed to hold his attention.

There was always the internet. Porn, sure, but that attraction had diminished. Sexual arousal seemed to be rare and he found it difficult to get interested in becoming aroused. It seemed like too much work, too much effort for the reward. He wandered across news and media sites and would eventually and inevitably gravitate to the bookmarks folder holding gun sites.

It was a couple of weeks after Carol left, he realized he hadn't done anything with the dog's bowls. They lay on a small pad next to the refrigerator. Easy to miss, he told himself.

The food bowl was empty but there was some scummy water in the other bowl. He stared at both for a while, the vacuum's cord half gathered in his hands. He finally attached the cord to the vacuum. James moved slowly and wheeled the vacuum cleaner into its closet in the hall. For a moment, he did nothing and just stared at the kitchen. He took a breath. Carefully, as if trying to avoid stepping on fragile things, he walked back to the kitchen.

James stood and stared at the bowls, at the dog's bowls.

Not the dog's bowls. At Brownie's bowls. Why haven't I thought of his name all this time?

All this time since I killed him.

His throat twisted into a knot and tears formed, blurring his vision. He angrily wiped them away. As he gathered the bowls and walked them to the dishwasher, a thought kept running through his mind like a closed-loop audio tape.

One more thing they did to me.

After dinner – some reheated Chinese from the night before – he settled in front of his computer screen. He wandered to scattered sites. One was the local movie theater but nothing offered held his attention. He would have been slightly surprised to learn he had not been to a movie in five months.

Political sites of a particular type held his attention, mostly by touching the deep-held anger he tried not to acknowledge. It did not matter what their ideology was; he spiraled in to them like a rock pulled planet-ward and, like that rock, he burned. It did not matter half of what he read was false and a good portion of the rest was misleading. For a few minutes he felt his anger, for a few minutes he felt something.

Specific issues did not stay with him. His viewing merged them together, grinded away all the supportive tissue their authors worked so hard to build and added them to a general sense of outrage. He did not challenge the facts. They did not matter. But all contributed, a little bit at every viewing, to a growing sense that something was very wrong and there was nothing to be done.

Nothing to be done about them.

He clicked on a folder of bookmarks and opened tabs for information on firearms. Reviews, shooting competitions, evaluations of gear of all kinds, and on-line sales. He compared rifles, shotguns, and pistols, studied formal reviews and forum comments, looked for sales and compared prices. He studied pictures, pictures of black and gray handguns, rifles that looked like they were something from a war or a science fiction movie, sights that magnified vision, let you see in the dim light found in darkness, placed a red or orange dot in your line of sight suggesting where the bullets would go if you squeezed the trigger now.

And again and again, he pictured in his mind what it would be like to have one of the black weapons in his hands and how he would appear to others. Forming the picture sometimes, and often for the only time in an entire day, brought a small smile to his face.

James had an accidental discovery at work. One day a yellow envelope used for conveying paper documents appeared in his physical mailbox stacked with the other narrow boxes used for the teams on his floor. Several such envelopes appeared a week and usually contained copies of flyers he was expected to post on his team's bulletin board. The flyers never had a "take down" date, only an order that they were to go up and join the dozens of other flyers gathering dust.

When he unwound the string holding down the envelope's flap, several pieces of paper slid out, each one marked at its top, Not For General Distribution, Copy 3 of 7. He glanced at the envelope; his office code was in the last box on the front; all the other boxes holding mail codes had been crossed out. James flipped the envelope over. Only a few of the boxes there had codes and all save the one for his supervisor had been crossed off.

At some point, the envelope had been addressed to him – he had no idea what for – and, after re-circulating, had been passed back to him instead of his supervisor. The mail clerk had seen his address, still not crossed off, and had not bothered to look on the other side to see who it currently was addressed to.

The first paper was a memo to the senior supervisors going over the criteria used for their evaluations and bonuses. He raised his eyebrows when he saw the size of the possible bonuses. The second page was another memo breaking down of the costs allocated to his and the other units; it was the basis for pressure from on high to reduce costs.

He took only a few seconds examining the list of costs for his team – they included personnel who did not work in his unit, a share of plumbing repairs for the floor below, and other things that did not make sense.

The third sheet confirmed that the raise in pay for line supervisors was not going to take place, even though James had been told "It's in the bag" by his supervisor. The last paragraph stated that senior supervisors were not to tell line supervisors of the decision "to avoid impacting morale."

James gathered up the pages and the envelope and hurried down the aisle to the copy room. No one was in it and he quickly made copies of all three memos. He folded the copies tightly and stuffed them into a pocket. The originals he put back in the envelope and walked down the hall to where the mailboxes stood.

Glancing around and seeing no one, he shoved the envelope into his mailbox and then walked back to his office. As he sat down, his phone rang.

"James Hardy," he said. "How may I help you?"

"Hey, Jim. Carl."

"What's up, Mr. Davidson?"

"Hey, have you checked your mail lately?"

"Looking at it right now. Just a couple of messages left to clear."

"Not email. Office paper mail."

"No, not yet," James lied. "Is there something you want me to prioritize?" "Prioritize" had been a word heavily used by management for a couple of weeks but then they moved on to different terminology reflecting the latest senior management in-service training, but James continued to use it when talking to management almost as if it was a kind of pushing back.

"No, no, nothing like that. We're checking to see if something was mis-mailed. You know, wrong addressee. Run on down and check to see if something like that happened. Stuff inside is confidential, private and personal. If you have it, there will be a 'Not For General Distribution' label, so close it up and address it to me, all right? I'll stay on the line. Let me know if there was anything. And remember, it's covered by client confidentiality, so don't…"

"Sure, no problem, understood, none of my business, got it," James said, standing. His mind was on a phrase the manager used: "We're checking…" As he walked down the hall, he wondered if the missing memos had put his supervisor's butt in the fire.

He paused at his mailbox and then pulled the envelope out. He slowly unwrapped the string, hoping someone would come by. As he did, one of the floor secretaries walked in and headed to a set of file drawers converted to holding office supplies. He nodded to the middle-aged woman as he pulled the top sheet out just far enough to see the warning.

"Got it," he said aloud. When she glanced at him, he shoved the paper back in and wrapped the string back into place. "'Not For General' and Davidson sent it to the wrong recipient," he said, shaking his head. "Big uproar."

"Keeps happening," she replied, her tone slightly bored.

"Yes, it does." He made a point of thoroughly crossing off his mail symbol and then flipped it over. "And there's the correct address." Shaking his head, he circled the code several times and tossed the envelope into the Out tray.

"Makes you wonder how anything gets done," he said. He nodded again and walked back to his office.

"Yes, it was in my mailbox," James said, picking up his phone again. "Your address was on the other side. Looks like someone forgot to cross off mine." He made a quick huff as if stifling a laugh. "Anna, floor secretary, said it keeps happening. Kind of old tech approach." Rumor had it the secretaries all reported everything up through their supervisors; he hoped the rumor was true and she remembered seeing him check the envelope and sending it on its way with its contents apparently unread.

"Well, thanks for finding it. I'll have a clerk run over and pick it up."

"It's in the Out tray, Mr. Davidson. Do you want me to hold onto...?"

"No, no, that's fine. No need to interrupt you further. Talk to you later."

So now he knew things management didn't want him to know. For a moment, he felt a vague satisfaction but it faded.

What did it matter what he knew? There was nothing to be done with the knowledge. They would do what they wanted to do. They always did.

And when they figured out he had copies, what would they do then? Probably make his life a little more miserable. He did not let himself take them out again until he went home.

Despite the danger his possession of them posed, he read the three memos after his brief dinner. Seeing they were lying about the raises for line supervisors came as no surprise; someone years before had told him that was standard. Get someone to take on a job, let them think it would eventually result in more pay or bonuses, and then just stop talking about it. At one time, line supervisors were paid more but that had disappeared as the company expanded. The bigger the organization, the more it tried to cut benefits to employees. James didn't much care, not anymore. He used to, but not anymore.

The one on management bonuses was all about employee production and reducing costs. Real money. He wondered if the department supervisors were screwed as much as the line supervisors. Probably not; they could get to senior management and strangle them with their own ties. He smiled briefly and turned to the costs allocation tables.

It didn't make sense until he realized that taking costs from one unit and assigning them to another made the first unit look better by reducing its costs. It was a way of favoring units whose supervisors were helping the elephant learn to dance. And making trouble-makers look bad, maybe bad enough to build the case for firing them.

Were they trying to get rid of him? Had he tried to protect the people in his unit too much? Or was this a way of applying the whip: "Look here, James, your costs are high – other units are doing more with less." Maybe that was it.

But maybe it wasn't. He had seen other unit leaders get pushed out. There were always ways. What could he do about it?

Nothing.

They had taken a big chunk of his life and now, maybe, they were getting ready to finish him off. What could he do, go to a stockholders' meeting and whine? Yeah, right.

They made other people suffer, grinding things down for the last fucking dollar, and they made jokes about setting circus tents on fire.

One of these days, someone should…

He tapped the papers together and held them for several minutes. Hanging onto them was a little like sticking his head into a bear trap. But just throwing them out seemed like a waste, though he had no idea how they could be used.

Maybe someone else could use them, someone who knew more about the company. He took a business envelope from a desk drawer. Carefully, knowing he was being paranoid – You're not paranoid if they really are out to get you – he used a kitchen towel to wipe down the memos and the envelope, wiping them again as he folded the pages so they would fit into the envelope, and using the towel to press down the self-sealing flap.

He took his old copy of the company directory and idly leafed through it. James hadn't looked at it in months. He was surprised at the number of people who no longer worked at the company. He saw his name. Carol's name was listed beside his. One more thing they weren't up to date on. Their mailing address and home phone number, his work email address and unit mail code.

He flipped back a page.

Alice North

The line supervisor, the Black woman who asked questions and had been with the company forever. Hell, why not? Send it to her. If she had any illusions left about the people she was working for, maybe the memos would take care of them. At least they would be out of his hands. Dump them in the trash, maybe someone would find them and be a good Samaritan, send them back.

James used his left hand to carefully print her name and address on the envelope. For a return address, he grinned and flipped the directory to the front. Most of the highest placed people did not have their home addresses listed but one did, someone in fiscal. He used the address and used a "forever" stamp for the envelope.

The next morning, he went through the local post office's drive through and dropped off the envelope, carefully holding it by its edge as he maneuvered into the outgoing slot.

At the very least, now it was someone else's problem.

Steven M. Silver

Chapter 12: The oak

Ellen did not use the word "date" when she agreed to dinner with Robert Blasingame. It was a regular thing, once a month or a little more, not quite as often as their weekend breakfasts, and no strings. It wasn't that Blasingame wasn't attractive and it wasn't that she didn't enjoy her time with him. What it was...

She could not define it. It was an unknown factor. She smiled slightly as she parked in the Italian restaurant's small lot. It was a known unknown, to use a politician's phrase. There were just too many things about Blasingame she didn't know.

More exactly, too many things she didn't understand. Blasingame had come into her life looking for a family heirloom, one belonging to his aunt but missing since her commuter flight crashed north of the small town of Coalville. Other people were looking for something on that flight, people willing to kill to find it. And Robert Blasingame turned out to be involved with them.

Involved? Ellen closed her car's door, looked around the parking lot, and spotted Blasingame's white Toyota SUV. He killed two very bad men with skills one did not obtain by watching the latest thriller at the multiplex. It was a killing Ellen never revealed to anyone, including her friend Karen Deevers. Silence was the promise she gave Blasingame and it had kept him, her, and a new friend alive.

Blasingame now was free of obligations holding him to a very powerful criminal, one who had sent him looking for the two men. But Ellen thought a part of Blasingame took on those obligations because they let him do something he...

She shook her head. Had he really enjoyed being bound to a criminal boss? Was there really part of him craving the risks and danger? And now, while he worked as a contractor restoring Pennsylvania's many old homes and buildings, he still took on jobs "finding things for people."

Things like the kidnapped step daughter of the leading drug boss in Philadelphia. And, what was she thinking? Ellen had helped him do it. Was his craziness contagious? She entered the restaurant with none of her questions answered.

She saw Blasingame as she stepped through the doorway. He was a tall man, muscular in an athlete's fashion, sandy hair cut short, and smile lines drawing your gaze upward to his pale blue eyes. They were curious eyes, always looking around, and they drooped at their ends as if weighed down slightly by some sadness. It was not an accident that he sat in a booth to one side with his back to the wall and could see everyone coming in.

He raised his hand and smiled, a gesture Ellen returned. She nodded to the waitress who stepped forward as if to intercept her.

"I'm with him," she said, a statement that brought a smile to her face, though not for the reason the waitress probably thought. She walked to the booth and Blasingame stood.

"Evening, Ellen," he said. Blasingame had a clear voice, as if it provided words used precisely.

"Hello, Robert," Ellen said as she sat down. She looked around. "Are we here because you've infiltrated the kitchen or are you operating on other intel?" Both Ellen and Blasingame liked discovering small, family-run restaurants, of which there were dozens in Chester County. He smiled.

"Neither," he said, passing her a menu. "Architect on a project I'm helping with suggested it. I looked and you folks don't have a review of it."

"Too far out from the city, probably. Did your friend recommend anything in particular?"

"He said the seafood was very good."

Ellen nodded and studied her menu. She settled on mussels and linguine and ordered a glass of the house wine.

"New project?" she asked Blasingame.

"Yes, major restoration. They had some fire damage last fall. Owner is trying to use the work to change a few things back to how they were in the 19th Century. I've been looking for things for a central fireplace."

"Where is it?"

"Cochranville. It's on the west side, a little separated from the town itself."

"Homeville Road?" Ellen was familiar with most of the roads around her home, the product of long drives of exploration.

"Yes. North side, back in the trees."

75

"I know the area."

While they waited for their food, they let their conversation take them in no particular direction. Ellen found Blasingame's restoration work interesting and he seemed to know how much he could talk about it before her attention became driven by politeness. They skimmed over local politics and Ellen talked about some of the stories she was working on. Their conversation turned to the food when it arrived – it was good – and they compared it to other restaurants they visited.

It was very normal and Ellen appreciated it. Her friends, and Blasingame was one, helped balance the stress of her job. She thoroughly enjoyed working in news but it tended to absorb everything you had like an ink blotter – you could be gone, nothing left, without realizing it. People lost relationships and encountered a host of other problems if they didn't find their balance point.

She smiled as she listened to Blasingame – it seemed a little odd but she did find balance in the company of what was certainly a very dangerous man. But what was that phrase? Ah... No better friend, no worse enemy.

"Did I say something funny?" Blasingame asked, his eyebrows slightly raised and a hint of a smile showing at the corners of his mouth.

"I just thought of something," Ellen said. She almost never tried to misdirect Blasingame; he seemed to have an additional sense useful for picking out truth and lies. "Something about balancing my life." She paused as a waitress removed their plates.

Blasingame cocked his head to one side and let the smile emerge. He held up his wine glass.

"Ellen, you are one of the most balanced people I know." He took a sip.

"Thank you," she said. She grinned. "Who am I being compared to?"

"Architects, antique dealers, computer nerds, and a professional cabinet maker and restorer."

"You run with a bad crowd, Robert," she joked. "I know the nerd and the restorer, I think." Blasingame, still smiling, nodded. "But if I share their level of life balance, I'd regard it as an accomplishment. You can tell them I said so. How is Ty?"

"He's doing fine and seems to be rejoicing in the title of 'nerd.'"

"He is my favorite computer guy," Ellen smiled.

"Well, he pulled down a service contract that's had him very busy but very well paid. His mother is beginning to bug him about going out and meeting someone, now that his business is growing."

"Uh-oh."

"She's forgiven all of us for taking him on our little adventure – she was torn between being horrified at what he was involved in and proud of his heroics in saving a little girl."

"She's settled on the 'hero' thing?"

"I think she's always thought of him as one, but it helped that he stopped working as a bouncer for a man of questionable business ethics."

"And you…?"

Blasingame's smile dropped away.

"I'm still helping people find things," he said slowly, "but my clients are a bit more upright nowadays than Ty's former employer."

Ellen raised her hand slightly off the table.

"I'm not judging, only asking," she said. "I worry a little about you."

Blasingame smiled.

"Score one for the good guy."

"Only a little. Don't let it go to your head." Her smile was wry; she really did worry about him.

Blasingame laughed and raised his glass for a second time and this time Ellen did as well.

She regarded Blasingame, and it had taken her some time to understand it, as a friend, like a brother she never had. Not a lover, not even what Ellen described as a very rare "recreational lover," a phrase she associated with community park programs. Sex would change everything and not in a good way. At least, not in a good way for her. She thought. She wasn't sure. It was selfish, she accepted it, but it was how things had to be until she was sure.

No better friend…

"Speaking of balance," Blasingame said, "how's the shooting coming?"

"Progress is slow," Ellen admitted.

"You are already proficient," he said. "You already had the basics down. Progress is slow from that point." He cocked his head slightly. "Or it was for me."

"You ought to come by sometime. I could show off and humble you."

"I already am very humble and I take a great deal of pride in it. Sure, I'd like to meet your instructor. Former state trooper, you said."

"Yes. He holds all kinds of instructor and coach designations…"

"I know, I looked him up." He raised his eyebrows. "Don't be alarmed. You waxed lyrically about him so much I had to find out what his secret was. Charles Dwyer's got the highest NRA instructor and coach's designations and was an instructor while in the State Police. Competes regularly, placed very highly in the statewide last year, has been married for forty-three years, and has the highest ratings by students at his range."

"You got all that from…"

"The web page of the range he teaches you at. Looks like he knows his business."

"My girlfriend referred me," Ellen said.

"Chernov." It was not a question. To Ellen's raised eyebrow, Blasingame nodded. "Former local police officer, former soldier, took down the Night Tripper, she would know about local firearms instructors." He smiled. "You wrote about her and Hannah, and that little girl. Good article."

"Just as long as you are not making calls to your CIA friends…"

Blasingame's smile widened but he said nothing. Whenever she mentioned anything to do with the intelligence agency, Blasingame became silent. After floating the occasional reference over the months, Ellen was used to his silence on what may have been, or may not have been, a previous venue of employment for her friend and used the three-initialed agency as a small joke. Blasingame did not seem to mind, and never corrected Ellen's agency attribution.

"When is your next session?"

"Saturday. I have his early bird block at eight. If it doesn't conflict with his daughter's birthday party."

"If you want the opportunity to show off, I can make it."

"I'd be delighted."

"I promise not to be a critic."

"Oh, no, if you come, I get to pick your brains."

"Seriously, it is usually best to work with just one instructor." Blasingame's expression matched his tone. "It's the same as improving in any sport. Good instruction, practice, and stay focused on the lessons you need to learn. Some instructors, you can work with them forever, always learning something new, something better. Others are great for a particular period – at some point, you grow through what they have to offer. But an instructor is always a good idea. It's easy to drift away from the fundamentals when you're involved in some advanced stuff, and a good instructor will get you refocused."

"That makes sense. All right, how's this? If you see something I should be doing better, you tell Charles and he can decide what to do with it."

"Sure, but I doubt if that will happen. Dwyer's qualifications and years of experience are off the chart. I'll probably just sit there, dumfounded by your expertise."

Ellen made a short laugh and turned the conversation, suddenly uncomfortable. Robert Blasingame, whatever his past might be, was now a friend and the subject of shooting, even at paper targets, felt like being on a boat that had been drifting quietly downstream but suddenly caught the edge of a twisting current and was thrust back, back towards dark waters she thought were left behind.

She mentioned Dwyer's ongoing joke about the Phillies. That brought a smile to Blasingame and the two of them talked for a while about the array of sports activities in Philadelphia, a place where the teams were referred to either with laughter or tears, and the river gently caught the boat and redirected it back downstream.

She didn't say anything about her agreement to ask Blasingame to serve as her body guard. The idea seemed too melodramatic, even embarrassing. But mostly it was the darkness their conversation had stirred that held her back. She had been too quick to volunteer Robert as her body guard. While she didn't believe she needed one, it was the business of asking him to return to that darkness. He would, Ellen understood, agree to do it, but that made her sense of responsibility feel even greater.

Ellen promised herself she would think about it more, a great deal more, before deciding what to do.

Ellen drove home – she lived west of Philadelphia, though not as far out as Blasingame – beneath purple skies giving way to darkness. In the corner of her eye, she saw a flash and, a few seconds later, heard the muted growl of distant thunder.

For no reason she was aware of, Ellen remembered her grandfather. Thomas Luther Parker had been many things in his life but the greatest number of his years was spent as a farmer. His farm became her childhood sanctuary where she learned much, including things she understood only with time.

She remembered an early evening. Distantly, beyond the broad Ohio fields now comfortably settled from the day into the slow blanket of growing darkness, well to the west of Butler County, a flash low in the sky announced something of power growing in the dark. Thunder, gentle for the moment, arrived seconds later and confirmed the announcement. Little Ellen and her cousin Eileen both stood from their perch on the porch swing.

But Grandpa Tom, sitting on the porch steps and his smile barely seen in the dark, gently waved them back.

"We'll go in before that big fella gets here," he said with his quiet voice and the girls sat down. Tom said nothing else for a moment, not until there was another flash.

"In the Army," he said, taking a sip of the one cup of coffee he allowed himself in the evening, "had a couple of Indian friends. One of them said they called storms 'father rains.'"

"Why?" Eileen asked. She liked to know things.

"Because they are like a lot of men. Tend to come on loud and sudden, maybe violent, and then fade away." He looked over his shoulder at the girls. "Some men are like that, they kind of store things up and then go off."

As if listening, another flash appeared. As the thunder arrived, Tom smiled.

"See what I mean?"

"If that's a father rain," Ellen said, "then there's probably a mother rain."

"Yep. It's steady, gets everything thoroughly wet. It's the rain that causes things to grow."

"Girl rains are best," Eileen announced, grinning. "They're the kinds farmers like."

"We sure do," Tom agreed. He took another sip. "But you make a mistake if you ignore the other kind because they'll wash you into the Ohio." He smiled. "Thing is, you don't always see them coming." Another flash, closely followed by its thunder. "That fella is trying to let us know he's coming and I think we ought to take him seriously, don't you?"

The three Parkers left the porch minutes before the first raindrops slapped the ground.

Her grandfather's face came into her mind. Well, Tom, I don't know if you were trying to tell me something back then, but I've encountered more than a few storms and I don't think I saw any of them coming.

She smiled as she pulled into her home's drive, arriving with the first raindrops.

The morning after the rain, Morrigan Kildeere told herself she just wanted to take a break from work, that entering the woods across from her house was part of going for a walk to clear her head and had nothing to do with her meeting with Jackie.

The road she crossed dreamed of being a gravel-covered farm road like it had been a hundred years before. It missed horses and wagons, Kildeere thought. The dream denied resulted in it shrugging off patches of asphalt in a haphazard fashion. Every other year or so the potholes would be filled in with a casualness that would have given engineers of the autobahn palpitations. Sooner or later, almost always sooner, the new asphalt would be hiccupped and end up in the shallow drainage ditches running alongside the road. The result was a road which kept road repair contractors solvent, vehicle speeds down, motorcycle riders cursing, and the strange sub-species of physical fitness idolaters who ran their miles on public roads away out of fear of turned ankles. A surprising number of Pennsylvania roads shared the same dream.

The trees facing the road had yellow Posted signs, all stapled high, at the very edge of her reach. It looked like she had used every second or third tree and she had. The people working in the hardware store up in Thorndale had begun making gentle jokes when she kept returning for more stacks of signs. One of them had pointed out most of the good hunters wouldn't go onto private property, especially one close to a house, and especially one with a Posted sign anywhere, and the bad ones wouldn't be deterred by a million signs. She shrugged and smiled and said something about playing it safe.

Despite what they said, every spring she did a long walk around, checking that there were no gaps in the signs. The wooded lot was hers, it came with the house, and she was determined to protect it. It was a sanctuary, a place given over to whatever wild could come back after two hundred years of human settlement.

Including herself, she thought.

Kildeere walked across the crumbling road carefully and paused when she made it to the edge of the ditch between the road and the woods. She looked in the direction of the housing development and saw several distant roofs, all the same pastel color, barely above the field-bordering trees. Like Jackie had done, she mentally drew a line from the roofs toward the woods.

She studied the trees. Well, if it had gone in there, it probably had little chance of being found. She walked through and around a thin barrier of blackberry bushes and picked up an animal trail she used when she went for walks and occasional lunches.

Once upon a time, the woods had been farmed. Sometime in the distant past the farming stopped, though the fields around it, stretching into the distance, continued to be used for corn and alfalfa. Trees came back and now were thick enough their shade kept bushes from becoming too thick.

Kildeere moved slow, her eyes spending as much time looking into the trees as they did examining the area around her. A failing drone probably would be snagged by some branch, she thought, long before it ever crashed into the ground. The trees seemed thick enough to snare everything except an agile bird.

But if it came down and missed the trees, would it have crashed? She had looked up drones on the internet out of curiosity. Some had the ability to fly home if they lost the signal from their controller and others would land. Well, maybe it tried to land, but she thought what she would find, if anything, would be blue and white shards of plastic.

Which got her thinking about a project and she stopped looking around as she went deeper into the woods.

Then she remembered what she had seen on the news and stopped. The woods suddenly seemed darker, almost threatening.

I didn't see any red ribbon. But there are other ways into this place.

Kildeere bit her lower lip and took a deep breath as old memories and dark images flowed through her mind as if from the devil's streaming service – all Hell, all the time. She closed her eyes tightly and her lips spread from clenched teeth. Part of her wanted to run.

Where? This shit is yours, woman. There's no place to go.

Morrigan Kildeere stood on the thin path, her eyes closed, hands clenched, and fought her flashback, driving it down, back into its dark hole, and, finally, took a long, deep breath. Her eyes opened, her hands unclenched, and she licked her lips. She knew the fight had only taken a moment but she felt like it had gone on for an hour or more.

The woods just looked like what it was, a gathering of trees, a small forest sitting in southern Pennsylvania, tops barely moving with a breeze she could not feel. Kildeere nodded and rubbed her hands against her jeans.

"Damn." The word was muttered, low, just for her own hearing. While not a victory cry, it was not said in defeat.

Kildeere looked around, seeking the drone, and didn't see it. She glanced at her watch. She would look for another fifteen minutes and then get back to work.

The path vanished, reappeared, then finally disappeared, but she knew where she was. The woods were more than her property. At times, they were a place of contemplation, a place to gather herself. And, if that was so melodramatic she smiled, it was a great place to have lunch.

She turned slightly and went deeper into the trees. In a moment, she was there.

A large oak, its branches broad enough to reduce growth around it to little more than grasses, had muscled itself upward from the center of the woods and served, more often than not, as her destination when having lunch. She paused, looking up at it, but saw no sign of the drone.

The raven caught up with her as she looked around the small clearing marking the boundary of the oak's presence. It landed on a branch and chortled some story while she searched.

"If you're so smart," she said, "why haven't you found it?"

The raven made no reply but looked into the sky, perhaps suggesting that looking for toys was beneath it. She shook her head, grinned, turned, and found the drone.

The drone was four small, ringed plastic propellers attached to a tiny fuselage, white and blue. It lay right side up, as far as she could tell, and showed no obvious signs of damage. She squatted beside it and did nothing for a moment as she studied it. Satisfied that she wouldn't break anything, she carefully lifted it with both hands and stood. She glanced at the raven.

It was looking at her and she thought, if it had eyebrows, it would have raised them.

I saw it all the time, she thought it was saying.

"Of course, you did."

Kildeere crossed the road, still gently holding the drone, and realized she did not know Jackie's last name. Well, he would probably come back. But what if she was not home? What if she didn't want to be disturbed?

She took the drone into her barn and placed it on a work table. She found a white trash bag and carefully put the drone in it. She pulled the bag's strings tight and tied them together with a bow.

A felt pen and a cardboard box panel made a sign she taped to the outside of the bag. Then Kildeere took the whole arrangement to the place where Jackie had left his bike and looped the bag bow around a post. She made sure the sign was firmly taped in place and then went back to work.

Jackie.
Here it is.
The raven found it.

Chapter 13: A perfect fit

The glass cases held handguns; the walls were covered by rifles and shotguns. The weapons seemed to turn the store into a tunnel whose walls of predominantly black and steel gray seemed to pull the glow of the ceiling lights into them, bringing out all the angular detail instead of allowing their long, dark shapes merge with one another.

Here and there, the row of stacked long guns was interrupted by brief spans of white peg board; each held several weapons displayed horizontally and all pointing to the viewer's right as if ready, maybe eager, to move in the same direction. James saw they were semiautomatic rifles that seemed related genetically, variations on a theme. Sharp angles over pistol grips, plastic stocks and flash suppressors, almost all were black but one or two wore dark gray or camouflaged patterns.

The clerk, a middle-aged white man handed James one and the weapon seemed to flow into his shoulder, pressed against his cheek, formed itself to his gripping hand, and its sights naturally aligned with his eye. For a second, felt like the sights were looking back into him.

"The AR-15 family comes with two kinds of operating systems," the clerk said, beginning what sounded a little like a familiar lecture.

"Gas piston and direct impingement," James said, his eyes still held by the sights. He swung the rifle slightly, sighting on a letter on a sign, then on the corner of a light fixture.

"Done your homework," the clerk said with a smile that might have been approving. "Do you have a preference?"

"Gas piston," James said, raising his head and studying the weapon in his hands. "Cleaner, I've read."

"Generally, yes, since the gas isn't pushing directly onto the bolt. But a little pricier, since you don't have the standardization you have with direct impingement. They are pretty much all built to the military standard, so interchangeable parts are more common, you can do a little more customizing with impingement if you are into that." He paused as James handed him the rifle. He laid it on the counter. "Might I ask, what did you want to do with it?"

"Target shooting," James said, though no real purpose came to his mind. "Maybe some home defense."

"Great gun for target shooting. Even the gas piston ones don't really have much of a kick, only a little more than impingement. And ammunition won't break your bank account. You can customize them to whatever you like with sights and scopes and whole match grade parts."

"What about home defense?" James asked, remembering an online article he had read.

"Most of the time," the clerk said slowly, "someone wanting an AR for home defense wants a short barrel. You know, for maneuvering through doorways in the dark and so on. But you've got to watch your surroundings. Take a 55 grain .223 caliber bullet; it will be moving at about three thousand feet per second at the muzzle. That little fellow will go through most ordinary house walls and continue on down the street."

"That wouldn't be good."

"That wouldn't be good," the clerk agreed, his smile returning. "For defense, you want ammo built for the task. Rapid expansion, you see? Stop at the wall." James nodded. "Hornaday makes very good ammo in pretty much all calibers, rifle and pistol, for home defense. Hit something and the brakes come on. Still want to be careful, of course."

"Of course. What about barrel length?"

"Well, defense in the home, you might want 16 inches. Out on the far range, a lot of shooters would vote for twenty for targets beyond 300 meters but I think that's mostly about terminal ballistics. The twenty will hit harder than the sixteen at far distance but, when you're talking about what an AR-15 rifle shoots, with a little practice, you won't have any problem shooting accurately out to 400. Among shooters, the 16-inch barrel is the most popular." He paused. "Have you done a lot of shooting?"

"None," James said. "But we all have to start somewhere."

"True enough." The clerk put the rifle up on its place on the wall. "Now, this one is," he said as he pulled a rifle down, "a Ruger, similar to the one you were just trying. But the stock is adjustable to six positions." He glanced into the rifle's chamber and handed it to James. "It is chambered for five-point-five six millimeter, which means it can also hold ammunition in .223 caliber."

"Not a good idea to go the other way around," James said, remembering his reading. He made a point of looking into the chamber and then raised the weapon to his shoulder.

"Not the best idea, no. You can adjust the buttstock with… There, you have it."

James tried the sights. It was not as comfortable as the other rifle. He adjusted the buttstock back a little and placed it against his shoulder.

It fit. No, shoes fit, gloves fit. The rifle *belonged* against his shoulder, the handgrip was exactly where his hand sought it, and the sights offered a clear view as if revealing something for his eyes only.

The clerk said nothing but smiled. He had seen others, not all men, suddenly find that link to a firearm when it felt perfect. Their nonverbals gave it away. This is what shooters meant when they referred to a gun "marrying up" to someone. It belonged.

"Very nice," James said, lowering the black weapon as gently as he might a kitten that fell asleep on his shoulder.

"It's on sale," the clerk said. "And I can give you a discount on any ammunition you buy with it, up to five hundred rounds."

"That sounds good," James said and, for the first time since entering the store, he smiled. "I think I'm going to need some lessons, though."

"Well, I know a retired State Trooper who gives individual lessons. Range is a little bit of a drive from here…"

"State Trooper? Sure, learn from a pro."

"I've got one of his cards, I'll attach it to your receipt."

"Thank you." James gently handed the black rifle to the clerk. "Seems like a good one."

"I think you're going to be very happy with what it can do."

"I think so, too."

James filled out the mandated paperwork for the Pennsylvania Instant Check System and it took only a few minutes for his background check to run and clear. The $25 PICS fee was added to the purchase price of the weapon and ammunition, cleaning gear, and a couple of spare magazines, and he paid for it all in only a little more time than it took to submit the PICS. With the AR-15 in its box behind his front seat, he drove home, feeling good, which was unusual enough he noticed it.

He didn't think about the why of it.

James set up an area in his well-lit basement for cleaning the AR. Though the light on his broad work table was good enough for most tasks, he set up three more lights, anchoring them by their clamps above him, carefully positioned to banish even the ghost of shadows.

In addition to the owner's manual, he had purchased during his searches on the web several books on the AR-15 rifle series. He had read each one – two he read twice – and he had one opened along with the manual. Next to them was an old computer tablet on which were offered numerous YouTube videos on the AR-15 and his particular make and model.

He very carefully disassembled the rifle and just as carefully reassembled it. He did that three times, teaching himself the particulars and the cautions. After the third time, he felt confident enough to give the weapon a cleaning, what some called in the videos a "field cleaning." Some of the more intricate assemblies remained intact as he broke the rifle down into its major components. He examined everything, both looking for anything that might be wrong and becoming more familiar with it.

It wasn't work, though he was studying every piece with greater intensity than he did with anything encountered at his job. He felt himself drawn into the weapon, into its finely crafted parts and rugged assembly, as if pulled into an elaborate puzzle. No, it was something more than a puzzle, but something with a puzzle's intricacies. A search for…

Answers? He did not know where the word came from but he paused for a heartbeat when he encountered it.

He smiled as he carefully ran a small piece of cloth down the rifle's barrel. Answers, sure, maybe, if he could only figure out the questions.

James loaded a large magazine with thirty rounds. Each was brass and reflected his strong lights so well they seemed to glow. Each round added its own small weight to the magazine until it was full. He hefted it in his hand. It seemed more substantial, more… Significant. Important.

He carefully inserted the magazine into the AR. It went smoothly, clicking into place without any reluctance, and the rifle changed in his hands. The mass of the magazine seemed to permeate the rifle, filling it, making it more than it was before. It still felt, as he raised it and pressed it against his shoulder as he sighted on the hot water tank, like it belonged. Now was added something else, something about power, about strength. Mastery.

James blinked and he lowered the rifle. Mastery. This was not a toy. It had to be mastered. The books, the videos, they were just an introduction.

He released the magazine and pulled the bolt back, checking no round was left in the rifle. Then he found the receipt.

Stapled to it was a simple white business card. Charles Dwyer, Firearms Instructor, it said. An email address was at the bottom. Several NRA-related icons for instructors lay in a row in the middle. James studied the card for a moment and then nodded.

Mastery.

Chapter 14: Too few to go higher

"How many?"

"Too soon. AP says one confirmed but also says it is an active…"

"I have a local station's website. They haven't posted anything."

"What we're seeing is from a helicopter. CNN is taking the feed from a Columbus broadcaster; local traffic bird doing double duty, you think?"

"All right, here it is. AP, taking it from that ABC affiliate. Shooter is dead, apparent suicide. Two nursing home employees dead. Chief of police, on the job just a few weeks, was responding to shots fired and the shooter got him as he approached the nursing home, but there's a little confusion still. Started early this morning, around nine."

"Four dead, then?"

"So far."

"First mass shooting for Ohio since, wait, I got this. Since 2004."

"All right, Jack, get on the wire but start laying it out. Where is Kirkersville?"

"Just a little east of Columbus. Less than six hundred live there."

"It comes to everyone. Ellen, set up the site to receive Jack's copy."

"How high do you want it?"

"Kirksville, only four? Medium unless it grows and be ready to let it go low."

"Okay. Jack, run your copy through me and I'll push it through the link."

"Understood. Bob, send me that 2004 stuff."

"You got it."

Ellen Parker studied her screen; four deaths were too few to put it any higher on the page and the story would probably be bounced down to the second page of the website as other news crowded it out. That's what the editor meant when he said it might go low. Besides, people looking at the website with phones probably would not bother to thumb very far down the page. They'd most likely stop at the story about the President's latest tweet – automatically, it was in the top quarter, sometimes the lead if it was loud enough, because, of course, it was the President – and whoever it was who died in and around a nursing home in Kirkersville, Ohio, would never be noticed.

The morning passed quickly. Kirkersville vanished, dropped in favor of other items. By lunch time, Ellen almost had forgotten it. She ate at her desk, working on a story about charter schools – her byline – and reviewing articles coming in from other people.

After lunch a flurry of activity broke out around an interview of the President; the editor coordinated everyone while Ellen took over shepherding several local stories onto the site. She set up the website to take the new material high up, talked with a reporter working a local story, got the reviews done and posted, called a charter school organizer to check some dates and enrollment numbers, sent a copy of story assignments to the editor, worked through her in-house email inbox by dashing off short "yes-no" responses to questions other staff had with only a few requiring a longer reply of several sentences, and did not notice the Friday afternoon's time melt away until it was gone and she was briefing some of the people who would be working through the evening.

She rode the commuter train from Philadelphia's Suburban Station out to Downingtown, studying the website on her phone and picking off a few incoming emails and text messages in the ride's hour. She took her car to the local YMCA and did a circuit of the weight machines. Since it was Friday, she pushed herself to do more than her scheduled repetitions; climbing onto a stationary bike for twenty minutes almost was a relief.

As she walked out to her car she checked for messages. Robert Blasingame had sent her one and she grimaced as she read it.

Working, sorry. Will be at the range tomorrow.

"Crap," she said as she got into her car. Well, the restaurant, a new one they were going to check out, was not going to go anywhere and they would get to it eventually.

Working. Robert liked to say he helped people find things. Some of those people, she knew, were folks more than one law enforcement agency monitored and hoped someday to sit down with and have a long and very pointed conversation. Folks who would find such conversations awkward could not very well turn to those agencies for assistance, folks like John Allen Douglas, whose step-child Nichole fell into the hands of a professional kidnapper and child killer. Robert found the child in the dark of a basement, with some help from Ellen and Tyrone Rydell, himself found under the unusual circumstances of having someone seriously considering questioning him with a blowtorch.

Robert was a dangerous man, someone it had taken Ellen time to trust, even after he saved her life. But he was an excellent companion for exploring restaurants around Chester County, worked at least some of the time as a restorer of old homes, liked Springsteen, and had learned interesting skills in the hills of Afghanistan. Maybe it was Afghanistan. And he was working, Ellen thought, because he was a little addicted to what those skills had taken him to.

Or maybe it was something else, maybe just a need to be good at something, maybe it was about doing something valuable, something worthwhile. Ellen's friends in the "Shot to Hell Club" referred to the need to be doing something significant in their lives after surviving what one of them called "Capital-T trauma."

It was a need Ellen shared. Maybe it explained hanging in the uncertain news business. Every other week another half dozen rumors appeared about everyone being sold to some consortium of terrible people and everything they worked for would be flushed into the Delaware River.

And maybe she did just so she could cover her mortgage. She smiled as she pulled into her driveway and watched as the lights came on over the garage and her front porch.

Maybe that was the secret, she thought. All the strongest needs came from needing first to pay the bills.

James Hardy walked out of the sporting goods store – it was larger than the grocery store he used – with another gun. It was a handgun and came in a blue plastic box with a built-in handle. When he got to his car, he put it behind the driver's seat with the other weapons he had purchased.

He smiled and shook his head. Buying the AR seemed to have unlocked something and he found himself buying more guns. Now he had six. One was a shotgun with an 18.5-inch barrel; they told him it would have to be registered as a "short shotgun" if it was less than a foot and a half, so the manufacturer added a half inch just to avoid the hassle. The stock could be folded and it had a pistol grip, both things making the shotgun very cool.

His latest purchase was his third pistol, a smaller sized Glock that he thought would fit in a jacket pocket without being too obvious. It was his second Glock, the other being a full sized 9-millimeter.

After work each day he would go to a gun store, almost never the same store twice, and would walk the gun displays. Most of the time he would buy nothing but, if the clerk had been attentive, he would get a box of ammunition. He ordered and bought guns only on weekends, and today was Friday so it counted, and only after doing what he thought of as research.

His web browser had more gun-related bookmarks than all the others combined. James liked the reviews but also scanned the forums for comments on makes of guns he was interested in. If someone in the military or police posted a comment about a gun he researched, he would study the remarks carefully. He was good at research, a carry-over from his skills developed on his job. At least he had gotten something good out of all that crap.

It was a chance remark on a gun site forum that opened up a new area for his research. Someone had mentioned a weapon used by a police SWAT unit and said it had been used responding to a shooting. The reply said the cops had been "out-gunned" and named the gun carried by the shooter. Someone replied to the reply and insisted that the shooter had used a different gun entirely. Then someone else said it was the most favored gun used by mass shooters.

What gun had he used? James looked it up and discovered the news media had called it an AR-15 but had not specified the manufacturer. He searched further and found a picture of the guns carried by the shooter. The picture had been released by the police and James suspected the caption was supplied by them. It was a Colt AR-15, no doubt about it.

What about the remark about what was the most favored gun? It took him only a moment to find a compilation of shootings put together by an outfit called "Mother Jones," whoever she was. The compilation started in 1982 and included shootings involving three or more deaths, not counting the shooter. And it could be downloaded and used as a spreadsheet.

Whoever put it together was a gun nut like him, James decided, smiling. The very first entry, from August 20, 1982, listed the firearm – a Mossberg 500 Persuader. Shotgun. He searched for it and found it. A classic, he decided.

He glanced at the spreadsheet. Eight dead, three wounded, all killed in a welding shop. Well, in a shop, close range, perfect for a shotgun. Probably anyone you hit would be killed, assuming decent sized shot.

James read the spreadsheet for a bit and then was surprised to see how late it was. He was going to meet with his shooting instructor in the morning and he didn't want to be tired. Though it was tempting to stay up and keep reading the spreadsheet, he shut his computer down. After all, he didn't have to stay up all night – it wasn't going anywhere – and he looked forward to taking his time with it. After all, there was a lot to be learned from it.

He turned off the lights and walked off in darkness.

Chapter 15: Center mass

Blasingame stood leaning against his old Honda's hatchback, his arms folded, legs crossed, and smiling slightly as he watched Ellen drive into the parking area. She nodded as she pulled into a slot.

After she gathered up a large, orange utility case containing gun cleaning equipment and boxes of ammunition, she walked across the lot to him.

"Good to see you found the place," she said. "I left bread crumbs."

"I was supposed to follow them? I thought they were breakfast."

His eyes hid behind aviator sunglasses but he took them off as she approached, revealing his sad-drooping eyes. Slightly faded jeans partially covered high top hiking shoes. A black Los Lobos t-shirt peeked (*Peace, Ese*) from beneath an open dark blue shirt he wore loose with the sleeves rolled up above his wrists. He reached inside the Honda and pulled out a blue tackle box with a pair of ear protectors held by a strap to one end.

Blasingame had on his tan baseball cap, an old one. It had a rectangle of hook and loop fastener over the bill and a longer rectangle of the same material in the back. There was even a little square of the stuff on the very top. Ellen thought there were supposed to be patches of some kind, maybe a name tag on the back, but he never had any.

He did not reach for her case. They knew each other well enough that he understood she preferred to carry her own things and she understood she lost nothing by asking for his help.

"Did you bring a pistol?"

"Found some rocks," he said, seriously, raising his blue case. "When I was a kid, I was pretty good at skipping stones. Never tried them on paper targets."

"I don't think Dwyer will let them on the range. He likes things to be neat."

Blasingame smiled and motioned to his shirt.

"Back at my four." He glanced at the Glock on her hip. "I try to be less demonstrative than some people."

"I just wear it to compensate for my sense of inadequacy."

"I thought as much."

Ellen led them into the large range building. A small shop, still closed, was to one side and faced a classroom on the other. They followed a short hallway with offices on either side. A sign for the indoor range pointed to one side but Ellen went in the other direction, passing a restroom and a small locker room.

They stopped in a room that had several tables with sets of chairs, a coffee urn, and machines with snacks and soft drinks. Charles Dwyer, sitting at a table near the exit to the outdoor range, raised his trooper's cup.

"Good morning, Ellen. You brought a friend?"

"Good morning. Charles, this is Robert Blasingame, an old friend. Robert, Charles Dwyer, my instructor."

Blasingame walked up to Dwyer and extended his hand.

"Glad to meet you," he said. "Ellen's told me a lot about you."

"Come to watch her shoot?" Dwyer asked as he shook Blasingame's hand.

"Only if you and she don't mind."

"Ellen?" Dwyer said, his eyes still on Blasingame. "Seriously, you all right with someone other than me watching?"

"It's fine. Is the coffee any good or should I have brought some from Starbucks?"

"It's better than Starbucks but then so would warm cat piss, pardon my French. You're ex-military?"

"Kind of," Blasingame said, a slight smile coming to him. "Was sort of a translator for a time."

"What are you carrying?"

"Springfield Armory 1911."

"You have a carry permit?"

"Yes, sir. Would you like to see it?"

"Ellen, your friend is offering to show me his county concealed carry permit for that large handgun he has. Should I take him at his word?"

"You do what you think is right," Ellen said, stirring her coffee as she leaned against the counter.

"You trust him?" Dwyer's small smile matched Blasingame's but his eyes did not leave the other man's face.

"With my life, Charles." Ellen suddenly realized she had decided to ask Blasingame to help protect her. *Well, Karen will feel more comfortable with him watching my back. I think.*

Blasingame looked at Ellen, his eyebrows climbing. She did not look away as she nodded but said nothing else.

"Well, then," Dwyer said, looking back and forth between Ellen and Blasingame, his own eyebrows making their own small climb. "I'm guessing we ought to go to work, young lady." He stood, drank the last of his coffee, and stretched. "When we go down the hall to the range, you'll have to clear your firearm. Range rules." He picked up his ear protectors and pulled on his baseball cap.

"Yes, sir," Blasingame said. "I saw some lockers on the way in…"

"Not necessary. And stop calling me 'sir.' I keep looking around for someone to salute. 'Charles' will do."

"All right, Charles."

As Charles led the way to the indoor range, he looked over his shoulder at Ellen.

"I don't have to tell you…"

"Cleared it in the car, put the clip in my case."

"All right, then," he said. He paused to turn on the range lights.

The indoor range consisted of twenty-five stations divided by short walls. The end of the range consisted of flat sheets of steel angled to deflect incoming rounds into a bullet trap. A powered, overhead cable system enabled each station to run targets out to any distance a shooter wanted and a hinged, red painted board blocked movement into the shooting corridors.

Blasingame glanced around as they entered the range room. There was no one else present. He stepped up to one of the stations and stood beneath a sign that admonished everyone to Keep It Down Range! as he ejected his pistol's clip and then pulled the slide to the rear, catching the round with his hand. Blasingame locked the slide to the rear, visually inspected the chamber to ensure it was clear, and then put the pistol in his case.

Folding chairs neatly lined the wall behind the firing stations and Dwyer pointed at them as he and Ellen walked to a station.

"You can sit there, Mr. Blasingame."

"'Robert' is fine, Charles." Blasingame, still smiling, sat down.

"Not 'Bobby'?"

"'Robert' is fine."

"Know what you mean. Always hated 'Charley' and I could never figure out who the hell was 'Chuck.'"

Blasingame freed his ear protectors and placed them around his neck as Dwyer and Ellen talked. He watched as they placed a pair of black silhouette targets on the arms of target holder. Dwyer ran the targets out to a white line running across the range; Blasingame estimated it was 25 feet away. As he did, Ellen worked on her clips, laying them on the wooden gate.

He saw Dwyer and Ellen put on their ear protectors – he saw she used the electronic kind while Dwyer's looked to be the old-fashioned passive type – and he did the same. Dwyer stepped back and looked left and right but they were still alone in the range.

"Ready on the firing line," Dwyer said loudly, perhaps compensating for his ear protectors muting the sound of his own voice, though the small microphones in Ellen's would carry his voice. "Shooter, begin your exercise."

Ellen picked up her pistol with her left hand and, bracing her grip with her right hand, began firing. Blasingame watched as she worked through a clip and then quickly reloaded. She resumed firing until the clip was empty.

Ellen dropped the clip from the pistol and secured the slide to the rear, checking that there wasn't a round in the chamber. Dwyer pushed a button on the dividing wall and the targets sailed back to them as Ellen picked up her first clip. The two took off their ear protectors as they studied the targets.

They stayed at the targets for several minutes, examining what Ellen had done. Dwyer pointed at holes, most of which appeared to be in the center of the silhouettes, would say something, and would use his hands to show her nuances of managing her grip.

Ellen seemed to follow her instructor intently, nodding, taking a small notepad out of her box and jotting things down, and occasionally asking a question, slightly leaning toward Dwyer when he answered.

She's really into it.

Blasingame thought for a moment.

Considering what she's been through, she ought to be.

They continued with the practice, pausing only to examine the targets and to quietly talk as Ellen made notes.

The last exercise had Ellen's pistol holstered and Blasingame saw her put a spare clip in her pocket. Dwyer checked the range and then did nothing, letting Ellen stare at the targets.

"Now!" Dwyer shouted the word loud enough that Blasingame could hear it even through his ear protectors.

Ellen, using her right hand and slightly crouched, emptied her pistol, the shots coming rapidly as she moved back and forth between the two targets. She dropped its clip, pulled the full one from her pocked and slapped it into the pistol. She let the slide go forward as she sighted on a target and fired. In a few seconds, the gun was empty. Her eyes still on the targets, she released the empty clip and put it next to her notepad. Ellen's eyes finally moved when she checked her pistol clear.

Dwyer said nothing for a moment, standing back with his arms folded. Blasingame was not sure what he was waiting for. Finally, Dwyer reached up and pressed the button, bringing the targets back to them.

Blasingame slightly raised his hand and Dwyer noticed and motioned him forward. He draped his ear protectors around his neck as he walked.

Ellen studied the targets silently and Blasingame looked closely. At some point, they had used black target tape to cover the previous holes over the center of the silhouettes but Ellen hadn't used the centers as her points of aim.

The heads of the targets were riddled, the paper torn like something angry had ripped through it.

Blasingame nodded. Something angry did, I think.

"The exercise," Dwyer said, glancing at Blasingame, "was about reloading from a pocket. Don't always have a convenient clip holder on your belt."

"Head shots?" For a moment, no one answered Blasingame's question.

"Just for practice," Ellen said. She folded each target. "Real life, center of target's mass." She looked at Blasingame and smiled a little. "I know. Practice like you fight. Any choice at all, center mass."

"It's good to have a choice."

"Damned straight," Dwyer said. "You clear on your homework?"

"Got it, Charles. More on the weak hand."

"It's coming," he said. "Patience. He looked at his watch. "I have to roll. Got a new client."

"Someone else for you to badger?" Ellen smiled.

"We don' need no stinkin' badgers," Dwyer said. He looked back at the range entrance where a thin man stood. "I think that's him with the AR. We'll be going outside. You two take it easy and I'll see you in three weeks."

"You bet."

"Have a good day, Charles," Blasingame said and held out his hand.

"You, too, Robert," Dwyer said, smiling, but his eyes were inquisitive and it was easy to remember he had made his living as a police officer.

Ellen quickly walked to the chairs and brought back a broad sweep broom and gathered up her casings. Blasingame helped her corral a couple that seemed intent on escaping. They put them into a zip bag and Ellen squatted beside her case, trying to make the folded targets fit.

"What did you think?" she asked as she finally succeeded.

"You're a good shot," he said.

"Any suggestions?"

"I like that he has you practicing with your weak hand. That was a big problem for me."

"Did it you get better at it?"

"Well, I sort of *had* to, but I don't recommend my method."

"What…?"

Blasingame pushed his right sleeve back.

"You probably saw this at one time or another."

A smooth, thin scar, about two inches long, made a twisted path behind the heel of his right hand.

"Ouch," she said.

"I recall saying something similar at the time," he said. "It made it almost impossible to maintain my grip."

"Were you shot?" Ellen held up her hands. "Sorry, I know I said I wouldn't ask about any of that…"

Blasingame smiled as he pushed his sleeve down.

"No, nothing dramatic. Tore it up snagging some barbed wire one night when I jumped off a wall. Some very nice people put it all back together again and I only notice it when I do *this*…" He spread his fingers wide and bent his hand back as if commanding someone to stop. "Just a little twinge thing and that's it. But, while it healed, I could only use my left. My penmanship was as bad as my accuracy. Several weeks of being a leftie did improve my shooting, though."

"'Translator,' were you?" She shook her head.

"Well, yes, kind of." He looked around. "When do people come in?"

"Let's get some of the house coffee and I saw what you did there, changing the subject and all."

They backtracked to the snack area. As they sipped their coffee, Blasingame heard shots coming from outside.

"Charles has a lot of students?"

99

"About a dozen regulars, I think, but that's not one."

"No?"

"New people, he'll spend their first session going over safety requirements, getting their history, shooting goals, all that kind of thing."

"And maybe figuring out what they're about?"

"Well, yes, a little. Last year a couple of Nazis tried to enroll in a course. Button-down shirts, regular haircuts, clean shaven, no visible tatts, very polite. Someone spotted some pamphlets in the back of their car. When told they weren't welcome, they got pretty upset and threatened law suits; the owner told them to go ahead and sue him because he said having them as customers violated his religious beliefs."

"Really?"

"Charles said Mr. Kellogg, he's the owner, believes in all Eleven Commandments."

"Eleven." Blasingame shook his head slowly. "All right, and the Eleventh is…?"

"Thou shalt not be a dick-head."

"I'm not sure that's Mosaic but anything's possible." He cocked his head. "I remember what you ran into. How big are those people in Pennsylvania?"

"Counting neo-Nazis, Klan, and others of their persuasion, we've got more racial hate groups than any other state." She took a sip. "Couple of small towns, they have a commanding presence. Very open, swastika flags, banners, scheduled meetings, billboards, try to appear as regular as Rotarians."

"I've known some Rotarians who would be offended at that description."

"Most people would be," Ellen said. "Pennsylvania's been through hard times. Old industries are gone, population was getting old as the young people left for greener pastures, all that. Infrastructure crumbling, drugs, for a while crime was rising. Politicians haven't been as useful as they might have been, lot of beating of the fear drums. Playing people off against one another. But not everyone went out and got a Klan card."

"My impression is," Blasingame said slowly, "most people around here are pretty solid."

"I agree. Biggest National Guard membership in the country, lots of veterans, lot of people who think the country is still something to work for. Looking for leaders. They went for Obama *and* Trump. Still looking, I guess. Hurting, some of them. Angry. Vulnerable."

"Fertile ground for someone claiming to have all the answers."

"So, we get our share of idiots."

"And some pretty good ones, too."

"I agree with that, too." She smiled slightly. "For a while there, everywhere I looked I saw monsters."

"You went through a few things…"

"Well, it was my job, too. We don't report on a lot of happy things."

"So how are the monsters now?"

"We have them outnumbered." Her smile broadened. "Just have to keep reminding myself."

Charles Dwyer had a notebook, an outline copied from the range's manual but with his own numerous notes inserted. He carefully checked each point as he talked to James – in the firearms instructor business, it was important to cover everything thoroughly.

He sat behind a small desk and James took the seat closest to him. Dwyer was glad to see the younger man taking notes on a yellow-paged pad he took from a brand-new blue range box. When Dwyer paused, James occasionally had a good question.

Dwyer liked that, too. A lot of people were afraid to ask questions but James closely followed what he said.

"All right," Dwyer said. "That's the basic info for the range. You'll find it repeated in that blue booklet, yeah, that one. Be sure to go over it at home. When we talked, you weren't sure about the specific courses you wanted to take. Since you brought that AR with you, I'm guessing you want to learn something about rifles."

"Yes," James said. He shook his head. "Guess I was a little eager and should have asked."

"Not a problem. I have some brochures about the courses for rifles that we offer."

"Well, I think I know what I want," James said. "When I saw the courses on the range's website, I looked them up on the NRA site."

"Modern technology is a wonderful thing. What are you thinking?"

"Well, I think I'm going to want some individual instruction in pistol. But what I think I ought to begin with is the Home Firearm Safety course and I would also like to enroll in both of the rifle courses you're offering, the orientation one and then the basic course." He paused. "And there are a couple of the basic pistol courses I think I need as well."

"There are courses all the time. Many are one day, anywhere from a couple of hours to pretty much the whole day. You can get through the basic ones pretty quickly. Of course, we're not the only place offering the courses you're interested in."

"Well, you're the closest to me and you came individually recommended."

"Me?"

"Fellow at the store gave me your card." James paused and dug into his jeans for a moment and brought out a business card. "He put his name on the back, name of 'John Campbell,' if I'm reading his handwriting right."

"You are. He sold you the AR?"

"Yes, he did."

"John and I go back a bit." Dwyer nodded. "Well, we keep the basic classes small but the ones you are interested in almost always have open slots. You probably saw the schedule on our site but you can reserve a slot by…" He flipped to the back of his notebook and freed a piece of paper. "By filling this out. Schedule is on the back." He handed it to James. "One of our folks here will enter it into the computer for you."

"Great, thanks," James said. He read the form.

"While you're filling it out, what got you interested in firearms?"

James looked up, his face blank for a second, then he frowned slightly.

"Well, sure, there was a self-protection part to it, I think that got me interested first. But as I did some reading; I mean, not just about guns but about shooting, I liked the discipline aspects. You know, it's something you have to pay attention to."

"True."

"I spend most of my time moving paper and reports around, that kind of thing. You know, on the job." He took a breath. "I think I'm looking for something that's a little more of a challenge, something I'm going to have to work at to be any good."

"Firearms can be a challenge, no question." Dwyer raised his eyebrows and folded his arms. "Some controversy about guns nowadays. You may find some of your friends think you've lost your mind."

James shook his head.

"Not a problem."

"They all gun owners?"

"No." James shrugged slightly.

Dwyer saw James' face flash a look of sadness and then go… Blank. Then he realized. No, because you don't have any.

Dwyer kept his interpretation, what he called "cop sense," to himself. His sense was pretty good, part innate, part developed by a Black childhood in a White society, but mostly from years as a cop. But he didn't drop it on James, didn't feel any need to show off. It was a tool, one he used automatically after all the years refining it. Revealing it to someone could be startling, so he saved sharing the insights for times it was useful, like when interrogating a perp.

Or messing with his family.

The thought of his wife brought a small smile to his face, one with the same dimensions as the one he had while talking with Ellen's friend but this time it was shared with his eyes.

"Well," Dwyer said, "just brace yourself. Somebody's going to decide they know what's good for you and that you are really interested in learning their wisdom."

"Sure. I know a couple of people like that."

"Humor them. It will drive them crazy, since they usually don't have a sense of humor."

That got a smile from James. It faded.

"One thing," he said. "I want to take these classes and all and get familiar with my firearms. But, eventually, I want to build on that, get some realistic training."

"Realistic?"

"I want to be as good as I can be with a gun." He paused and the silence stretched. "If I ever have to use one, I want to be prepared, and I think that means getting some training oriented towards the real-world."

"I see."

"That's why I wanted to get in touch with you. I saw you are one of the instructors who does self-defense training beyond the standard courses. I want to do them but I think, if I'm serious, I think I'll need to learn more to really master shooting."

"I see. Well, I do that kind of teaching but a lot of it is on your own."

"Homework."

"Exactly. Takes time, dedication."

"Discipline."

"That it does. I do work with a handful of people."

"That lady you were with today." James shook his head. "I didn't mean to sound like I was snooping but I saw her going through like a drill."

"Not a problem, the range is open. Yes, like that lady. And it was a drill."

"She seemed pretty good."

"She is. She's worked hard at it. Lots of 'homework'."

"Well, I'm willing to put in the time."

"Let's get together after you do those courses and, if you're still interested, we'll set you up."

"Sounds reasonable."

"Now, since you're here, why don't I take you out to the outdoor range and show you around? That is, if you've got the time."

"Sounds great," James said. He put his pad into his box and stood as Dwyer did. "I appreciate you taking the time to do it."

"Glad to," Dwyer said. "Gets me off my butt and gives you some exercise hauling that big box of yours."

"I guess I overdid it."

"Better too big than too small. You have some ear protectors in there?"

"Yes, sir." He smiled and shrugged. "And all my cleaning gear, boxes of ammunition, everything I could think of."

"Do the same thing myself." Dwyer let the way to the exit. "Pack rat. Sooner or later, I fill my box up and get to go buy a new one. Some kind of conspiracy."

James laughed. It wasn't much but it wasn't forced. To Dwyer it sounded a little like the kind of laugh you would hear from someone out of practice.

Chapter 16: Back watching

"What do you think of her?" Janowski's question hung in the car. It was not the first time he had asked it and Chernov knew it would not be the last; whatever else one thought of him, Janowski was persistent. A good quality for a police officer, at least in the abstract, Chernov was willing to accommodate her partner as he worked through his thinking about Kildeere.

"You mean since yesterday?" She smiled as she replied. "A little on the strange side." She flipped a page on her clip board, reading notes she had taken before coming on shift.

"Anything more?" He looked both ways before pulling out onto State Route 896.

"I'm not getting alarm bells." She looked up; the day was gray which meant nothing; it might rain, it might snow, it might be sunny and clear, all before lunch, maybe even all at the same time. This was, after all, eastern Pennsylvania. "She has a patch of woods in front of her house. Our bad man favors woods."

"Another datum. Everywhere you go in Chester County there are patches of woods. But, yes, I saw that and kept looking for a red ribbon or something." Janowski fell silent as he studied a car in front of them. "But I've got a faint one. Something not quite right with her."

"You mean her art or her?"

"Yeah, the art... I'm no expert, but I know what I dislike. No, not her art. It's weird enough, but not her art. Not entirely. There was something about how she responded to your questions."

"You keep saying that. You pin down what it was yet?"

"I'm not sure. She volunteered a lot of information. Remember how she briefed us on where she was, where 10 was, where the housing development was, how the roads connected?"

"I remember."

"We didn't ask. Someone might assume we knew where the hell everything was. We're cops, we live here, you know?"

"True."

"Why all the info?" He shrugged. "I think she might have been trying to direct us away, maybe toward, something."

"Like...?"

"Don't know. And then she said she wished she had seen someone."

"I remember."

"Maybe trying to show she was on our side?"

"Maybe."

Chernov looked up from her notes.

"When we first got there, she was expressionless. It was only when we talked about the raven that she loosened up."

"Neutral subject, she felt safe," Janowski said. "Which means she didn't feel that way when we arrived."

"Lot of people are guarded when we arrive."

"Or are a little too happy to see us, trying to convince us nothing is going on. But, yeah, she didn't act happy. Didn't crack a smile until the raven thing. Guarded." He glanced at her. "Was there anything else?"

"Something she didn't do."

"Didn't do?"

"Most of the farms we've stopped at, whoever is home has invited us in. Cup of coffee, a little hospitality. Stay long enough, they'll break out their phones and show us pics of their grandchildren. Farmers, it's how they are. People living alone. Like her."

"She didn't, you're right. Unusual. Not even into that studio of hers." He paused. "People tend to relax around a female cop, and sometimes lower their guard with an old guy like me. She did not seem to."

"I wonder why not."

"Me, too."

It was Monday before Ellen called Blasingame.

"Are you busy?" To Ellen's ears, her voice sounded distant, as if she was trying not be involved with her question. She adjusted her grip on her phone, as if the action made things, not just her voice, clearer.

"No," Robert Blasingame replied. "What's going on?" That was Blasingame, a question going to the center of things.

"Something is happening and people think I might need protection. I doubt that I do but..." Her voice, carefully casual, trailed off and

Blasingame did not fill in the silence. Ellen felt the conversation with Deevers had crept up on her, slowly taking her in its arms without her noticing until they were talking with Dwyer.

"It's this child killing thing," she said. "He spotted my name on one of our articles about him. He's contacted me, twice. FBI's involved."

"They have some very good protection specialists."

"They do. And if you aren't available, they said they'll do it."

"Your idea to use me."

"Yes."

"I imagine your friend Karen was not terribly happy with that."

"She would prefer to use people she's worked with but, mostly, she wants me safe. Big sister thing."

"I understand; I'm the same way. Except for the sister part."

"My editor said she'd try to get some kind of payment for you but finance might balk since the Fee-Bees offered to do it for free and…"

"I'm easily bought and come cheap. Don't worry about it. Between jobs. I'm going to ask Tyrone to assist, if that's all right."

"Delighted. I'm at work."

"Stay there. Don't go home. I'm going to pick you up. In the meantime, I'll have Tyrone look your place over."

"He has one of my keys, I think, from running cables for me last month." She paused. "You think that's needed?"

"It gives him something to do with his free time." It was his turn to pause. "Yes. He might be interested in more than just talking to you. No point in taking unnecessary chances. About the key; if Ty doesn't have one, we'll meet halfway and I'll give him mine."

"It's just a precaution. Karen says they don't think he wants to harm me yet. He sees me as his audience. Only if he gets cornered might he feel a need to strike out and I'm not likely to be anyone cornering him. They're still working up their profile on him and they may decide that protection isn't really needed."

"Love the 'yet.' Let's go ahead and do this until they decide that. I've got Tyrone on my other phone. Hold on."

Ellen sat watching her computer screen, an article she was editing unchanging under her gaze.

"He's in Paoli just finishing. He knows what to do and will call when he's had a chance to look around. He said he does have your key."

"All right." She paused and glanced at the time. "I'm wrapping up for the day." She took a breath. "I've been dragging my feet asking you."

107

"Because…?"

"I don't like the idea of needing someone to watch over me."

"I get that, I think. You're pretty good at taking care of yourself."

"I've been totally at someone else's mercy, and that bastard didn't have any." She took a breath. "Sorry."

"Don't be. Some things are worth anger."

"Didn't mean to spill it on you."

"Didn't. I agree with you. My perspective is, I'm glad to do it. Another set of eyes is almost always useful. I feel honored."

Blasingame said it like he might have mentioned that it was a sunny day. No drama. Maybe honor was something a natural part of him. She hadn't thought of that.

"For now," Ellen said, "they want me covered 24-7."

"I have a bag already packed and will use your couch. We'll set something up for when you're at work." Ellen heard a car door slam. "I'm on my way. Stay where you are. Should be there in forty minutes."

"All right," she said and then Blasingame was gone. Ellen turned her phone off slowly, as if there was a need for precision. She looked at its screen for a moment longer and then put it down. Then she used her desk phone to let security know Blasingame was coming.

She returned to editing the article on her computer screen and, for several minutes, pretended that a killer of children was not a part of her life.

Ellen looked around as people began leaving and arriving. She had not realized how much time had passed. One of the other reporters waved at her as he headed to the elevators, a phone pressed against his head. She waved back, he grinned, and pointed. She turned and looked.

Robert Blasingame stood leaning against a support pillar, a slight smile on his face competing emotionally with his pale blue eyes. She noticed that he was taller than most of the men coming and going. As always, he favored well-broken in jeans, Wranglers, usually, and ankle-high French hiking boots. A dark blue hooded windbreaker was open, revealing a buttoned dull green shirt of indeterminate age.

He nodded and his eyes followed people coming off the elevator and from the stairway. Ellen got up, feeling relieved and a little angry with herself that she did.

"Thanks for letting security know I was coming," he said. Now his eyes were on her, chasing away the anger. "They were very helpful."

"You didn't Taser them, did you?" She smiled as she said it, but she knew he had done that and much worse to people.

"No. As I said, very helpful. I'm parked down the block."

"Let me get my stuff. Is Ty at my place?" Blasingame followed her to her desk.

"Yes. And I'm trying to remember to call him 'Tyrone.' His mother caught me using 'Ty' and she delivered a lecture on the need to maintain appearances encouraging the perception that he is a competent professional."

"He must have been embarrassed."

"It was all he could do to keep from laughing his ass off."

"Really?" She picked up her bag and made sure she had her phone.

"He had tears."

"Mothers can be serious about their children."

"Then she told me to eat all my greens."

"Really?"

"Well, they were good and everything. She had thrown together a late dinner for us. But at that point she was just playing with me."

"Like a tiger with a rabbit?"

"Pretty much how it felt. Didn't help he laughed. So did she. Desert was worth it, though."

"I'm all set," she said. She led the way to the elevator but he stepped in front her as it arrived. It was empty. They walked in and Ellen pressed the ground floor button.

"When we get to the car," he said, "I'll want you to give me all the details you can."

"Well, I'm not asking you to catch him."

"Not the job," he said as the elevator stopped. "Just watching your back is the contract."

Before she could say anything, the doors open and he stepped out. He made a small motion with his hand and she followed. She remembered a dark night when Blasingame, Tyrone, and she had rescued a very young girl; Blasingame had used hand signals then, a silent way of communicating, and it was almost reassuring to see them again.

Then, unbidden, the picture of almost the first time she had seen Blasingame, before being chased by killers, before trying to save the little girl, at a place with no foreshadowing of what was to come, a small B-and-B in the middle of nowhere, watching him as he did push-ups, unaware of her gaze – was he, Robert Blasingame, really unaware? – as the sweat worked through his shirt and it revealed the contours of his back muscles.

Watching his back...

On his very first day of instruction, James found he loved it.

There was no equivocating, no faking, in shooting. You hit the target or you did not. You handled a gun right or not. You practiced or you did not. It was totally unlike work; everything at work was like trying to navigate through a thick fog on a ship that you steered by rumor while strange sounds were your only guide to whether or not it was taking on water and some of the crew didn't seem to know their jobs.

"The basics," Dwyer said, "are the foundation. Everything you do is built on that foundation. Yes, there are special skills to add onto that foundation but if it isn't right, if you don't have it rock steady, you might as well throw your rifle at your target."

It made sense and James raised no objection but not just because of his instructor's logic. When Dwyer spoke, he sounded like the words were fresh, spoken not for what was probably the hundredth time, but spoken to him as something new. The 'new' was, he understood, Dwyer. Another man, a man with authority and competency, was interested in him, was helping him.

Dwyer used logic, humor, but never mocked James' efforts. He always was encouraging, even when correcting. That was his teaching style, to be sure, but it reflected a growing interest in James. The young man was very serious, something Dwyer appreciated when guns were involved, and intensely interested in everything Dwyer said. He seemed a little like Ellen Parker, whose intensity came from dark experiences in her past. James came from, Dwyer thought, from a need to be doing something, something that mattered.

The why of that need puzzled him only a little; he thought it was probably the same thing that brought some young men to the range, the need to have something in their lives that offered them clear feedback of success or failure, something that wasn't easy.

Dwyer's "cop sense" never had encountered someone like James Hardy before; its calibration was off, misinterpreting signals like a submarine sonar operator hearing an unusual sound from the dark depths and thinking it was nothing alarming, just a familiar object moving in a familiar way, perhaps echoing its signal off unseen chasms.

Nothing alarming.

Chapter 17: Visitors

The drone vanished, gone the next day while Kildeere wrestled with a piece of metal that was not at all sure the small sculpture she worked on was its truly best abode. She heard the raven say something, probably rude, but it was not until the following day, morning coffee cup in hand, she sat on the front porch steps and noticed the drone bag's absence. All that was left was a small pennant of remaining tape, idly stirred by the morning breeze.

Well, good. He wouldn't be back and one less distraction…

She saw the car coming from the east, moving slower than it had to, given the road's condition. There wasn't much traffic on the road and she tended to notice when there was. Everyone in the housing development, Kildeere thought, went in the other direction, bound for their fortunes in Philadelphia.

But the blue SUV was coming west, slow enough it gave the impression its driver was looking for something, maybe house numbers, of which there were none since there were no houses other than hers, or was lost. It did not turn south at the intersection and kept going until it was passed the fence. Then it turned into the short length of gravel driveway ending in her barn.

Kildeere got to her feet as it slowed and stopped. She did not recognize it and could not see the driver through the glass. She put her cup down and walked over to the driveway fence, stopping at the gate next to the barn.

A woman stepped out from the driver's position, said something to someone in the car, and then walked around the car and stopped at the fence. She was White, short, and had long hair in an unnatural shade of blond.

"Good morning," the woman said. Her expression was blank, maybe guarded, and Kildeere wondered what she was selling. As Kildeere approached, she held out her hand. "My name is Ginny, Ginny Flinthill. I'm Jackie's mother."

Kildeere stepped up to the fence and shook her hand, careful not to grasp too tightly. White people could be alarmed easily when first meeting someone Black and her grip was stronger than most men's.

"Morrigan Kildeere," she said and wished she had brought her coffee mug, both for something to drink and for something to fill the silence.

Flinthill turned to the car and nodded. A door opened and Jackie came out. He walked slowly and stood beside his mother. She watched him, waiting, and Kildeere wondered what was going on.

"Thank you for finding my drone," Jackie said. The sentence sounded rehearsed and she realized what his mother was doing.

"My pleasure," Kildeere said. When the boy held up his hand, only slightly angled upward to clear the fence, she shook it, again gently. "No problem."

"We appreciate your help," Ginny Flinthill said. "Where did you find it?"

"In the woods," she said, making a short motion towards them. "Just lucky it landed out in the open."

"Yes." Flinthill eyed her. "I really do hope it wasn't any bother."

"None at all. I was taking a break, just stretching my legs, and thought I'd see if I could find it. I was surprised, thought it might have been hung up in some tree and I'd never see it." She surprised herself with how much she said and realized it had something to do with the presence of the boy.

"You work here?" Flinthill looked at the pieces of sculpture in the yard and then settled on the tower. "Someone told me you were an artist." It was almost a question. Then she said, and it was almost bashfully, "My sister is an artist, a painter."

"Yes, I am. Would you like to see my studio?"

"Yes, yes I would. Would it be all right if Jackie...?"

"Sure." Kildeere opened the gate and walked with her to the front of the barn. She slid one of the big doors back wide enough for them to walk through and turned on the lights.

"Wow," Jackie said.

"Don't touch anything," his mother said, using the mothers' eternal supplication.

Kildeere expected a quick tour but Flinthill had questions about everything and she spent a lot of time looking at projects in progress as well as finished ones.

"This is really incredible," she said, shaking her head. She held a worked piece of stone of a turtle's head emerging from a rough-cut stone and gently put it down. "You've been doing this for years."

"Some days it feels like that," Kildeere smiled. "All in the same day."

"My sister is going to be so jealous that I got to meet you. Do you have a website where she could see your work?"

"No." She said it with a little emphasis and then tried to cover it. "I beat on rocks and bend iron; I'm not much on modern technology." Flinthill smiled. "But I'm in a couple of galleries in Philly. She might see some of my stuff there."

"Which ones?" Almost magically, a cell phone was in her hands. Kildeere named two galleries and Flinthill's thumbs blurred. "Wow," and Kildeere learned where Jackie learned the expression. "This is really something." She looked up from her phone. "Is it okay to take some pictures?"

"Sure," Kildeere said, though she felt uncomfortable, as if she was revealing too much too fast.

Later, she walked with the two back to the SUV. Flinthill waited until Jackie entered and closed his door, then turned to Kildeere.

"I guess I was checking you out, a little," she said. "He's been a little down lately. Some of the boys he knows, plays with online, have moved away or something. He hasn't talked about it much. Anyway, when Jackie came home with his drone, well, there've been some things going on."

"I've heard." Kildeere took a breath. "Better to be safe."

"Well, the kids, they have stories." She smiled. "You've probably heard them."

"No, not really."

"Oh, made up stuff. Too much Netflix. But Jackie's convinced you're a 'good guy.'"

"Rather than…"

"Crazy. Or a witch." Flinthill looked her in the eyes. "Kids' ideas. It's not what Jackie thinks."

"Being a crazy witch might be fun," Kildeere said. "But I don't have the strength for either. They require too much focus. Me, I just beat on rocks…"

"And bend iron." Flinthill nodded. "I appreciate you giving us the tour. I'll be seeing you."

Then she and her son were driving back down the road. Kildeere saw a small arm emerge and wave. She did not return the gesture but walked back to her cold coffee and emptied the cup. Trying not to think, she walked to her kitchen and refilled it.

Kildeere opened her refrigerator and studied the contents, more to distract herself then to find something. She took out a hardboiled egg and stood over the sink. With a quick twist that was almost violent, she tore the egg in half with very little debris dropping away. She carried the two halves in one hand and her coffee in the other as she went out to the front porch. She didn't see the raven but thought it was close by and lobbed a half egg to one side of the porch. She sat on the edge, her feet on the steps.

A rustle announced the arrival of the raven. It barely took the time to study the egg before using its large beak to tear into it. It would pause about every ten or fifteen seconds (Kildeere had, in the past, counted, fascinated by the big bird), look around, look at her, and then return to the egg. It finished by annihilating the shell, as if it had the goal of leaving behind no piece of any appreciable size. Then, apparently satisfied, it faced her and the other half of the egg.

The raven always knew when Kildeere held back a half. She tore a small piece of the egg out with her thumb and ate it, pretending she didn't know the raven watched her. Then she took a larger piece and tossed it half way to the raven.

The raven looked around as if bored and then it slowly walked forward, looking in every direction except the egg piece. It might have been inspecting the porch, concerned with building permits and such. It stopped, standing over the piece. Then it lunged down and swallowed it quickly.

It knew how the game was played. It looked at her with black eyes that seemed to be amused and waited. Kildeere reached towards the bird and spun the egg in its shell like a top. Then she watched as the raven pounced, making one flap with wings suddenly extended, then tore into the egg. She grinned but the smile was quickly gone as she picked up her cup

You are not exactly maintaining a low profile.

The thought came and she grimaced.

Out of sight, out of mind.

"At least," she said aloud as she looked up to the sound of an approaching car, "the police haven't come back." Kildeere raised her cup in a mock salute to the car, a police car, the one that had come before.

"Damn," she said so quietly only the raven heard.

"Welcome back to weirdsville," Janowski said.

"You're not much of an art lover," Elizabeth Chernov observed.

"Who told you that was art?" He paused as he shifted into park and turned the engine off. "Sure, some of those things are all right. Yard decorations for fancy places, museums, like that. But that tower is awful."

"You mean badly done?" Chernov smiled and unbuckled herself.

"No. No, she's got skills, not saying she doesn't. But that thing looks like a cell phone tower for hell."

"Maybe that's what it's supposed to be." She winked at him – he missed it – and got out.

Janowski paused in the middle of opening his door and thought on Chernov's comment for a few seconds. He shrugged and stepped out of the car.

He stayed by the car, door open, hand clear, and listening for anything coming over the radio while his eyes watched the woman on the porch stand. Beside her was the raven they had seen on their first visit.

Hell, it might be that raven. She might have a whole menagerie of the damned things hanging around. How can you tell them apart?

He smiled as if encountering something amusing but his eyes stayed on Kildeere and avoided the tower.

"Good morning, ma'am," Chernov said as she walked up to the fence.

"Morrigan is fine, or Kildeere; 'ma'am' has me looking around for my grandmother."

"Very well, Ms. Kildeere." She waited as Kildeere walked to her. "We're doing a follow-up with all the people we talked to before to see if there's anything they might want to report."

"Not really." Kildeere took a sip and tried to ignore how hard her heart was beating. "Been trying to keep my eyes open but…" She shrugged.

"We appreciate it." She paused. "We're a little more specific about the time we're interested in. At night. Especially after midnight."

"Well, I think I can figure out the why of that. I do sometimes work late and often keep the doors open for the cool." She shook her head. "Haven't seen anything that caught my attention, not in the past few days, not since you were here last."

"It's a long shot, but we try to check everything we can."

Chernov looked at her partner and then back at Kildeere but said nothing, just raising her eyebrows. Kildeere frowned slightly.

"Sergeant, would you like to see my studio?" Her voice was very formal.

"Hate to have you take time from your work," Chernov said, "but I saw your name on the list of artists in the Chester County Studio Tour last year."

"You came by?"

"No," she smiled. "I got swamped. What was it, around 60 studios, somewhere north of a hundred artists?" She shook her head. "Mostly saw painting, some clay, West Chester on down to Kennett Square. Tried to get to places a little distant from New Joyton. I saw a blacksmith in West Chester but no one actually sculpting in metal."

"Sure, I know him. Lot of wrought iron." Kildeere said. "I'm on a break. You can pull in the driveway and I'll get the doors open."

In a moment, Janowski guided the car slowly down the road. He glanced at Chernov and smiled.

"Isn't this where I say something about a spider inviting a fly in or something?"

"We don't know if the perp is a man or a woman," Chernov said, watching Kildeere push back one of the barn doors as they approached. "Odds on it's a man, right. But we're not certain of that and we have a woman living alone in the country and a chance to see what's she's doing without having to have probable cause." Chernov smiled without humor reaching her eyes. "Besides, gives you a chance to ask about that tower from hell."

Janowski said nothing; Chernov was no one's fool. She'd been an MP in the Pennsylvania Army National Guard and helped bring down a monster called Doctor John while saving a little girl said monster and his allies tried very hard to find. "Bring down" was how it would be phrased in the next county history book – she, along with another woman, had shot his ass dead and, it was said, she made sure the last thing he saw on earth as he bled out was her face.

Janowski thought someone should make a movie about her.

He paused as they climbed out of the car. Kildeere pushed back the second of the doors. He looked over at the house. It had a front porch and a side porch facing the barn. The asymmetry seemed to work. There was a second floor to the house that looked like it had been added late in the house's life. Small, ground-level windows, one backlit by a dim white light, marked a basement. White paint with green trim did not disguise its age but Janowski liked old homes. This one looked comfortable, kind of comfort that came from being lived in for generations. He thought it a place that had known solid families, their joys and sorrows, and, for a second, Janowski remembered his childhood home.

He smiled as he folded his sunglasses and hung them from a shirt pocket; his wife said he was a "romantic" when he talked about things like he was thinking about Kildeere's house. Maybe so.

He followed Chernov as Kildeere took them around the studio. It was a small barn but thought had gone into arranging it. The floor was concrete and a blacksmith's anvil stood like a sentry to one side as they entered. Welding tools and tanks were against one wall, stone working tools were opposite, the middle had massive work tables adorned with vices of various sizes, all under LED lights that could be raised or lowered to supplement banks of fluorescents. A partial second floor held supplies of various kinds while the back wall overlooked blocks of stone of various colors and pieces of metal from someone's giant jigsaw puzzle. Chernov seemed to know about her work and Janowski noticed Kildeere tended to deflect answers about her career and steer the conversation towards subjects like the studio tour and other art forms.

He wondered what she was trying to stay away from.

"About that tower…" Janowski said in a lull. "What's it all about?"

"Tell you the truth," Kildeere said, looking through the open doors at the dark structure, "I'm not sure." It did sound like the truth, like she was still thinking about it even after however long ago she had built the thing.

"You're the artist, though." He raised his eyebrows.

"Yep," she nodded. "I think most artists have an idea of something they want to happen when someone encounters their work, sure, but the very first thing they want to have happen is a reaction. You know, something that keeps whatever they did from fading into the wall like a Holiday Inn painting."

"Sure, makes sense, but that thing…" He shook his head. "What did you want to happen?"

"It usually satisfies the first thing," Kildeere said with a small smile. "But I think my head was in a pretty messed up place when I started on it. I think I wanted to convey some of what that messed up place felt like."

Janowski said nothing for a moment, still looking at the tower. Finally, he nodded.

"I think you succeeded," he said, his voice very serious. "Did it help? I mean, some things we have to get out. Did it help you do that?"

"I think so," she said and looked at him. "That's pretty insightful." Her voice was equally serious and Janowski wasn't tempted to add …for a cop.

"Thank you for taking the time with us," Chernov said, glancing back at Janowski.

"Not a problem." Kildeere made a small smile. "Nice break to the morning."

"What did you think?" Chernov's question went unanswered for a moment, the only sound the whisper of tires on pavement.

"She said her head was messed up."

"'Was'."

"Right. I'm wondering if she's one of those people who straightened things out by venting it on others. Pressure builds and, pow! Someone's in a ditch somewhere." Janowski shook his head; both of them had seen the ugly debris left by such things.

"There are people like that but I didn't make her for one of them."

"I'm not sure I do. It's just…" He fell silent and Chernov did not jump in. Janowski had good cop instincts and she had learned to let him think things through.

"She's hiding something," Janowski said. "I don't know what. Yeah, it's hard to like her for those boys, but… Something."

"What she said, the tower, was there anything else?"

"You mean, did I see anything in there I would want to have a bunch of forensics people jump all over? No, but there was…" Again, the pause and again Chernov remained silent. "She asked if you wanted to see her studio." He shook his head. "Small thing. Tiny. Not her house, not a cup of coffee. Her studio."

"That is tiny."

"Maybe most people who invite us in it's to their kitchen."

"Maybe. Maybe living rooms are as far as they take us. Never done a count."

"Right. Never had an artist take me into their studio. But do artists do that?"

"You mean, usually they want to keep stuff out of sight until they're ready to sell it?" Chernov shrugged. "She did that because why? Keep us out of the house? That what you're reacting to?"

"Tiny, yeah, I know. And the profilers said it's not likely to be a woman. I know. But those woods… Our perp likes woods, maybe is comfortable in them. The profilers told us that as well. Across the road from her is that big patch of woods. She owns them. Got the whole place Posted. Is it just a coincidence? I don't know, not really. But she's sitting on something."

"She might be," Chernov said. She spoke slowly, like someone working their way through a minefield. Woman, sergeant, fast-track, talking to man, lower rank, older, probably as far as he was going to go in New Joyton's police service; yeah, minefield.

"Michael," she said, "she might be. But it's damned thin. Yes, something, but, remember, she told us there was something that had her messed up. Far more likely she's talking about something that happened to her rather than something she's done, like killing kids." She paused. "And she's a Black woman. We're cops. White cops. She's out here in the country, all alone. Maybe we have her on edge just for that."

Janowski nodded and held up the fingers of his hand from the steering wheel to acknowledge her. She used his first name, a signal used at certain times, times when he was probably wrong but she didn't want it to be Sergeant – Corporal official.

He took a breath. She was right. It was damned thin. Something happened to her and she wasn't specific? Maybe she'd missed paying her taxes. Maybe someone had tried to beat her to death. Maybe sexual assault. Maybe the list was endless.

Maybe it was Black talking to White cops with guns. Janowski knew everyone was nervous talking to cops but… Yeah, a Black woman talking to White cops might be dealing with something he couldn't fully get into.

But, still, something more was going on with Morrigan Kildeere.

Kildeere watched the police car disappear following the road west towards Route 10. Then she slowly walked up the gravel driveway to the barn doors and pulled them closed. For several minutes, she leaned against them, her arms folded.

What did they see?

What do they suspect?

She had no answers.

Blasingame drove Ellen home saying very little, letting her tell him what was happening. Only occasionally did he ask a question, something she did not notice as the words seemed to pour out of her. Without noticing the transition, she described her growing anger at the killer for using her as a messenger. Finally, she paused and shook her head.

"You don't need to hear that stuff," she said. "I'm just pissed off."

"It's all right," he said. "You are not the kind of person who wouldn't take all this, well, personally."

She smiled and started to say something when she heard his phone ring from its holder on the dash. Blasingame stabbed it with his finger.

"I'm here," he said, his eyes on the road.

"Ellen with you?" It was Tyrone.

"Hi, Tyrone," she said. "Thanks for helping out."

"Glad to. Listen, don't go to Ellen's house just yet. We have something to talk over. There's a pizza place near the Coatesville high school. Little Anthony's, just before the railroad overpass. Wait for me there, I'll fill you in then and we can decide what to do."

"Understood," Blasingame said. "We're on the by-pass. Probably be there in fifteen." He reached to tap his phone but Ellen put her hand on his, pausing him.

"What's wrong?" Ellen asked.

"Looks like you've already had a visitor," Tyrone said. "Not a nice one. I called Agent Deevers and her people are coming here. I'm leaving to keep the crowd down. Talk to you when we meet."

Ellen released Blasingame's hand and looked at him.

"Do you think…?"

"You're a reporter. Maybe lots of people are interested in you. Hold on until we talk to Tyrone."

Ellen's lips remained tight all the way to Little Anthony's. As they pulled into a parking slot next to the pizzeria, Tyrone's white van appeared and parked beside them.

Tyrone, a strongly built Black man who Blasingame believed collected computer qualifications like some people collected stamps, got out of his van smiling.

"Hey, lady," he called to Ellen. "I'm glad I had your key."

"Hey. What's going on?"

"A lot," Tyrone said, "but let's sit down. I've got to get something to drink."

Ellen's question was deferred as the three went into the pizzeria, though it clearly took her an effort to not push for an answer.

In a moment, they were sitting in a booth in a corner of the shop.

"All right," Tyrone said, after taking a long draw on his soda, "I took a look around. No one near your residence. Waited down the street, looking for someone doing circuits around but saw nobody. Since I had my gear and your key, I thought I might as well do a quick sweep of your house for active devices." He looked at Blasingame. "No harm in it and, like I said, I had my gear."

"What did you find?" Ellen's question was carefully spoken.

"Your house is completely clean," Tyrone said. "You've got that protection service going and no one not a pro could tackle it to get in. It's running fine. I checked that no one had messed with it or anything else. Scanned for bugs. Everything came up clean."

"Then why are we here and what was all that about a 'visitor'?"

"When I came down from upstairs, I looked out the window at your garage. I thought I saw something in that woodpile that's against it. You know the one I mean."

"Yes. I've finally put a tarp on it after we finished with it. A little too green to use."

"That's it. Neatly stacked by an over-qualified but incredibly handsome young man."

"I think I bought you breakfast for your help last month."

"That you did. And that's why I remembered how we arranged all that fire wood. The pile had been changed and not because of the tarp. I went out of the house by the front door and went down the street, keeping the house between me and the woodpile. At the corner, I hung a left and walked up into the wooded lot behind your and the other houses. Once I got into the trees, I walked back to your house and approached it from behind. Very carefully got to the woodpile and took a look. Someone's put a game camera in there."

"What is that?"

"It takes pictures when triggered by motion. This version has a flash but it's switched off. Built-in night vision. You come home, it notices and takes a picture. Actually, it's set to take three at three-second intervals. It will download its pictures to anyone nearby who has a coded Bluetooth device, like a cell phone with the right app and password. Range about 30 feet, say, about where the street crosses in front of your house."

"Power?" Blasingame asked.

"This kind of camera uses rechargeable batteries and can take an external battery, which it has further down in the pile. But even with the external, its duration is pretty limited. Probably good for maybe 72 hours."

"If he put it there…"

"He'll be back." Blasingame thought for a moment. "Glad you called Ellen's friend."

"Agent Deevers?" Tyrone grinned. "She was delighted to be encountering the Three Musketeers again. But here's the thing I passed on to her. Two things. First, the camera's little power indicator suggests it's almost out. According to its numbers, it will shut down around two AM tonight. Second, I probably set it off just moving things in the woodpile around it. I figure the guy is going to notice, when he gets in range, the pictures he gets are not what he was expecting and will keep right on going."

Tyrone was silent for a moment. "Yeah, I called Agent Deevers before I called you. She got me to promise that I would keep you away." He looked at Ellen. "I don't think she's forgiven us for taking you on that little trip to get Douglas' daughter."

"Step-daughter," Ellen corrected him automatically.

"I understand the guy Agent Deevers is looking for is a really bad one and it would be nice to personally bust his ass. I would have liked to check with you two first but this is serious stuff and I figured we needed to move as quickly as possible. Let the pros take this mother down and…"

"I'm not arguing. It was a good call. Really. And I'm not in a hurry to have a confrontation with some serial killer again. So, yes, good call." Ellen held Tyrone's gaze. "Absolutely, a good call."

"What do they want us to do?" Blasingame asked, still smiling.

"Nothing other than stay away until they call. If I'm right about the power thing, he'll have to come by no later than tonight to keep it going with a new external battery. All kinds of people plan on greeting him then." Tyrone raised his eyebrows. "This means that guy may have been monitoring you for some time."

"A very creepy idea," Ellen said. "Glad you didn't wait. They'll need all the time they can get to set things up."

"She's right," Blasingame said and Tyrone nodded. With the nod, Ellen understood that it was Blasingame's approval Tyrone was looking for.

You get like that when someone saves your life. She almost started when she realized the thought applied to her as well.

Ellen looked at Blasingame. "Plan B; I guess I get to use your couch tonight."

"Dinner at the diner?" Blasingame asked, looking back and forth at his two friends. "They've gotten used to seeing Ellen and me at breakfast."

"Country meatloaf and you're buying?" Tyrone stretched. "Lovely, but then I have to drive home."

"Shoo fly pie for me," Ellen said. "Celebration – if they grab the guy, it will be party time."

"Probably be two in the morning when they do. Please, don't wake me with the good news." Tyrone stretched, his big arms going back, as if he had put down a heavy load. "Let's go, early dinner."

Ellen and Blasingame followed Tyrone to a country diner not far from Blasingame's house and one they'd used in the past. Dinner was delicious, though Ellen found herself distracted. Had the killer been watching her since his first call? It was more than creepy. And was it really this easy? Tyrone makes a call, the FBI deploys the troops, and the monster is looking through bars before dawn.

She decided against the shoo fly pie and went for an apple cobbler instead. She was close to finishing it when she felt her phone silently vibrate.

"Call," she said and looked at the screen. She recognized the number; Karen Deevers was calling. Even with nothing said, Ellen felt her breathing slow down. She tapped the screen and held the phone to her ear.

"It's Ellen," she said and closed her eyes. She listened to Deevers, nodding silently. There was a pause. "No doubt at all?" Her eyes were still closed and she shook her head slowly. Finally, she opened her eyes.

"I got it, I'll let them know. Thanks. Right, yes, of course." Ellen turned off her phone and looked at the others as she put the phone away.

"It was Karen Deevers," she said. "The camera was from a peeping Tom, a guy from down the street. He came early, didn't see me come home and thought it was a good time to change batteries. They had just set up, positioned people, had some watching from the woods behind my house." Tyrone nodded as she took a breath. "He's been doing this for the past month. They went to his house, he's cooperating like mad because, for some reason, he doesn't want to be mistaken for a serial killer, and they found lots of pictures of other women in our neighborhood. Hundreds of pictures, maybe two dozen women. They've turned it over to the local police and the FBI is trying to fade into the background as quietly as they and their automatic weapons can."

"No shit," Tyrone said.

"We're back on Plan A," Blasingame said calmly. "I'm with Ellen. Ty, go on home and come back to Ellen's when you can. Set up a recorder she can use on her house phone, nothing that taps into the wiring, simple recorder she can use with the handset or on her cell. Just in case she gets called at home on her land line."

"Why not into the wiring? I can make it all automatic that way."

"Sooner or later the FBI folks likely are going to want to do that and I don't want you to have to remove any of your stuff."

"Gotcha, not a problem." Tyrone looked at Ellen. "Simple thing. Turn it on and press the mike against the handset or your cell phone. Talk normally. Turn it off when you're done."

"Okay."

"I'll stay with Ellen," Blasingame said. "If your schedule permits, we'll set up shifts after the weekend. Call me tomorrow and we'll talk that over."

"All right. I'll set up a time to bring the recorder over." He looked at Ellen. "You want your key back?"

"No," Ellen said. "Safety in having a friend hold a copy, just in case."

"Thanks," Tyrone said.

They finished their deserts in silence. Blasingame paid for dinner, part of a running joke among the three, and then they drove out into the gathering night.

Saturday came glowing, sunlight almost splashing across the houses near Ellen's. She watched the morning evolve from her living room, her feet curled under her, a hot cup of coffee in her hand. Blasingame was already up, had his coffee with her, and was now making use of the shower.

Blasingame... He was, to use the hackneyed phrase, a perfect gentleman and Ellen found herself sometimes wishing he wasn't. He made not even a hint of a pass. If he did, then she would have to decide about him and maybe resolve her own mind. On the other hand, part of her did not want to make that decision – her relationship with him was shaded with many colors, some of them fairly dark.

While he had saved her life, he accomplished it by killing two men. She was not drawn to killers. Dark highwaymen quick with rapiers were the stuff of romance novels. Ellen knew people who had taken lives. Some saw it as grim necessity. Others, like the killer of boys, seemed to revel in it. She did not know what Blasingame thought of his actions. And she was reluctant to push for an answer.

She didn't really know what to think of her own decisions; a dead deputy sheriff, killed by her using his own shotgun, no longer lived in her dreams, but therapy had not left her with a solid moral stance. "Doing what she had to do" did not seem to be much of a guide to life. That complicated her feelings for Blasingame. If it wasn't for his killings...

She thought Robert Blasingame was someone she would have been very, very interested in. On the other hand, if it wasn't for his killings, she and a friend would be dead and buried in unmarked graves beneath rows of corn. She sighed.

Complications.

Once or twice a week, they routinely shared breakfast. Some of the guarded distance Ellen maintained was less than it had been. But there was a need to do something to cause movement. If nothing happened, if they kept things the way they were, then they'd probably slide into the static category of "friends." That might be all there was for them. And having Robert Blasingame for a friend would not be bad. But Ellen wondered if the two of them were not meant to have more, to be more.

Every day, she felt the need to get closer growing, in spite of all her self-imposed cautions. Blasingame was, she thoroughly understood, a dangerous man. Well, she wasn't exactly harmless herself if push came to bloodshed. He had a past; so did she.

He seemed content to wait on her. Or maybe he wasn't interested? It was not the first time Ellen had the thought. She didn't believe it; one of her friends, a woman who had served in Afghanistan, used an expression she thought described Blasingame. He had "a sniper's patience." He was waiting on her; she was sure of it. What she wasn't sure of was, what did that mean?

Ellen filled her cup and pondered life while Blasingame completed his tasks in her bathroom.

A few minutes later, she dressed and went into the little room she used for an office. Her laptop came to life and she looked at her email, wondering if Karen Deevers might have sent something longer than a phone text. Whatever Deevers was doing, she hadn't sent anything. There was email from Elizabeth Chernov, however. It had arrived within the past hour.

Ellen read the message from Chernov and shook her head. Was her friend getting overtime for working on a Saturday? Only reporters and baby doctors had hours as bad as police sergeants.

The name was not familiar to her. Morrigan Kildeere. She typed it into her laptop and saw the same information Chernov undoubtedly had found; a Google is a Google is a Google. Artist, more or less based in Philly, successful, more or less. She dropped the name into the newspaper's database.

Some of the same links Google had found reappeared, along with links to various in-house newspaper articles in which the artist's name appeared. Nothing else popped up. She read the bio the paper updated more or less regularly. Date of birth, born nearby, Drexel alum, career took off when a very sharp gallery owner named John Faraday linked up with her and became her representative, which Ellen took to mean working as her agent. Besides in his own gallery, he got her featured in a number of the most prestigious galleries in the tri-state area, and really moving into the big time. Then... Nothing. Well, no, not nothing, but the big features stopped. Still active, yes, still showing in local galleries, but fewer of them and almost none of the big hitters, the ones that were part of the national and, sometimes, international scenes. Ellen frowned and backed up. What happened? Why the low profile? She kept reading.

Ah, her representative, Faraday, died. Drowned. Drinking a bit too much at a party, the coroner said, and dropped his super-agent body into the Schuylkill River. Found under the South Street bridge. Was his death what kept her from breaking out into the big-time art scene?

What about John Faraday? She clicked links, read for a while, and then entered the newspaper's background files after entering her password. These were the files compiled by reporters over the years and consisted of information not meant for publication. Sometimes they were just notes, side issues, things not published as irrelevant to whatever the story had been at the time. Sometimes the words were more. Ellen tapped in John Faraday's name.

Most of what she saw at first matched the published information. A hard charging gallery owner with a small but successful branch in New York City, John Faraday worked with an elite of young, Philadelphia-based artists. He seemed to have an excellent eye at identifying up and coming artists of exceptional talent. He also seemed to know everyone important in the art world; gallery owners, art critics including some of Ellen's coworkers, museum buyers, high status collectors, and others with the power to make an artist famous and rich. His artists were known in New York City, Dubai, Tokyo, wherever money lay in great big piles and people wanted to put it somewhere. Ellen smiled.

Rumors... Twice divorced. Driving while intoxicated in New Jersey, an incident quickly resolved with only a hint of some grease applied to sliding him out of the public view.

Sexual harassment? The phrase showed up but no one was able to go anywhere with it. A woman on his staff got a lawyer, there was brief, one-time coverage in the city pages, and then it all vanished. Then another note, not published, a rumor that something may have happened at a party on the Main Line. A young woman, some drugs, all of a sudden there was a non-disclosure agreement and the story evaporated. Another incident of the same kind a year later with a source claiming there were others. A rumor, nothing more, nothing confirmed, of several NDAs. The source suddenly and only said "No comment" and disappeared from sight. Some months after Faraday became Kildeere's representative, he fell into the river. Ellen thought for a moment.

The artists Faraday represented were public knowledge, nothing hidden there. She copied the names and pasted them onto a blank text page. Then she searched each one. Some were still represented by Faraday at the time of his death, some weren't. Most were in New York or Los Angeles – bigger art scenes – so it followed… No, it didn't follow.

Of the eleven names on her list, the only artists still using him when he died were male. A few of the men previously had left him and all of the women had, other than Kildeere; he was still representing her when he died. There looked like there was a pattern.

All right, a male with lots of money, highly successful, maybe figuring he was entitled to whatever he wanted. Steps off a bridge or rolls down a riverbank from drinking too much and drowns his well-deserved ass in the Schuylkill. Couldn't happen to a nicer guy. Ellen paused and then backed up.

Nowadays, Morrigan Kildeere didn't have representation. Why not? She has all those strong reviews, her gallery rep dies, wouldn't she run out and get another? If she was in the same class as the other artists Faraday represented, there would probably be gallery representatives calling on her as soon as his body was found.

Was this usual? Ellen thought for a moment and then opened up another window. She looked up a name, checked the time, and then used her phone.

"Mr. Jonathan Tipton, if he's available," she said to the person answering the phone. "Ellen Parker of the Inquirer."

A moment later, a sprightly voice – Ellen always thought of Tipton as a man dancing through life – came on the line.

"Ms. Parker, good morning, good morning. Good to talk with you again. What might I do for you?"

"Good morning, Mr. Tipton. I'm doing a little background gathering and could use your expertise. I don't know if this will be a story but I want to get some things straight."

"You mean I won't get a chance to advertise my gallery? I suppose I'll have to satisfy myself with spreading gossip about my competitors." He chuckled and Ellen heard the slight tinkle of a cup meeting saucer;

someone else was still working on their coffee. "What do you need to know about the Philadelphia art scene, dear child?"

"Do you know an artist named Morrigan Kildeere?"

"Oh, yes. Sculptor. Stone and some incredible metal work. Fine sense of balance. I mean in the Calder sense. You know. What about the lady?"

"I understand she is still active."

"Yes, one of the best of our local artists."

"She was represented by John Faraday until his death."

"I think that is correct. Let me check." His voice trailed away. "Yes, yes, she was. Poor woman."

"What do you mean?

"I knew we'd get into gossip. One does not wish to speak badly of the dead but Johnny was, how to put this, a pig."

"I know of some rumors about sexual harassment."

"He was an insult to his gender, my dear. But, really, surfacing that after all these years? Slow news day?"

"No, no, not interested in him all that much."

"Good taste on your part."

"But Kildeere. She doesn't have representation now?"

"Ah, no, I don't think so. Let me check. Hold on one sec." There was silence and then Tipton came back. "Officially, she does; a gallery down the street from mine represents her. But they're not doing much about moving her work anywhere else. Of course, she's well known locally, doesn't need anyone to do much representing her around here."

"Is she bound to them because they represent her?"

"Pretty much. Don't think of a gallery representative as a literary agent, not entirely. You write a book, a literary agent finds a publisher, and the money pours in. But the agent doesn't publish your book. A gallery representative sells your art, you see. It's like the representatives are the publishers and the agents both. Now, a gallery representing you will usually be exclusive in a particular area, but, in any case, gets a cut of everything you sell, even if a rival gallery sells it. On the other hand, the representative will work to get you known and get other galleries and museums handling your art, especially in markets where you and the representative might not be. Your success is their success."

"How long does that representation last?"

"Usual contract is six months or a year. Typically renewed when both gallery and artist are doing well. If I was an artist's representative, my gallery would get about half of whatever the artist's art sold for."

"Fifty percent? That's pretty good."

"It sounds good, doesn't it? But don't run out and become one of my competitors. Gallery representation has a big overhead. Unlike literary agents who get a publisher to look at your manuscript, they don't have to pay the rent on a big building, finance publicity, and all that. Art like painting and sculpture can be very big-ticket items but can also be very slow to move, so that fifty percent you are salivating over might be pretty infrequent." Ellen heard another clink of cup meeting saucer. "Philadelphia is in the shadow of New York. In many ways, we're more like a small-town gallery system. Lots of local artists, buyers, in some ways less formal. Fewer lawyers, may they all burn in Hell."

"Gallery representation, then, is that's how it's done exclusively?"

"Well, not entirely." Tipton sounded hesitant for a moment. "Things are changing. Some artists, those who can't get gallery representation or those who are pretty successful, are doing it themselves. You know, all that Instagram – Facebook – website nonsense. And there are some people calling themselves 'agents,' though a lot of them are thieves. Lawsuits tend to be among the flotsam and jetsam in their wakes. I haven't seen any numbers, but I think most artists prefer to get gallery representation of some kind to take the load of the world of business off their shoulders."

"So Kildeere still has representation, just kind of low-key. She hasn't taken it on herself, even though she's successful."

"My point exactly. Her gallery, the owner is her representative, would do the talking with someone who wanted to commission a work, do the negotiating, arrange the advance and paperwork. If she's needed to schmooze the client, it's easy for her to drop in, smile, and go home. No problem."

"Well, she lives out here in Chester County, so, no, not in Philly."

"Philadelphia. You would never write 'Philly' in one of your articles."

"You're right. But, as I understand things, she was poised to really make it and then he died. Her current representation seems to deliberately focus only on the local area."

"I am a bit surprised at that. She's excellent. Johnny was a pig, but he knew talent. And he was aggressive in getting it into the big venues outside of Philadelphia."

"Big as in large galleries?"

"Big as in large money. Remember, he would have made a fortune off her. He had tight contracts with his artists. Galleries, museums, private collectors, whatever. Everything went through him and he had all the contacts. If he hadn't died… Well, even if he had, she probably had a dozen heavyweights fighting one another to represent her. People with Johnny's contacts and better manners." Tipton paused. "It is odd, now that my attention is brought to it. To use your word, she really was poised. It's like she just decided to back off, to adopt a low profile for some reason." He paused again. "Oh, no, she didn't get married or something, did she?"

"Not that I know of. No, that's not in her file."

"Someday I'm going to ask you for a copy of *my* file."

"Happy to share if you buy lunch. But an artist in her situation, her position, if her representative died…"

"She would have briefly mourned and picked up a new one and could be bringing in the GDP of Brazil."

"Really that good?"

"Really that good. Still is. I can only assume she's imposed the limits on her representative. I imagine they wish she wanted to be a superstar." Tipton sighed theatrically. "But it can happen. Maybe burn-out. Maybe the work was too much. All the things around the work, the socialization, might have been too much. Faraday might have been spurring her on and, when he died, she decided she didn't want all that fame and fortune after all. Didn't want to be spurred. Remember, it's not like she's abandoned art. She's still creative, still represented, still doing very good things. I would like to have some of her pieces but they are a lot fewer nowadays and she tends to use her representative gallery, of course, and a small handful of the same galleries. Familiarity, I suppose. But I don't know. I've never seen someone get that close and decide to back away. I suppose a psychologist might have ideas about it, if you believe in psychology."

"Maybe insecure and losing her protector…"

"Johnny was no one's protector, dear. He was, in the worst sense of the word, a dick. And there you go with the psychology business, just as if it was real. No, really, by the time an artist gets to where Kildeere was, is, they've had to wrestle with their demons. They usually don't chase them away completely, but they deal with them, they handle them. I don't think Ms. Kildeere would have been that insecure about her work by then but, who knows? Everyone has demons. Now, have I been helpful enough?"

"As always, Mr. Tipton. As always. Thank you for help."

"You're quite welcome. Write something nice. Philadelphia," he emphasized the word, "could use it."

"Yes, sir."

Ellen leaned back in her chair. On the edge of becoming super successful, Morrigan Kildeere took a big step back.

How was this helpful to Chernov? Ellen grinned. Her friend, like Karen Deevers, was a cop and would tell her what was going on 'cop time,' which might be never.

That didn't mean she couldn't do a little investigating on her own.

Chapter 18: Convergence

The list was not long and the crossing off of five names, well, there was satisfaction in seeing only two remaining. Accomplishment, yes, that was part of it. For a purpose.

But what to do when the purpose was attained? Then what? The question nagged but it offered only mild resistance. Then it came back. It always did.

He smiled – someone had told him many years before he had a great smile and it had become his default expression through practice – and took a long breath.

Where are we? Five down, two to go, if needed, and maybe even if not needed. Progress. Accomplishment. No sign of any interest in him. What could they know?

He had not bothered to use a female voice in his calls. He believed the FBI's profilers would be certain he was male very early on so why bother? Then the first item was they believed him to be male and they were correct.

But they would not be absolute in that belief. A high degree of faith in their profile, but faith, and he smiled again, was seldom absolute. Especially for people like the bloodhounds in the FBI; they would try hard to keep an open mind, allow for the unexpected. He nodded.

Of course, they would. But what difference did their profile make? Half the planet was male. So what? Did they know the important why of the list? The question received an emphatic shake of his head. Absolutely not. It required an exquisite knowledge of coincidental contact, a sharing of space and time, and all of that simply was not available to them.

They would be busy estimating. That would be the best they could do. Estimating his motivation, his reasoning, his desires, but they would not know. It was too complex. He would succeed. They had not come close in New Jersey where everything was, and he had to be honest, pretty obvious. He would succeed.

Then what? He smiled. There it was again.

Well, at the very least, he would find something to do with his free time. He always did.

Three people converged on Kildeere's home as the Saturday sun beat down in an unexpected foretaste of summer. Two used their day off to seek clarity.

One was Ellen Parker, driving her car and glad it was retrieved from the commuter train parking lot where she had left it the day before. Beside her, Blasingame gazed at the late morning hills and the cars around them with equal calmness, his pale blue eyes always moving.

Somewhere, under the same sun but considerably closer by, a serial killer might, or might not, be interested in finding Ellen; other than his constantly moving eyes, Blasingame showed little sign of alarm at the idea. Ellen took no comfort in Blasingame's calmness, having learned some time ago he showed little when the situation became threatening, less when it increased. Given his current presentation, she thought he might be expecting, oh, say an EF3, possibly a 4, tornado.

For herself, she was glad to be out. Ellen had thought she might have to convince Blasingame of her need to follow a possible story, but he had simply nodded and reminded her they needed to pick up her car. She took his stance as evidence he understood she was an adult with experiences in the real world of violence and not likely to deliberately seek out suicidal danger. Also, there was a reasonable chance he was saving his authority, such as it was, as her bodyguard for those situations he believed really were dangerous and would try to impose boundaries. Ellen promised herself she would listen if and when he raised objections to where she might go.

Ellen had contacted Chernov and given her the information she had on Kildeere. Chernov was, as expected, careful not to say much about it, other than offering a brief thanks. Neither Ellen nor Chernov realized the information would send the second person toward Kildeere's home.

Chernov was covering the New Joyton police department's desk during the Saturday shift when she talked with Ellen and was glad to see her partner in civilian clothes come in.

"You like the coffee here so much you came in on your day off?" she asked Janowski. Her hands were posed above a computer keyboard; Saturday shift supervision was a good time to catch up on paperwork.

"Need to get my PT clothes," he replied. "Going to drag them behind my truck."

"That will help." Janowski had taken to running before or after his shifts and his gym clothes were the source of small humor.

Janowski disappeared down the hall to the locker room and came back in a few minutes, a blue Adidas bag in one hand.

"Anything new?" he asked.

"Not much. Task Force found a camera some stalker had set up to take pictures of the newspaper contact. Thought it might be our guy but it was just a peeper."

"Pictures of your buddy Ellen Parker?"

"The same. Anyway, she got some information on your favorite sculptor for me."

"Yeah? Anything interesting?"

"Still reading through it but it looks like Kildeere is fairly well known, highly regarded as an artist. She had representation by a very high-level guy; the kind whose clients are pretty famous in the art field. Owned his own gallery. But he died and she seems to have settled for just being a local star."

"She coulda been somebody?" Janowski did a fair imitation of Marlon Brando but you had to have seen the movie to appreciate it.

"That's the story. She's doing really well and, if she wanted it, she could be doing a lot better. But, nope."

"Artists make a lot of money?" Janowski paused, his hand on the exit door crossbar. He looked thoughtful.

"Ellen didn't give any numbers, but you remember that turtle head in Kildeere's barn?"

"On the middle table. Sure."

" I saw she sold one through a gallery in Philly that handles her nowadays for a little over 15 thousand, according to their website."

"Really? She was working on things a lot bigger than that."

"A lot of things. I've looked at the gallery's site and they have their catalogs for the past couple of years. She's in all of them and her prices are up there with everyone else. And that's just one of the galleries Ellen listed as carrying her stuff."

"I'm impressed." Janowski grinned. "And I put all my talent into looking handsome."

"Good luck with that."

"See you Monday," he said and was gone.

The third person, then, approaching Kildeere's home was Michael Janowski, a decision he reached while talking with Chernov. He drove the back roads of Chester County with the ease of someone born and raised among the crisscrossed and interwoven interstate highways and turnpikes, numbered state roads, and 17th Century cow paths that followed wandering American Indian trails and served as the foundations of county roads. He used his own vehicle, a four-wheel drive, capped, green Ford F-150 pickup adorned with fishing decals, an old NRA emblem, and two bumper stickers. One said, "Proud Parent of a Soldier," and the other claimed his dog was smarter than your honor student.

On the passenger seat was a very good pair of binoculars and an aerial map of Chester County, now carefully folded so Kildeere's house was displayed in the center. After talking with Chernov, Janowski studied it carefully and looked for a place to park that would keep his truck hidden. The south edge of the wooded area below the woman's house would work. His early curiosity about Kildeere led him to discover the woods were her property, something that was one more light strum of the chord hinting at something unusual about the artist.

Janowski followed Route 10 south until he was below Kildeere's house and then turned east. A four-way stop marked his turn north towards the woods and he drove up the road with farming fields on either side.

At the edge of the woods, an old trail formed a divider between the trees and a green-fuzzed field, he thought it might be soybeans though it was early to tell, and he turned in. He stopped and then waited. It was a hot day but he ignored the weather as he looked around and listened.

The fields around him generally were flat, hiding nothing, though far to the south hills rolled like ripples on a blanket. Scattered in the distance, he could see buildings, farm houses, and a powerline, its towers looking like creatures frozen in midstride as they held onto cables, facing east and west without giving a clue to their starting or ending points.

Janowski reached behind the passenger seat and brought out a small backpack camouflaged in grey and green digital squares. It was heavy with a full water bladder. His son had bought it for him from an Army exchange.

He stepped out of the truck and put an arm through a backpack strap, content to let the load hang slightly out of balance. His police issue Glock pistol was in the pack. The binoculars went around his neck and, pausing again to look around, he walked around the truck and entered the woods.

Raspberry thorn bushes formed a barrier almost as effective as concertina razor wire – he thought they were more effective than the yellow Posted signs someone seemed to really love – but it did not extend down the lane very far before he found a gap that he could negotiate without suffering too many small stabs.

The trees were dense enough to limit the amount of undergrowth but visibility was still limited. He used his phone's compass to check from time to time but he had a good sense of direction and did little straying from a straight path. After a short time, he found a large oak tree off to his left and used it to orient himself.

Janowski saw the trees opening up ahead, allowing glimpses of the sky. He slowed down and almost instinctively bent over as he approached the northern edge of the woods. He made the last few yards almost squatting and stopped while still within the trees but near enough to the edge that he could see the road and, beyond, Kildeere's house.

He sat down and took a long drink of water from the pack's tube coming over his shoulder. Then he studied the house and barn with his binoculars. The sun lit up everything so it looked like some kind of postcard, though that damned tower spoiled the view. He shook his head. Kildeere was not visible but her car was sitting on the gravel driveway.

Janowski had no plan, other than to watch and see. There was something about Kildeere pulling his attention, like the first scent of smoke of a wild fire. As the days passed after his first meeting with her, he became increasingly unsettled. A growing sense of something being wrong with the sculptor slowly filled him.

It wasn't the tower; at least, it was not only the tower, that weird painted metal pointed up at the sky. Multiple times he went over the two conversations Chernov and he had with her. Nothing specific leapt into his awareness but there was something wrong, something in her responses. She was quick to answer questions. Too quick? He wasn't sure. Something about her was hidden, something dark, he thought, even while part of him thought it highly likely he was more than over reacting.

The conversation with Chernov, though, with the information about Kildeere's finances, added questions. She could be rich but here she was hiding out in southern Chester County. Something was not right with the picture he had.

Janowski was the kind of man who worked at keeping himself in balance, never giving away to the extremes of elation and despair life seemed to bring by the shovelful. But his reaction to Morrigan Kildeere had tipped his balance and he came to watch her from the trees not to find evidence of her wrongdoing but simply to find some kind of internal peace, a resolution of the uncertain signals he felt deep within. He watched trying to capture understanding.

He sat on a fallen branch and looked around a large tree, carefully studying the house and barn while he sipped on his water tube. Other than the damned big black bird Chernov had identified as a raven, there was little going on.

Then he saw a car drive up to the house. It came slowly, as if searching for the address. It stopped at the front gate. An athletic White man came out of the passenger side. He looked around calmly, seeming to be as interested, or uninterested in everything equally. Janowski did not recognize him. After a moment, a young woman emerged.

Janowski had never seen Ellen Parker before except for a picture on the internet; Chernov had talked about her once, about a dark night made darker by a sadistic killer named John Theron, also known as "Doctor John." Ellen had taken a bullet to distract him so Chernov and another woman could kill him. Janowski had looked up the story and come away impressed with both women.

Now Ellen Parker, followed by the man and shading her eyes with a hand as she walked around the fence, was visiting Morrigan Kildeere. What was going on?

Ellen walked slowly and adjusted her shoulder bag. Her thin blouse seemed like a coat as it held the heat. The sun pressed down with sufficient power to discourage rapid movements and it wasn't summer yet. She put a hand over her eyes but could see nothing behind the house's dark windows.

"She might not be home," she said.

"Maybe in the barn," Blasingame said.

She heard faint music came from the barn – her friend had good ears – and Ellen followed the fence to the driveway. She saw a large black bird sitting on the house's side porch. The bird, maybe it was a crow, was fooling around with a pan of water sufficiently large to handle a good-sized dog, ducking its head into the water, shaking droplets in all directions just for the fun of it, she thought, and pausing to take a quick drink.

The bird, big enough to be a raven, stopped playing and studied her. After a moment, as she reached the driveway, it decided she was unworthy of its attention and it went back to splashing the water around. Ellen watched it as she walked and smiled. Then she heard the barn door slide back.

The first thing Ellen thought was Morrigan Kildeere looked taller than her file pictures. Then she realized it wasn't so much Kildeere's actual height as how she carried herself; erect, like some of the military people Ellen knew. They did it from a blend of authority, pride, and a sense of competency, and she wondered if it was the same for Kildeere.

Then she noticed Kildeere's strength. She pulled the heavy barn door closed with one hand, almost casually as she looked over at Ellen, and the flannel shirt with its rolled-up sleeves did nothing to hide her broad shoulders and muscled forearms.

"Morrigan Kildeere?" Ellen asked as she stepped onto the driveway. "I'm Ellen Parker, Philadelphia Inquirer. Do you have a minute?"

Kildeere, the door closed, said nothing for a moment, but her face emptied of any expression as her eyes swept over Ellen and Blasingame.

"I might," she said slowly. "Are you selling subscriptions?"

"No, though we won't turn one down. I'm gathering some information for a possible article and a gallery owner I know mentioned you."

"Who?"

"Jonathan Tipton. He owns…"

"I know his gallery." Again, Kildeere paused. "How is the old smuggler?"

"Still has his fingertips on the carotid artery of the Philly art world."

Kildeere smiled as Ellen walked up to her.

"I may tell him you said that. Why did he mention me?"

"I was asking him about local artists. He said you were an excellent artist." It was close enough to the truth that Ellen did not feel the bite of a lie.

"And your friend…?"

"Robert Blasingame," he said and held out his hand. "I just help Ellen with navigation."

Kildeere shook his hand and looked at his face closely. He had smile lines beneath gray-blue eyes that drooped slightly at the corners, as if he carried both humor and sadness at the same time. His hair was cut military-short and what was left was sandy-colored. But his eyes had your attention; as big as he was, his eyes, calmly studying you and learning more about you than you might have volunteered, made her feel a little nervous. She grabbed the feeling and pushed it down.

"Are you a reporter, too, Mr. Blasingame?" She smiled, trying not to give anything away.

"'Robert' is fine, ma'am," he said. "Or Bob. No, I'm not a reporter." He looked toward the porch. "Is that a raven?"

"Yes, he is." She paused, as if considering other questions but she turned back to Ellen. "Jonathan's a pirate but a nice one." Kildeere glanced at the sky. "It's a bit warm today. Let's go inside." She opened the barn and Ellen stepped into Kildeere's studio.

It was warmer in the barn than outside but Kildeere walked through it silently and exited through a door facing the house's side porch. The raven stopped splashing and walked to the steps, as if challenging their approach.

"Don't mind him," Kildeere said over her shoulder. "If it is a him. He's just trying to get a handout."

"What's his name?" Ellen asked.

"Don't know," Kildeere said, shaking her head. "He's never said."

"Taciturn, then, is he?"

The raven made a sound like it was trying out something between a squawk and a yodel as the three came up the steps.

"Actually, he likes to debate significant issues, but I find his arguments specious. That's why I think he's a him."

"Odd to find a raven with that trait."

"It is odd." Kildeere opened the screened door and held it for Ellen.

"I've read they generally use Socratic logic," she said as she entered.

They walked into a kitchen and Kildeere waved at a beat-up table with handcrafted chairs. She noticed Blasingame sat in the one that did not have its back to any doorways.

"That's what all the sources say," Kildeere said, her arms crossed and leaning back against the sink.

"What sources are those? I need attribution in the news business."

"Wolves. Ravens are known as 'wolf birds.' Apparently, they and wolves have worked out a cooperative venture of some kind. But wolves aren't much for interviews, what with the solitary thing."

"And eating their interviewers."

"Greatly exaggerated but it does discourage visitors. I may take it up." Kildeere smiled broadly, enjoying the exchange of quips with Ellen.

"I don't mean to intrude," Ellen said automatically.

"I'll throw you out if I summon up the energy. Do you two drink coffee?"

Ellen said she did and Blasingame nodded. Kildeere pulled a carafe from her coffee maker and looked at it suspiciously.

"Still seems hot," she said. She took cups and filled them, one at a time, and put them down in front of Ellen and Blasingame. As she poured her own, she motioned with her head toward the refrigerator and told Blasingame she had fresh cream.

He was up and back down, placing the cream pitcher between Ellen and Kildeere.

"Thanks," Ellen said.

"Local dairy folks, southwest of here, make a little cream on the side. I've taken a liking to it."

"It's pretty good."

"You know cream?"

"Spent a lot of time on a farm when I was a kid in Ohio. Grandfather's place. He wasn't dairy but there were a fair number of dairy farmers around. When I was with him, we always bought local. He claimed he could identify the farm the cream came from." She took a sip. "This takes me back."

"What do you want to know?" Kildeere asked sharply.

Ellen realized Kildeere was concerned about what Ellen's interests were. Maybe. But the question and Kildeere's tone turned on her reporter's hearing. For the first time, Ellen wondered what Kildeere had to hide.

"We're looking," she said slowly, "at a possible article on artists in the local scene. Mostly those who are highly regarded by other professionals. Get a cross-section on the best of Philly."

"How did my name fall into the mix?" Kildeere's voice was more relaxed but Ellen thought she might be trying to hid her anxiety.

"Just the result of a big sweep, looking at what's happening in galleries, talking with people like Jonathan, that sort of thing. We've got several different ways we might go with it, assuming we get to go at all. But we're at a point where talking to the artists themselves is the next logical step. So here I am."

"I see."

"I noticed, when we went through the barn, that you're quite busy. It looked like you were in the middle of a couple of projects in stone and several more in metal."

"The large stone things are commissions," Kildeere said. Her tension, now that she was talking about her work, seemed to fade away. "Some of the metal things are just small mobiles, part of a series." She paused. "Would you like to see them close up?"

"Sure," Ellen nodded.

"Bring your coffee." Kildeere stood and Ellen and Blasingame followed her.

"Maybe I can get a little background about you to give it all context."

"Background?" Kildeere asked as she led the way out the door. The raven was gone. "Like what?" The tension was back.

"Well, what got you into art?"

"Desperation, mostly," Kildeere said, after a stride or two towards the barn. "It turned out I had to do art, but didn't know it. Just something that was pushing at me." She paused and turned all the lights on.

"I think," Ellen said as she looked around, "you're lucky if that's the case. It can help propel you through the disappointment."

"You've talked with artists before."

"Yes." While Blasingame held back near the door, Ellen walked around the studio, frequently pausing. Kildeere stayed with her, not saying anything unless Ellen asked about a piece. Ellen realized the woman was letting her have her own reaction to the work without putting a filter of interpretation in the way.

Ellen was drawn to the stone sculptures. Some were still emerging from the rock while others were in the last stage of smoothing. She started to touch one but stopped and looked at Kildeere who smile slightly and nodded.

The rough of the rock turned smooth like something growing from the stone and Ellen was fascinated. She had seen stone sculpture before but, first time, she was seeing rock giving up the beauty within. And the nearly finished pieces, one as tall as she was, seemed to convey that process as if recounting their rough births from stone. Kildeere's work reflected where it came from, it respected it's past.

Almost in counterpoint were the creations in metal. The mobiles balanced themselves lightly as if seeking a breeze. Some were small enough Ellen could lift them with one hand. Two were large and hung from the barn's crossbeams. Again, glancing at Kildeere first, she touched the tip of one. The mobile sprung to life, gently turning and dipping, so finely balanced the whole piece responded.

"Wow," she said. "Is this hard to do?"

"Not really," Kildeere said. "You just sketch it out, find the materials, cut them to shape, do some welding to assemble it, discover something isn't right, and spend months trying to figure it out while you bang your head against the wall. The head banging is critical."

Ellen chuckled.

"I guess," she said slowly, "what with the head banging and all, there's some kind of link to heavy metal rock."

"That's an awful joke, but you might be right." Kildeere smiled. "There are computer programs that can do it all for you, all except ordering the steel."

"You don't use them."

"No, I don't, but how did you guess that?"

"Well, same reason the best potters don't use molds. The point of art is that a human created it."

"Well, you may be right, but there is an elephant that some zoo has trained to paint canvases."

"I don't think we can get an elephant to do what you do."

"Job security." She looked at Blasingame and then turned back to Ellen. "You two want to go get a beer?"

"Sure," Ellen said, expecting to go back to Kildeere's kitchen. She was slightly surprised when they went through the big barn doors and Kildeere unlocked her old SUV.

They left the doors open for a moment to let the heat escape and then quickly lowered the windows. In a moment, they turned out of the driveway and headed west.

The bar had an inside and an outside. The inside was cool, dark, crowded, and noisy with patrons cheering on college teams doing something to each other, perhaps in athletic competitions. Since there were about two zillion colleges and universities in the Philadelphia area covered by the local television stations, ten different television displays showed six different games at the same time, which made for lots of cheering and groaning, though Ellen thought some of the cheers and groans had more to do with the beer than the sport results. With silent agreement, Ellen and Kildeere moved out to the wide patio and refuge under a table's canvas umbrella. Blasingame stayed inside but Kildeere noticed he sat at the bar, where he looked through a wide window and saw the whole patio.

The patio was another world. A creek ran around two sides of it and, with the bar doors closed to preserve the air conditioning, conversations could be heard without much difficulty. Ten tables and a scattering of individual chairs and benches covered the patio's flagstones and, though they were well populated, all the customers seemed to have agreed to keep their voices down.

"Nice place," Ellen said. "I knew of it but have never been here."

"Sometimes I come for their dinners. A little pricey, but good food, especially if you've been doing beans and dogs for three nights in a row so you can get back to work." Kildeere drank from her bottle. "You live around here?" She pulled a phone from her jeans and checked it.

"East. Up near Thirty."

"How did you get this assignment?" She didn't raise her eyes from her phone but her fingers tapped it silently. "Just luck of the draw or do you regularly cover Philadelphia's art scene?"

"No, usually I don't. We've got a couple of people who really know it. But, since I live out here in Chester County, I get tagged with doing some of the leg work when there's something going on out here."

Kildeere didn't say anything, though her eyebrows went up. She tapped her phone and put it away. She picked up her bottle and glanced at the bar; Blasingame was watching her and Ellen.

"'Leg work' require a bodyguard?"

"Usually not," Ellen said. Kildeere looked at her for a moment.

"No, you don't cover the art scene, whatever that is. Your byline shows up on a number of articles and none of them have to do with art." She took a swallow as if needing to make herself pause. "So, really, why are we talking?"

"You're an anomaly." Ellen shook her head slightly. "You were about to go national, maybe international, but you didn't. You chose to stay pretty local. The impression some have is you could have had it all but you chose not to go there. That's unusual, so I thought I'd check it out. Might be a story in it."

"One of their best reporters has the time to take a look at why someone decides to avoid the big time?"

"Well, it's Saturday." She tried a small smile. "And thanks for calling me one of our best."

"That's why you talked to Tipton?"

"Yes. I already had your name from a source and talked to him to get some background. He really does think you are one of the top artists in the area."

"This is just about why I didn't go for something larger?"

"It might be. We haven't settled on whether or not there really is a story here. And we won't do it without your cooperation."

"Uh-huh, just like in real life."

"No, really. This isn't about busting the butt of some slum lord or politician on the take. Maybe we can do an article on local artists. To do it, we have to sell it."

"Sell it?"

"To our editors. Lots of possible stories out there, we can't do them all. To even take a shot at doing one we have to show it will get some interest. Look at it from my point of view. You are an artist who everyone agrees could be a superstar but you've decided not. You don't think people would be interested in that?"

"What are the boundaries?"

"Boundaries?"

Kildeere took a deep breath. "Maybe there are things I don't want to get into. What happens then?"

"Look, I'll ask questions. You answer or not, right? I'm not looking for an expose, I'm not trying to ambush you, there's no hidden agenda here."

"Really?" Kildeere's lips went tight for a second. "You don't want to talk about John Faraday?"

"Your old representative?" Ellen shrugged. "I'm not trying to embarrass anyone. He's a part of your history, but I'm not interested in his drinking and how it may have contributed to his drowning. Sure, I am interested in how his death influenced your decision not to grab the brass ring, if it did. As I said, that could be something people would be interested in if it was relevant." She took a sip from her beer; the brief spasm of guilt she felt – there was no story, no pitch to give her editor – she pushed away with the thought that maybe there really was a story here.

"What do you know about Faraday?" Kildeere looked down at the table as she asked her question.

"Big-name gallery owner, a good number the artists he represented have international reputations. He was everywhere, knew everyone in the art scene, and could spot talent." Ellen took a breath, unconsciously mimicking Kildeere. "But he had trouble holding onto artists. At the time of his death, you were the only woman he still represented, and about half the men he started with had left him."

Kildeere, her eyes still down, nodded but said nothing. Ellen waited.

"Maybe," Kildeere slowly said, "I wanted the freedom to go my own way. After he was gone, I understood the big scene eats up a lot of your time, your life. Pressures to do things other people want, perform in ways other people want, you know? When he died, his gallery fell apart pretty quickly. No one really took it over. It gave me time to think. I'm not into the whole party, glad-handing thing. I wanted to do art but I thought being a big name would just get in the way. I found a gallery to represent me that doesn't push." She looked up. "Does that work for you?"

"Sure. I think a lot of people can identify with taking control of your own life."

"All right," Kildeere said. "That's what I'll talk about. Not about his problems with his artists or his drinking."

"Agreed." Ellen held out her bottle and Kildeere grinned and tapped it with her own.

"Now," Kildeere said, and finished her bottle, "I've got a question for you."

"Go ahead."

"What's with the bodyguard?"

"You don't believe he's my navigator?"

"Answer my question. You want me to answer your questions…"

"Probably nothing," Ellen said. "People are concerned that a man who has called the paper to talk to me might want to get a little closer than that."

Kildeere said nothing, but brought out her phone again and closely examined the screen. She flipped through several pictures and her eyes widened.

"Shit, lady, you've been talking with a monster." Kildeere put her phone away. "That is insane. I looked at your name on the site but didn't read the articles, didn't even pay attention to the headlines. What is all that about?"

"He called to correct something I wrote. He's called back. I can't go into details but it's no big deal."

"No big deal, but you've got a SEAL following you around."

"Robert wasn't a SEAL."

"Whatever. I don't need to know what it was he was, or is, but he's watching everything you do, everyone who comes near us." She shook her head. "Yeah, some of it might because he just likes to look at you, I get a little of that vibe, but mostly he's in full sheepdog mode."

"Sheepdog?"

"Friend of mine, 'way back, said most people are nice and normal but there are wolves out there and most people can't deal with them. But some people, they're like sheepdogs, they protect people from the wolves." She smiled. "That's what I meant earlier about being a SEAL. My friend, he was one of them. They have a look. Kind of, 'Here comes the tsunami, ho-hum, another day at the office, and, while I'm up, do you need me to buy some milk?' And, like I also said, he likes looking at you, so your boyfriend is a sheepdog."

"He's not…" Ellen fell silent.

"Oh, man," Kildeere said, "I think I finally met a woman whose head is more screwed up than mine."

Ellen laughed and, after a second, Kildeere joined in.

Chapter 19: Intruders

Janowski watched Ellen's arrival, disappearance into the barn, emergence and encountering the raven's inspection. Then there was nothing for his binoculars to show him except the raven messing around in a big dog bowl of water. It stopped splashing after a moment and stood on the porch. Oddly, it looked in his direction, though he doubted it could see him from so far away. It launched suddenly into the air and was gone.

Then the three came out of the house. They weren't leaving; they returned to the barn. Time seemed to crawl until they emerged. They all got into Kildeere's car and turned south at the intersection. He hoped they wouldn't notice his truck.

He had not seen Kildeere lock the door to her kitchen, something often not done by people living in the country. Janowski crouched in the hot shadows of the woods, considering possibilities as the car drove away. When it was out of sight, he moved almost by reflex. As he opened the fence gate, part of him told Janowski this was really, really stupid.

But he already had seen the inside of the barn and there was nothing there to answer the question he shared with Ellen Parker; what was Kildeere hiding? If there were any answers to be found, they had to be in the house.

The raven had left shortly after the women and man came from the barn and the water it had scattered as it played was mostly gone. Janowski was careful not to step on any that remained.

The door opened without hesitation and he saw in the corner another door, one leading to the basement stairs. He quickly went to it and it was as he thought. His hand found a light switch and Janowski flipped it up.

He went down, looking around as he went. To one side he saw an exit out the back, to the other was an oil-fired furnace and a hot water tank. An old washer and dryer sat together on the concrete floor and took up a large portion of the wall next to the stairs. A heavy-duty utility table dominated the center. The walls were painted white and basement was dry. He stopped at the foot of the stairs.

Well, there was no plastic sheeting, nothing for wrapping small boys. Janowski really hadn't expected to see any. He tried the door for the exit and it revealed steps up to a set of Bilco steel doors, similar to those found at the back of every farmhouse between the Atlantic and the Continental Divide. He closed the door.

Next to the door was a floor to ceiling set of shelves holding tools, small plastic boxes of screws, an old cast iron frying pan, some empty glass jars used in canning vegetables, and a box of electrical extension cords so old they were two-pronged and dust covered.

Beside the shelves, mounted on the wall, a grey internet connection box glowed green pinpoints of light. Below it, side by side, were two large storage boxes. The first held winter clothing. The second…

Letters in envelopes, photo albums and a shoebox of ancient photographs and their negatives. He shook his head. Welcome to the Twenty-First Century, Ms. Kildeere. Don't you know everything is digital? A college yearbook stood against one side. Several folders were propped against it. Each held announcements of art shows arranged year by year. He flipped through them quickly; Kildeere's name was one of many in the oldest but was the only name in the latest. But the latest was six years old. He shook his head and reached down for another folder. He opened it and looked into the eyes of a smiling man.

The man's image, captured in glossy black and white, smiled with teeth almost brilliant with hands occupied holding a pen and paper as he gazed into the eyes of Janowski or anyone else looking at the publicity photograph. His picture displayed intelligence (head slightly tilted as if considering a question) and humor (the smile capable of freezing deer crossing a highway). It was the kind of professionally prepared photograph that seemed incomplete not to have the subject's signature in a corner but it was unsigned. The back revealed the name. "John Faraday" was no one Janowski knew but the stamp included the phrase, "The Faraday Gallery", and he understood the connection.

The folder was filled with items about Faraday, all collected in the days, Janowski saw, following his death. Death? Skimming quickly through part of the pile of newspaper clippings, he spotted Kildeere's name in an article as one of his "up and coming artist" clients; other articles confirmed the relationship.

The other newspaper clippings followed Faraday's death and the subsequent investigation of what was quickly termed an accidental drowning. No letters, email print-outs, copies of contracts, birthday greetings, none of the debris that might follow a professional relationship, much less a personal one. Had it not been for the notation in the clippings, the folder might have been taken for the work of some freak who liked to collect information on accidental drownings.

Accidental…

He paused and read the clippings more closely. Kildeere's name appeared in several places during the investigation. Apparently, she had been waiting in the nearby 30th Street train station when Faraday fell into the river. They were supposed to take a late train together to New York and meet with representatives of a famous – even Janowski knew the name – museum. Business details were not covered, but he assumed the museum was interested in some of her big stones. Maybe even that ugly tower out in her front yard. Serve New York right to get that damned thing. But he had not joined her and she did not go alone. He read all the clippings but there was nothing else.

She had pictures besides the one of Faraday. All from the newspapers. There was one of the front of the Faraday Gallery. No, two, from two different newspapers. A couple of the bridge, one showing with an arrow where the police thought Faraday had gone over, about a third of the way out from the train station side. Oddly, she, or someone, had hand-drawn a small circle on the bridge railing much closer to the station side. He looked closely but there wasn't anything there. Might have just been a doodle.

Why had she not gone on up to New York by herself? Big museum, big money. He shrugged as he thought. Maybe it was nothing.

Why did she keep this stuff? Nothing personal, nothing professional, just stuff on Faraday's death.

And the investigation.

Janowski frowned as he carefully reassembled everything and put all the folders back into the box. She did not seem to be the kind who might be possessed by morbid curiosity but, as he stepped back and looked things over, you could never tell what would push some people's buttons.

He walked up the steps and paused before stepping into the kitchen but no one had returned. Janowski carefully closed the door and stepped out onto the side porch. A quick look up and down the road showed no cars approaching and he jogged back into the trees.

It was a lot hotter going through the woods, a heat emphasized by its contrast with the cellar. At one point, his cop sense went off and he looked around. For a moment, there was nothing to see. He realized he stood in part of the woods where everything was silent – the song birds had shut down. Just enough of a change to catch his attention. Janowski kept looking, pretty sure his own movements had not been responsible – after all, he had heard chirping up in the trees coming and going to Kildeere's place. He saw nothing, other than that big black bird, or one just like it, from Kildeer's porch. The raven was silent as it looked at him and cocked its head. But, other than the big bird, Janowski saw no one else. He turned and resumed walking.

He grimaced as he made his way past the big oak he had seen earlier. Going into Kildeere's house was an incredibly stupid thing to do and what had it accomplished? Right, she was, or had been, interested in the death of her agent. A little fact from six years ago that seemed to mean zero.

What else had he learned? That newspaper woman, Ellen Parker, was interested in her. Enough to come out on a Saturday. Right, reporters, like Joyton police officers, worked on Saturdays, though he thought Ellen actually was official while he was a complete idiot who put his job and future at risk. Janowski shook his head as he worked around the barrier of thorn bushes.

All that risk for nothing. Maybe, and he smiled as he climbed into his truck, she had just liked seeing her name in print. Some people were like that.

Still, she had been interviewed by the Philly cops. Janowski idly wondered if the interview notes were still around. Probably nothing of interest in them, certainly nothing that might finally shut off that almost compulsive need to know more about her. He looked both ways and drove the big truck back the way he had come.

Might not hurt to find out. Six years, they might not even exist, but old sayings of turning over every stone came to mind. Hell, he could request them officially and not put his butt in the wind. He smiled and shook his head a last time. Yes, do it officially and finally get that damned itch scratched. Case fucking closed.

It was a Saturday, so no one expected him to be working. That meant some freedom to scout possible sites, something that gave him a small thrill. Small, but that was better than nothing. On the other site, scouting the last names on his list was a problem on weekends. If they were home, usually so were other people. If they weren't, there was little way to know where they were off to.

Weekdays were better. After school but before parents came home from work. He would shadow and then move. Always a fair amount of tension involved, of course, but he liked the feeling. It was part of the anticipation.

He had two places he wanted to examine as sites. He had learned not to depend on his memory. Chester County, looking a little like a wedge of Pennsylvania pie jammed against Delaware and Maryland, was largely as he remembered it, but that was not the same as unchanged. And it was important to be sure.

Today he drove through Octoraro Reservoir, traveling down 472 from Lancaster County. The Reservoir bordered Chester and Lancaster County and had a number of small, isolated places around it on the Chester County side. But none were very far from the busy traffic on 472. He shook his head; he thought there had been much less traffic in past years, back before he moved to New Jersey.

Well, they didn't all pan out. But, since he was in the area, there was a county park just a little further south close to the Maryland border, the Mason-Dixon Line. He had never visited Nottingham County Park before – Chester County was very large, large enough to have some hidden features even if you'd been born there – but he liked that U.S. 1 slipped past it. He also liked, if the county website was correct, all the space in the park that was away from watching eyes on the circling roads and picnic pavilions.

It might be wise to use a place he had never, ever, visited in the past. No class trips, no scouting outing, no family reunions, nothing linked him to the park. No connection.

Nottingham County Park had lots of people doing whatever it is people do in parks but did not give the impression of being crowded. He nodded to himself. For a Saturday it seemed wide open. He followed the roads around, just letting himself wander. He lowered his window. The heat didn't bother him and he felt it put him more in touch with the park's potential usefulness.

He pulled over in an area well away from the pavilions and their picnicking families. The trees held the heat of the afternoon which probably explained why no one used the nearby hiking trail. He stepped out of his car, stretched, and looked around.

He saw an almost dried-up creek skirting the small parking area. He looked around; there was no one. Smiling, he walked along the banks of the creek. Here and there a small puddle appeared but there was very little water. He decided it was really just a drainage ditch, an impression reinforced as he encountered grey rocks of the same size used to line the sides. He frowned – trying to dig through them would be a major chore.

He stopped where the ditch curved to the right and looked back. His car was invisible. He stepped out of the ditch and examined the ground. It was mostly earth covered by a few weeds and generations of dead leaves.

It would do. Do? It would be wonderful. He felt the feeling, *the* feeling grow as if a small body wrapped in plastic lay at his feet. It grew to a level that he could almost taste but then it stopped. He pressed his lips together tightly.

This was just anticipation. It wasn't the real thing. This was just a promise of what might be. He nodded, looked around one more time, and then walked back to his car. He would have no trouble finding the place again, even in the dark. The knowledge was spiritual, a part of him, and he would not need maps or GPS to find it again.

It was, after all, his calling.

Brown looked up from his computer screen and stretched as he nodded at Karen Deevers. An informal tradition in the short life of the task force held that people working on the weekend, which was almost everyone, would dress informally. His normal coat and tie were replaced by coat and knit shirt, both conservative FBI-blue, which did nothing to make him appear to be anything other than an FBI Agent. Deevers, however, wore a summer blouse and blue jeans whose relaxed appearance was somewhat disturbed by the holstered, canted slightly forward .40-caliber Glock pistol on her waist.

"I agree," Brown said before Deevers said anything. She smiled slightly and cocked her head to one side.

"With…?"

"Your email. I don't know when you sleep, the thing arrived at three this morning."

"I woke up and, while I started to read an eBook, it occurred to me there was a possible source of information we had not explored. I sent it to you and then, duty discharged, slept soundly."

"It's a good idea," Brown said. "I've been looking and there aren't any public records of past church members for Saint Barnabas. That boy, Philip Lang, he attended school there before his family moved, that clearly connects him to two other boys who still were in school at Barnabas, but none of the other victims ever attended Barnabas. Your idea that other people who had also moved away from the parish about the time that the Lang family did might know something about Lang and some of the other boys not otherwise connected to the school is worth checking."

"Long shot," Deevers said. "I have no idea how many families that might be."

"I agree, long shot, still…" He shook his head and reached for a cardboard tube of coffee he had brought in from Dunkin' Donuts and took a sip. It was room temperature but he didn't care.

"We don't have much else to check out," Deevers finished his sentence.

"Other than wait for another murder and hope we can tease something out of it." Brown shook his head again. "I hate waiting on that son of a bitch."

Deevers said nothing. Hunting serial murderers often involved waiting for the next death. That would give them more information, some of which might be useful. But… She shared Brown's impatience with waiting. Everyone was pooling ideas, even knowing it was quite likely none would provide any breakthrough. She and Brown had sat down with state and local task force officers, encouraging them to make suggestions.

Of course, most of what was suggested were things already tried or still in process, such as monitoring sites. But, even when no one had any new ideas, in spite of all the frustration, every day all the cops came in, picked up their assignments, and went back out.

At its best, being in the police was a calling, almost religious in its nature. Deevers thought for a moment and then smiled to herself. All right, it was religious, for it required faith in the idea of the law as an approximation of justice. You had to have something you believed in to keep going when everything seemed to be nothing but a series of dead ends.

"We need some names," Brown said. "Give Barnabas a call and see if they can give you some to check out." He paused. "If they are willing to give some out. I don't know if Catholics regard forwarding addresses as privileged communication or something."

"One way to find out," Deevers said, heading to her desk. "If we get any names, let me see if I can find a local to go with me."

"Good idea." Brown went back to his computer screen as Deevers sat down and flipped to the back of her notepad where she kept telephone numbers. It was time to intrude on someone's day off.

153

"No, no, not a problem at all," the young man in the administrative office of Saint Barnabas said to Deevers. He looked young enough to still be in college, an appearance emphasized by the ready smile his Oriental eyes seemed especially designed to support. The effect was probably also enhanced by his David Bowie t-shirt. "Glad you called my cell; as it happens, I'm at Saint Barnabas today." He laughed politely. "No, the sisters aren't making me stay after school. We've got a couple of work orders going out and our contractor called yesterday and said if we could have them ready by Monday, he would pick them up then. Oh, yes, that's it exactly. Puts us higher on the list than if we mail them out later in the week. What is it you need?"

He fell silent and made a note on a piece of scrap paper. He nodded.

"No, not a problem, but I don't think it's going to be a very long list. Other than the family of the poor Lang boy, I can only recall two or three other families who've moved away or otherwise dropped out in the past couple of years." He smiled. "It's not something I monitor closely, being more on the financial side of things but I can get the information together for you. Can you give me a half hour to wrap up what I'm doing and get the list compiled?" He nodded. "Great. See you then. 'Bye." He hung up.

"What was that all about?" A white man with grey hair and a deeply lined face asked from his desk without looking up as he studied his computer screen. His chair was draped by a sport coat but his shirt did not have a tie. He looked over the top of his glasses and hit a key with emphasis. "Done," he announced, obviously pleased. "Sending the numbers to you right…" he paused and quickly typed on his keyboard, "…now." Another key was struck with meaning. "You got it?" He looked at the young man.

"Yes, thank you." The young man's fingers moved quickly, almost dancing to music no one except he could hear. Even as he worked, he answered the older man. "That was Agent Deevers, one of those FBI people we talked to."

"Oh, yes, I remember." He had reached back for his coat but paused. "She has another question?"

"Sort of. Looking for other people who've left Barnabas in the past couple of years. Probably wants to find out if they knew any of our boys."

"Sounds like something they should have done earlier."

"You might be right." The young man did not want to argue as he copied and pasted the numbers he needed into the work order; he thought the police had had enough to do questioning everyone any of the three boys

154

might have known at Barnabas. The list of classmates and shared school activities involved well over two hundred other children. What could someone add who had left Barnabas two years ago?

"You need anything else for the work orders?" The older man was impatient to get back to his Saturday, probably because the Phillies had a double-header. He stood and shrugged himself into his coat.

"Nope. Hope your Phillies do well."

"Oh, it's early, they always do well at the start of the season." He offered a smile. "Then they break your heart. You'll let Father Oliver know the work orders are done?"

"I'll email him with copies right after I print out the contractor's, which is to say, right now." In a style similar to that of the older man, he hit a key and then another. A printer in the corner of the office stirred itself to life.

"Okay, you have a good one, Bobby," the older man said as he walked to the door.

"You, too, George."

Bobby Flynn went to the printer and picked up the work orders. He read them as he walked back to his desk and did not look up to see his coworker, George Mayfair, take out his phone as he walked down the hall.

Mayfair waited until he was in the staff parking area. His and Flynn's cars were the only two but he stopped and looked around before doing anything. He licked his lips and raised the phone, his eyes continuously moving.

"Something's going on," he said when the connection came to life.

Chapter 20: Pieces

Bobby Flynn smiled as he let Karen Deevers into the building. She was alone, having failed to find a local police officer who wasn't tied up with work. It was a small thing, but when talking to locals she liked to have local law enforcement present. He tried not to look at her pistol.

"Sorry about that," Flynn said. "I forgot to ask Mr. Mayfair to set the door to the unlock setting when he left. Did you have to beat on it very long before you called me?"

"No, not really," Deevers said, politely smiling. Her knuckles were sore, a sensation that would take a while to fade away and she accepted the pain as a penance for not thinking of her phone immediately. "Thanks for staying."

"Not a problem." He led the way down the hall to the administration office at the end. "Anything we can do to help. Anything at all." His smile was gone. "If it helps catch that monster…" He shook his head. "I cannot imagine what it must be like for you, being involved with this kind of person."

"You learn how to handle it," Deevers said, "and you build some really solid anchors in your life." She surprised herself by being so open with the young man but it was the truth.

"That sounds like a good philosophy for life in general."

The hall was fairly long and Deevers glanced at the small black domes of surveillance attached to the ceiling. Flynn noticed her glancing up.

"We still have them," he said. "We still do our drills. Part of what you need in a school nowadays."

"I remember them from my earlier visits. I hope it wasn't difficult to find the information I requested." Deevers felt like she was depressing the young man and wished his smile returned.

"No problem at all. I had just sent it to my printer when you called." He gestured toward a good-sized printer along a wall and walked to it. "Glad we're not emailing this around. I'm always concerned someone, probably one of our kids, is going to hack into our computers and mess with our records."

"I hope not." She glanced at the page Flynn handed her. "Six families have left Barnabas in the past year?"

"More than I thought." He grimaced. "Sometimes people have to move, jobs, opportunities of all kinds, and sometimes people just leave. Those last two names are in that category. Pulled their kids out of school and left, both before any of the boys… Any of the boys were taken." He seemed distressed.

"Then these addresses are the ones they had at the time their children attended Saint Barnabas?"

"Right. If they moved, we weren't notified of a forwarding address." A small smile appeared. "You probably can find them."

"We've been known to do that," Deevers said, smiling. She held out her hand. "Thank you."

"Not a problem, happy to lend a hand. Let me walk you out."

Flynn kept up a light chatter, mostly talking about the school and how the deaths had impacted everyone he knew.

"The students, of course, and the teachers, but even people working in administration." He shook his head. "Like Mr. Mayfair, my boss, a lot of people have been walking around in a daze. So, any time you need anything, anything at all, just let us know."

Deevers hit the exit door's crossbar and paused at the top of the broad stone steps. Flynn looked around, perhaps a little surprised that he had walked outside with her.

"The school takes up a lot of space," Deevers said as she looked at the printout.

"Oh, yes, the church, the school, the old convent. Now that building is used by the diocese, but that's where it all started. They gave the sisters a farm, you see; lots of space. They started the school and the first church. Over there," he pointed beyond the school, "we have baseball diamonds and two soccer fields."

"I see," she looked up and then back at the printout.

"Really first-rate facilities," Flynn said, obviously glad to be talking about something that wasn't about death. "In fact, both the county soccer and baseball leagues used them for their tournaments and playoffs. You can just see the far baseball field, just to the left of the diocese office building. We get some income from our snack and hotdog stand but we let the leagues use the fields for free. Kind of an ecumenical gesture, I guess. Only problem is, this is all the parking area we have and it really filled up when all the soccer and baseball fields were used at the same time." He grinned. "We had kids everywhere, tons of adults, the county had some deputies directing traffic."

"A little quieter today."

"Oh, yes, it really is." His smile faded and he shook his head. "All that was before everything happened."

Depressed again, he offered his hand to Deevers and unlocked the door to return to his work.

Deevers one-handed the speed dial process. As she waited, she looked up. The school might be named after a saint, but it had closed circuit video cameras on its walls. Trust but verify. Who said that? Agent Brown answered her call.

"A few more names than he expected," she said. "Had a couple of families drop out somewhat abruptly. Sounded like that was unusual." She walked down the steps; someone standing close would have noticed that her eyes swept over the empty parking lot, the thin tree line bordering it facing the road, and the baseball diamonds bordering it on another side. On the other side of the road a single-story office building, surrounded by a thin parking lot, sat in the heat with only a handful of cars to suggest anyone had a reason for working on a Saturday.

"Telephone numbers are given, yes, we can start with those." Her free hand folded the paper and slid it into her other hand. "All right, see you in a bit."

She looked into her car as she approached it, a bit of carefulness that was automatic. Deevers unlocked the driver's door, opened it and paused to let the heat out, and then entered.

As she drove away, his eyes followed her from the office building parking lot. He made no effort to follow her; trying to tail a trained FBI Agent, especially one as alert as she was, would be incredibly stupid and he prided himself on not being that. Instead, he smiled and used his binoculars to watch her disappear. It had been a good move to bring his binoculars. The close-up view he had of her in the parking lot, studying everything as she walked to her car, a solid and professional appearing pistol on her hip, revealed her to be a very dangerous woman. As much fun as it might be to have her in his power, he knew that was just the stuff of dreams.

In the old days, as he termed his activities in New Jersey, he ignored any woman who appeared to be watchful. Why run risks when, with a little patience, you could find one much, much easier?

No, he had priorities. His list, for example. Actually, not the list of names, but what those names were doing on the list, what they possessed; what, he suspected, just one of them possessed.

He waited until she was gone and then drove onto the road. He deliberately turned away from the direction the dangerous woman had gone. It meant taking the long way home but one could never be too careful. Besides, he now knew what one of them looked like. While that knowledge might not ever prove to be important, it certainly could be fuel for a fantasy evening. He smiled.

It had been a slow end to a Saturday. Ellen had felt a compulsion to fix something for dinner and so they stopped at a farmer's roadside stall and bought vegetables. Blasingame helped with the bags, though he paused to use his phone to talk to Tyrone.

"Anything going on?" Ellen picked up several red onions and put them in a bag.

"No," Blasingame said. "Ty said your wi-fi was pitiful and he fixed it. He also changed your password. He said he left it in your hidden drawer in your big, big desk. The double-big is a quote."

"What was wrong with my password?"

"Do you want another quote?"

"Does his mother know he goes around changing women's passwords?"

Blasingame chuckled as Ellen looked over some zucchini.

"Oh, don't tell her that. I've gotten him in enough trouble."

Ellen smiled and paid the teenager behind the plywood counter; he smiled as he listened to the two adults and wondered if he would ever be comfortable enough around a girl to talk like... Friends. His flash of insight went unnoticed by Ellen and Blasingame as they carried the bags back to her car, still lightly joking with one another.

Ellen fixed something she called "Italian-Mexican" lasagna. Though it smelled delicious as it baked, Blasingame managed to look dubious every time he glanced at the stove.

"Come on, Robert," Ellen said as she poured glasses of wine, "with all of your running about, you must have eaten some really awful things."

"Survival school," he said as he tried a sip of the wine. "Eglin Air Force Base. We made a soup from baby squirrels. When I go to someone's house to eat, I try to remember that's the standard they have to beat."

"Okay, no appetite," Ellen announced and led the way to her small living room. As she sat down, she looked at him and raised her eyebrows. "Did you just reveal some of your past? Were you in the Air Force?"

"No," he said, sitting in an overstuffed chair that allowed him to see her, the front door, and the kitchen's back door. "I told you, I wasn't in the military. But they have an excellent survival training establishment there, or did. I don't know about nowadays."

"Ty thinks you were a CIA agent."

"Nope." He looked at her over the rim of his wine glass. "And that's it for yeas and nays. Are we at the point where we share our pasts?"

Ellen put her glass down and then shook her head.

"Nope," she echoed. "I'm happy to hear anything about you'd care to tell me but a history course is not required."

"I think I told you I worked originally as a language specialist. Not CIA, but one of the alphabet agencies that supported the people on the ground. Mostly the people who needed a translator and didn't usually have any of their own."

"Why didn't they?"

"Usually, they weren't the people you sent when you wanted to talk to someone." He smiled slightly. "People like me got some training so we could keep up and know how to get in and out of a helicopter without embarrassing ourselves. That training was supplemented by what we were taught on the ground." He took a sip.

"You've got some skills; I've seen them."

"Mostly, I'm very good at being observant and patient, things I think I had before I ever got involved. But the real pros, they trained all the time when they weren't actually on a mission, and I managed to go along and learn things. Don't confuse me with one of them, though. Mostly, I talked to people, gathering information. I led a small team of intelligence gatherers. Sometimes, I was a part of interrogations."

"What was that like?"

"The interrogations?" He smiled. "Not like the movies. Usually, people were scared to death. Their own propaganda made them think falling into our hands meant they'd never get to heaven, that we'd eat their sons and daughters, real horror stuff. Many of them would tell you everything they knew, everything they thought they knew, and would make up stuff if there was a pause in the conversation. It was just taking the time to get to know what they wanted, what they needed. Often, it was just knowing they could get in touch with their families, something easy."

"What about the tough ones?"

"Sometimes the smartest ones would tell you what you wanted to know the easiest. Egos, sometimes, thinking they could spin a yarn that would take us in, that sort of thing."

"What about someone who just wouldn't say anything?"

"We'd tell them not to say anything, that we just wanted to fill them in on the situation, and we'd do a dog and pony show that made it sound like we knew everything about everyone. Depending on the individual, we might play it as if we thought they didn't know anything, too minor to think about. They'd start to get worried that if we didn't think they were of value, someone was going to take them out the back door and leave them by the side of the road. They'd start to talk, mostly lies, but never quite understanding we learned from their lies."

Ellen went silent and sipped her drink. Blasingame made no effort to fill the silence.

"All right," Ellen said, "I know what you're expecting me to ask but..."

"No," Blasingame said. "I never tortured anyone. It happened, but not while I was there. Despite what you see in the movies, that kind of thing doesn't work very well. People make up stuff to get it to stop. They'll say anything. Sure, sometimes we'd leave someone in isolation for hours, letting the tension build, but usually we had to work quickly. Information is often time sensitive, so you can't fool around."

"Listen, I don't care about all that," Ellen said. "I mean, I care about it. You can't be a reporter without having some kind of ethical stance. What I mean is, you've proved to me that you're a good guy." She took a breath. "A friend. I don't need testimony. I'm always interested in knowing more about you."

"'A friend?'" Blasingame smiled broadly. "I think my tail feathers are on fire."

"I don't have a lot of friends," Ellen said.

"Me, neither." His smile faded.

"When I say you're my friend, it feels like I'm saying something important."

"You are."

"This is not a good time to get into this, but here we are." Ellen paused. "Robert, I like you. I think you are a good man and I want you for a friend.

161

'Way back in Coalville, I thought there might be something else between us but now I'm thinking clearer and that something, whatever it might have been, isn't really there."

"Do I still get dinner?"

"It's more than I can handle, so, yes, sure."

"Great. It smells delicious."

"And you, what do you think about what I've said."

"Kind of mulling it over," Blasingame said. "Yes, I felt something for you, but I'm a little slow on letting myself get involved with someone. The brakes are on, not a problem, and, yes, maybe we can be friends. I think, now that I'm thinking, that's the direction we were moving."

"You're not just saying that?"

"I'll say anything for a free meal, but I think I'm telling you the truth."

Ellen nodded her head and slouched against the back of the couch.

"What do we do now?" she asked, her voice low.

"We have dinner," he said. "Maybe a little more wine. Maybe watch something on Netflix. Tomorrow, you'll make your bed and I'll straighten up the couch. I should have asked earlier. Do you go to church on Sundays?"

Ellen laughed and, oddly, so did Blasingame.

Dinner was delicious.

Chapter 21: The firing line

With Dwyer's close attention, James found his accuracy improving rapidly at first and then more gradually but always getting better. There were instants when he had the black dot of a bullseye balanced on the tip of the rifle's front sight and framed perfectly within the circle of the rear sight and knew as the rifle fired precisely where the bullet went without having to look. It was like magic, Zen, the Force, some damned thing where the melding of firearm, bullet, target, and him – most importantly, most impressively, him – doing something not just right but close to perfect.

James liked coming to the range, even for the "homework," and it became part of his after-work routine. Depending on what time he arrived, there were usually other people on the hundred-meter rifle range. He would wait for the ceasefire call and then walk down to the barrier in front of the earthen berm and staple up his target. Depending on his assignment, the target was either a simple black circle or a stylized black silhouette.

He would return to the firing line and take his position – prone, sitting, kneeling, or standing – and wait for the range safety officer to make her call.

"Is the line ready?" A pause waiting for someone to indicate they needed another moment. "Ready on the right, ready on the left, all ready on the firing line." The last check. "Commence firing."

Then he would get to work. It was work. Sometimes it was as hard as anything he had ever done. It was easy to get frustrated, it was hard to overcome the frustration, but that was part of the homework. No one else to provide encouragement. Overcoming things, overcoming himself, was something no one else could do. If he wanted to be better, then he had to control himself. The rifle was far easier.

The work carried over. He never thought of his job in terms of his official occupation, the specialist title he had earned through study and experience, just the endurance for a paycheck, the thing rotting at the core of his life, the experience eroding relationships, grinding away at his sense of himself as anything more than the replaceable cog in a machine his employers wanted him to believe he was. It lay like a heavy hand on the scales of his life, pulling the pan holding the painful negatives of an ordinary life down hard, making the pan with the balancing weight of whatever good there was in his life seem like it was empty. The job continued with its humiliations, petty and large, but...

James' sense of things changed with a quickness that surprised him. He first noticed the change while sitting in his supervisor's office, waiting for the man to look up at the papers he studied, pretending that the papers were important, perhaps something James should be worried about. The first thing that came to him was how small his supervisor was. Not in size; his supervisor was actually taller than James. But, as he sat in the man's office, it was if he observed him from a distance, from sufficiently far away that the supervisor seemed small, not much more in importance than his office furniture. It was a strange perception, one that was a little startling.

The second thing he noticed was he was not thinking about whatever it was the supervisor was trying to do. James wasn't running through the list of the management techniques that were current in the company, trying to anticipate whatever was coming and brace himself for it. Instead, he was thinking about the previous evening's target practice and how he might improve his skills.

And he was thinking about Charles Dwyer. Dwyer's comments about his shooting, his encouragement, were important, more important to him than avoiding whatever psychological warfare technique his supervisor was going to use. The thought made him smile.

His supervisor looked up from his shuffled papers and saw James' smile. He stopped, the serious expression on his face, one he practiced in accordance with the company's middle management training courses, fading in a momentary confusion. He fumbled with the papers and then tried to pick up on his script.

"Do you know why," he asked with a pointless question designed to disquiet his underling, throw him off-balance, "I've called you here today?" His presentation, he knew, was poor, damaged by hesitations and pauses. Why is he smiling? What does he have to smile about?

"Not at all, sir," James said. His tone had the serious quality his supervisor's question lacked.

But the smile stayed.

What does he know?

Charles Dwyer stood behind James and watched the young man fire his pistol in the indoor range. He nodded; the young man paid attention to coaching and improved steadily. After days of steady practice, it showed.

True, it was all formal target shooting – approach the firing line, use the same targets, use the same clips with five rounds loaded into each, work on the sight picture, all of the basic things for beginners – but Dwyer strongly believed in being solid in the fundamentals. Everything built on them. Before learning combat skills, you had to know how to use a firearm, make it an extension of your hand and eye, your will.

Dwyer liked most of his private students. Hell, he admitted, he liked all of them. But, as he explained to his wife, some he particularly took a shine to. Ellen Parker was one. That lady might have spent the rest of her life running in the opposite direction of anything resembling a gun, given everything she had been through. She didn't, she went after shooting, not just to master it, but maybe, he thought, to master herself.

And James Hardy. The White man reminded Dwyer, and this was something he never explained to his wife because it wasn't entirely clear to him, of some people hurt by "the machine," his title for society as a whole. A lot of those people Dwyer met on the job, people who retreated into pain and anger until finally they lashed back, and you could spend days gathering the body parts.

Dwyer blinked. Well, James didn't seem like the kind of person to go out of his way to hurt anyone, didn't seem to nursing any grudges, just wanted to add a little discipline, a little challenge, to his life.

James ceased fire. He cleared his pistol and visually checked the chamber was empty. Then he pressed the button to retrieve his target. People in the other lanes continued firing as James studied his target. He made a brief note in a small, spiral-spring notebook and looked over his shoulder at Dwyer. He grinned.

Dwyer said nothing; both men wore sound suppressing earphones. But he made a drinking motion and pointed in the general direction of the break room. James nodded. He would have to wait until the range secured and everyone could sweep up their brass from the concrete floor.

Dwyer saw Ellen Parker sitting with Robert Blasingame as he entered the break room and waved. Ellen waved back and Robert nodded. Dwyer went to the urns and fixed himself a good-sized coffee in his State Police mug. He paused as if checking the coffee's temperature but his eyes flicked towards Blasingame. There was something a little off about the man. His cop sense wasn't sounding any major alarms. It was just like there was a part to Blasingame that stayed a little out of sight. Probably nothing, but Dwyer felt a little protective towards Ellen.

He walked over to their table and Ellen motioned to an empty chair as he approached.

"How goes it, folks?"

"Slow and steady," Ellen said and Blasingame nodded as he sipped from a can of soda. "How has your day been?"

"Pretty good," Dwyer said. He looked over his shoulder and waved at James Hardy standing in the doorway. "Come on over," he said.

James, still wearing his earphones, grinned and took them off but left his yellow tinted safety glasses on. "Coffee," he said, and walked over to the urns. A moment later he sat down.

"How are you all doing?" James asked.

"Not too bad," Ellen said. She looked at the punctured target James had placed face down in front of him. "How's the shooting going?"

"Well," James said slowly, "not too bad for a blind man." He turned the target over and his face was carefully neutral.

"Nice," Ellen said.

"Thank you," James said in a tone completely sincere as he eyed the target. His face relaxed. "It seems to come slowly." He looked up at Dwyer. "I mean, I'm a slow learner."

"It can come in fits and starts," Dwyer said. "You're on track. You want to watch you don't get in your own way." He shook his head. "People become impatient, get dissatisfied with their progress." He smiled. "I think most of shooting isn't about sight picture and trigger squeeze; it's about letting yourself do it."

"You're right about that," Ellen said.

"I've seen you shoot," James said. "You're pretty good."

"Thank you."

"Have you been doing it long?"

Ellen frowned slightly as she picked up James' target.

"My grandfather taught me," she said, still studying the target. "I was in my teens." She looked up. "Some friends of mine, military, law enforcement, they did a little more teaching but Charles was the first person I've worked with regularly."

"Do you do a lot of shooting, Mr. Blasingame? I don't think I've seen you shoot."

"Please don't call me 'Mister,'" Blasingame said. "I keep looking over my shoulder for my father. Robert is fine. And I do a little."

"I'm James." He held out his hand and Blasingame shook it.

"Robert," Dwyer said, "was professionally trained and has kept up his skills." It was a guess, but Ellen's raised eyebrows and Robert's slight smile provided him with confirmation.

"I didn't mean to pry," James said. "Other people that I've met on the range, here at the club, some seem a bit guarded about how good they are, how they learned." He shrugged. "I guess I'm still learning the culture."

"Well, no one wants to sound like they are showing off," Dwyer said. "The shooting speaks for itself. You don't have to wear a jacket with a bunch of competition patches on it, though some people do, maybe for reassurance when they get into a slump. But you'll find some people who talk the talk, same as with any skill."

"I enjoy it," Blasingame said, slightly surprising Ellen with volunteering something about himself. "Some of it feels like some kind of meditation, makes me clear my mind. But, I think, beyond the utility of the skill, the discipline shooting requires is a thing I find important." He took a sip from his can. "And it's fun, much of the time. Competing with myself, trying to better what I've done in the past. Coming up with new challenges. That sort of thing."

James looked at Blasingame closely, as if hearing more than was said. He nodded.

"Discipline, yes," he said. "I get that. I think I'm seeing some of that in my life, kind of as a spin-off or something."

"Mental exercise," Dwyer said. "That's what most of shooting is. Exercising some of your brain muscles. Maybe make you a little stronger in places besides the range." He smiled broadly. "We need a shrink to comment on that."

"I'm sure some would agree," Ellen said. "In fact, I'm positive."

"What kind of work do you do, James?" Blasingame asked.

"I'm a line supervisor in a managed health care system. Mostly pushing case files and paperwork around. You?"

"Restoration work, mostly. I help folks find things needed to make their new houses look old." He smiled. "Work with architects, antique people, and a whole lot of very skilled people."

"Chester County is the place for that," Ellen said.

"Pennsylvania stone houses are cold in the winter and hot in the summer," Dwyer said, shaking his head. "I love my aluminum siding and a roof that doesn't leak."

"Don't tell people that," Blasingame said. "If they ever realize it's all a giant con, I'll have to find honest work."

Dwyer chuckled.

"I work in Philly," Ellen said to James. "Newspaper stuff. Mostly pushing paperwork around."

"Oh, no," James said. He smiled, almost shyly. "You don't. You're with the Inquirer, you've gotten a couple of award nominations." His mouth closed suddenly, almost quickly enough to make a sound.

"You've checked?" She still smiled but her eyes narrowed.

"Someone here mentioned you as another one of Charles' students," James said quickly. "I have a folder of online news sites and on one they had a piece written by Ellen Parker. I just wondered if it was you and they had a picture of you at a journalist class talking to some students. It wasn't a very good picture but I thought it was you. I didn't mean to pry."

"I know the picture – for me, it was good. I don't take good pictures. It's not prying." She grimaced. "I'm only a little in the public eye but I've already had a few unusual people contacting me."

"Well, I'm only a little unusual," James said. "I think. I could be wrong. It could be a lot." He grinned and Ellen's smile returned.

"No harm. Can I sell you a subscription?"

"Ah, sorry. All my news budget is taken this year already by the Post and The Guardian. Call me next year."

"What do you think of our web site?"

"I really like the layout," James said, hitching himself forward. "The tabs are great, especially for getting to local news. But I think books ought to get more coverage. Washington's got the Post and New York has the Times and both do a great job about books and reviews. Philly should have the same thing." He grinned. "I'm a huge eBook fan, so I'm always looking for reviews, recommendations, that kind of thing."

"I think I agree," Ellen said. "You said you thought you were seeing some of the effects of shooting in your life, the discipline?"

"I think so, yes. My job..." He shook his head. "It sucks, like a lot of them do. Anyway, there have been days when I was close to really blowing up. Frustration, mostly. But I think I'm seeing less of that kind of reaction." James paused. "Not, not less of a reaction. Things still suck. But the level of my reaction is less. I think I'm managing myself better." He paused again, the tip of his tongue emerging between his pressed lips as he thought. "Yes, that's it. The job is the job, but I'm handling it better."

"And that's from the shooting?" Ellen asked.

"From the training." He glanced at Dwyer out of the corner of his eye and then looked back at Ellen, smiling. "Mr. Dwyer is a cruel taskmaster and he can be brutal."

Ellen laughed.

"He's a brute," she agreed. Dwyer shook his head.

"Oh, all right, if you two are going to gang up on me, I'm going to pick up my toys and go home." Dwyer stood and lifted his mug towards the others in a mock toast. "Stay safe," he said. "It reflects badly on me if you shoot your own toes off."

"But it's all right," Ellen asked, raising her eyebrows, "if we shoot off those of someone else?"

"Ms. Parker…" Dwyer dramatically sighed, smiled, shook his head, and walked away, waving as he stepped into the hallway.

"I haven't taken lessons before," James said. "He seems like a very good instructor. He catches a lot."

"He's very good," Ellen says. "I get frustrated, sometimes, and he is so patient, I find myself copying him. Very good teacher."

"You know, I think you're right. He's helped me a lot, even when I'm having trouble grasping something. I've never seen him get frustrated with me, even a little bit. And that thing you said about copying him, yes, I think I do that, too. I came here wanting to learn how to shoot well and I think Charles is teaching me some other things as well."

"He's a pretty good man," Blasingame said. "Solid, someone to depend on. Doesn't rattle easily. An anchor."

"You're right," James said. He stood. "Well, I've got to get some things for dinner. You all take care."

Ellen nodded and Blasingame made a small wave with his hand and they watched James leave.

"Sounds like," Blasingame said, working on finishing his soda, "he's got a crappy job."

"Sounds like."

Chapter 22: Conversations

James Hardy looked at his supervisor and kept his face totally still as he wondered what a high velocity bullet would do to the man's skull. As the supervisor spoke, James had little difficulty imagining what would happen for there were places on the internet where you could see gunshot wounds. He had found those sites almost by accident.

Almost.

And now, often after he came home from work, he thought about what it would be like to find his supervisor and the other people running the place dead, scattered in their offices and hallways, maybe even in the parking lot as they tried to flee. Oddly, he found the imagined images of death, the pools of blood, the bits of bodies, sometimes he found it relaxing.

The images had never come to him while he was at work. There was a boundary of where his mind was when at work and when at home, but that boundary dissolved as he met with his supervisor and listened to the man talk bullshit. It was the same as always; more was expected, greater numbers of cases moved along, all because of the unspoken need to get the director, maybe the CFO, a bonus.

Part of him wanted the supervisor just to say it, trim it down to the miserable core. But, no, no solid turds were provided, it was all made up of diarrhea. Even when they handed out shit, they emphasized volume, as if more was some indication of quality. The thought brought a slight smile to his face in spite of his tight control of his anger.

"Did I say something funny, James?"

"No, sir," James said almost casually. A 5.56-millimeter round would cause his lower jaw to disintegrate… "I was just thinking I was glad I had begun a review of my team's procedures, looking to see if we could work a little smarter, a little outside the box. What you said, what was it?, three weeks ago stuck with me. I think we're going to hit the ground running on this."

The supervisor's eyebrows rose like a pair of caterpillars working together like a drill team. He said nothing for several heartbeats and James sat in his chair calmly while he worked to pull his mind away from images that he didn't really want to see in real life.

Not today.

"Well, good, James, glad to hear that." He did not look like he was glad. The supervisor looked down at his desk, at the single-page outline of what he wanted to say, and realized James had moved his talk to the last item. "Good, good. Always happy to hear when one of my line supervisors takes our messages to heart." He smiled but it was tentative and did nothing to remove the narrowness of his eyes and the touch of fear it revealed. The narrowness increased as James smiled broadly.

"I'm glad to hear that, sir," James say as he stored the images away. "Sometimes it's a challenge, trying to translate theory into practice," he added, quoting a line from an "all hands" email, "but I think I have a handle on the outcome you and the other stakeholders want."

"Good, that's what we want. And remember, your team are also stakeholders, so this is something you want as well."

Sure, I remember you asking us what the hell we wanted, James thought, but he just nodded, though his grin was savage.

Later, James went to his team members and explained what they were going to do.

"They want to increase work units." He paused after the first sentence of his explanation as each member handled the bad news in their own way. The word "fuck" was quite popular, usually said as part of a resigned sigh. "When you do your daily workload report, what I want you to do is break down activities into components." Another pause with a puzzled expression the most common response. "'Telephonic communication' goes into work unit report with a designation as to whether it was less than five minutes, five to ten minutes, ten to twenty, and so on, right?" Silent nod. "Usually, if you make a call, you would record '78' for the call, and then, say, point three if it was ten to twenty minutes long. What I want you to do is break that workload entry in two. Put down two '78s', one for point one, the other for point two. They total the same but you increase your reported work units. Got it?" Eyes widened, unless they had already figured out that trick. "Don't overdo it, don't do three-point ones off of one point three. Too much of a change and that will attract attention and you want to leave some space in case they up the work unit requirement again. And they will, sooner or later. Aim for an increase in your work units of an average of eight percent. They want five." Then another pause. Usually, they would just nod silently. Some smiled. James would smile back.

There was no work unit credit for a line supervisor teaching a team member how to game the system.

After work – a half hour after work – James left his desk, got into his car, drove down the hill from where he worked. He pulled into the parking lot of a conveniently located pizza place, looked around to make sure no one was watching him, and then he gripped his steering wheel so hard his knuckles showed. His face twisted as his lips pulled back revealing clenched teeth.

And the images in his head came like a dark spring's flood, sweeping everything away in front of it, trees and grown grass, leaving only glistening black and jagged rocks where nothing could grow.

When the images passed, he sat with his eyes closed and only slowly released his grip. James looked around as if discovering where he was, but it was a place he came and for the same reason. He licked his lips. Then he got out of his car and went into the pizzeria and said hello to the Jordanian people working there and had a large soda with lots of ice and a baked veggie with hot peppers. He took his time, watched the evening news and the sports reports, and left them a good tip.

They waved as he left – he seemed like a nice guy, worked up the hill, a little on the quiet side, and he really seemed to like the food.

Everything was normal.

"Did I catch you at a bad time?" The voice was metallic, just like in the past.

"No, not really," Ellen said. "I was just getting ready to go home." She held up her hand, attracting the attention of the FBI woman who was sitting next to Blasingame.

"Oh, working late?"

"A little. You know, deadlines, have to get stuff in."

"I know what you mean. A job can be pretty demanding."

"Yes, it can."

"Consider yourself fortunate. You do most of your work at your desk, right?"

"Pretty much. Sometimes get out. You?"

"Haven't seen my desk in days. But that's not why I called. I wanted to say 'thank you.'"

"You're thanking me?"

"A simple acknowledgment. You passed on what I told you and they recovered those bodies. I'm glad that got done."

"You are?"

"Of course. Closure and all that. For the families, I mean."

"And for you?"

"I don't think I can go there with you. Let's limit to saying that now they are paying attention."

"Attention to what? I mean, lots of people are pretty focused on you, you know."

"I didn't mean those people, your police friends."

"Who, then?"

"Well, no, I can't go there either."

"You're making it hard to understand you."

"I'm really not interested in your understanding, Ms. Parker. You are just a line of communication. Under these circumstances, that is all you are."

"What would be other circumstances? What's so special about these circumstances. ...Hello? Are you there?"

"I am. You cannot grasp the significance of these circumstances. Reporters, journalists, whatever you are called, you have no higher belief than the next story that will sell. Too cynical, too wrapped up in the moment, in the worldly moment. Spewing words out without understanding. No faith in anything. What do you believe in, Ms. Parker? Anything?"

"I... Shit."

Ellen looked up at the FBI Agent. "He hung up on me."

"Nice job holding onto him as long as you did," the Agent said. Her name was Zahra O'Brien. She was young and looked like her people might have built pyramids in the past. She took out her own phone and walked away, talking quickly. She held out her free hand and raised her thumb, but what she was indicating was not clear.

Ellen went back to work, trying to clear her head of the residue left by talking to the murderer. She glanced toward the side and saw Blasingame still sitting with his back to the wall where he could see her and the elevators and stairway door. He raised his eyebrows in a silent question. She shook her head negatively, signaling she didn't want to talk. There would be enough of that after the FBI studied the recording of the call and came to her with questions that she probably didn't know the answers for. Then she would have to brief Blasingame, who probably would not have any questions.

That was Robert. Define the problem and then resolve it, quickly and quietly. What was that old phrase from spy movies? Yes, "with extreme prejudice," if that's what it came to. Something that didn't apply if the problem was a flat tire. She smiled, imagining Blasingame coming to her aid if she'd had a flat.

He would probably appear out of nowhere and definitely would have no questions. He would study the situation and quietly find the spare and the tools. The lug nuts would come off quickly as he used some technique that he probably had learned from some secret Army truck battalion and then he would vanish. And all her tires would be, now, whitewalls. She would not know how he had done it.

Ellen smiled in the middle of editing a column; she would have to ask Robert if Army motor transport units were involved in covert ops somewhere. He would probably deflect the question and start talking about the change in seasons. She finished the column and looked up to see O'Brien coming back carrying two diet sodas from the snack room.

"Is that my reward?" Ellen asked as O'Brien put them on her desk.

"The Coke is yours," O'Brien said, smiling, "the Mountain Dew is mine because I know it is an offense against your religion."

"I've worked hard to educate you members of the FBI on proper diet sodas." She paused to open her drink. "My efforts have been for naught. So, what do your people think?" She took a sip.

"You didn't catch any phrasing that reminded you of someone?"

Ellen shook her head.

"No. I still don't think he's anyone I've ever met."

"'Your friends.' He might know you well enough to know you've been involved with law enforcement before."

"That's not private information. If he's checking up on stories I've written, then he knows I have police for friends."

"That might be it, or he might be using the term more casually. But, no, the thinking of our profilers is, he doesn't know you."

"Good." Ellen took another sip. "I'm glad to hear that. What led them in that direction?"

"He doesn't know enough about you to hurt you with what he knows. The profilers think he has a history of targeting women, we told you about that." Ellen nodded. "Even though he's going after boys now, they don't think he could avoid trying to hurt you. Say something someone close to you might know. Problems in your life, things about your family, that sort of thing. Pain for the sake of pain. He did take a shot at diminishing you. 'Just a line of communication.'"

"Can't resist the opportunity to keep his hand in."

O'Brien nodded silently and took another sip.

"Anything else you can share?"

"Power; that's what the business of closure is all about. He doesn't give a damn about the families. He likes the control. And recognition. We think he was upset that he wasn't getting enough credit for his killings."

"I caught that," Ellen nodded.

"He did throw in something new. The references to faith. Agent Deevers said she thinks that is at the base for his change in victims. She's talking it over with the Quantico team and they are going to be spending time listening to him, but she believes he made a major slip."

"Well, she was a profiler herself."

"A good one, everyone says."

"Anything different I should be doing?"

"No. Stay alert. Everything we've been saying." O'Brien paused, thinking. She looked up. "Listen to your briefing. Remember, if he feels the walls closing in, we think he'll respond. In New Jersey, he relocated. Maybe he'll do that again if he thinks we are close. On the other hand, maybe he has no place else to run to. He might lash out at whoever he can reach. You are a public figure so we have to believe you are on that list."

"Thanks for the reminder." Ellen grinned. "I've always had a need to be the center of attention."

Chapter 23: Weaving threads

"Did you hear Alice North retired?" Terrence – Something said.

James looked up from his computer monitor and blinked.

"I didn't know her first name was Alice." After using the directory, that wasn't true but it was the kind of thing someone who knew him might expect him to say.

"I'm serious," Terrence said as he leaned into James' office. He looked out into the hallway and then came back. He kept his voice low. "They made her go through a bunch of interviews for that division slot and then gave it to some weevil with about a quarter of the time with the company."

"That's too bad, she seemed to be pretty good."

"She really was." Terrence looked back for a second. "She could have retired years ago. One of the people I know in fiscal says she doubled her savings purchases of company stock when it was first offered, something like a zillion years ago."

"Hell, that started ten years before I was hired. She probably owns the place by now."

"Don't know why anyone would want to, but, yeah, she's probably not feeling any pain." He looked down the hall again and then back at James. "Look, don't tell anyone I told you about her."

"Lips sealed, partner. Fuck the weevils."

"Peace, *esse,*" Terrence held out his fist and James lightly punched it with his own and the Black man walked away.

Terrence Ridgway. The man's last name suddenly appeared.

James looked at his monitor without seeing it. Did Mrs. North's retirement have anything to do with the files he sent her? He thought for a moment and shrugged. Probably not. She probably had thrown them out. It sounded like she'd had enough with being jerked around.

Well, good for her. And good for all the other people he had heard left. Better than going crazy. Or drinking yourself to death.

Or come to work with a shotgun and see how many in first tier management you could get before the cops broke in. There had been stories that a couple of people had threatened their supervisors and ended up being cut loose, no benefits, no medical, and escorted away by the local police. He shook his head.

Could he leave? Maybe they would offer early retirements to lower the work force, something they'd done in the past. But he didn't have enough years to take advantage of that even if it ever happened again.

Why did he stay? Part of it was his team, though he realized his efforts to serve as a buffer, to protect them, were less and less effective. Part of it was the job itself, something about making a contribution, though he couldn't really say he was doing much of that anymore.

Mostly, he didn't want to give them, whoever they were, the satisfaction. Not that anyone in "The Quad," top management's name for itself, knew he existed.

He didn't want to leave. He didn't want to just leave. James thought for a moment.

What he wanted was revenge.

The thought was startling in its clarity, like a beam of blue-white light stabbing through the darkness, almost like a stroke of lightning. It seemed to fill him with its energy.

With an effort, James made himself read the document on his display, fighting to direct his attention some place other than inside his own mind.

Not now, not now, not now.

Agent Brown waited as the assignments were passed out.

"All right," he said and every officer's eyes focused on him. "Xylazine is a drug that's supposed to be used on animals. Our perp uses it on the boys he takes. You all know that. We've been aware of it since the first autopsy had those odd results in its drug screen. Here's what we didn't know. Lights."

The lights in the conference room went out and a projector relayed his laptop's display, at first slightly out of focus, and then self-corrected. What it showed was a map extending from Lancaster County, the county west of where they all were sitting in Coatesville, east to the New Jersey shoreline.

"You know from our earlier briefings that xylazine is not a controlled substance and it supposedly is only available to veterinarians. We all put in a lot of hours checking on every animal clinic in the area, on everyone who worked in one of them, and we came up with nothing. No leads. But the folks in New Jersey who think our guy was killing women there took a look at our results, thought about it, and exhumed some of those women and then they dug them all up." He took a sip of stale coffee.

"Time and embalming, cremations, and so on affected their results. What they did with the xylazine positive results is they and our people compared them with our cases and dated them and mapped when and where the bodies were found. This led to this map. Red dots are dead bodies confirmed to having been exposed to xylazine. That's the first thing I'm going to show you." Brown stepped out of the way and red dots, one after the other, appeared in New Jersey, from the southern Pine Barrens up to just outside Atlantic City.

"I'll pause it there for a moment. What we're going to see next are the women whose death matched the others but they didn't find xylazine. They are in orange." A handful of orange dots appeared. "You saw the sequence, all in that general band through New Jersey, okay? Now these next dots are blue. Here they come, all over Philadelphia. These are overdose deaths and go back to the early '90s.' Yeah, this crap has been around for a while. This is actually important for a reason I'll get into in a moment. Now, it's about five months since the last New Jersey death..."

Red dots appeared in Chester County, one after the other.

"No more in New Jersey, except in connection with illicit drug use. It's used to cut addictive drugs of choice but long-term use can cause a lot of damage, as we noted before, and, since it is a depressant, pain killer, and muscle relaxant, people can OD with it. When that happens, it is often not recognized as the usual screens pick up on the drug, or drugs, that the victim thought they were paying for. The screens see heroin or meth fine, but don't pick up on powdered sugar or xylazine. While the official count is somewhere around fifty OD deaths from the stuff here in the States, because of the lack of detection we think the real count is higher. But all that is mostly an issue for our DEA friends. Lights."

"What does all this mean? Well, it's on the street, just like everything else, and that's the point I mentioned earlier. Our focusing on veterinarian clinics was a good idea and one we had to check out but, because of that street use, we need to go to the street with our DEA friends and see what we can find. Consider that a lead. Who is handling xylazine and how are they getting their hands on it? Here's the thing – our perp is using pure xylazine, nothing else, no cutting of it. Not homegrown. When we went to those clinics, we were interested in who might be a recent arrival and had access to that drug, right? We found no one. Now our question is a little different. Who working at those clinics might be selling it to the street? This is something we've seen before with PCP and a host of other drugs." There were nods around the room.

"While our DEA buddies and their local drug investigators go onto that street I keep talking about, we're going back to the clinics with our slightly different question. We want to know about inventories and how they control them. We are looking for stuff leaving the clinic that isn't accounted for. None of the people we talked to in our earlier round with those clinics matched our profile or even came close, right, but now we want to know who has set themselves up with another revenue stream."

"Here's our problem. Pennsylvania took a shot at setting up a mandated drug reporting system back six, seven years ago. The state veterinary association shot down four of the five proposed bills; all four would have required reporting of drug and considered the vets to be a prescriber, someone whose sale and handling of the drug would be monitored. The fifth bill specifically omitted vets. There are no records reported to the state."

"We have to look at each clinic and see what records they've chosen to keep and see if it helps us find missing xylazine. I suspect we're going to have better results looking for clinic members who are selling drugs to drug people; that's a scenario we've had a fair amount of experience with. Maybe one of those buyers is our perpetrator. Lights."

The lights came on and the projector went dark.

"We've tried to make sure you are not going to clinics you've been to before, just to keep those places a little off-balance." He paused, frowning for a moment. "The thing I want to stress is, this is a lead, a new avenue for us to explore. I think we all know the clock is ticking before our ass-wipe takes another boy. You don't need any kind of motivating speech from me, right? This is what we all are in business for. Let's get it done."

Brown stepped away from the table serving as his podium and team leaders stood, drawing their small groups together. He looked at Karen Deevers at the back of the room and waited while she talked with a team leader, a plain clothes detective from one of the larger towns. Brown had worried, despite his earlier work with Deevers, that she would mostly just be a monitor of his work, passing word up the chain of command. She might be doing that – he could live with it if she was – but she also proved to be highly valuable to the task force. Her experience with the Behavioral Science unit had led her to suggest working with New Jersey in building the time-lapse occurrence of xylazine cases. If they needed something to beat authorities over the head that the killer in Pennsylvania was the same one in New Jersey, they had it. Too many people in authority seemed to need to pretend that if it wasn't happening now, it was over, gone, nothing to be concerned with.

There had been talk of disbanding the New Jersey task force hunting for their serial killer. After all, the murders had stopped. Maybe he was dead, maybe in prison. Out of circulation somehow, maybe even magically. And there was no proof that he was next door in Pennsylvania – the victims were different, after all.

The talk was silenced; he may have left the state but he knew New Jersey and nothing said he would not return there. Wishful thinking didn't stop serial killers.

Politics. Brown shook his head. You never escaped it if you worked in law enforcement. Never, ever, ever, a chant from his childhood surfaced. He smiled just as Deevers looked at him and her answering smile was tentative, not understanding his.

Brown motioned for her to stay where she was and walked across the room to her. The team leaders had just about finished specific assignments and a trickle of officers gathered their computers and note pads and made their way to the door.

"Are you having a good time?" Deevers asked. Her smile was still tentative.

"Thinking about politics," Brown replied. "It took me to my childhood."

"Easy connection." Her smile became firmer.

"We now have third links between the killings in New Jersey and here. Same methodology, the thing that first alerted everyone to the idea we had a common murderer."

"Method of death, burial, use of drug," she nodded.

"The time line suggests a link. Starts and stops in New Jersey, a pause, and then a resumption, but in Pennsylvania."

"Women in New Jersey, boys here. That's not terribly common, changing victims."

"I agree with your analysis of his latest call to Parker. Some higher purpose explains the change in victims. Call it the third link." He nodded. "My question is, did that new purpose cause him to leave New Jersey or did he run from their pursuit and found it once he got here?"

It was her turn to nod.

"My best call is, he found it here."

"I have an idea why you think that but tell me."

"I think he was chased out of New Jersey," Deevers said. She returned a wave to a pair of uniformed officers leaving. "When I talked to Dave Hanks, he was certain their monitoring of his dump sites came within a hair of catching him on one of his visits."

"I read his report. They really did seem to come close."

"You should hear him on the phone about it. One of the locals was seen, he thinks. Messed up their placement."

"I get why he left that out of the report; he still has to work with them."

"And they are in the center of ground zero for his dumping, so it's critical."

"Politics."

"Politics." She made a small shrug. "The incident fits the time line for when the killings stopped."

"He goes to a place where he dumped at least two, that bridge, with a plan to play with himself and sees a cop back in the trees."

"A cop car, gray and orange, middle of the night."

"So much for camouflage."

"They think another car coming around the curve to the bridge highlighted it. He starts up, does a quick turn, and takes off. The local needs to get out of the woods, get up and over the bridge, and, when he comes down the other side, the suspect car is merged, they think, into the cross-traffic. Apparently, the local didn't know the car had pulled up to the bridge shoulder and parked. The bridge blocked the line of sight."

Brown said nothing for a moment.

"I didn't realize they had been that close."

"If it was the bad guy and not someone night fishing, but the timeline is right."

"What did he find in Pennsylvania to give him a calling to focus on boys?"

"Had to be something major, not just opportunity. He probably wanted to pick up on women again, maybe expand his target attributes if he had to, but he encountered something while he was planning and scouting that changed target values."

"Early on, then, before he started up with women again." Brown pursed his lips. "What would he see while touring the county, picking future grave sites? Something not found in New Jersey, maybe?"

"Farms, small towns, all that kind of thing is basically similar with Chester County."

"What would he do, what would he encounter here that would be different?"

"As a part of scouting and planning? Hard to say." Deevers thought for a moment. "And his cover. He's going to need employment and a way of camouflaging himself."

"Look like everyone else," Brown said. "He quits his job in New Jersey and has to find a new one here."

"Might contribute to the pause in murders. Or the pause might simply be due to relocating, packing and moving. Maybe his company transferred him. Or maybe, yes, he was dealing drugs and the pause was about having to re-establish his business."

"It might. Getting back to building his cover, trying to be just another local guy. To get next to the women, he appeared ordinary. He wasn't living in the woods like the Unabomber, or walking around unbathed with filthy clothes and long hair. Boys would probably take off if he looked freakish."

"Middle class, cop, someone they might see as ordinary, something like that."

"Maybe your friendly neighborhood drug dealer."

"Explains his connection to xylazine. Buys it from the clinic people, uses it on his targets, maybe moves other drugs."

"In Chester County? Lots of eyes. If he's moving weight in any kind of major way, he'll be dealing with a man named Books."

"I remember the briefing. Low profile, as close to a boss as there is in the county."

"Doesn't dabble in small stuff." She frowned, remembering. "Took over the meth trade a few years ago from the old boss, named Tallman. Has a series of garages, including several that are a part of a legitimate chain. Supposedly, he personally took out Tallman but the locals aren't sure."

"The briefing said he runs the meth trade."

"We think he moved the manufacturing out of the county, maybe down into Maryland. Maybe not. He has a link to Philadelphia's Douglas."

"The guy whose daughter was kidnapped?"

"Step-daughter, but yes."

"I was on the task force working with DEA trying to bring him down." Brown shook his head. "We almost had him."

"I remember."

"Tallman… Wasn't he the guy who sent those people after the kid that Sergeant Chernov was guarding and you intercepted them?"

"Yes," Deevers said. "She wasn't a sergeant then, at least not with New Joyton."

"I'd forgotten the background to that shootout. You did a very good job."

"Thanks, but there was a lot more to it than that. Those friends of Ellen Parker's settled everything."

"It's coming back. That Parker seems to have gotten into a number of situations."

"I agree."

"She and her boyfriend rescued Douglas' step-daughter."

"I'm not sure Blasingame is her boyfriend."

"Whatever. And now she's been contacted by our perp." He smiled and shook his head. "Do Chester County criminals wait until she's free before committing illegal acts?"

"I don't think so but I could ask her."

"No, please don't. I don't think I want to know."

"Well, this time there's only one bad guy and he came to her."

"Only one."

James Hardy looked around the small snack bar as he sat down but he was alone. He concentrated on sliding his tackle box containing his pistol, ammunition, and cleaning gear under the table, carefully placing it so no one would accidentally trip over it. Then he took off his ballcap and his yellow-tinted shooting glasses; the cap went directly onto the table in front of him and the glasses, folded, went onto the soft cap. The precision of his slow, careful movements reflected his struggle to maintain control.

He rose from the table and went to the soft drink dispenser. He punched a button without paying attention to what it would deliver, picked up the can, and then returned to his seat. James did not open the can but stared at it as if it was something important, something he had to figure out.

James looked around suddenly, like someone breaking a trance. It had been an awful day at work – the description was one he reserved for the worst days – and he had come directly to the firing range after work. But he did not want to shoot at targets.

Not at targets.

"James, how's it going?" Charles Dwyer's deep, warm voice seemed to fill the room as the instructor walked in. He headed for the always-on coffee urn, his state police mug already poised to receive whatever was in it. James had to swallow before he trusted himself to speak.

"Not bad, Charles," he lied. "How're things with you?"

"Same. Just wrapped up a class. Where did they hide the creamer?" He answered his own question, pulling the container down from a shelf and shaking some powder into his mug. Then he added coffee. He looked at James as he stirred and the younger man motioned to a chair at his table. Dwyer nodded as he walked over and sat down.

"You getting in some more practice?"

"Thought I would. But, you know, long day at work, more tired than I realized, so figured I'd contribute to the fund, have something to drink, and then go home."

"That is not something to drink, James. That color is not found in nature."

James looked at the can and realized it was a flavor that he found too sweet. He pried back the tab any way.

"Well," he said, "it's probably good for my heart." He raised the can in a toast and Dwyer returned the gesture. James took a sip and almost shivered in response to the taste.

"Don't joke about your heart," Dwyer said. "My doctor has given me several very severe lectures about mine. Got me on pills, a diet, a fitness course, all that." He shook his head. "My wife loves it, gets to bully me every day."

"Is it serious?"

"No, not really. Preventative. Something that runs in my family. Have to pay attention to it. Probably too much fatty food back when I was a statie. The job kicking you around?"

"Oh, yeah, they're trying to turn us all into elephants or something."

"Elephants?"

"It's just how the administration thinks. Trying to find ways to make us perform and make us think it's our idea." He took a drink without thinking and winced at the taste. "That crap is awful." He put the can down with more emphasis than he intended.

"Good decision on your part," Dwyer said, leaning back in his chair. "Feel like your head is messed up, sometimes throwing rounds down range is not a good idea. Sometimes it is a great way to relax because it gets your head out of all that and focused on something pretty demanding. One of the other instructors said it's a Zen thing. But you have to know yourself. The range is not where you want to be distracted."

James nodded and took a deep breath.

"Yep, I agree. I appreciate the compliment."

"Happy to give it." Dwyer took a sip. "Besides, I think we may be getting some rain in a little bit."

"I hadn't heard."

They moved from the weather to other topics and James didn't hide his reaction to his next sip and they made jokes about Mountain Dew and they laughed, Dwyer deeply, James tentatively, and they had a normal conversation, something James seemed to experience only at the range and mostly with Charles Dwyer.

As Dwyer got up to leave, Ellen Parker and Robert Blasingame came in. Ellen had a rolled-up tube of targets and Dwyer spread them on the table to study and they talked about shooting. James asked a couple of questions and Ellen answered as if she had no hidden agenda and wasn't trying to get him to agree to something that would make life more miserable for the people on his team. Dwyer left and James' eyes followed him from the room.

"It has been," Ellen said, "a long day." She took a sip on her can of diet soda and James noticed it was not what he was drinking.

"At least you avoided drinking the green stuff from hell," he said and held up his can.

"'Way too sweet for me," she said. "And I don't know what that stuff is supposed to taste like."

"Bought it by accident," James said, quickly, suddenly thinking he had sounded like a clown.

"'Green stuff from hell,'" Ellen repeated. "I'm going to remember that."

James smiled; he wasn't a clown. Maybe not.

"Come here from work?" Blasingame asked.

James nodded. He looked at Ellen's targets again, not wanting to talk about his job.

"Pretty good shooting," he said.

"The good one is Robert's," Ellen said. She pushed it aside. "Like I told Charles, these are my weak hand efforts."

"Oh, yeah, but, still, these aren't bad. Not that I know that much." He looked at Blasingame, wondering if he had said the wrong thing but the man just nodded as if in agreement.

"Thanks," Ellen said. She held one, studying it. "I get to trying too hard and then I shoot worse, all over the map." She looked up and grinned. "I probably shouldn't go to the range after work."

"Charles and I were talking about just that. He said it can help you relax but if your head is messed up, if you're distracted, it's not a good idea."

"I think he's right." She looked at Blasingame. "It doesn't seem to affect your shooting."

"The trick," Blasingame said slowly and took a sip of his coffee, "is to do nothing at work. Then you come to the range fully refreshed."

James smiled but said nothing, not sure of how to respond.

"Robert cheats," Ellen said, the grin still with her. "He uses magic and doesn't bother to aim."

"I do keep my eyes closed – all that shooting is too scary to watch."

"I think Mr. Dwyer said you were good with a handgun," James said. "Do you practice a lot?"

"I have to," Blasingame said, "because I'd be better off throwing it at the target." He smiled. "I can get by with a pistol but I'm more comfortable with a rifle."

"Really?" Ellen asked.

"Really. I'm only fair with a rifle, though. I've seen some real pros with long guns and I am nowhere near as good as they are."

"Snipers, you mean," Ellen said. "Like SEALs and Rangers."

"Like that," Blasingame nodded. "But I am a bit better with a rifle than a pistol."

"You know SEALs?" James asked, his eyebrows climbing. "Were you one?"

"No, I wasn't."

"Robert was a translator overseas. He supported military personnel."

"That was me, hiding under a desk, the guy they called on when they wanted to talk to someone." He smiled. "It wasn't just they were good shots. They were. The key, though, was when they could do it."

"When was that?"

"Whenever it was needed. Lots of people are great on a range. Those people could do it with other peoples' bullets kicking sand in their faces." He shook his head. "Incredible."

"I guess so," James said. "Makes me wonder what I would do if I ever had to do it for real."

"Hope you don't have to find out," Blasingame said. "But don't under-rate all the practice. Once you decide that you have to do it for real, the training helps. A lot."

"'Once you decide…'" James nodded. "That's a big decision."

"A very big one," Blasingame said, but he was looking at Ellen. "One of the biggest there is."

"How do you do it?" James frowned. "I mean, how do you decide? I mean, until you're really faced with a situation, how do you know what to do?"

"Good question." Blasingame shrugged. "If you can, you study yourself. What are your rules, your right and wrong? You can't always identify specific situations but you can figure out what your values are. Some people would rather die than harm another person. If that's where you are, and you're sure of that, then all this shooting we're doing is just for sport. But if you can identify reasons why you would take another life, to protect yourself, to protect others, whatever, then you've got a lot more thinking to do."

"You can't always anticipate," Ellen said, her voice low. "What you think you know about yourself might get turned upside down when you are actually in the situation. You might discover what your values really are." There was something in her brown and gold eyes, something that flashed like a hard reflection.

"I read your story," James said. "After that first time we met. You were kind of famous. That killer... You could have gotten away but you saved the county deputy and the woodworker's lives."

Ellen said nothing but nodded slowly.

"I really did want to run away," she said. She smiled slightly. "I had the shoes for it. I think I hoped he would give up when he saw the shotgun but I knew he wouldn't. He liked killing, he liked hurting people. I think he saw how afraid I was and took that to mean I wouldn't shoot."

"But you did."

"It was for the deputy, his name was Morgan, and the cabinetmaker, his name was Klemmer. Maybe mostly for Klemmer. I just couldn't run away. I didn't realize that until I was in it. I don't think I had ever thought about things like that before, not about me, I mean." She paused, thinking. "I had a cousin. She was killed when were just girls. Stray bullet from a gang fight. I knew about violence but I never thought of myself in it, having to make decisions about it. I think maybe I didn't want to think about it. Then one day I had to." Ellen nodded. "Robert is right. Think about it. Try to get your mind around it beforehand."

"I will," James said. "You sound like someone whose judgment could be trusted."

"Oh, no, not me," Ellen said, and the grin came back. James noticed her eyes softened. "I'm just a southern Oh-hi-a farmgirl," she said, her voice now graced by a gentle accent. "I can milk a cow, drive a combine, but when it comes to philosophizing and fine judgment, I am totally at sea." She cocked her head to one side. "Besides, didn't anyone ever tell you not to trust a member of the news media?"

"Well," James said slowly, "it is all fake news…"

"There you go," Ellen agreed, nodding, the grin still present.

"Seriously," James said. "Thank you, both of you. I appreciate hearing your thinking."

"You're welcome," she said, her grin gone. Blasingame nodded, his expression serious.

"Working with Charles, I really like that," James said. "I work for idiots but he makes sense. It's like he's figured out life and has nothing left to prove to anyone." He shook his head. "Not even to himself."

"He had a tough job," Ellen said. "Saw some bad things. But he told me once he found a balance point."

"Like I said, he's figured it out. The people I work with, it's like they are so crazy they think they're normal. Screwing people over seems to be everything they value. Not just customers but the people who do the job for them. And pretend it's all fine, all normal."

"Sounds bad," Blasingame said.

"It's like working in a pressure cooker, 'cause you have to pretend you're onboard with them, even the really stupid stuff that eventually will cost more. Even the stuff that's just mean for the sake of humiliating people." His lips tightened for a moment. "It's like they want people to blow up or quit or punch someone out. It's really, really stupid."

"How are you handling it?" Blasingame asked.

James laughed, a short bark with no humor in it.

"End of some days, I can't see any reason to come back the next day, you know? I was hanging on, trying to protect my work team. They're good people, all of them, scared shitless, and it helped me to know I was taking care of them, even if only a little bit. But the administration was making it clearer and clearer there was nothing I could do, not really. If they wanted to screw my people, they could. Life at home, well, it went away. Nothing left. It really helped to come here, make myself work at something I'd never tried before. Get me out of my rut, so to speak. Charles, like you said, he's got this balance point and just being around him helps me get things in balance for myself."

"Let a little steam off, too?"

"Oh, yeah, that, too." He smiled. "Probably freak out my supervisor if he ever heard that I was taking shooting lessons."

"Any chance you can change jobs?" Ellen quickly added, "That place you work sounds like a real snake pit."

"I'd love to, but the whole health field is kind of imploded, at least around here. Recession thing. But, yeah, you're right. When things open up a little, I'm going on down the road." James smiled again. "Believe me, I read your paper's 'Help Wanted' section every day."

"But no leads yet?"

"No, no, you all do have openings, but there are so few and so many applicants that moving over is really hard."

Ellen looked at James for a moment and then took her wallet from her small purse. She took out her card and pushed it across the table to him.

"That's my email address at work," she said. "If you'd like, send me a copy of your resume and your current position description and I will see if I can find something for you."

James looked at the young woman as if he was seeing her for the first time. His lips moved apart as if he was going to speak and then they closed.

"Really? You'd try to help?"

"Really. I know a few people and it probably won't result in anything. But it won't hurt anything."

"Wow. I don't know what to say."

"Just send me your stuff. Maybe what you'd prefer to be doing."

"Anything."

"I kind of thought that, but you know your field. Might as well put together a dream sheet, okay?"

"Sure, yes, okay." He looked at Ellen's card as if it was made of something very fragile but had the secret to the universe inscribed on it. "Right away."

"Good. Us gun nuts have to stick together." She looked at her watch. "We've got to go. Running late." She looked up. "I'm serious, James. If I find any leads, I'll pass them to you."

James stood up and held out his hand. Slightly surprised, Ellen stood and gripped it. He shook hands as if sealing an important agreement and she thought he might be. He shook Blasingame's hand as well.

James watched the two leave and stood until they were gone. He sat down and rubbed his face with both hands.

He had lied to Ellen Parker. He had not looked for other jobs in his field or any other. He did not know why he had not; it was as if he had been infected by some kind of paralysis keeping him from trying to escape. Decisions. Now he had to decide if he would send her the papers she wanted. Already his stomach tightened. If he didn't, he would be ashamed every time they ran into one another.

He could always quit coming to the range…

No, he couldn't sever what felt like a lifeline. He would send her what she wanted. Do it tonight, as soon as he got home, get it done and out of the way. Maybe she wouldn't find anything, maybe she would forget, maybe she was just being polite and had no intention of helping him. And if she gave him a lead, he could always say it wasn't right for him or he failed the interview or something.

What was wrong with him? It was like the job was inside him, controlling him. She offered him a chance and all he could think about was how he could get away from it. How crippled had they made him?

He pushed himself back from the table and reached down for his gear. Decisions.

As the two walked back to Ellen's car, she shook her head.

"Am I reading too much into what Hardy said? He seemed, I don't what word I'm looking for…"

"Troubled, for a start." Blasingame was in overwatch mode, his eyes sweeping the parking lot. "He seemed to me to be someone who's been kicked half to death and doesn't have much strength left to dodge the next one."

"That was my impression. I've heard of places like that. Treating their employees like abused dogs." She shook her head as she paused at the back of her car. "Assholes."

"If what he said is how things are, then he's right. His supervisor would drop a log if he knew James was taking shooting lessons." Blasingame smiled slightly. "Whoever that person is, they probably know what happens when a dog is abused enough."

"I am not sure," the woman said, her voice as taut as a pulled bow string, "why you want to talk to us." Her name was Patricia Trace and her anger had her lips tight.

Her husband, Paul, sitting beside her, lightly laid his hand on hers and she tightly squeezed it. A beam of morning light lay across their couch and made their hands glow.

"The police," Paul said to her, "have to be thorough." He looked at Deevers and Chernov. While his wife looked angry enough to throw both women through a window without bothering to open it, he looked exhausted, his face lined, but there was a thin line of anger behind his words. "You said you needed to talk to us about what's happened at Barnabas." Both women noticed he didn't use the word "Saint." He cleared his throat, perhaps to give his wife a little time. "We left the school and church before all the deaths happened."

"As you said," Deevers said, her elbows on her knees, her hands together as if begging, "we have to be thorough. One of the boys, Philip Lang, was in the same class as your son, and we're just trying to see if…"

"Now you show up," the woman said. "We couldn't get anyone interested before, but now, more than a year later…"

"Peg," her husband said. It sounded a little like a plea. He turned back to the two women. "Look, we had good reasons for leaving that place. I can only guess what Philip's parents are going through, but we've had enough of Barnabas."

"What was the problem there?"

"It had nothing to do with the killings," he said, making a small wave with his hand.

"It has nothing to do with them," his wife said. Her voice rose, the anger taking it louder. "It's still going on. Little Paulie is still…"

They saw him lightly squeeze her hand. Her lips tightened but she stopped. He didn't release her hand until she nodded.

"You're right," she said, her voice quieter.

"No one at Barnabas said anything to you," Paul said. It wasn't a question. "Of course not." He said nothing for several seconds and Deevers let the silence stretch. "All right, all right," he said as if conceding to an argument no one else could hear.

"Paulie, our boy, was molested by one of the priests at Barnabas. Bastard's name was Hemley." He looked back and forth at the two women. "Our doctor confirmed it and we reported it." He took a breath. "Paulie had nightmares, afraid of the dark, all of it. I was laid off, insurance cancelled, lawyer from the church said they'd make an offer, a settlement, cover his therapy. I wanted to see that fucking priest hang…" His lips tightened and his hands clenched and this time it was his wife's hand on his. Paul closed his eyes for a second, nodded, and continued.

"We took the deal. Had to wait three months to see a specialist, three damned months of nightmares every night, him losing weight so he looked like one of those kids from a concentration camp, three months because she had a waiting list of other kids like Paulie." He shook his head. "Not her fault. Once she got to Paulie, she saw him every day, did that eye movement therapy thing, she was wonderful. We got Paulie back. He's in school and everything. But," and he said his words like strokes of a hammer, "I will not allow anyone to take him back to that shit. No damned one."

"I understand you, Mr. Trace, and we do not want to bother your child. We're trying to learn more about Philip Lang. We're not involved with any of the investigations into church misconduct."

"'Misconduct...'" the woman said and shook her head.

"I'll be right back," Paul said as he stood up and left the room. Chernov glanced at Deevers and wondered what was happening; the FBI Agent sat calmly, as if people she interviewed walked out of the room routinely. Patricia said nothing and leaned back into her couch and crossed her arms, her eyes looking down but her mouth a tight line. It was several minutes before Paul returned with a beige file folder. He opened it as he sat down next to his wife.

"Class photo," he said, taking out a large glossy photograph. He handed it to Deevers. "That's Paulie, second row, right there on the right-hand side. The Lang boy, yes, you're right, he's directly behind Paulie. The kid with the goofy smile. They were friends. Hell, Paulie was friends with everyone. But pretty close to Phil. They did some projects together, we carpooled with the Langs a couple of times, school plays, that kind of thing." He fell silent as Deevers and Chernov studied all the small faces.

"Here's the deal," Paul finally said. He looked at his wife and she nodded assent to his unspoken question but her lips remained tightly pressed together. He looked back at Deevers. "You can talk to Paulie. You can ask him about his friend. He already knows Philip is dead. In spite of everything he's been through, he went to the funeral." His lips folded tightly and tears filled his eyes. "My boy, he's got the heart a lion." He said nothing else for a moment as he took out a handkerchief and wiped his eyes. He made a small smile. "And that therapist is worth her weight in gold."

"Mr. Trace," Deevers said slowly, "we appreciate..."

Paul cut her off with a raised hand. He shook his head.

"If it helps, we'll do what we can," he said. "Enough kids in that damned school have been hurt." He stood and left the room.

It seemed he was gone longer than the first time, though her watch told Chernov it wasn't. She wondered what Paul could say to his son. As the two came into the room, Chernov followed Deever's lead and stood. She noticed that the father and son were holding hands, something she guessed the boy had grown out of years before.

"These are the police officers I told you about," Paul said, motioning with his free hand towards Deevers and Chernov. Deevers stepped forward and held out her hand to the boy.

"Paulie," she said as the boy took her hand tentatively, "I'm Special Agent Karen Deevers." She shook the boy's hand as if it was a natural gesture. "And this," she nodded at Chernov, "is Sergeant Elizabeth Chernov of the New Joyton Police Department." Chernov held out her hand and the boy took it. His grip was tentative, as if he didn't know what to do about a woman in a dark blue uniform with a large gun on her hip.

Well, most men didn't, she thought.

Everyone sat down. Deevers did not let the silence grow.

"Paulie," she said, "we're investigating..."

"Phil," Paulie said, interrupting. "You're trying to find who killed Phil."

"That's right," Deevers said. "We're talking to anyone who might know any of the boys who have died." She paused as if waiting to see what reaction Paulie had and then continued. "Because you changed schools, none of our investigators talked to you, is that right?"

"Yes, no one's talked to me. No police talked to me." He looked up at his father and then back at Deevers. "Just Bonnie, but she's not a police officer."

"Bonnie is his therapist," Paul said.

"Did Phil ever tell you there was someone he was afraid of?"

"No. Phil liked everyone. Everyone liked Phil."

"Did you and Phil know any of the other boys who died?"

"Not really. Well, sort of. I mean, some of them went to Barnabas. I was gone from there before it happened, but I didn't know the guys from Barnabas."

"Did Phil know any of the other boys?"

"Oh, sure, he knew a couple. They played computer games with each other. I don't know if he knew all of them. He played games with me."

"When was the last time you saw Phil?"

"At the play-offs."

"The play-offs?"

"I wasn't in them; I just went to watch." He looked at his mother. "I went to see if I had triggers. It was a test. Bonnie and Mom went with me. It was Saturday and really crowded. We watched the soccer teams playing. I like soccer and used to be on the Barnabas team. I'm on a team now, the Blue Ducks, we're junior league."

"You saw him there?"

"Yes. He was in Little League and they had a couple of games going on. I went to the rest room and he was getting popcorn, so I did, too. We goofed around a little before he had to go. He said he missed seeing my ugly face and I told him he was uglier."

"Was that the only contact you had with Phil?"

"What do you mean?"

"Did you see him at any other time?"

"No. Not really."

"Not really?"

"Well, online, sure, but not in real life, you know?"

"I understand. What did you do online together?"

"Games, mostly. We did a lot of GW2…"

"GW2?"

"Guild Wars 2?" Chernov asked.

"Right," he smiled at Chernov. "I was a ranger, Phil was a guardian. Do you play?"

"Did for several years," she said, smiling. "Level 80 elementalist. I played with a group of friends."

"That's the best way. He and I would do different games, some co-op, some free to play. But he played a lot more than I did." He glanced at his mother again. "I just play two nights a week. I think he was doing a lot more than that. He has a clan he plays with… That he played with. Some of them were at the games we were at."

"The soccer and baseball teams?" Chernov asked, getting a nod from Deevers.

"Yes. Some were on those teams, others just came to, you know, cheer for their teams. League playoff stuff."

"Do you know the boys in his clan, the ones that were at the games?"

"No. Well, I knew of some of them he mentioned but I never met them. They were at Barnabas. I already said that. He said a couple were from Barnabas, which is how he joined them. The others were from around here, some of them, anyway." He smiled. "You know, you get into a clan, there can be people in it from everywhere. But the other guys, the ones he knew, he knew some of them in real life, you know? And they knew other guys from around here, and they were kind of a mini-clan within his clan because sometimes there's adults or older kids and they tend to go with one another on a raid or something." He looked at his mother again and then back at Chernov. "Phil said they had done a raid during the games."

"What do you mean?"

Paulie shrugged and looked down.

"I don't know. Phil just said some of his guys were at the games and they did a raid while everyone was at the games."

"What kind of raid did they do?"

"He didn't say."

"Clan stuff is sometimes secret," Chernov said.

"That's right," Paulie said, nodding.

"You guys were best friends." Not a question. Paulie nodded silently. "I tell my best friends things I might not tell anyone else." She paused. "What did your best friend tell you that was secret?"

Paulie shook his head negatively.

"Paulie," Chernov said gently, "sometimes it's the smallest things that help us find the really bad people. Sometimes it's like a giant jigsaw puzzle and you don't know how important a really small piece might turn out to be. You might have a piece like that, something Phil told you. It might help us get the man who hurt him. It might not. If it does not," she said, and her voice became firmer, "Paulie, I swear to you," and she put her hand over her badge, "we will keep anything you tell us secret forever." She kept her hand on her badge as Paulie looked at her.

"The guys in his clan, some of them, did a raid on Barnabas," he said. "No one can know 'cause some of them would get expelled."

"What kind of raid was it, Ranger Paulie?"

"I was, I am, 'Clinton Barton.'"

Chernov's eyebrows went up.

"Hawkeye?"

"Because he doesn't have any super powers, he's just really good with his bow. How did you know?"

"In the movies, he's my favorite character," Chernov said. "For just that reason. An Avenger who wasn't invulnerable." She paused, smiling. "I've spent too much time at the movies. So, what was the raid all about?"

"They snuck into the administration and took something."

"Saint Barnabas administration?"

Paulie nodded.

"And it was what?"

"I dunno. Phil didn't say." His gaze swept across the adults looking at him. "It wasn't anything big or anything. Phil said it was like pirate booty, something you could stick in a pocket, you know? Not a laptop or anything worth anything. He said he couldn't tell me what it was and made me promise not to tell anyone." He looked at Chernov and, for a second, a look of panic swept over his face. Then his control snapped in and his face was totally still and Chernov had a glimpse of what he would look like as an adult. "But I told you."

She put her hand over her badge.

"You have my promise."

"What's your online name?"

Chernov's eyebrows went up again.

"I'll tell you, but it's a secret. Police officers have to be careful about who knows who they are online, you know?"

"Sure," he said, nodding. "I won't tell anyone."

"Promise?"

"Promise."

"All right, Clint. When I played, I was 'Red Alessia.'"

"Cool name."

"Thanks."

"What's it mean?"

"Well, 'Alessia' was my grandmother's name. She was Italian and it means 'protector.' And 'Red,' well, that was my division overseas, 'The Big Red One.'"

"You were in the Army?"

"Yes." She paused. "You know how you were checking on triggers?" Paulie nodded. "That's kind of why I made that part of my online name."

"I get it. Soldiers get PTSD, too."

"That happens."

"Bonnie told me about you guys. Soldiers." He nodded. "Do you still play?"

"Not much anymore." She grinned. "Police sergeants do a lot of night work."

"Too bad. It helps to not feel so alone."

"You may be right."

"Are there any other questions?" Paul asked, looking back and forth between Chernov and Deevers. Deevers looked at Chernov and then turned to Paul.

"We're good, I think," she said as she stood up.

They said goodbye to everyone, making a point to shake hands with both Paul and Paulie.

As Chernov backed their car down the driveway, Deevers smiled.

"I always wondered at the 'Red'."

"You thought it was my progressive leanings?" She looked up and down the street and shifted into drive. "At least I didn't give our name away."

"'The Shot to Hell Club' playing D-and-D probably would have raised more questions than the answers we got."

"And raised eyebrows."

"What do you think it was?"

"Something small, fits into a boy's pocket. Pen, maybe. Does Saint Barnabas have engraved pens? That might be inviting as loot."

"They might. We'll check. I don't know that it would have anything to do with our case."

"A pen wouldn't." Chernov went silent as she negotiated an intersection. "Maybe no connection at all." She paused. "Computer kids. Something small. Smaller than a laptop."

"A phone? It would fit in a pocket."

"Phone, an old iPod, something like that." She was silent for a mile. "I don't think someone would kill a bunch of boys for a phone. But they might do it for something else."

"Like?"

"Information." She nodded slowly. "Like what might be stored on a thumb drive or a phone."

"Maybe. But horse and cart. Maybe there's no connection. Whatever it was, if it was, maybe it has nothing to do with the deaths."

"Maybe not. I don't think, even if it was something like a thumb drive, that it would be anything that would be important enough to kill kids to get it back."

"Financial records," Deevers said, remembering her recent visit to the administrative offices. "Church and school memberships. After school activities. Contracts." She shook her head. "Got to watch we don't leap ahead of where we are."

"Still," Chernov said, "he gave us a connection, those sports groups using the Barnabas fields. I'm betting it's going to tie the Barnabas boys with the others, the ones not students at Barnabas. The thing the boys picked up in their 'raid,' that may turn out to be nothing, at least not as important as the linking of the sports programs." Chernov lifted a tablet from between the seats and started typing. "I'll get Report of Contact of this into the task force database as soon as we get back."

"It's worth checking out." Deevers looked at Chernov out of the corner of her eye. "Brown will want to include your ROC in tomorrow morning's briefing." She paused. "But you think they picked up something in their raid they should not have and now they are being killed for it."

"Sounds farfetched when you say it out in the open like that." Chernov grinned. "In the movie they're going to make about you, Jodie Foster would say something like, 'Sometimes you gotta go with your gut.'"

"I'll never make it to a movie. Maybe a cartoon. Daffy was always my favorite."

"But, yeah, I think someone is hunting those boys who raided Barnabas."

"I've always liked Pennsylvania." He looked up at the late afternoon sky and admired, for a moment, a contrail following a glint of silver silently racing south.

"Well," said the veterinary clinic clerk as she tapped the face of her tablet, "it's got a little of everything."

"That's the secret." He looked at his smart phone. "Got it and forwarding now." He tapped the phone's screen. "Order should be delivered next Monday." He looked at the young woman and wondered what it would be like to murder her slowly. "Tell the boss his standing order is on schedule for delivery in two weeks."

"Good," she said. "Did you say you used to live around here?"

"I was born here," he said. "Lived near Oxford."

"I know Oxford, my cousin lives there."

"Small world." He put his phone away. "You have my number, so if there's any problem with your order, call me day or night, weekends, weekdays, always available."

"Thank you. Have a good one."

She spun in place and disappeared into the small clinic. He smiled, watching her for a few seconds through the large window that had pictures of pets by children across its bottom. He thought she would be a fighter. It would be fun.

But he had things to do. He walked across the parking lot to his small van and slid the door back. Various sized sample boxes were secured to shelves. Giveaway merchandise – pens, sticky paper notepads, a handful of insulated cups with the company's logo, treats for dogs, cats, and horses, and a large number of dark blue baseball caps with the same logo – also filed boxes.

He did a quick scan and raised an eyebrow. The pens were going faster than expected. Greedy bastards in those clinics. He brought out his phone, quickly tapped in an order, and sent the message on its way. Then he got into the driver's seat. Beside him, an insulated cup held his Dunkin' Donuts coffee and he sipped on it as he thought about his next move.

He glanced over his shoulder and saw no one near his van. He reached under the passenger seat and brought out a laptop computer. He looked around again before raising the lid. He opened a folder on his desktop and brought to life a video.

It was in excellent color; it had been a bright day. The seven boys ran up the concrete steps, headed for the doors. He paused the video. Oddly, two were in baseball uniforms and one wore shorts and a t-shirt with broad, green and white stripes. Only one thought to look around and none looked up at the camera. The one looking was already accounted for. Bruce Vickers. The green and white shirt was from his soccer team. Wouldn't be playing that sport again. No matter; it was a pretty boring sport. He smiled and he let the video continue.

The software blinked at the splice and now the view was in the administration building hallway. Though the color dimmed from a lack of bright lights, the detail was fine enough that the boys were easy to identify, if one knew who they were. He froze the frame. The person who was the source of the videos had identified several, all now accounted for. None had what he was looking for.

But, helpfully, what they did have was some of the names of the boys not from Barnabas. The Sneaky Snakes who could speak answered his questions but the drug he used tended to make consciousness and speech difficult.

Nonetheless, he had made progress. There were two boys left, both identified. Sneaky Snakes indeed, he thought, because it had taken questioning the other five to get the last two identified. Five down, two to go, and he still did not have what he needed.

Was this a test? The thought had occurred to him before. He pushed it away; there was no way to be sure but completing his task was the important thing. Completing the mission, following the will of God, all would follow that.

He closed the video and then opened two images taken from it. One was a little brat named Marc Gramm. He shook his head. Of the two remaining boys, Gramm was not his current target. The path of faith included mysteries, he thought, and Gramm had been identified perhaps uselessly. The boy who surrendered the names, who admitted to the theft of a small thumb drive, also said the other boy, a "computer freak," had the drive.

The other image, that freak, was the key. Get him, carefully ask his questions, and don't allow him to depart until he revealed exactly where the small drive was, that was the next step.

He had scouted sites for disposal – an enjoyable task in itself – but mostly he just wanted to let things calm down. That is what he told himself and he did not seem to realize that his calls to Ellen Parker had the opposite effect.

The deepest part of him, the part of him that didn't care if he was just slaughtering people or on a mission from God, did not want things to be calm. It, he, wanted a firestorm all around him, wanted to be the firestorm, wanted to see the world burn but knew it would never be that fortunate, so it would settle for killing children. Or women.

Someone.

A little research was needed. He needed to get to know a Sneaky Snake named Jackie Flinthill. And then have an entertaining question and answer period with the boy.

Chapter 24: Breaking glass

James Hardy sat very still, listening to his supervisor describe what was to be done. The man smiled while talking but occasionally raised his eyebrows in a gesture that was supposed to mean something. Regret?

"You know your team," the supervisor said. "You're their leader. Management decided to tap into your knowledge and experience on this project."

The "project" was identifying which of his team members would be reassigned to positions designed to get them to resign or retire.

"Here's a list of the twelve." He reached across his desk and gave James a single sheet of paper. On it were twelve names, nothing else. "It will be up to you to pick the four and notify them of their transfer out. Then it will be up to them."

James stared at the names. There were only twenty people on his team, some specialists, others working a little bit of everything. The selected twelve had been with the company longer than the rest, which meant they were highest on the pay scale; probably that was the reason for trying to get rid of them.

"We're not trying to get rid of anyone," his supervisor said. "Emphasize that. But we've got to do some down-sizing and we'd prefer they make their own decisions about staying or going." He shrugged. "They're not being fired. But their transfers to Personnel where none of them are particularly qualified or experienced should encourage them to go someplace else, once the boredom sets in. And, if they don't take the hint in three or four months, I'd guess the Personnel Manager will find some cause for letting them go eventually."

He waited for James to say something and frowned when he remained silent.

"Do you have any questions?"

James shook his head. He stood and turned for the door, pausing when his supervisor quickly said more.

"Listen," the supervisor said, "you don't have to tell the four that you selected them. Just get the job done as professionally as possible, understand? If there's a problem, if HR or Personnel has to get involved, probably everyone will get the details of all this and that will make things uncomfortable."

James looked at him for what seemed like a long time before leaving the office. He went to his desk and sat down. There was a slight tremor in his hands; clenching them seemed to make it stop. Waves of anger swept over him again and again, making it hard to think.

Finally, he picked up his telephone and called each of the twelve, asking them to come to his office. They arrived in a trickle but they all came in a few minutes. James held up the list and explained what he was supposed to do.

"You twelve have the greatest amount of time in the company," he said. "I think that's what this is all about."

"Figures," someone said.

"I don't know how to do this," he said. James felt his eyes water. "I really don't. And I don't want to do it." He looked at the page of twelve names and turned it around and around. He looked up. "I told you where they were going to send you and what they planned to do if you didn't get fed up in three or four months and leave. Let me ask a couple of questions."

He frowned and shook his head.

"Anyone want to retire?"

Several people smiled, thinking he was joking. But one person held up their hand.

"James," a short Hispanic woman said, "put me down as one of the four. I'll retire after I get there. I've got the time in grade, I'll be all right, and I think they'll probably be gunning for me anyway. That's how they work. They've done this kind of thing before."

"Thank you, Cathy," James said and made a small check beside her name. "Anyone else?"

"I hate this place," a man said. He was White and bald with deep lines on his face that might come into use if he smiled. "I've been looking for a reason to leave. Yeah, I've been talking to headhunters and I've got a couple of things. Didn't want to leave the team, enjoyed working with you guys even when admin turned into complete assholes, pardon my French. James, put me down and I'll roll out when I have something lined up. And, young man, you want to think about getting your own butt out of here. They're going to kill you."

"Jake, some days it feels like that," James said. He made another checkmark. "Any of you need a letter of recommendation, please let me know. And your French is pardoned, Jake."

James looked around.

"Any other volunteers?" But there was only silence. "You are all good people. You all do good work. It looks like I'm going to have to pick two more. I think I'd rather jump out the window. I'll make the final decision by close of business today unless someone else volunteers. Please don't come by to plead your case. Once I decide on the last two, I will let them know and then I'll email everyone on the team. Any questions?"

"James," Jake said, "I wasn't kidding. You look like you're about to have a heart attack. You got to get out of this place. Talk to my headhunter, see what's out there."

"Jake, I don't want to leave the team. I keep hoping things will change."

"They won't, man. You're not fooling them, they know you're not a company man, but you keep the trains running on time anyway. Sooner or later, they're going to get rid of you and probably do it in a really shitty way, pardon my French."

James nodded. He said nothing, his jaw clenched, and stood as the twelve left his office.

In less than an hour, he made a call.

"Sorry, John, but I'm putting you on the list."

"I was afraid of that. Did you just flip a coin or what?"

"No. You're the youngest of the twelve, you've got an MBA, I'm hoping you have the least difficulty landing a good job."

"I should. I can say, 'Do you want fries with that?' in three different languages."

"God, I hope you can get something better than that. Remember what I said about the letter. Again, I'm sorry. I have to make another call."

"I get it. I think your job sucks more than mine." They hung up and James punched in another extension.

"Sorry, Carol. I've put you on the list."

"God dammit. Why me?"

"You're almost the youngest of the twelve, you have the some of the best evaluations even before you came to my team, and you've got an advanced degree. All that gives you a better shot at pulling down a new job."

"John's got a graduate degree."

"He's on the list. I'm really sorry about this."

"Yeah." The woman seemed to be breathing deeply. "This is really shitty. I feel like going back to your office and screaming."

"I wouldn't blame you. I should have found some way to protect you all."

"Whoa, James, I was joking. Yeah, this is lousy, but they are really messing with you, not just us. I guess they're hoping that if one of us decides to go all postal we'll stop at you."

"That's what it smells like."

"Listen, you do good work and I know you tried to protect us. But this place is a snake pit. They ought to burn it down and sew the ground with salt. You know, Carthage stuff." She paused. "We all know what this has done to you and your life. Jake is right. Even if I was staying, I'd tell you to get out before you go crazy."

"Or crazier. Thanks, Carol. I gotta get an email out. I'll let everyone involved know when the details come to me."

"Talk to you later."

James sent out an email to the team telling them of the transfers. Then he sent one to his supervisor with the four names.

A half hour after that, management sent an email to each member of his team saying they had reviewed his decision and intervened so that only three would be transferred. They made it sound like the transfers had been his idea. Management named Cathy, Carol, and Jake. When he went to use the restroom, James noticed half his team avoided eye contact with him. He spent the rest of the afternoon staring at his desktop.

Charles Dwyer suffered a heart attack that evening. He was sitting on a lawn chair in his backyard reading an eBook on his tablet when it struck. His wife found him fifteen minutes later and she did not think he was asleep. She dropped her iced tea and ran to him, punching 911 into her phone as she did.

A former nurse, she was still doing chest compressions on her husband's body when the paramedics arrived. They used a defibrillator immediately but too much time had passed. Nothing worked.

His wife and daughter organized their calls in a fashion that Charles would have found well organized and a reflection of what he had done in his own life.

A notice was posted on the firing range bulletin board, his coffee mug was taken away to be given to his wife, and it seemed even the shots on the range were muted. Ellen walked in and saw the handful of people in the break room standing around not doing much of anything. She nodded to a woman who looked familiar and the woman motioned with her to the bulletin board.

Ellen read the notice, twice, though tears blurred her vision the second time. Blasingame stood beside her, grimaced, and then asked if she wanted to go home.

She said she did not and went outside to one of the pistol stations. Blasingame stood beside her, not saying anything. As she slipped on her yellow lensed shooting glasses, she looked at him.

"I told Charles I would."

Blasingame nodded. Ellen worked on her weak hand.

She didn't cry until Blasingame drove her home. It was brief and light, nothing dramatic, but she sat in her chair not doing anything for almost an hour. Finally, she looked over at Blasingame.

"He was a good man."

"I think you're right," he said.

The funeral, quiet, family only, took place four days later. After talking with some of Charles' friends, his wife decided to have a gathering of his friends, family that had not been able to get to the funeral, and any of his range club students who wanted to come.

Having met Ellen Parker months before, she asked Ellen to post an invitation to his students at the range.

"Tell them we're calling this a wake," she said. "To hell with when it's supposed to be."

"I will," she said. She offered help, which was politely refused.

Ellen made a notice out of some light green paper she had; she did not remember the brownie recipe. She went to the range after work and posted it next to the sheet of paper with the notice of Dwyer's death and a clipping of the obituary from the Philadelphia Inquirer. People were reading it before she left.

James Hardy came in a few minutes after Ellen went home. He had not been to the range since the last disaster at work, so he had not seen the earlier postings. He learned of Dwyer's death, funeral, and wake all at the same time.

He sat at a table across the room and alternated staring at his folded hands with staring at the bulletin board and its terrible notices.

After an hour, he took a small notebook from his case and walked over to the wake notice. He copied the information and double checked it. Tears blurred his vision as he checked but he did not look away until he was sure he had it right. Then he gathered up his gear and drove his pickup home.

He had a great deal of difficulty getting to sleep and, though part of him wanted howl with sorrow, he did not cry a drop. Just before dropping off to a thin sleep, he felt something fall, emerge, into the awful empty hole of loss, something hard, something on the verge of becoming, of bringing a powerful response.

If he had been awake another minute, he would have thought it was like feeling a cocked pistol hammer form inside of him. But he fitfully slept.

Chapter 25: Missions

The one good thing, he decided, about Flinthill was the little bastard was only a few miles away from where he lived. The bad thing was he never seemed to come outside. Prowling through his neighborhood – parking outside Flinthill's home was not an option – invited attention, even with using a different one of his three vehicles. Probably every mother in the development was on high alert. Here it was, a perfectly ordinary Saturday, and he was spending it looking for Jackie Flinthill, hoping he would wander out of his house and reveal himself. But that hadn't happened.

There had been The Temptation. Of course. It was always present, pushing for his attention. He found himself trying to justify diverting from his mission and taking a woman. Or two. To "jar things loose." That was nonsense, of course. And thinking that maybe finding that Ellen Parker bitch and having fun with her was foolish in the extreme. The police probably were all over her. Temptation, temptation, temptation, all because he felt frustrated in completing the mission.

He shook his head as he thought it through. No one had forced the mission on him; he volunteered for it. Accidentally, yes, but he volunteered. Building his cover meant doing normal things. None of this, "he was a quiet man who kept to himself" silliness. In this modern, hyper-socialized culture, isolation and low profiles, he was convinced, attracted attention.

He mowed his lawn, subscribed to a newspaper, helped his neighbor with his deck, and went to church. He smiled. Volunteering to gather books for the St. Barnabas School sale benefiting its library had meant talking to people, letting them get to know him, while he thought about when he might resume his activities. And one person in particular.

George Mayfair, the administrative chief of the school and church was a talkative person who really did try to be a friend to everyone. That made adding him to the cover operation easy. And George, good old, sensitive George, was so damned easy to read. When he was happy, it showed. When he was worried, it showed. One day it really showed, even though he was just sitting in at the meeting of church volunteers – boring as hell, but there was always great cake.

George clearly was troubled and an impulse, probably just a desire to enjoy George's suffering, led him to try to engage the older man in a conversation. George almost ran from the conference room and he saw the panic in the man's eyes. It was wonderful and he wanted more. He caught up to George in the parking lot and turned on his act of concerned friend, but he could have approached walking on his hands and singing Italian opera and George wouldn't have noticed.

George didn't reveal the problem, not then. But he came by after work a few times during the following week and George went with him one late afternoon to a nearby Ruby Tuesday's. Carefully, he avoided questions for a time and just yakked about his job, visiting animal hospitals and clinics, selling supplies, drugs, and how much he liked helping the veterinarians do their jobs. George had stared at his glass of half-drunk beer, silent, looking like he was going to cry at any moment. It was wonderful to see.

Finally, George started talking. At first, he was very roundabout. But something was very, very wrong, and the man had no idea what to do about it. "We're in real trouble," was all he could say, repeatedly. Something had been stolen. And that was it for details. It would take another after work meeting at Ruby Tuesday's before George responded to his, "George, if there's anything I can do to help, just let me know. I can be totally discrete."

The "something" was a thumb drive. Why was it important? Silence. Avoiding eye contact. Taking a swallow of his beer so large he almost choked. Finally, and slowly, George told him. A report. About priests. And young boys.

He almost had laughed. Was that all? That particular horse had fled the barn and then came back to burn it the hell down. The Pennsylvania Attorney General had revealed the results of a two-year grand jury investigation into priest abuse of children. Over three hundred priests were named, publicly, as molesters of over a thousand children. Six Dioceses were involved. The newspapers, the broadcast news, seemed to have a new story every weekend on that particular subject.

But, no, this was worse. There was a network, George explained. Priests, bishops, protecting priests, that was known and in the AG's report.

But what was on the thumb drive were the records of a different network, a network of pedophiles up and down the Church hierarchy, all across the country. It wasn't the Church leaders who wanted to protect the Church from bad press, though there was a list of those idiots. No, this was the central contact information of pedophiles in every Diocese in the United States, 145 of them. People to call for assistance when it was time to move on. People to call to select churches where there were potential targets.

He was astounded and amused. What was all this information doing on a stupid thumb drive laying in George's office? It had been Father David Hemley's. He was the center of the network, had compiled the contacts over the years, never stored them on any computer, kept all the information on one little thumb drive that could be, if needed, thrown into the nearest fire. That hadn't happened because dear Father Hemley, recently retired from leading his flock at St. Barnabas, had up and died in the spring. The thumb drive had been found by George, found it while assisting with cleaning out Hemley's living quarters, and he put it in his pocket to inspect later and then forgot it.

He fought to keep from laughing. And when did you discover what was in it, Forget-Me-Not George? A week after the Attorney General's press conference. There it was, sitting in the bowl for his keys on top of his chest of drawers. So, not thinking it was anything more than some drafts of sermons, he brought it to work, plugged it in and had a moment where he did not understand what he was seeing and another moment where he tried to return to that lack of understanding.

Names, addresses, email addresses, telephone, by church, by Diocese, even, in some cases, preferences. Another list of bishops who could be relied on to try to cover things up, pay people off. Some names, surprise, were on both lists. Hemley had developed his files over the decades of his service.

Why wasn't the thumb drive ash? George hadn't known what to do. Was it the only copy or were there others laying around? Then he discovered it probably was the only copy.

That revelation came with the calls and the emails, all for Father Hemley. As the St. Barnabas administrator, George automatically had all calls and emails for Hemley diverted to him. Every day there was at least one, often more. Other priests asking for a referral in some area for an unspecified reason, wanting to know who might be "friendly" or "supportive" for a request to be reassigned. So many that George had a copy-and-paste response ready.

Suddenly, it seemed like a gift, the calls and emails stopped. Word had made it around the network. It was over. George determined that it was time to destroy the drive. But when he came to work, it wasn't in his desk drawer. In fact, the drawer wasn't locked. He had screwed up, gotten in a hurry to get out early on Friday, and slammed the drawer shut but didn't lock it. When he came back on Monday he wanted to die. The only clue he had was the imagery captured by the security cameras.

George quickly made copies of the imagery, of the seven boys slipping into the building, and then erased the originals. The Micro SDs the cameras fed would be written over multiple times in the coming weeks but that didn't tell him which of the boys had the thumb drive.

He nodded attentively. Yes, this was a problem. It could be a disaster. More embarrassment for the Church, for St. Barnabas. He was delighted – the oncoming train wreck would be amusing to watch.

Then he learned that George's concerns were about more than embarrassment. Barnabas had its own scandal. Money had changed hands and the news was stifled. But yet another scandal, a revelation that Barnabas was the center of a spider's web of pedophiles, especially after the AG's little dance, then a huge hammer was likely to come down on Barnabas. Reform was in the air and it reached, so people said, all the way to the Pope. George could find himself out on the street, essentially unhirable by anyone for anything. Never mind his age; stained by a relationship to Hemley meant his life was over.

And there it was. A mission. Take it on, recover the thumb drive, and a bargain would have been struck. He would be, for lack of a better word, protected. He was in the right place at the right time and had the necessary skills – this was not accidental. He could do the mission and put some time between him and New Jersey. Things had gotten a little tight there, he was sure of it, and taking on this mission would give him useful distance from the whores while keeping him in practice.

He suggested he might be able to help and George almost wept. He turned over the memory card he had copied all the imagery to. He wasn't any help in identifying any of the seven but he matched several faces to the team photos of the teams that were using Barnabas' facilities that Saturday. Then he went to work.

He told George nothing at first, even when the first reports of the "red ribbon killer" appeared. George didn't ask about the boys. He told George that a cover story would be needed to misdirect the investigators. George said nothing. When the FBI showed up, George called, almost panicking again. When he suggested staying out of their way and letting Bobby Flynn deal with them as much as possible, George grabbed onto the idea.

It might be a good idea, he thought, when he completed his mission, to put George deeply into one of Pennsylvania's flooded quarries. It wouldn't be a lot of fun, more like work, really, but George did not seem to be a rock of reliability.

He drove his middle-aged Chevy sedan into the Wawa store parking lot just north of the development and filled the tank with gas. As he watched the numbers turn over, he considered his options and found them to be very few.

Yes, nothing had gone public. The Snakes had stolen the thumb drive but seemed not to understand what it was or, if they did, did not know what to do with it. In any case, nothing had happened. While that undoubtedly was appreciated by his George at Barnabas, it really didn't guarantee bad news not arriving at some time in the future.

He smiled at the thought. Maybe George realized the thumb drive was a time bomb and was walking around with his stomach in a knot, waiting for the headlines to appear. Well, if that happened, his mission would come to an end and he would have to find another outlet for his energies.

Maybe the damned thing had been lost. Isn't that what children did? He shook his head as the pump stopped.

He buttoned up the pump and his car and pulled up to a regular parking place, still thinking. All five boys so far had given up the names of the other Sneaky Snakes and acknowledged stealing from Barnabas. Well, not all. Some were overwhelmed by the xylazine and never provided him with any answers. That was a shame. On the other hand, the boys who responded to his questions all corroborated each other. Who knew what the unresponsive ones would have said? Maybe the same thing, maybe something different, or something additional. Something like, they dumped it into the mail and sent it to their local police, or the Pope, or the FBI. No, that would have produced a tsunami of newspaper headlines.

That last boy said Flinthill had it, that young Jackie was a "computer freak," so it had been passed to him. Find Flinthill, get the device, and he could complete his mission. Marc Gramm would never know how close he had come to having his young life evaporating while wrapped in plastic.

Back to the subject. He had hoped cruising Flinthill's neighborhood might reveal the boy. But there seemed to be nothing but houses. No gathering places for children, no playgrounds, soccer fields, baseball diamonds. Nothing to contest staying at home and online. Well, nothing in the housing development itself. Maybe on the periphery?

He unfolded a map of Chester County, though he didn't need it. The development mostly was surrounded by farm land. The exception was where he was parked. A small cluster of gas stations, fast food places, and the Wawa, all huddled around a crossroads. He looked up. Lots of cars, no bicycles or other indications of gatherings of children.

Probably Flinthill was locked in his room chasing dragons or porn with his computer, whatever it was boys did nowadays. But, if he went outside, where would he go? Had the kids found a place for socializing, somewhere that adults didn't intrude?

Maybe it would be a good idea to circle around the development rather than sneak into it. Sure, it wasn't likely to result in anything useful and he would end up having to slip into the boy's house. He was good at that and it was very exciting, but it was so risky it had to be the last choice. He smiled. Chasing down brats wasn't really his thing. He had learned quickly how to hunt boys but his primary skill set was for different prey. He needed to stay within his limits, his experience.

Look for the simplest solution first. It might not be likely but it would be safer. He nodded to himself as he folded the map. A little more exploring was called for.

Kildeere stood back from the rock and studied it. For a piece of stone, it was being pretty pig-headed about revealing itself. No, actually, that was stone's standard behavior. You think the grain is going one way and it goes another, so you have to be very careful not to offend it so severely it cracks up. She turned and looked out the barn door toward her house's side porch.

Jackie Flinthill sat on the steps, throwing bits of boiled egg to the raven. The raven, well able of snatching them out of the air, acted as if it didn't see them, or Jackie, and then hopped onto the white and yellow pieces.

The boy seemed delighted, totally focused on the raven. He had taken to calling it "Raven," and Kildeere thought it was a reasonably appropriate name. The raven appeared not to mind. Of course, it frequently ignored the humans around it, name or no name.

She stepped to the doorway and the raven, Raven, looked at her, a bit of white dangling from its bill. Then it looked toward the road. Kildeere followed its gaze. A gray, nondescript car slowly drove down the road. It almost stopped at her driveway but, accelerating slightly, it continued on.

She looked back at Raven. It was still looking at the car, ignoring the last bits of egg Jackie offered.

Kildeere walked to the porch. Raven looked at her and lowered its head, twisting it slightly sideways, as if watching her, the egg bits, and the car now in the distance. Jackie looked up, grinning.

"He ate most of the egg," he said.

"He'll eat all of it when you're not looking. I'm getting a soda. You want one?"

"Yes, ma'am."

She went into the kitchen and returned with two bottles of locally made root beer. She handed one to Jackie as she sat beside him. Raven busied itself hunting for bits of egg, though it occasionally looked at the two humans as if expecting them to supply some kind of entertainment.

"Warm day," Kildeere said. She took a drink.

"Good flying weather," Jackie said, nodding at his drone laying against the wall behind them. A recharger was plugged into an outlet and linked to the drone. "I got some good video of the sculptures."

"Can I see?"

Jackie reached behind him and brought out his controller, moving quickly, as if he had hoped she would want to see the results of his flight. He did. He flipped up a small screen and passed it to Kildeere.

"Just hit the play," he said.

Kildeere watched the video, nodding and smiling slightly.

"This is pretty cool," she said. "Really different way of looking at things. It's like flying through some kind of canyons."

"Keep watching," Jackie said, sipping on his bottle, as he watched Kildeere's reaction to the video.

"Wow. You flew right through that one."

"Big old donut, pretty easy. Keep watching."

"Oh, now, that's impressive. Climbing and circling the tower. All the way to the top. That's really good."

"I've been practicing," he said. "The circling while still pointing at the same thing was really hard to figure out. I started using a chair on our back porch. Then I added rising."

"Can I see it again?"

"Sure. Hit that button, yes. Now play again."

They both fell silent as Kildeere saw her sculptures be revealed by a gliding perspective. She finally handed the controller back to Jackie.

"Thank you," she said. "I've never seen my stuff like that. You've got a good eye."

"What does that mean?"

"It means you know how to show something to people watching the video. You could go through everything and make it all blurry or something but it's all clear. And you presented those sculptures in a way that was not how people would usually see them but still wasn't showing off how you could fly. It was like you respected those things. You had to fly very, very well to do that, but you weren't bragging, you were displaying the art."

"Well, I guess so. But I did fly through the donut."

"It had it coming. Did I explain what I meant about 'a good eye'?"

"I think so. It's like I'm running a museum and I want people to appreciate things from how Raven sees things."

"I think that's what it's like." She took another swallow. She looked at Jackie out of the corner of her eye. "How are you doing?"

"Okay." He looked at her. "Did you think I wasn't okay?"

"You remember when your mom brought you out?" He nodded. "The next few times you visited, you were a little quiet."

"Yeah. Some of my friends went away so I was a little down."

"Where did they go?"

"Mostly, they just left. You know, stopped being online." He fell silent. "We don't watch the news much but one of the guys I played online with…" Again silence. "Listen, you can't tell my Mom about this, all right?"

"Jackie, I can't promise that. It might be something she needs to know. She's your mother."

"Yeah, I know." He took a breath. "We have a clan, the Sneaky Snakes. You know what's been happening to those boys, the red ribbon thing?" Kildeere nodded. "A couple of them were Sneaky Snakes. One, Bruce Vickers, I knew."

Kildeere said nothing while her mind raced. On the other side of Jackie, Raven looked at her, its mouth opened wide as if to shout a warning.

"How do you know they were Sneaky Snakes?" she asked.

"I only know two. Their names, I mean. Bruce got me to join so we could play online, you know? When we went on that raid, I was told another guy's name. Michael."

"What raid?"

"At St. Barnabas. A bunch of Snakes were there for the baseball tournament or the soccer games, whatever, though we didn't know it because we don't know each other in real life, just online. But one guy knew one guy and he knew one guy and Bruce knew me. We all got together and called each other by our Snake names. It was pretty cool. I met Mike Jones, he told me his real name and I told him mine but it was a secret. All seven of us went on the raid."

"What was the raid, Jackie?"

"Just something to do. One of the guys went to Barnabas, maybe more than one. Anyway, they took us around and we found a door that was unlocked, which was really stupid, what with all the kids around. We went in. We were calling each other by our Sneaky Snakes names and that was fun. When it started to get boring, someone said we were on a raid like in Guild Wars or something, so we started sneaking around. It was just a bunch of offices and desks and stuff. One of the guys found a thumb drive and we pretended it was loot from a cave or something and we all escaped." He shrugged.

"A couple of guys knew Bruce was really into computers and gave him the drive but he gave it to me because I was, too. I think it was mostly he didn't want his parents to see him bringing home something stolen." He hesitated, looking at the bird, but he did not add more details about St. Barnabas. He took a breath.

"Anyway, a couple of weeks later one of the guys from the raid didn't show up for a raid we were planning." He looked up. "An online raid. We got a substitute and went ahead. Then Bruce dropped out. People drop out of online stuff all the time. But I knew Bruce and he was on the news, like I said, one of those red ribbon boys. Then someone told them where to find Mike Jones and I knew his name."

"Jackie," Kildeere said slowly, as if examining wires to a bomb's detonator, "did you tell any of this to your mother?"

"No. Not really. I told her the part about some of the Snakes dropping out. I didn't say anything who they were or about them being the guys on the news."

"It would be a good idea to let her know what's happened."

"I don't want to get anyone in trouble. That thumb drive was tiny and we didn't take anything else."

"I don't think that's the main issue. If someone hurt Bruce and Mike, and you knew them, you might know something that would help the people who are trying to stop whoever it was that hurt them." She took a breath.

215

"I don't think they're worried about kids sneaking into St. Barnabas, not when compared to someone hurting boys, you know?"

"You don't think she'll be mad at me?"

"You know how you thought I might be crazy when we first met?" She waited for Jackie's nod. "Well, when it comes to their children, mothers can be really crazy. It's because they love them. You understand?"

"I think so." He thought for a moment. "Would you come with me? It might keep her from going too crazy."

Startled by the request, Kildeere did not answer. She looked at the yard and wondered what to do. Raven hopped a foot into the air and landed in front of her.

"What do you mean by 'crazy'?" Kildeere asked

"She might ground me forever. She told me I was spending too much time online with the Snakes. I had to cut my online nights back." He looked miserable as he watched Raven, then he took a breath. "No, you don't have to come. She's not really crazy. You're right. Maybe she'll call the police."

"Might be a good idea."

"You could be right." Jackie sighed. "Things are really weird, you know?"

"Tell me about it."

Persistence.

On the day of the wake for Charles Dwyer, of which he knew nothing, he had cruised the development, repeating a tactic from previous days but with different vehicles. No success. Sitting in the Wawa parking lot had not helped. The problem was a lack of information. Where would boys of Jackie Flinthill's age congregate? He had found nothing. The housing development had no nearby playing fields, the small strip mall was not inviting, and there wasn't even a community center in struggling competition with PlayStations and Xboxes. The pattern of disappointment continued as he drove through the housing development.

Yes, he had the boy's home address. Thanks, George. Useful, but it did not give him the boy.

Frustrated, he finally turned west. He was not defeated. He was never defeated. He would come back. He nodded at the thought as he left the development for farm fields and occasional plots of woods and isolated farm houses.

Then he saw Flinthill.

It was just a glimpse, something in the corner of his eye triggered his head into swiveling and there the boy was. He was on the house's side porch, next to a black bird and a Black woman. He was showing her something. But it was Flinthill.

It was a struggle not to slam on the brakes. He took his foot off the gas pedal for a few seconds, confirming what he thought he saw. It was not wishful thinking. Deliberately he looked ahead and gently accelerated the car, hoping no one, other than the bird, noticed him.

Ugly bird, beak wide open as if screaming at him. Right next to Jackie Flinthill. This was wonderful. What else had he seen?

A yard full of strange ornaments. Across the road a dense plot of woods. What else? A bicycle leaning against the fence. Jackie would be going home on it, would have to peddle on it all the way by himself.

A plan began to form. But it depended on being able to observe the boy without being seen. He looked ahead, trying to find a left-hand turn and realized there wasn't one. He slapped the steering wheel and let himself quietly curse his luck when he finally came up on Route 10.

He savagely turned left, south, and sped down the road, looking for another left. It seemed that he had driven miles, almost the whole distance to his own house, before he found a road. He turned, cutting in front of an oncoming car, and drove as fast as he dared. Up ahead he saw another road and he turned left again. Now he was pointing right at the house Flinthill had been visiting.

Not a good idea to expose himself but there were the trees he'd seen. One of those abandoned clumps of trees. And there was an old farm track bordering it. Wonderful. Everything was falling into place.

Without knowing he was following the trail of a New Joyton police corporal, he pulled onto the track and quickly got out of his car. There was no one around. The house and Jackie could not be seen from where he stood. He plunged into the woods.

Thorn-covered bushes tore at him, saplings and roots tripped him, it was like a nightmare where things were pulling at him, trying to hold him back. Relief came when he almost fell into a clearing dominated by a large tree. In it was another large, black bird – not likely to be the same one he saw on the porch – which stared at him, its head lowered. It did not startle, showed no alarm, but it looked at him as if he was prey.

"Fuck you," he panted. He looked down for a stone to throw at it but there wasn't one.

Almost immediately a shadow slipped silently over him and then he was back into the woods. He looked behind but the big tree and whatever bird might be on it was gone. The woods, though, remained, and he continued to fight his way through.

He stopped when he saw the roof of the house and crouched. He took a breath and tried to calm down. Then he moved forward on his hands and knees, knowing he was probably ruining his slacks. Like him, they were not designed for this.

He reached a point where he could see the house. The boy was gone, along with the bicycle. Not that it mattered, so was the bird and the woman.

Quiet curses returned.

He sat against a tree. Dampness creeped into his pants but he stayed still, watching the house.

Jackie Flinthill had been at the house; he had no doubt. That wasn't a mirage he saw. What he didn't know was why. If he understood what the boy was doing there, he might be able to predict when he would return.

Yes, if he had to, he could go into Flinthill's house. That could get very messy, very complex. Many unknowns. Far better to snatch him off the road. With just a little luck, there might be no witnesses, no alarms.

Depending on what the boy told him, it might be necessary to go into the house. He would never be so blessed that the brat had the thumb drive on him. But he would know everything the boy knew. Everything. That would greatly improve the odds, perhaps even erase them.

He would come back and sit here at this time every day that he could, until he spotted the boy. Maybe bring something to sit on, better clothes, some boots. He smiled. It was always good to plan and be prepared. Then he would see what could be done.

He sat there for most of an hour before he got up. As he expected, his slacks were patched with patterns of damp and spattered with mud. He paused, brushing as much of the dirt away as he could. At least he would not be in a hurry getting back to his car. He smiled at the thought. Maybe he'd get another shot at nailing the black bird with a rock. His smile broadened.

Kildeere watched Jackie pedal away. She did not know what his conversation with his mother would be like but his mother seemed like a reasonable person. She stepped onto the front porch and paused to look at the "donut" rock sculpture Jackie had flown his drone through. She smiled. The kid was all right.

There was a movement in the trees across the road, one that did not match the slight breeze. Kildeere walked into the house and closed the door. A small pair of birder's binoculars sat on an end table and she picked them up as she backed further into the unlit room.

She used them to study the place where she saw the movement in the trees. Something was still there, further back among the trees. She saw something move and then there was nothing. Whatever it was, it was gone. The moving thing might have been someone's back. She frowned.

Had the police come back, were they suspicious enough of her to place her under surveillance? Had she slipped and said something, or had Ellen Parker found something?

Did they suspect what had actually happened that night in Philadelphia?

For several minutes, Kildeere sat in the gathering darkness, her hand clenching the binoculars tightly, and stared at the trees and wondered what they hid. She tried to carefully review everything she had said to the police but she only remembered fragments. Had they ever mentioned John Faraday? She did not think so.

A sweep of her binoculars picked up something on the yard's fence; a trailing piece of tape she used to put up Jackie's sign. She shook her head and walked to the door. She had meant to pick up that thing but kept doing other things. She walked through the yard, stepping around sculpture, until she came to the corner of the fencing. It took a minute to free all the tape.

Kildeere looked at the north-south road bordering the woods. The wood lot's corner kept her from seeing far down the road. As she watched, an older gray car backed into the northbound lane. The angle prevented her from seeing it, but she knew it was coming out of the lane bordering the wood lot on its south side. The car pulled forward into the southbound lane and was quickly lost to sight.

It didn't look like one of the vehicles used by her southern neighbor, a farmer whose field of growing green skirted her woods. Hunter? She had lots of yellow "Posted" signs up, each one with "M. Kildeere" and her street address carefully printed along the bottom. Most of the time hunters abided by the signs and it wasn't hunting season for guns or bows. Maybe it was a hunter scouting for a stand. Maybe one of her signs had come down and left a gap.

She put the binoculars down and walked back to the barn. She picked up her stack of Posted signs and a heavy-duty stapler. A moment later, she walked down the road checking the signs. They all seemed in place.

Kildeere turned into the lane. It was clear where the car had parked; the crushed weeds showed its path, along with a trail going into the woods. Hunter, looking for a stand?

But the signs were where she had put them, close enough no one could go into the trees without seeing more than one. Probably not a hunter. Maybe not a hunter.

She could not recall seeing the car before. Maybe her neighbor had gotten his daughter her own car; Kildeere remembered encountering his wife while shopping and they had talked about possibility. The wife, Kildeere remembered, was against the idea.

Maybe they had given her one anyway. Why would she bring it here? Wasn't she off at school?

Maybe it was a cop's...

She shook her head as she walked back. She had not let anything slip. There was no reason for the police to be taking an interest in her now.

But Ellen Parker... The reporter knew about John Faraday. Had she really been interested in a story on Kildeere's art work or was she after something else? Kildeere cursed. It was a good cover, talking about art. If she had found something, though Kildeere had no idea what it might have been, would it have been enough for her to talk to the police?

Maybe her friend, Blasingame, wasn't some kind of boyfriend-bodyguard hybrid. He looked like he might be a lot more. Maybe a cop?

Kildeere shook her head. She was building towers out of straw. Maybe it was just a deer. A running deer. Maybe. She wanted to believe it.

She had to believe it.

Jackie pedaled home at a pace slower than usual, trying to think of what he was going to say. He parked his bike in the garage breezeway and went into the kitchen. His mother sat at the kitchen table working up a shopping list when he came in.

"Hey, Jack," she said as he came in. "How'd it go?"

"All right," Jackie said. He sat on a chair next to his mother. "Mom, I think I have something to tell you."

His mother said nothing, just nodded as she put her pen down. Part of her dreaded what she might be about to hear but did not let it show.

"I know some of those boys, you know, the boys that have been killed." There were tears in his eyes. "I played with them online."

Jackie did not say anything about the raid on the administration office, nothing about the thumb drive, because it was stolen and he was afraid and because he was a boy encountering death. And he didn't want to get anyone in trouble.

His mother asked him about the other boys, about playing with them online, about his guild, and Jackie answered her questions. Her mother, worried about his withdrawal during the past few weeks, thought she understood what it was all about, and did not understand something very dangerous was coiling about her home and son.

She made the decision to call the police. She took the number from the card that almost every family with a child at St. Barnabas and families with children at other schools the murdered boys attended had been given. In a moment, she found herself talking with an officer in the task force. What she did not know was the task force was receiving calls on a daily basis from families whose children, they discovered to their horror, knew one or more of the murdered boys.

"Other than the two boys Bruce Vickers and Michael Jones, did your son know any of the other boys?"

"He thinks he did. He thinks some of them were in his online group."

"Yes, the Sneaky Snakes, you mentioned them. But he doesn't know any other names?"

"I don't think he does."

"I see. Would it be all right if I talked to him?"

"Yes, I think so. Hold on." She held the phone close to her body and looked at Jackie. "Jackie, they would like to talk to you. You don't have to, but it might help. Do you want to?"

"Sure," Jackie said, acting with a child's nonchalance while his heart beat hard enough he thought the police officer would hear it without needing to use the phone. He reached out and took the phone.

"Hello."

"Hello, Jackie. This is Sergeant Joe Ackerman. How are you doing?"

"Okay."

"Good. Listen, your mother filled me in with some of the information you gave her. I just need to check out a couple of things with you. Okay?"

"Sure."

"Great. She told us about Bruce and Michael. When did you first meet them?"

"I met Bruce in soccer league a couple of months ago, whenever the season started."

"That would be about May, would it?"

"Yes. No, actually, I think it was March when we went to sign-up. Practice started on April Fools."

"And what about Michael?"

"At the league playoffs at St. Barnabas. Early last month. It turned out we were both Sneaky Snakes but I hadn't known his real name."

"How long have you been in the Snakes?"

"Since I met Bruce. He told me about them. We play Guild Wars Two together."

There was a pause, the sergeant noticing the use of the present tense for someone dead, something children did. He was becoming very familiar with the language of children confronting death and he hated it.

"How did you learn Michael was a Sneaky Snake?"

"Bruce knew both of us."

"He introduced you to each other."

"Yes."

"Jackie, do you know if any other Sneaky Snakes have been victims?"

"I'm not sure."

"You're not sure?"

"People leave the Snakes. You know, 'cause they go on vacation and stuff. Get bored, drop out, join another clan." Jackie paused. "Some of us, the younger players, we called ourselves 'The Next Generation,' because the older guys tend to go on raids with each other. We scheduled our own raids and stuff. Some of the TNG Snakes have dropped out. I don't know what's happened to them."

"You don't have their email addresses or anything?"

"No. Our guild officers do, I guess. You know, for news and schedules and stuff."

"Jackie, do you have any messages from your guild officers or other kids?"

"Sure, I save them all."

"Jackie, I'd like to have our police officers come on over and see some of those messages, if that's okay."

"Well, we're not supposed to share them."

"We can swear the officers to secrecy so no one will tell anyone anything. We're not interested in the content of the messages, your plans or anything like that. We just want to see the email addresses."

"There aren't any. It's all a group email. One of the leaders set it up. We can all use it."

"That's great. We can work with that."

While the sergeant's voice was calm, he had raised his hand and was waving it. Another officer hurried to him and listened as Ackerman whispered in his ear.

"I need one of the tech people." Ackerman uncovered the phone.

"Jackie, as I said, I'm going to send some of our officers to your house to talk about the Snakes and your email system, if that's okay with you and your mother. All right?"

"I guess."

"Good. We'll try and get him to you pretty quickly. Can I talk with your mother again?"

"Sure." He held out the phone to his mother. "He wants to talk to you."

Ackerman nodded to himself and called up the spreadsheet for interviews. He looked for someone with sergeant's rank to accompany the officer who had a technical background. He was still looking when Jackie's mother came on the phone.

"Hello?"

"Ma'am, Sergeant Ackerman again. Here's the situation. You heard what Jackie said. We need to find out if other members of his online club know any of the victims. He said they are using an email group service. I'd like to have one of our computer folks take a look at their messages and then we can use that information to find the other members and see if they are okay and what they might know."

"I see. Do you need a warrant?"

"Only if you need us to get one but it would go faster if we didn't have to do that paperwork."

"No, it's all right. I just didn't know how these things are done. Of course, you can see the messages."

"Great. Thank you. I've got your address from when you introduced yourself and I'll give that to our people. I'm filling in the information to schedule the interview and it looks like a Sergeant Elizabeth Chernov is available to accompany our technology officer, that will be Officer Jacob Ahmed. Sergeant Chernov is from New Joyton and Officer Ahmed is out of Downingtown. How does the day after tomorrow at one PM sound?"

"We'll be here." She paused. "I suppose you have a fair number of children who knew one or more of the victims."

"Yes, ma'am, unfortunately quite a few. You never know, though, if someone has some piece of information that will help. We try to talk to everyone, just in case."

"I see." She paused again as she looked at her son. "Day after tomorrow, 1 PM. We'll be here."

"Thank you again, ma'am, and please tell Jackie 'thank you in advance' for me, please."

"I will."

Officer Jacob Ahmed was a Black police officer who had been through courses on cybercrime and he understood what Ackerman was asking for.

"I don't think," Ackerman said, frowning, "there's any panic to this. It sounds like we might be able to identify some of the Sneaky Snake leaders and they can give us a roster of their members. We get to them and maybe they might know some of the victims."

"You never know," Ahmed said but did not sound hopeful. "We'll probably need to get a court order."

He put a tablet on Ackerman's desk and tapped its virtual keys, alerting the task force leadership to anticipate his request for a court order. "Most outfits that provide group email services to groups like the Sneaky Snakes don't release names and email addresses without one. What we will get then is the list of email addresses and whatever user names they signed on with." He scratched his cheek idly. "With those email addresses, though, we can go to their ISPs and find out who they are."

"Another court order." Ackerman, White, and somewhat old school in that he was convinced all this computer bullshit did was make things more complicated, was impatient with almost everything. His own typing for his Report of Contact was much slower than Ahmed's; he watched as Ahmed's fingers moved quickly and then tapped the message send tab again. Ahmed looked up.

"They won't drag their feet – with kids involved, they'll respond quickly. They almost always do." He tapped his tablet and then grinned. "You'll be happy to know the Sneaky Snakes have their own website. Looks like they play together in several games. Run their group email through the hosting server."

Agent Brown appeared in front of the two officers, his phone in his hand.

"I just got…" His phone made a faint chime. "And another. Officer Ahmed, you are going to wear your fingers down to stumps." He paused to read both messages. As he did, his phone chimed again. He grimaced but kept reading. "All right, we need the group email service so we can turn it over to the lawyers. I'll let them know what's coming." He looked up. "We've had good cooperation from everyone so far, though we haven't had reason to ask for a lot. I've lost count of the number of parents we've called in like," he looked back down, "Mrs. Flinthill."

"Not sure she's a 'Mrs.'," Ackerman said, leaning back in his chair and stretching. "Just used her first name and didn't refer to a 'Mister Flinthill.'"

Brown nodded. "Maybe a single mom. If she's the only eyes-on her son, she might be a little over-reacting." He shrugged. "Hard to see how a parent couldn't react to a situation like this. Who is going with you?"

"Sergeant Chernov."

"Her partner, too," Ackerman said. "Janowski, also from New Joyton."

"They're out at the moment," Brown said, involuntarily looking at his watch. "I think they have tomorrow off. I don't like the delay but I don't see this amounting to a lot and we can use the time to get the order. Make everything tighter that way." He looked at Ahmed. "Chernov will have the lead." The FBI liked to have everyone clear on hierarchy.

"I met her a couple of weeks ago," Ahmed said. "I'll grab her for a sit-down about what we're going to be looking for before we go to the Flinthill's."

"Good. And don't grab her."

Ahmed smiled. "Nope, not engaging in inappropriate conduct with any other law enforcement officer of whatever gender."

"Happy to hear that," Brown said, shaking his head slightly. Everyone was a comedian. "You two have anything else for me?"

"No, sir," Ackerman said as he sat upright. Ahmed echoed his words.

"Great. Let me know how it went when you get back." Brown turned and walked away.

"Well, there I go, scoring points with the task force commander."

"He's a fed," Ackerman said, raising his eyebrows. "They tend to be sensitive about all that appropriate workplace behavior stuff." He watched Ahmed start to protest and held up a hand. "But he was just trying to keep you alive. She shoots people who behave in a sexist manner towards her, you know."

"Oh, that Dr. John stuff." Ahmed nodded. "I remember that."

"With the women around here, it's a tradition." He leaned towards his monitor and acted like he was reading something on it. "You do know, of course, our assistant task force commander has shot a number of men." He looked up. "All, or mostly all, in the line of duty, of course."

"Hey, wait, I wasn't really going to grab her. Man, it's just an expression of speech."

"I'm sure she'd appreciate your explanation as she reloaded."

"I'm going back to my desk and possibly hide under it."

"Good move, officer," Ackerman said, no longer hiding his smile. You had to make your fun whenever you could.

Chapter 26: Quiet curses

James Hardy stood in front of his supervisor's desk – he had not been invited to sit down – and did not wonder why he was there. Sooner or later, he would learn why he had been summoned and there was nothing he could do about being required to wait.

The supervisor looked at his monitor, glanced over at Hardy and frowned, and then typed something on his keyboard. He looked back at Hardy.

"Are you sick? You look terrible."

James shook his head negatively.

"Anyway," the supervisor said, pivoting his chair toward James, "we're going through a restructuring. Should be done in a few days." He picked up a thin stack of stapled paper and held it out to James who took it but did not read it.

"It outlines," the supervisor said, a touch of exasperation in his voice, "the restructuring for your team." James still did not respond. "We're doing away with several teams." He waited for James to say something. Finally, he shook his head. "Your team will continue. I really went to bat for you and your people." The usual lie and both men knew it. James still did not say anything.

"That document," the supervisor jabbed a finger at the pages in James' hand, "lists the people that will be removed from your team and transferred to other teams. Since we're eliminating three teams, we have supervisors with no or few people, so we're going to restructure. All the supervisors will have more or less the same number of people. All that's on the second page, supervisors with their new team counts." He waited for James to leaf through the pages but he did not.

"Naturally," the supervisor said, "this means some of the supervisors, that is, people who were supervisors in the past, will have supervisees below the threshold needed under Tier Four position descriptions to qualify as a supervisor. We'll do what we can in the future to see about restoring those numbers." The last sentence was said quickly, as if a foreign language phrase recited from memory, vowels and consonants forced together without any understanding of what was said.

The supervisor waited for James to say something. But James was barely listening, understanding he was witnessing theater, an act. A response from him simply was the supervisor's cue to make his next statement. Whatever was going to be said, whatever manipulation, would take place whether he summoned up the energy to play his expected role or not.

Some of his team was taken away; it really didn't matter. He had failed to protect them. The administration had worked to demonstrate his powerlessness while trying to make it seem he was responsible for whatever disaster was dropped on them. And they probably had set it up for him to lose his supervisor rating while being required to carry out supervisory functions. Of course. They had done that to others and it was a bit odd it took them so long to do it to him.

The supervisor had little patience or maybe he just had other people stacked up waiting outside his office. He took a breath.

"You're still," he said slowly, as if trying to be dramatic, "a Tier Four supervisor. It was a fight but I got it done for you." He smiled as he held out his hand for James to take. He expected congratulations for doing nothing. James reached and gripped it indifferently and released it quickly.

"Is there anything else?" he asked. The supervisor shook his head and James left.

Back at his desk, James read the stapled pages. They had taken away members of his team arbitrarily, it seemed at random. Smaller teams would, he knew, be required to maintain the production they had before. Costs would go down. Management's bonuses would go up. They would get away with it.

Someone, James thought, ought to blow their brains out. Each and every one of them. Someone needs to hit them so hard the whole damned company would have to sit up and take notice. Finally.

It wouldn't be hard. Plans came to him; how to stash weapons around the floors, in a vehicle truck, how to carry enough ammunition. Then his thinking focused.

Do it on a Wednesday or a Friday when the top tier of the administration would have their regular meetings on the top floor conference room. Senior supervisors, directors of operations and fiscal, their favorite toads and weevils. More than a dozen of them. No need to hide lots of weapons all over the building if they were all in one place at one time. Just ferry in some ammunition to his desk, a rolled-up gym bag to carry it. A couple of pistols could be concealed without a problem. All right, bring along the shotgun and the AR. He'd paid enough for them. He smiled. Break them down and put them in the gym bag. Then up to the fifth floor. Rest room to the right, go in, assemble everything, then down the hall to the conference room. Just the one door. Stay in the doorway and kill them all. Keep firing until there was no more ammunition. Or you were dead.

You wouldn't get away with it. Of course not. Someone would get a call out and the police would arrive. Nowadays, after so many shootings, they would not wait outside. They would be coming in as fast as they could. But it would take them minutes to arrive, minutes to come up to the fifth floor. Maybe he'd let the cops kill him, maybe do it himself. Not going to hurt anyone other than the top tier.

Wouldn't get away with it. Just as well. Everything sucked. Might as well go down, eyes on the tier, wondering what had they done to bring down all that destruction. The word would get out. Everyone would talk.

He looked at the time. Almost quitting time. And it was Tuesday. Wake for Charles Dwyer tonight. And then pain to the pain makers tomorrow.

James was not sure what he felt but it was, strangely, a little like hope.

"Looks like it's going to rain," Blasingame said as he looked up at the clouded sky. There wasn't much daylight left and the dense clouds smothered a lot of it.

"They said there was a chance," Ellen said. She paused at the driver's door. "You know, it would be all right for you to come in."

"No one there knows me and I wasn't one of his students. I wouldn't want to disturb anyone with wondering who I was." He opened the passenger door and paused. "You're going to be in a crowd. If he's one of them, then the reality is he can strike before I could do anything about it."

"You've mentioned that cheery idea before."

"On the other hand, if I see someone dragging an elephant gun behind him trying to go in, I might have a chance to dissuade him."

"Of course." She shook her head and took her seat. As they merged onto U.S. 30, she tapped the radio to a classical music station.

They were pulling up to the curb across from Dwyer's home when the rain started.

"You might want to hurry," Blasingame said. "We're getting a little lightning to the west."

"All right." Ellen, wearing a brick red dress and flat shoes, quickly got out and dashed across the street. Blasingame watched her reach the front porch just as the rain shifted into a higher gear.

"Great timing," he said.

There were more people in the house than Ellen expected. It turned out many of the first arrivers were local friends. Neighbors, fellow members of his church, and fellow retirees from the Pennsylvania State Police, more than half of whom had brought food and drink, had the house feeling full. Students from the range arrived after Ellen did.

Mrs. Dwyer – who insisted Ellen call her Janet – drafted Ellen to help out as they spread casseroles and the plastic cups around the islands of ice in bags and various different sized and colored bottles. Other people joined in and their activity seemed to signal everyone that speaking was acceptable. Conversations began and the house was filled with relieved voices.

"I think," Janet said, leaning towards Ellen, "I am going to end up with three weeks of leftovers and five days of dishwashing."

"There will probably enough booze left you won't notice all the washing."

Janet smiled. She took Ellen's arm.

"I appreciate your help," she said.

"My pleasure. Charles taught me a lot." She paused. "And I don't mean just about shooting."

"He was very impressed by you. Did he ever tell you that?" Ellen smiled slightly and shook her head. "He bragged to me about you all the time. That's why he invited you to dinner those times. Wanted me to meet 'this incredible lady.'"

"'Incredible'?"

"Everything you'd been through and you still managed to be a good person. He was impressed."

Ellen's eyes watered and Janet leaned in.

"Don't you start, Ellen Parker, or you'll have me doing it and the whole place will be flooded." Ellen smiled and wiped her eyes.

"No, ma'am."

They were interrupted several times by people coming up to Janet to say something, exchange hugs, and nod at Ellen, who only the students, and not all of them, recognized. A very thin Black woman came up and she and Janet hugged. They talked for a moment; Ellen thought they had worked together at Janet's church.

"We parked down the road a bit," the woman said.

"Oh, I hope the rain eased off."

"It has. It was really bad and then it just slowed down. There's someone in a pickup truck down just ahead of us, down the street past the light. Young White man, I didn't recognize him. I think he was coming here but he didn't follow us." She paused, glancing at Ellen. "He might be…" Janet nodded.

"Ellen, if the rain isn't bad, would you see if it is one of Charles' students from the range? If it is raining, there's an umbrella to the left of the door on the front porch."

"Got it," Ellen said. He guessed Janet and her friend thought the White man might be hesitant at coming in because most of the people coming into the Dwyer's house were Black.

She found the umbrella and opened it as she stepped onto the sidewalk. The rain was steady, suggesting it was planning on going on for a while. A streetlight illuminated the corner and a handful of cars parked on the next block. Ellen looked ahead and only saw one pickup.

Ellen thought she recognized the pickup from the range, something confirmed when she saw a membership decal on the rear window. The interior light was on and she recognized James Hardy as she approached the driver's door. He did not seem to notice her, so she reached up and lightly tapped the glass.

James startled as his head spun toward her. For a second, his hand fumbled with the controls before the cab became dark.

But for that second, Ellen could see clearly a handgun on the seat next to James and a shotgun and black rifle in the space behind the passenger seat, braced by a gym bag. After the light went out, James took off his ball cap and dropped it on the handgun.

As Ellen motioned, James lowered the door window.

"Hey, James," she said, bending over, "are you coming in?"

She saw he had been crying. Well, there was plenty of that going on.

"How're you doing?" James asked as a greeting. He wiped at his face.

"Raining. You'll get wet." Ellen realized she had lowered the umbrella as she leaned towards James.

But there was something else, something very wrong.

"Are you coming in?" she asked again, speaking slowly. "Mrs. Dwyer asked about you."

James smiled though his eyes were hollow sockets.

"I better not. I don't think I would be good company for anyone tonight."

"James, what's going on?" Rain was soaking Ellen's hair and dress but she ignored it. She sensed danger in the air, like static electricity foreshadowing a lightning strike.

"Nothing, really," James said. He looked forward, over the steering wheel, as if something important occupied the dark, empty space in front of him. "Same old, same old."

"What do you mean?" She spoke slowly, trying to understand her own feeling that danger was very close, perhaps sitting in front of her.

"You know," James said, his eyes still forward, "Charles, he was quite a man."

"Yes, he was." The rain was covering her face as if a dozen people were crying above her.

"He was brave, you know? I looked him up. He earned citations and everything. Saved a woman's life." James glanced at her and then his gaze went forward. "Kind of like you. Put his life on the line but for something important. Not just trying to show off. Serious. Dead serious, you know?"

"I think I do. James…"

"My whole life." He shook his head. "My whole life has been about losing things. It's all dribbled away. My wife, she left." Again, he shook his head. "Wonderful. Best thing in my life. Couldn't hold onto her. No strength. Couldn't figure out what to do. And my dog." He fell silent but Ellen saw his jaw clench. "Couldn't save my team. Powerless. Sucked dry? The job, you know?"

"James," Ellen said, "what happened?"

"Same old, same old. Screwing us because they can. No point to it, not really. Probably costing them more than they're saving. Shitty morale, messed up homes, all of it." He nodded. "Charles would not have put up with it. Right? Not that kind of man. I tried to. Put up with it, I mean. Tried to take care of my people, take care of my life. Let it all turn to shit. I really messed it all up. I let them get away with it." He nodded one more time. "But not anymore."

"James," she said, raising her voice a little, just enough to get him to turn a little in her direction, "What are you going to do?" Ellen remembered the weapons that hid in the darkness.

"Should have done it a long time ago. Slow off the starter blocks."

"What are you going to do?"

"He really liked you, you know?" Now James turned to her and studied her face, half hidden in the dark. "You are a lot like him. Took a stand, put it all on the line for other people. I read the stories. He knew them. Thought you were special."

"I'm just me," Ellen said. "What are you going to do?"

"What I should have done a long time ago, you know? Stop them, make them pay, take a stand." He reached down and turned on the ignition. James looked back at Ellen and made the same small smile she first saw in the range break room. "I got to go," he said, and the truck started to roll forward.

Ellen reached in and grabbed his arm while her feet scrambled to keep her upright. The upside-down umbrella made pointless circles on the ground as her freed hand clenched the window sill as tightly as she could.

"Stop it, James," she said sharply. "Right now."

The slowly moving pickup braked so hard Ellen almost fell. James looked at her, his face like a mask, emotion gone.

"I can make you let go." His voice sounded like someone else, like someone she had never met. He smiled and it was ugly and twisted by hate. "Let go."

"No," she said. "I'm not letting go. I'm not."

"You're stupid."

"No, and neither are you. What are you planning to do? James, are you going to kill someone?" Even in the dark and rain, the question seemed almost ridiculous.

"Trust me, it's no one you know."

"They've hurt you; I get it."

"And everyone around me. Made me into a piece of shit." He took a breath. "I even killed Brownie. My dog. I killed my dog. I hit him and he died." His voice choked.

"I'm sorry, I didn't know." Ellen struggled, trying to think of something to say.

"He was just a dog, you know? But I lost him. I lost my wife. Last straw. She denied it, but it really was. I thought about killing myself, you know, but... But it was like I had one last chance for redemption, to take care of the people I worked with, you know?"

Ellen nodded.

"I failed at that, too." James made his ugly smile. "Something I couldn't have ever done right. Time to end it all."

"You said you read about me?"

"Sure." The ugly smile smoothed into something else. "You did some good things. Saved those guys, those women and the kid. That was something."

"Did you read all of it?"

"What do you mean?"

"How messed up I was?"

"Yeah, you got shot…"

"Not about that. How messed up in my head I was?"

"There was something about that."

"I was scared of the dark, scared of people with guns, scared of loud noises, I tried to bunker in my home, didn't want to come out."

"Scared of guns? I met you at a gun range."

"Only because I decided that I wouldn't let the fuckers win."

James looked at her as if studying something behind her eyes.

"You were brave…"

"I was scared out of my mind, before and after. Especially after. It didn't seem to matter that I'd made it through those situations. It didn't matter that anyone was saved, not the deputy, not the carpenter, not those women, not the little girl. Not even me."

"You were traumatized."

"I was ruled by them," Ellen said. "'Traumatized' is how I felt. But they were winning. They were in my head. Keeping me from doing what I wanted to do, making me do what I didn't want to do." She paused, wishing she knew a short prayer, but there wasn't time for even that.

"They won," Ellen said. "Both of those bastards. Because even though they were face down in the dirt, they controlled me."

"Welcome to my world." He licked his lips.

"Exactly. What happened to me is pretty much what is happening to you. The particular history is different but the important part is they won."

"They don't win if…"

"If you don't let them take you over," Ellen interrupted. "Killing them doesn't do it. The fight is inside you, you see? It's about you and who you are. They get you to go crazy, they win. They get you to hide, they win. They get you afraid, hate filled, killing people, killing yourself, they win. You see?"

"You thought about killing yourself?"

Ellen fell silent and looked down at her feet. Slowly, she nodded.

"I don't like to admit it. I… My shrink knows. A couple of friends. Yes, I thought about it. For a long time."

"But you didn't."

"I didn't." She smiled slightly. "Good of you to notice."

"Why not?"

"Like I said, I didn't like them winning. I decided the best winning would be to have a good life." She took a breath and let it out slowly. "It felt like starting over, you know?"

James said nothing, still looking at Ellen's face.

"Starting over. That must have been hard."

"It was," she nodded. "Real hard. But winning was so great."

"How did you know you won?"

"Couple of things but the most important was that I realized, all of a sudden, I was doing stuff I liked. And I hadn't thought about them for weeks and weeks."

"I'm not sure what I like."

"Well," Ellen said slowly, her voice sliding into an Ohio drawl, "you sure as hell know what you don't, or are all those guns in back just early Christmas decorations?"

James laughed. It was a bark at first, as if it had to fight its way up and out, and then it settled into a chuckle. He wiped his eyes.

"Oh, shit," he said. He shook his head. "You throw some big ideas around."

"Maybe. But, listen. Mrs. Dwyer really was concerned about you. How about going on in and talking with her or something?" She took a breath. "And then maybe you and I can talk a little bit more."

"All right," James said. "Watch yourself." He backed his truck up and shut it down. He climbed out from the cab and looked at Ellen. "You're all wet."

"My readers say that all the time. Listen, go ahead. I'm going to get a towel from my car and wipe down a little. I'll catch up to you."

"I can do that," James said. "Hang onto that umbrella." He looked around in the darkness. "I think the rain is lifting." He walked down sidewalk toward the streetlight.

Ellen walked behind the pickup, intending to cross the street, and found Blasingame standing in the dark, his hand emerging empty from his jacket.

"I don't think I needed a bodyguard, Robert."

"I didn't either until I saw the guns."

"When did you see them?"

"When he said he wouldn't be good company. He was pretty focused on you."

"Did I ruin your chance to be a hero? I don't think I was in any danger."

"What did that lady sing, we don't need another hero? I'm not one." He shook his head and looked to one side. "Hell, that's the way it's always been. Someone sees things the way they are and decides, finally, and maybe scared almost to death, that they will step up and do it themselves." He looked at Ellen. "That's a hero, if there is any such thing. Someone putting herself between the big bad and the ones she would defend, and doing it so scared she pisses herself."

"And you're not like that." It wasn't a question.

"Hell, no," Blasingame said, his voice sounding ancient with self-understanding. "But you... Woman, that's what you are."

"I wasn't in any danger, Robert."

"Not in any physical danger, no, but if it had gone sour, if he had taken off and hurt someone, if he'd blown out his own brains, all of that is dangerous. Dangerous to you, your heart and mind."

"I need a towel." She led the way back to her car and discovered her memory was accurate. A small hand towel lay on the backseat and she ran it through her hair and face.

"Am I presentable?" she asked Blasingame. He handed the umbrella back to her.

"Probably," he said. He watched her walk back to the wake, shook his head, and returned to the passenger seat.

The rain was drifting away.

Ellen saw James talking with Mrs. Dwyer and smiled. Whatever disaster had been about to happen seemed at least diverted. She moved around, absently listening to conversations, occasionally talking to someone she knew.

James came up to her.

"I want to say thank you," he said. "I got to get straight on a few things but I think I figured one thing out. I'm getting a new job."

"That's a pretty big decision."

"Doesn't feel like one. It feels like, I don't know, a pretty obvious thing to do, something I've known I should do for a long time."

"Might be a good idea."

"I think so. There's another thing." He paused and seemed embarrassed. "Listen, I've got all my guns in my truck."

"Really? All of them?"

"Yeah. I think it might be best to put them a little out of reach for a while, you know, until I get things settled down."

"Sure."

"So, can I give them to you to watch for me? I know it's an imposition but I don't want to take them home just now."

"Sure. You want to do that now?"

"If it's no bother. I feel like going home and thinking things through."

"Just let me say good-bye to Mrs. Dwyer."

"I'll stand by."

Ellen spent a moment with Janet, exchanged hugs, and, for a moment, couldn't find James. But he was on the front porch, waiting for her.

"I'm across the street," she said. "I'll drive up to you."

James nodded and held the door open for her. She was in her car quickly and eased it forward.

"What's up?" Blasingame asked.

"James asked me to hold onto his guns. We're going to pick them up."

Blasingame nodded but said nothing. In a moment, they were alongside the pickup. Blasingame got out, said hello to James, and opened the back hatch of Ellen's car. He and James cleared the weapons as they were placed in back. All were loaded with rounds in the chamber. Blasingame didn't say anything at first but James looked up as he emptied the shotgun.

"Sorry about this," he said. "Really stupid, I guess."

"Not a problem," Blasingame replied. "Nice rifle."

"Thanks. Ruger."

"Are these all of them?"

"You mean, do I have a couple stashed at home?" James shook his head and took a deep breath. "No, I grabbed every single one I had. Loaded them like it was a ceremony. No real point to it, except each one made me more certain what I was going to do…" He shook his head again. "I was just going to have to unload them to break them down. Idiot." He looked at Blasingame. "That lady of yours, she kind of got to the heart of things."

"She has that ability. But I don't think she's my lady."

"Yeah, she does." He paused and tried a small smile. "Thanks for lending a hand."

Blasingame walked to the passenger side while James and Ellen had a short conversation. James tapped the car roof and went around his truck. Blasingame sat down and locked his seat belt as Ellen drove them down the street.

"A rifle, a shot gun, and four handguns," he said. "All locked and loaded. I think he was serious."

"I think he was, too."

237

"Hope some things change for him."

"I hope so, too." She shook her head. "It can be tough when you're all alone."

"I don't think he is," Blasingame said, looking at Ellen's silhouette. "Not anymore."

Chapter 27: Unforeseen

It would be an extremely rare situation where Kildeere might be in conversation with another person. But if they said they experienced a dream, in Kildeere's memory The Dream immediately appeared. It was the only one she consistently remembered. It was always the same, no details different one occurrence to the next, and every one an exact replay of what happened, except...

She has The Dream the same night Ellen Parker helps James Hardy find a way not to kill a dozen people. If Kildeere had known about Parker and Hardy and their words in the rain and a pickup with death behind the seats, she might have felt a link between her dreaming and their conversation, for a part of her was spiritual enough to deny coincidence, especially given the subject matter. But she did not know.

In The Dream, it is six years ago. She is waiting in the near midnight dark outside of Philadelphia's 30th Street Station. She is expecting to meet her agent, John Faraday. He lives in an upscale apartment building catering to young singles and, if a person like Faraday, older single males with a lot of disposable income. It is within walking distance of the train station and he has told her to meet him on the bridge over the Schuylkill River. She likes the bridge and has told him how much she enjoys watching the river flow past. Later, she will realize he never forgot anything she said about likes and dislikes and used that information to always present himself as if having the same preferences.

"We'll start our celebration on the bridge," he had said, for her break into the New York City art scene had come. They would catch a late train north, get some quick hours of sleep, and then sit down in the morning with the owners of one of the top galleries in the city.

He has a late opening for one of the other artists he represents and will be late and is that all right, given that your life is about to explode with recognition and work and riches and fame and things she could not even imagine. She is so thrilled with the news she doesn't even notice that he has not invited her to the opening and it will be later she learns there was no such happening.

She is on the south side of the bridge; the traffic coming from the station is funneled into the boulevard's single lane and there is little of it. The two lanes going towards the station have only a little more. Philadelphia has a night life but it is not near 30th Street Station.

Kildeer is in her favorite position, watching the water silently move away from her so smoothly it makes it seem the bridge is moving. Hollow rails of metal connect pillars of concrete blocks and she wedges herself against a pillar with her elbows on the top rails.

As the dream goes on, she remembers she has dreamed this dream before but it makes no difference. What is happening locks her into place as an observer. All she can do is anticipate and that does not make the dream any less of a nightmare.

Kildeere sees Faraday coming, easy to make out even in the distance. There are no other people on the bridge and he is just walking onto the bridge and then he is next to her.

He says what she knows he is going to say because she has dreamed this dream before but it is still a shock, for she has not heard him say these things before. He is slightly drunk but he knows what he is saying, what he is doing. He is claiming her on the eve of her coronation, a phrase he uses twice, and she has a debt to pay for all his work and knowledge and contacts. He wants her to know he expects to be paid with her body and her heart and her soul when they get to their hotel but, for now, he will settle with handling her in any way that pleases him.

She tries to cajole him, deflect him, promises to talk about this with him, tries to be reasonable. Her words, spoken six years before, were heard and rejected then; in the dream, her mouth moves but nothing is said.

He grabs her; she pushes him away with her sculptor's arms and he hits the sidewalk butt first, which enrages him. He meant her to be humiliated and she is an almost incoherent list of names that he spews at her like vomit and he gets to his feet. Her roller bag almost trips her as she tries to back down the sidewalk and her large, broad strapped leather tool bag, filling in as a handbag because she doesn't have one, is awkwardly in front of her and hampering her right arm as she tries to raise her hands to block him as he comes at her again.

Faraday is not groping, not pawing. His hands lunge at her neck and the violence of his grip is shocking. She tries to pry his hands away but her right arm is restrained by the bag's strap and weight and her left is not enough.

He drives her back into one of the concrete pillars and her breath is gone. She shoves her left arm in front of her face, forcing one of his hands to loosen its grip. Her right hand is tangled with the bag, has been driven into it when she tried to push him away.

And her hand finds, at the bottom of the leather tool bag, a hammer. It is Italian made with a soft iron head and only weighs a pound and a half but she grips the wooden handle as if it was a prayer. She pulls her hand back, out of the bag and behind her ear, and then she slams it forward towards the barely seen white blob of Faraday's face.

The hammer strikes his lower jaw, almost a glancing blow, but it is enough shock and pain to cause him to release her throat and stagger to one side, trying to get away from her, and his momentum carries him into and over the railing.

He does not fall into the indifferent river. One arm catches the railing and he cradles it under his arm while the other clumsily tries to grab on, his own feet and legs moving as if doing some slow, unsynchronized dance as they seek a hold on the bridge but seem to only succeed in pushing him away and interfering with the grasping arm.

She cannot hear him; her own heartbeat is all the sound in the world. But she knows he is cursing her even through a mouth spitting blood. There is no expression on his face except a terrible hate. She knows he will soon gain his coordination of legs and arms and he will save himself and then he will destroy her. Perhaps she knows that is what all his curses are about.

Kildeer turns and faces him. Then she raises the hammer, a hammer used for fine precision work, a hammer used for adding beauty to the world, and she brings it down on his forearm harder than she has ever struck stone or steel and the arm's bones shatter. Her second blow misses his arm and strikes the railing. Faraday starts to scream but chokes it off as he realizes he is falling. He reaches for the railing but the closest arm is useless and the other is raised to just graze the railing; she might have touched the reaching hand but she does not.

She looks at him, tries to see his face, but he falls backward into the dark and his face is gone from sight well before he strikes the broad, moving back of the river. She barely hears the splash. It is several minutes before she has the strength to throw the hammer into the river as far from her as she could.

Kildeere was not there when Faraday's body was found. She had picked up her tool bag, found her roller bag, and gone into the train station and taken the SEPTA train out to Chester County. Rain, which had threatened all evening, obscures whatever might have been seen from the train and continues well into the morning.

But the one imagined part of the dream is of the finding of the body. She sees it from over the shoulder of several uniformed Philadelphia police officers.

He lays on the muddy embankment and stares at her, his face locked forever in hate, and his dead mouth is moving, though he cannot speak because, of course, he is dead. She wonders why he doesn't realize that.

When she wakes up the next day, she does what she often does when The Dream visits her. After breakfast, she goes down into her basement, turns on the lights, and re-reads the clippings covering Faraday's death. Most of her time is spent staring at one picture that shows his probable path off the bridge. It is incorrect; they have it too close to the center of the bridge.

But where he did go over, where she used her hammer, she can see, she thinks, even in the grainy newspaper photograph, the top of the railing where the second hammer blow landed. A dent, maybe, or some missing paint. Some kind of mark. And she wonders if the police will ever notice it and wonder who might have an Italian-made, square, iron-headed, pound and a half, precision sculptor's hammer. For the past six years she has wondered.

Sometimes she sits in the basement until noon. But not today.

She fixed herself breakfast, which began with getting coffee brewing. While that happened, Kildeere scrambled eggs and peppers. She also hard boiled a pair of eggs; Raven's supply in the refrigerator was down to the last one, the result of periodic visits by Jackie Flinthill. She exchanged three hard boiled eggs still warm for the cold one in a plastic bowl in the refrigerator. Then she sat down and organized her plan for the day while eating breakfast.

When she finished, she did the dishes quickly – she hated having them stack up – and then walked out to the barn. Morning still had its cool from the night and she enjoyed the warmth of the coffee coming through the big mug she used. Raven was not around, or perhaps he, or she, was near, but was busy doing whatever the hell it was ravens did in the morning. As she opened the barn's side door, the sound of tires on county pavement caused Kildeere to glance toward the road. She felt a slight touch of relief when she saw it was not a police car; The Dream usually left her with some tension.

It was just an ordinary gray car whose driver – it looked like a man – was apparently apprehensive about the road and was taking it a little slower than the average. She paused, searching her memory. The gray car seemed familiar but she did not know why.

It turned at the intersection and soon was hidden by the trees. She stepped into the barn and went to work. A few minutes later, Kildeere's phone buzzed her.

Ellen Parker's phone had demanded attention before Kildeere's.

"Looks like your friend is ignoring you."

Ellen smiled and shook her head as she looked at her phone. Her editor had the damnedest sense of humor.

"I take it he hasn't called," she said as she waved at Blasingame. He had his shaving kit in one hand and was reading an eBook reader in the other.

"No. They, your friends from the FBI who have been kind enough to bring in another coffee maker, thought there might be an interval pattern and figured him to call late yesterday. He didn't. Did they talk about their idea with you?"

"Nope. Something else going on?"

"Out of left field. You know that cover story you used with the sculptor, Morrigan Kildeere? Well, Big Sam heard about it and he thinks it might be a place to start for an 'arts of Philadelphia' series."

"Really?"

"Don't panic. He doesn't want you to do it. We've got a couple of good arts reporters. What he wants to do is a follow-up with Kildeere and maybe save our people a trip out to the wilds of Chester County."

"Okay. Does he have particulars?"

"In the email I am forwarding as we speak. It's just a few things that go a little beyond the notes on her you have."

Ellen reached over and lifted the lid to her laptop – she preferred to read email on her laptop's bigger screen – while taking another sip of coffee and using her shoulder to hold the phone in place; such were her reporter's skills that she accomplished the task without spilling or dropping anything.

"I got it. I see he wants this done today before I come in." She grimaced. "Kildeere might be out of town or something."

"Leave her a message if she doesn't answer and then come on in. I've got some things for you to do if your life needs direction."

"Thanks, boss. I'll call her when normal people wake up and, if I have to schedule it later, I'll notify you."

"Silence indicates success. My life is becoming simpler every day."

"Wish I could say the same," Ellen said and her editor laughed and hung up.

"Are you going to be in there forever?" Ellen called loudly but got no response from Blasingame. She put the phone down, but not the coffee, and walked to the small downstairs bathroom he used. She could hear the shower running.

She went upstairs to the big bathroom, used it, and then dressed. She was surprised to see James Hardy sitting on her couch when she came downstairs. Blasingame was in the kitchen, leaning on the doorway, coffee cup in his left hand, right hand almost innocently hanging at his side, slightly holding open his windbreaker. She knew what the jacket hid. James stood up.

"I brought donuts," he said.

"Wonderful. How do you know where I live?"

"I didn't mean to alarm you," he said, raising his hands chest high. "I was up all night, thinking about our conversation." He paused, noticing the expression on her face. "About where you live. You have medical insurance. I work in the medical field. I looked you up. Sorry."

"You did that why?"

"I wanted to tell you that you got me started thinking." He paused, frowning. "I don't think I've been doing much of that. I wanted to tell you what I decided to do."

"Please, sit down. Or stand up and get a cup of coffee. I'm going to get some more. Tell me what you've decided." She walked into the kitchen and Blasingame moved to one side but never looked away from James.

"Do you have any milk?" James followed her. "I've been drinking coffee all night. If I have any more, I think my heart will disown me." He paused and looked around. "That was a joke."

"It's early yet. I look forward to what you say later. Milk is in the fridge and there are glasses in that cabinet. Did you really bring donuts?"

"Yes. Robert put them on a chair. Not all donuts. I didn't know what anyone would like, so it's a little of everything. The carrot cake muffins are unbelievable but that might be because I haven't eaten anything since lunch yesterday. No, I didn't have lunch. Breakfast."

Ellen poured herself a cup and used the jug of milk James had gotten out for it. She looked at Blasingame, who was slightly smiling.

"What has happened, James?" she asked.

"I quit my job," he said. "Went to work early and used the computer to write my resignation, sent email copies to everyone, and printed it out, signed it, and left it in my supervisor's mailbox. I managed to be very polite but it won't matter. I wasn't going to ask for a letter of recommendation from any of them anyway."

"How are you now that you've done that?"

"Well, I made a joke for the first time in maybe six months." He sipped his milk. "You and Robert were the first people to hear it."

"You were really out of practice, so we won't penalize you anything for the effort. What are you going to do now?"

"Look for work. I don't know what the market is like." He looked at Robert and then back at Ellen. "I remember that you said you'd keep your ears open if you heard anything. I think you were trying to encourage me to get out of there before I did something really bad. But I was stubborn, hoped somehow everything would get better. It didn't. I think I want you to hold onto those guns for a while."

"I don't have a good lock-up for them," Ellen said. "Robert will take care of them, if that's all right."

"Plenty of space in my gun safe," Robert said.

"That's fine," James said. "Listen, something I have to ask. Robert, are you some kind of security guard and you've been hired to protect Ellen?"

Blasingame said nothing but, smiling, raised his eyebrows and looked at Ellen.

"He's a friend," she said, "and, yes, he's watching my back."

"A professional, though, right?"

"Semi-pro," Blasingame said. "A little double-A, played outfield, nothing serious."

"Pretty serious," James said, smiling. "You looked at all the places someone might be carrying a gun when you let me in, put the donut box out of my reach and handled it yourself but only with your left hand, and I think I saw the edge of a holster on your right side."

"What do you make of that?" Blasingame asked. He seemed amused.

"Ellen's in some kind of trouble and it's probably something to do with that red ribbon killer." James looked back and forth between the two. "We forgot the donuts."

"Let's go into the living room and sit down," Ellen said. She led the way and paused to take something from the donut box. Then she sat down.

"James, I can't go into what's going on. There's probably no danger to me but it seems reasonable to have someone around."

"I understand." He nodded. "When this is all over, I'd really like to hear the whole story."

"Only if you bring more donuts."

"Deal."

"I've got to make a call," Ellen said, and went back into the kitchen.

"What kind of work do you do?" Blasingame asked James.

"I organize medical programs of all sizes, from identifying positions needed and personnel to fill them, to setting up the logistics and finding properly located buildings. Everything from major hospitals to 'doc-in-the-box' clinics in malls, from downtown to Third World projects. And the evaluative process used in monitoring and goal setting." He leaned back in the couch. "Most of what I've been doing for the past couple of years has been with developing cost-cutting schemes for health care outfits trying to increase their profit margins." He shrugged. "We're not making people better, just improving bottom lines."

"You said Third World?"

"Mostly advisory contracts, some from US Aid and like that. We helped a non-profit set up a pilot series of women's clinics in Afghanistan."

"How did that work out?"

"Taliban blew up one, some other nuts burned down two, but last I heard, the non-profit thought the model worked and was setting them up all over the place."

"They could use them. I'd like to talk more with you about that project."

"Who could use what?" Ellen asked as she came into the room. "I've got an appointment with Kildeere. She's standing by. She said she may have a young visitor, boy by the name of Jackie Flinthill, but she didn't mind if I didn't. I don't."

"Would you mind if we brought James with us?" Blasingame asked. "He's been involved in a project I think I know about and I'd like to hear more."

"Fine by me. Going to be crowded at Kildeere's, so don't eat all the donuts. You'll probably be bored waiting for me. James, you up for being interrogated by Robert?"

"Sure, fine, why not? I'll probably bore you with the details, but sure."

As James bent forward to take a donut, Ellen looked at Blasingame, who made a nod so subtle that she might not have noticed it if she had not been looking.

Well, if Robert thought it was a good idea for James to come along, then it probably was. Maybe he needed to be doing something with people.

After a couple of the donuts were taken care of, they decided everyone could use Ellen's car. She drove as Blasingame, sitting in back, asked Hardy about the Afghanistan project. Ellen was a little surprised with how much Blasingame knew about such projects and the medical non-profit Hardy had assisted.

Small world.

"Have a minute?" Elizabeth Chernov, a print-out in one hand, leaned into the doorway of Karen Deever's office.

Deevers looked up from her desk and waved in the general direction of one of the few chairs in her office.

"Good morning, have a seat," she said, reaching for a tall cup of tea, the only thing she trusted the Starbucks near her home to make. She took a sip and leaned back. "Hope you enjoyed your day off yesterday. What's up?"

"I saw Janowski and I were logged to take one of our tech people to talk to a Mrs. Flinthill."

"I saw that," Deevers said and her free hand slipped into a small, neat pile of paper. "Her boy..." She fell silent as she reviewed the print-out. "Her boy Jackie knew two of the victims, part of some online group. Right."

"Yes, I read his note in the log. Pretty similar to the interview you and I had with Paulie Tracer. He knew one of the boys through his online play as well."

"It is possible there is a connection," Deevers said. "We've had a good number of interviewed kids who knew some of the victims online as well as at school and other places. But maybe Jackie Flinthill's access to the group could turn into something." She took another sip. "What are you thinking?"

"The first boy we talked to, Paulie, he didn't tell us the name of the group he knew about. And Jackie, while he named the group he was a part of, he didn't say anything about taking something."

"The Something-Snakes, right." She looked at the paper again. "Maybe the victims Paulie knows aren't part of Jackie Flinthill's Sneaky Snakes."

"That might blow my idea that this is about something those kids took from Barnabas."

"It might."

"It occurred to me," Chernov said, "I might want to call the Traces before talking to the Flinthills, see if Paulie knows the name of the group."

"If it is the same group. Remember, we have had a lot of online references during our interviews, especially with all the kids from Barnabas we talked to. But, yes, give them a call. If it is a different group, then your idea might have just gone belly-up. If it is the same group of Sneaky Snakes, then we might be getting to something like motivation."

"Maybe more than that," Chernov said as she stood up. Deevers nodded.

"Make the call," the FBI Agent said. "If Paulie identifies the Snakes, then other boys in that group are targets and we will want to get to Jackie and his mother right now."

"On it," Chernov said as she left the office. Deevers picked up her office phone and hit the button for Agent Brown."

Quickly she explained the situation.

"We didn't ask Paulie for the name of the group," she said. Deevers was silent for a moment, listening. "Right. If the two boys are talking about the same small group of boys and something was stolen, then the killings are not random. And that means Jackie Flinthill is not just an information source. He may be the next victim." Deevers listened, nodding.

"Sergeant Chernov, Corporal Janowski, both of New Joyton, and Officer Ahmed from Downingtown, are scheduled to meet with Flinthill and his mother this afternoon. I'm going to contact the mother and request she and Jackie remain at home and then go with the three uniforms. We may need to set up a security arrangement. Yes, I'm glad we get a chance to get ahead of this bastard, too." She hung up her office phone as Chernov stepped into the doorway.

"Paulie was talking about Sneaky Snakes," she said. "It took them a minute to find him and ask but he remembers that as the name of the group."

"See if you can go to the Flinthill's now. Call the mother. They might be away, since they're not expecting you until later."

"Right," Chernov said. "Janowski is here and talking to Ahmed, so we are set to go."

"If she's home, don't delay. One of you can let me know you are rolling. I'll brief Agent Brown what we are up to. Check back in when you get there."

"Understood." Chernov disappeared and Deevers reached for her phone again.

Always careful, today he left his gray car at home and used the white minivan carrying his job supplies. He had seen Kildeere as he drove past the house but there was no boy.

Kildeere. It was a lovely name. Morrigan Kildeere. Chester County's web site took him to ChescoViews and a satellite view of her house and wooded lot, the property carefully outlined in yellow and the parcel number, highlighted with the acreage beneath, enabled him to find the name of the present owner. Lovely.

Probably too early in the day for the boy to be around. He turned at the intersection and went south. He was taking time from work but felt pressed to look for Flinthill. He pulled into the track behind the woods and shut his car down. Time to do some thinking.

In New Jersey, no one expected him to work late at night. The advantage in being a veterinary pharmaceutical representative was that his work was largely in his control. But he couldn't just stop visiting clinics. He opened his laptop and saw the places he had to contact. Nothing beat going face to face, shaking hands, socializing. He had an idea.

He called up a list of clinics and their purchasers. He nodded and smiled. A number of the clinics on his list for today had recently made orders and it was unlikely they would be giving him any additional business today. He picked up his phone and carefully entered a number.

Pausing several times to unnecessarily clear his throat, he talked to the clinic's receptionist.

"Got a little frog in my throat," he said. "But I wanted to check in with you to see if you needed any help and to see if all your orders have come in on time." He paused, nodding through the expressions of sympathy. "Well, thank you, I appreciate that. As long as you have what you need. But if anything comes up or the doctor would like to talk about anything, you've got my personal number, so please use it. In the meantime, I'm going to burrow into my house and not risk spreading this around any further." More sympathy and he smiled. It was too easy.

He repeated the same script several more times and had cleared his morning schedule. Only one clinic had a problem and he said he needed to

249

gather their invoices and would it be a problem if he came by sometime this afternoon? Of course, it wasn't. And they thanked him.

All right, that opened the day a bit. He could do a little cruising around before lunch. But not enough to attract attention. Just cover the Black woman's house. Maybe she was a baby-sitter or something. Weird, all that yard stuff. Maybe she was one of those hoarders who picked up junk from all over and brought it home.

But if the kid's bicycle was around, he was going to have to move. It would be too great an opportunity to lose. That's what he focused on, trying to ignore the growing need. He hoped the boy would be there. In his car's glove compartment was an old automatic pistol he had bought in a bar near Atlantic City. He didn't care what it might have done in the past. Very carefully he kept it clean and a pair of gloves – gloves in the glove compartment, it was too obvious – would ensure he left no fingerprints on it. If the boy was there, he'd kill the woman and take the boy. Some time tonight he would wrap the boy and put him in the ground, but only after getting the answers his mission required.

He nodded. It was a warm feeling to know that he was in control of everything.

Chernov let Janowski drive so she could brief him and Ahmed.

"Use our flashers," she said to Janowski. "We need to make some time." The big, midnight blue SUV lunged as he picked up the speed as they turned south out of Coatesville. "Use 82."

"On it," he said.

"I called his mother," Chernov said, pivoting in her seat so Ahmed could clearly hear her. "Virginia Flinthill, and explained that we had to talk to her and Jackie right now. She said Jackie had just left on his bicycle to visit Morrigan Kildeere."

"The artist you two talked to?"

"Good memory. Yes. Virginia Flinthill said she would call Kildeere and have her send Jackie home. He'll probably be waiting for us by the time we get there."

Ahmed nodded; that was good news.

"We found the Sneaky Snake website," Ahmed said. "My partner, he's been with the task force since it was formed, is going through it, but it's very large. Multiple pages, including a bunch with member stuff."

"Names and photos?"

"We should be so lucky. No, only online names. But a few apparently real photos. Robinson, that's my partner, he's trying to match them to people like Jackie Flinthill."

"They have their own web site? Isn't that expensive?" Janowski asked as he slowed, but didn't stop, at an intersection.

"Not really. Only a couple hundred a year. It looks like there are some adults involved. I'm guessing they're the founders and they carry the expenses."

"Adults? Sarge, could one of them…?"

"Possible. Right now, though, we think it is a local man." She turned to Ahmed. "Are you up on this?"

"The Snakes stole something from St. Barnabas and someone is after them for it," he said, nodding. "I think Janowski might have something, though. I can't think of anything they might have stolen that would be worth killing kids for."

"You might be right as to motive. I didn't know the Snakes had adults. But why would one of the males in that group, if he was a predator, wait until now? We're going to want to find out if any of the adult males are near this area." Chernov frowned. "The business of what they took has had us questioning the theory. A predator in the Snakes, yeah, that's another possibility. First thing we have to do is make sure Jackie is safe and then we can start digging deeper."

Chernov leaned back in her seat. Giving up on a theory was common in police work. It took discipline to follow the evidence and she had to admit they had none suggesting anything the Snakes grabbed in their real-world raid was a motive for murder. And predators prowled the internet.

First things first. Secure Jackie. Get the message data off his computer and get into the Snakes' website. Then grind everything down and see where it took them. It would take time but they had some things to work with and that was always good news.

Bobby Flynn pushed himself away from his desk and frowned, not sure what to do. A landscaping outfit scheduled to work in the area around the sports fields had some questions and Flynn didn't have the answers. George Mayfair, his boss, usually was the man to go to for answers but he was out today.

George had been out a lot recently. Sometimes he came in for a couple of hours, sometimes he didn't come in at all. He didn't look good when he was at his desk. Exhausted, maybe a little jumpy, sometimes just sitting and staring into space. Flynn thought George was dealing with something pretty serious and didn't want to disturb him at home.

The only other person in the administrative section was an elderly secretary, Helen Smaltz, and technically she worked for George and Flynn, so he felt foolish about asking her about border widths around the soccer fields, things he was supposed to do since he had written, probably written, the damned contract.

If I was a collection of survey notes, where would I hide? Flynn had no answer to his question. He stood up and walked over to George's desk. It was locked tight, as Flynn expected. Sometime in the recent past, George had begun to be compulsive about locking his desk; as they got ready to go home, he had seen George check that every drawer was secure three and sometimes four times.

Flynn broke down and asked Helen if she knew where George might have his notes about landscaping around the sports fields but she didn't. She didn't think they would be in his computer, since "George always took notes by hand rather than wasting time hunting and pecking on a keyboard." She suggested Flynn check the ancient metal file cabinets that lined a wall.

The things probably had been bought before Flynn had been born. All had had their locks removed, a reasonable move since no keys still existed for them. When Flynn had been hired, there were still paper folders in them holding records of various kinds going back to the middle of WW II. Over the years, those files had been trashed, burned, or recycled, depending on the year, to make room for copies of print-outs of relatively recent business.

An hour of pushing and pulling drawers resulted in nothing. Flynn shook his head; this was not a good way to start the day.

"Have you checked the TV closet?" Helen asked, as her 60-plus year-old fingers raced over her computer keyboard. "I saw him working in it some time ago, right after that big league thing we had. Remember?"

The "TV closet" was what had once been a janitor's closet and now served as the center for their security camera monitors. No one used it for much else as it tended to be pretty stuffy. Flynn walked over and opened the closet door.

A large utility table almost filled the narrow space, leaving barely enough room to move a chair. A bank of monitors lined the edge of the table, all controlled by a small and old laptop. It was asleep, its lid closed. An external broadband modem, about the size of a small paperback, connected to it. It had a single blue light providing the only way to tell it was alive.

Flynn flipped on the lights and sat in the chair. He saw a couple of sheets of paper and his hopes rose. They turned out to be numbers, maybe dates, times, but were unlabeled, though in George's handwriting. He pushed them to one side, shaking his head.

The monitors were black and white, though Flynn remembered from a briefing that the video was recorded in color. While the laptop's SD card stored a copy, all the imagery was compressed, encrypted, and sent to the cloud owned by the security outfit that installed the surveillance system. He looked at them for a while but all they showed was school children coming and going. And it didn't look any of those kids knew where the hell he could find information on the landscaping issues of ball fields.

Flynn rose, picking up the sheets of paper, meaning to throw them out. As he reached for the light switch, he looked closely at the two sheets to make sure he wasn't about to dispose of something that would later turn out to be important.

George had neat penmanship, you had to give him that. His records were always meticulous. There was the date, same date as the baseball and soccer league events St. Barnabas had supported by providing its ball fields. Good PR and they made a few dollars with t-shirt and hotdog sales. Numbers formed a pair of columns under the date; the second page was blank, empty. Apparently, whatever George was working on, he had resolved it using only one sheet of paper. Hooray for George.

The numbers were, Flynn realized, times using a 24-hour format. Date and time. Of course, date and time coding for the video surveillance system. George had looked at several brief periods and then his last sample, the fifth one, he had looked at for twelve minutes and twenty-seven seconds.

Curiosity won, outweighing landscaping contracts easily. He sat down and pulled the laptop closer. The small laptop was dedicated to handling the security cameras and storing their footage on the SD card. He quickly called up the date and times from the card's storage. The first four were all from the same camera, the one in the administration office. There wasn't much to see and George had not spent more than a minute or so on each.

The fifth time segment wasn't there. He tried the start time; it immediately leaped ahead to a time just beyond that on the paper. The same thing happened when he asked for times between the start and end. Flynn frowned. This was odd. The only way the recorded video was removed from the SD card was when it ran out of space from new recordings and the fifth part was too recent for that to have happened. Yes, a timed segment, even several days, could be deliberately erased, but the procedure was elaborate to prevent accidents.

George was no friend of computers and Flynn knew the older man never checked the security video system, except this one time. He probably used the manual in the desk drawer, carefully following it step by step. But why? Why erase twelve minutes and twenty-seven seconds of imagery?

Clearing it off the hard drive didn't get rid of it. After all, it all went to the security company's cloud.

Did George remember that?

Flynn clicked the icon for security software; two more clicks and he looked at the icon for the cloud storage. He clicked it and a window opened. Six-hour long segments, labeled by date and time, formed a long list in a new window. He found the one encompassing whatever it was George was interested in and clicked it.

A new window opened. Did he want to download all six hours or did he want to specify a time to view or did he want to cancel? He clicked the second option and yet another window opened, this one asking him to specify a start time (Use 24-HR Time Please). He did and clicked Enter. Nothing happened and he wondered what he had done wrong. Then he remembered that the recording was compressed and encrypted and it might take some time to send it to him…

Then a new window opened. It was the administration office. For a moment, Flynn saw nothing as a timer in the lower right corner spun the time in seconds. Then he saw boys.

There was no sound. They came into the office, clearly intent on fooling around. Some were laughing. Others appeared to urge the laughers to hold it down. One or two looked at peoples' desks; one of them picked up a folder on Flynn's desk. Flynn stopped the playback, freezing the picture, his tongue between his pressed lips. Was that…?

He found the control to expand the picture and reposition the center of the viewing area. He centered on the boy who had the folder. Flynn recognized him. Michael Jones. One of the St. Barnabas boys killed by the red ribbon killer. It was not the full-face, smiling picture used by the FBI in their questioning sessions but it was Jones.

Flynn covered his mouth with his hand, his eyes wide. Slowly returned the picture to its normal size. Then he let it run. Some of the other boys he thought he recognized. Then he saw another.

Philip Lang.

The boy had left Saint Barnabas. Something had happened; Flynn thought it might have been a disciplinary issue. But now he was back. What was this about?

The images kept moving. One of the boys sat down in George's chair and Flynn thought the old man would have had a stroke if he had known...

He had known. But what was there to know? Philip Lang and some friends found their way in the administration office? All right, but it wasn't a big deal.

Then it was.

The boy in the chair, who looked familiar but Flynn could not come up with his name, idly pulled at the desk's drawers. Methodically, while the other boys walked around in the background or tossed a soccer ball back and forth, he tried to open all the drawers on the right. None moved; George always locked everything. Then he tried the middle drawer and had no success. Then he tried the drawer on the left and it slid out smoothly, surprising the boy.

The kid reached in, looking like he was pushing things around. Flynn shook his head. George would know someone had been in his desk. The kid paused and then brought out his hand. He clenched something in it and he held it up for the others to see.

They gathered around him and he stood up, his back to the camera, apparently to show it to them. They were all smiling, one was laughing. Then they all exchanged high fives. The boy closed the drawer and they all ran, smiling and laughing, out of the office.

Then the office was empty and the clock continued to run.

Flynn sat back in the chair and stared at the video that now showed nothing. Then he carefully shut everything down, until the solitary icon of the security software remained. He looked around, stood up, turned off the light, and left the small room.

He walked to his desk and sat down, folding his hands together on his desk. Somewhere in the background he heard Helen's fingers tapping quickly in the silence. Flynn looked at George's desk for a moment. He slowly shook his head and took out his wallet.

He quickly found what he was looking for. He laid the small card in front of him and picked up his office phone, paused, hung it up, and took out his personal phone. He tapped in the number. He did not have to wait long.

"Special Agent Karen Deevers, please," he said. "Yes, it's Bob Flynn at Saint Barnabas. Tell her I believe I have information on the murdered boys. No, all of them. Yes, I'll wait."

Chapter 28: Last hand

It was like a riffled deck of cards, one laying on the other, a sequence that seemed to be fast, almost violent, and, looking back, impossible to vary without entirely different outcomes.

It is the morning in which Morrigan Kildeere awakened from The Dream, spent some time looking at her files on the death of John Faraday, and then had breakfast. As she finished and reached for her phone, Corporal Michael Janowski drove Sergeant Elizabeth Chernov and Officer Jacob Ahmed, lights flashing, to the Flinthill residence.

Kildeere's call was from Ellen Parker to set up an appointment for an interview that morning. She wasn't bothered by Jackie being a witness and Kildeere decided dodging an interview might not be a good idea.

The interview request granted, Ellen, accompanied by Robert Blasingame and an eager for company James Hardy, drove towards Kildeere's home. For James, the morning was a continuation of the dark, raining evening in which he decided not to kill every supervisor at his place of employment. He carried a shallow box of donuts and put them on the seat beside him; Blasingame carried at least one handgun. Blasingame talked with Hardy about humanitarian services for women in Afghanistan.

Bobby Flynn told Special Agent Karen Deevers he thought he saw the images of dead boys, shadows and light, on digital video stored in the cloud and there was nothing of the metaphor about the horror sweeping through him. Deevers asked for a copy even as she sent an agent to get a search warrant useful in establishing a chain of evidence for the other two agents she sent to Saint Barnabas.

The next card was very private, not seen at that moment by the other cards snapping together. George Mayfair, unable to sleep the previous night, unable to discard the growing belief his effort to protect his Church had resulted in unleashing Satan's wrath on children, finished a very long letter to his family. He emailed it to all of them, his two children pursuing careers in Arizona and North Carolina, his estranged wife who never divorced him because she adhered deeply to Catholic beliefs, his younger brother teaching in a Catholic university in Cleveland, and his youngest sibling, a sister close to retirement from the Air Force. Before the day was out, all would find their hearts torn apart. He did not think to make a call to the killer of children and, perhaps, call him off of his next target; as usual, George mostly was concerned with his own problems. He went into his basement, accompanied only by his favorite pistol. He put the muzzle to his temple and killed himself. It would occur to more than one member of his family that his sins were concluded by his committing suicide, the worst sin, but George was spared that last realization.

The killer drove his white minivan up to the intersection with the road in front of Kildeere's home. His impatience with waiting on the track bordering the woods was odd. He prided himself on his patience, understanding the virtue helped keep him safe. Once moving, though, he relaxed. He stopped at the intersection and, almost idly, he looked to his right. In the far distance, coming slowly, perhaps enjoying pedaling in the late morning, he saw Jackie Flinthill.

He made his decision quickly and turned away from Jackie and, almost immediately, turned into Kildeere's driveway. He got out of the van quietly, careful not to close the driver's door. In his sport coat pocket, he had a syringe and a small bottle of xylazine. In his gloved hand, he had an old .38-pistol he believed untraceable. He walked slowly to the barn, found the sliding door already open just enough to squeeze through. Old barn, heavy construction; he nodded. It would muffle a gunshot. He walked across the studio to the door facing the house and waited. He smiled and crouched in the shadows; Kildeere had stepped out onto the side porch. Everything was perfect.

Kildeere paused, stuffing a black bandana into her back pocket so she could take her second call of the morning. She listened to Jackie's mother ask her to tell Jackie to turn around and return home. It was very important, she explained.

"I can drive him back," Kildeere said.

"I don't want to inconvenience you. And his bike…"

"It will fit in the back, no problem."

"All right, that would be great," Ginny Flinthill said and saved Kildeere's life.

They hung up and Kildeere looked up as a shadow passed over her. It was Raven, unusually early.

"Nothing for you, come back after lunch," she said, and, instead of going into her studio and encountering an already planned gunshot, she headed for her hatchback to make sure there was enough room in the back for Jackie's bicycle.

He heard her side of the conversation and realized he was out of position as her footsteps went towards the cars. He quickly walked to the sliding door facing the driveway.

Kildeere was thinking about Jackie. His mother always called before he came by, making sure it was all right with her, perhaps sensing Kildeere's desire to be alone. But she never said no. The little White boy always brought his drone and kept himself busy flying it around and over her house and barn while she worked.

He had questions about art, about shaping stone, about cutting and welding metal. She gave him a sheet of metal and some sheers that were too big for him. He used them anyway, cutting bits of metal while making a mobile. It took him little time to grasp the principles of balance he needed and, perhaps oddly for a boy his age, already had the patience to trim and shave the ovals of metal. Kildeere, pausing with her own work to slip into the role of teacher, found she enjoyed it. Jackie listened and did not forget what he was told. He seemed to know when to let her work.

Coming through the fence gate, she saw the white minivan, parked as far forward and to one side as it could be, invisible until she reached the gate. What the hell? She opened it and walked forward. She did not recognize the van and wondered...

He stepped out of the barn and struck her on the side of the head with his pistol. Kildeere dropped, folding in on herself, and did not immediately die because he did not wish to risk the sound of an outdoor gunshot.

Also, it felt good to have a woman in his power again. He missed that. Well, soon, now.

He thought about dragging her into the barn and finishing her but he looked up and saw Jackie approaching the intersection. As he crouched, he felt her jeans' pockets and pulled out her cell phone. He dropped it on the ground and looked at the Black woman.

"Maybe later."

He waited for Jackie to get closer. He heard the boy yell something but wasn't sure what it was.

259

"Good morning, Raven," Jackie called as he leaned his bike against the front fence. He didn't seem to notice the white minivan.

Raven sat on the front porch roof and looked at Jackie and then at the front of the barn. It looked back at Jackie as if expecting a response but the boy just kept coming. It opened its beak and called in a way Jackie had never heard before, a shrill cry that turned into a growling gurgle that seemed dangerous.

Jackie stopped, his breathing slowing down. He had figured out that Ms. Kildeere was not a witch, but ravens... Ravens ran with wolves, he had read, and there was something about them, even about Raven, that might make them as strange as any witch or wizard.

Raven called again, this time with a voice that was deep and raspy, and Jackie stepped forward.

Then he heard someone calling him, a man, near the cars in the driveway, calling for help.

"There's a woman down," the man called, "I need your help."

And Jackie, believing it to be Ms. Kildeere, one of his few friends still alive, ran to do whatever he could.

...Wondered why she was on her face on the driveway. Then Kildeere felt the pain on the side of her head. She reached up and felt the wound just above her hairline. Kildeere got to her knees and looked at her hand. It was smeared with blood and there was blood on the ground.

She got to her feet, swaying slightly, and looked around. There was nothing to see, no explanation of how she had been injured. She looked toward the intersection and saw the back of a white minivan disappear behind the trees as it went south.

Kildeere, feeling blood slowly crawl down the side of her head, walked to her studio's first aid kid and clumsily opened it. As she tore open a gauze pad and pressed it against her head, she remembered the white minivan in her driveway. Still holding the pad against her head, she went to the barn door. The minivan was gone. She looked back at the intersection, which was empty, and then noticed the bicycle.

Jackie.

Somewhere Raven was shouting at her to get moving. At least, that's what she thought it was saying.

She reached for her cell phone, couldn't find it, and then saw it crushed in the driveway. She picked it up anyway but it was dead. She dropped the bloody pad and phone, biting her lower lip, trying to think through the cloud of pain in her brain. Kildeere forced herself to organize her thoughts.

She could go back into the barn and get another pad. There wasn't enough time. Did Raven say that or was that her? And why wasn't there enough time?

Someone had Jackie.

The bandana. It was still in her back pocket and she slipped it around her head, pulling it tight even as she walked to her hatchback.

Raven was still calling at her and she raised her left hand in a small wave.

"Let me be, I got this," she said, but Raven, now calling in a rhythmic fashion, seemed intent on ordering her onward.

Keys. Were on her keyring on her belt. She opened the car door and cleared an old leather tool bag off the driver's seat by tossing it into the passenger footwell. Kildeere sat behind the steering wheel and was pleased to see her hands move in an accustomed, automatic manner as she started the car; it was like she was an observer of her body.

In a moment, the seatbelt warning bell gently chiding her, she was backing out of the driveway. She turned at the intersection, in the direction of the white van, and pushed the gas pedal down as far as she dared. The only long-range thinking she was doing was solving the problem of how to get her seatbelt fastened as her speed went well above the legal limit for a back-country Pennsylvania road.

"Is that Kildeere's car?" Ellen asked as she approached Kildeere's house. She saw the hatchback disappear south from the intersection as she drove through it.

"I missed it," Blasingame said, turning back from his conversation with James. "It's not in her driveway."

Ellen pressed her lips together and accelerated slightly only to have to slow down as she nosed into the driveway.

"She's gone," she said.

"Hold on," Blasingame said and was out of the car and ran to the barn to look in. He turned, shook his head, and then crouched on the drive. He picked up a shattered phone and then touched the ground with his fingertips. He ran back to the car.

"Go back to the intersection," he said as he buckled his seat belt. He held up a cell phone, its face shattered. "I found this and there is fresh blood in the driveway. And that looks like a boy's bicycle against the fence."

"The blood, how fresh?" asked Ellen.

"No more than ten or twenty minutes. Could be a lot less."

"How do you know that?" James asked, holding the back of Blasingame's seat as Ellen turned sharply at the intersection.

"Mis-spent youth," Blasingame said.

"He's spent time around people who bleed."

"That and a class on tracking. The instructor had a lot to say about blood trails."

"No shit," James said.

"I don't see anything," Ellen said, looking ahead. She floored the gas pedal and her Honda whined in mild protest.

"She could be in pursuit and getting ahead of us." He turned in his seat. "James, we go through any intersection, you look left, I'll look right. You see a blue hatchback heading away from us, yell."

"Got it."

"While you're waiting," Ellen said, concentrating, "call the police. Use my phone. It's set to speed dial to Beth Chernov and Karen Deevers."

Blasingame said nothing but picked up Ellen's small purse and took out her phone.

"Hello, Agent Deevers," he said and James' eyes went wide.

Chernov cut their emergency lights as they approached the Flinthill house. No sense in attracting a crowd. Still, their tires chirped as they came to a halt. Chernov already was unbuckled and she was first out of the car. She half ran up to the front door which opened as she arrived.

"Is Jackie back?"

The question was answered by Ginny Flinthill's shake of her head and sudden terror in her eyes. Chernov turned, about to issue orders, when her phone buzzed her. She took it out and pressed against her head.

"Chernov."

"Deevers here. Have Ahmed stay there and have him call you and us if Jackie comes back."

If.

"What do you want…?"

"You and Janowski proceed to Kildeere's house. We were called by Robert Blasingame; he's with Ellen Parker. He said Kildeere is not there, nor is Jackie, but Kildeere told Parker she was expecting him. They saw

262

what might be Kildeere's car, a blue Honda hatchback, going south through the intersection just before the house. They are trying to find it. They found what might be Kildeere's phone, smashed and nonfunctional, on the driveway, and fresh blood." She paused.

"I understand," Chernov said, trying to keep her voice calm in front of Ginny Flinthill.

"If possible, catch up with Ellen and take over the pursuit. We believe the perpetrator has Jackie and Kildeere is following him. I am mobilizing people here. Go. Stay in contact."

"Understood. We're moving now." Chernov put her phone away. "Ahmed, you are to stay here. Ms. Flinthill, if it is all right, I'd like you to show Officer Ahmed your son's computer. Officer Janowski and I are going to see if we can find him."

Ginny Flinthill could only stand and nod her head, tears forming in her eyes. Ahmed wanted to ask questions but saw there was no time and he desperately wanted to know why there was no time.

"Call base if you find anything," Chernov said over her shoulder to Ahmed. She and Janowski were running before they were halfway down the yard.

As they snapped their restraints into place, Chernov explained what they were doing and were the last in a parade of vehicles that might, or might not, be in pursuit of the killer of boys.

Janowski said nothing. He remembered Kildeere's basement and her collection of articles on John Faraday. Somehow, the death of Faraday and what was going on now, whatever was going on, were connected, and he wondered if she was on the side of the angels or something darker. As they got onto the road heading to Kildeere's, he decided it didn't matter. Chernov was just the person he wanted to be with no matter how dark things got and he promised himself he'd cover her back no matter what they encountered.

He had taken Jackie quickly; his moves were well thought out and, by the time he met Jackie, practiced. The boy called out but there was no one to hear him and the xylazine had its intended effect. Jackie collapsed and he carried him to the van. He used plastic zip lines to bind his ankles and wrists behind him. and a quick piece of tape over his mouth, leaving an easily grabbed tab if he needed to remove it in case the boy vomited. None of the other boys ever had but you never knew about animal tranquilizer effects on humans. He stepped in, slammed the sliding door shut behind him, and quickly backed the van down the driveway.

As he approached the intersection, he saw a car coming from the development. He turned and picked up his speed. He looked behind him and saw the car go through the intersection and nodded. They weren't looking for him. Probably just going to Route 10. He kept his speed up; he wasn't concerned with any pursuit but he was eager to get to work.

He was about to win it all; most importantly, as his, well, not exactly "friend," but perhaps colleague was the right word. He nodded. As his colleague George Mayfair told him, he was winning God's gratitude. He smiled. Mayfair insisted someday it would be very important. He laughed and shook his head. Old George was such an idiot, so scared of what might happen if dead Father Hemley's trip guide for pederasts ever appeared in public view, so afraid of God.

He chuckled. He would return it to Old George – after all, he had given his word – but maybe he would keep an electronic copy. And then, just when George thought the danger was past because he had destroyed the thumb drive, he might just pass it on to that newspaper bitch, Ellen Parker. She would love that.

Of course, he would have killed Old George before that. Can't leave loose ends around. And maybe the Parker woman, too, but only after she wrote her story. Do her because, according to what he had read, she had managed to get out of peoples' crosshairs in the past and taking her down would be an achievement. Yes, like climbing Everest after other climbers had failed. Score one for the team.

He glanced in his rearview mirror and saw a car far in the distance. He did not recognize it but he added a little more speed. The car did not get any closer and seemed to lose ground. Good. Probably not following him.

He thought about taking a few turns, just to see if the car followed, but side roads were few and, besides, he was getting close to home and fun with Jackie. After all, he thought while smiling, didn't he have God on his side?

He kept going.

The white minivan became smaller. Kildeere resisted the urge to go faster. She had kept the hatchback at its maximum speed until the van came into sight and then reduced her speed, trying to maintain her distance. Now the road was straight and seemed to go forever. She could give it a little distance.

And then what? She had no phone, no way of calling for help. She had nothing. Then she saw the minivan slow down and turn east. Turn or not? If he saw her, what would happen? Where was he going?

She knew these roads. Long drives to clear her head, take a break, see the spring growth, the fall leaf colors, she had been on these roads. What was down the road he was on now?

Nothing. It ran straight, maybe for a mile, and then descended in a curvy path to follow a good-sized creek. When the road turned north, there would be a T-intersection. East would go to one of the main north-south roads. West hit a single-land bridge and then followed the creek while working northwest. Nothing in that direction except a few widely separated small houses on hillsides overlooking the water. The creek narrowed…

Kildeere shook her head as she approached the side road. There was only one thing to do.

"I still don't see her," Ellen said, keeping her voice controlled.

"Has to be in front of us," Blasingame said calmly.

"There she is," Ellen replied. "I see her."

"I don't see anyone in front of her."

"Me, neither. Let's not run up her back until we know what's going on."

"Hold on, she's going behind those trees."

"I lost her." Ellen shook her head. She licked her lips. "I'm going to speed up until we can see her again."

No one said anything as the hatchback hurried down the road. The trees were on the left, a dense line that followed the road on both sides as it made a gradual turn first left and then, only slightly more tightly, to the right.

"Anyone see her?"

"No." Blasingame looked down at the map in his lap. "There's a turn to the left in a mile and a half and then no cross roads for two miles further south."

"Got it."

"I think," he said slowly, "if she went straight, we would see her."

"I'm not sure," Ellen said. "The left road, how far does it go straight?"

"About a mile."

"All right. We're turning. Hold on, we might be going a little fast at the intersection."

"Holy shit," James said as they hit the turn. "Sorry," came as they survived it. "I didn't think you could do that turn in this car."

"A cop taught me how to do that," Ellen said, shaking her head. "I wasn't sure the wheels would stay on. I'll have to tell her about it."

"I think," James said as he looked behind them, "you lost a hubcap."

"I'll buy you a new set," Blasingame said.

"I'll go halfies with you," James said, grinning.

"I don't see anything in front of us."

"Couple of houses on either side. I'm looking right, James go left."

"Got it."

"Road drops ahead and follows a creek," Blasingame added, as he studied a small house and barn they raced past.

"I think I know it," Ellen said. "Lots of curves, visibility is going to be short. Houses are scattered, a few on long lanes that might hide any cars parked there."

The white minivan vanished. Kildeere ignored a spasm of panic. As she drove towards the creek, she quickly looked at the houses she encountered on either side. Even if the van had hidden in one of the barns, there was not time for whoever it was to close the doors and hide it.

Who was it? The question dropped on her. She felt like she was operating on reflexes, not really understanding what had swept her up, not really thinking things through.

Was the white minivan really being driven by the man killing those boys? What evidence did she have? Maybe Jackie had wandered off, looking for his damned drone again.

Her foot very slightly rose from the gas pedal.

Maybe the van was driven by someone Jackie knew and they were just going for a pleasant drive in the country. Maybe she was making a mistake.

Maybe she was going to be the little Black dot on a microscope slide that every cop in a hundred miles was going to focus on and, interested in her once more, this time not miss the clue left on the bridge. And then they would have her.

Her foot felt like it had lost all sensation; she could not tell if it was pushing hard on the pedal or it was floating away.

The bridge.

John Faraday had tried to kill her. She had known terror, the horror of being alone while madness destroyed her world.

Was that what that little White boy was feeling?

For the first time in six years, Morrigan Kildeere wanted to pray. But God wouldn't listen to her. She was a murderer. God wouldn't listen. Her mother said God heard every prayer but, sometimes, the answer was, "No." She shook her head. That was not a helpful memory to spring to mind at the moments. He probably wasn't expecting any calls from her anyway.

If You are listening, then know this. Her lips tightened as the words formed in her aching head. I am going to save Jackie Flinthill and if You don't want to lend a hand, that's fine, I'll do it anyway. But I'd appreciate the help.

Kildeere smiled a little as her foot pushed hard on the pedal.

She covered the last quarter mile before the road began its descent and turned abruptly to the right, but she anticipated the turn.

Black woman to the rescue, huh? She had no answer to the question. And what are you planning on doing once you catch up to this monster, if it is who you think it is? Gonna throw your tool bag at him, your spare tire? Call him names?

If I see where he's stopped, then I'll keep on going to the next house and ask to use their phone. And maybe the house after that. She shook her head. Whatever it took.

The twisting road matched the creek turn for turn and trees reached overhead, putting both road and creek in shadow. Kildeere drove as fast as she dared, cutting the curves, hugging the turns, fighting off the growing fear the van was getting further and further away.

She came up on the intersection sooner than she thought she would and slid to a halt. Which way? Kildeere pulled hard on the steering wheel and almost immediately was crossing the single-lane bridge. As she drove off it, the road immediately followed the creek again.

She passed a house perched high on her left but there was no sign of the white minivan. The creek was to her right, down a steep but short bank, and was showing rocks piercing its surface. It was getting narrower.

Another house on the left. A trailer home, its short driveway blocked by a pickup with a green cap with ladders neatly secured to its roof. No room for a white minivan.

A driveway to the right, crossing the creek with a cement culvert. The house, a dark brown that almost hid it in the trees, lay on a broad swath of flat land as the hills back away from the creek. An attached garage was open. No minivan.

The trees ended and suddenly the creek and road were flooded with sunlight. Kildeere saw ahead, framed by wild blackberry bushes, another small culvert carrying a dirt and gravel driveway going fifty yards away from the creek. A rust-red, two-story house lay at the end of the drive.

267

Dust hovered over the driveway and Kildeere stopped, her plan to drive on and find a phone immediately dropped as her eyes saw the rear of a white minivan almost hidden by the house.

At the mouth of the driveway, she parked next to an old, black mailbox precariously clinging to a wooden four by four sagging slightly to one side, losing its fight with gravity. She looked for the van but the angle was bad and the bushes hid most of what she had seen.

Even as she wondered what she was going to do, Kildeere grabbed her old leather tool bag and got out of her car. Crouching, she moved to the edge of the bushes and looked down the driveway. Now she could see the van's rear.

She tried to reason what to do. Let's say he took Jackie inside. He's busy with the boy, not looking out his front window. Now's the time. Kildeere came out from behind the bushes, took a breath, and then jogged down the driveway. Her feet, clad in her heavy work boots, kicked up small puffs of dust but she didn't notice. She watched the house, looking for any sign of life, waiting for something to happen, something that might bring pain and death to her and Jackie. She kept running.

"We took the side road," Blasingame's voice came from Chernov's phone.

"We thought you did," Chernov replied and spoke to Janowski. "You were right, they turned left."

"Be there in a second," he replied. Chernov glanced at the SUV's GPS and then studied the map in her lap.

"How far down that road are you?" Chernov asked.

"Just starting down to the creek."

"We're a couple of miles behind you."

"You probably already know but Kildeere has a blue Honda hatchback. We've looked at the few houses near the road but haven't seen it."

"Yes, we have that." Chernov relayed the information to Janowski as they slowed for the turn onto the side road.

"We'll keep our eyes open anyway," he said.

For a moment, no one said anything.

"We're at the creek and now are running alongside it. I think there's an intersection ahead of us."

"Stand by," Chernov said. She reached down for the microphone.

"Dispatch, One-Seven update," she said.

"One-Seven, be advised we are tracking you. We have Sam Nine-Three approaching from the east on Glenrose."

"Roger that. We will turn left, west, at the intersection with Glenrose Road. Please relay."

"Will do, One-Seven." She put the microphone down as Janowski grinned.

"Hurrah for the deputies, he said. "Cowboys.""

"Blasingame, when you come to the T-intersection, turn left onto West Glenrose Road. Sheriff's Deputy is coming from the east. They have not seen Kildeere's vehicle yet."

"Understood. Do we have other units converging?"

"Probably, but transmissions are not encrypted, so the task force dispatcher isn't saying more than he has to." She paused. "Sam Nine-Three is the county Sheriff's Service."

"And they have one possibility closed off. Got it. We'll be turning west, toward that bridge I think I see."

"We'll follow. Any point in asking you to wait for us?"

"Probably not."

"All right. Stay sharp. He isn't taking these back roads because he has nothing better to do. He's got some kind of hidey hole and I don't think it is far away."

"Ellen says she agrees, if you didn't catch that."

"I didn't. Don't go in without backup."

"Absolutely," Blasingame said. Chernov did not know what he meant and decided not to ask.

The front of the brick-red house had a roofed porch with a few old chairs and a child's ancient rocking horse. Between faded and peeling paint and accumulated grime, Kildeere doubted any child had ridden it since before she was born. Moving as quietly as she could, she moved around the house, heading for the minivan. She paused to look through the ground floor windows but curtains kept her from seeing anything.

Well, if I can't see him, then he can't see me. It seemed like a thin straw to grasp.

When she got to the minivan, she moved over to the side away from house. Other than the sliding door being open and wire racks holding steel drawers lining one side of the van's interior, nothing appeared sinister. The drawers were filled with various brochures, pens, and advertising giveaways, like baseball caps with embroidered veterinarian and pharmaceutical emblems. He was a veterinarian? She shook her head. No, probably someone who supplied drugs to vets.

Behind the driver's seat was a steel box secured to the floor. It was locked and Kildeere thought it was probably used for drug samples. Then she saw the small, plastic-capped bottle. She reached in and picked it up.

It was a bottle for an injectable medication. There was still liquid in it. She looked at the house. Had he used something on Jackie? Wasn't there something in the news about the boys being drugged? She shoved the bottle into her jeans pocket. She had to get into the house.

Cautiously she approached the back door. It was protected by a storm door and she very carefully opened it. Then she pressed against the door, listening, but there was nothing.

Kildeere looked down at her tool bag. Why was she still dragging this thing around? She crouched and put it to one side of the door. She started to get up but stopped. She flipped up the cover and felt inside. It would have been nice to find a bayonet or an assault rifle but there were only small chisels for fine work, a Dremel tool with a box of attachments, and a few hammers, most relatively small.

Her hand found the head of the biggest hammer in the bag. It was only a two-pound, medium-sized Trow and Holden stone hammer, its head blunt on one side, wedged like an axe on the other. The last time she used it she had managed, in spite of its fiberglass safety handle, to slip and cut herself with it.

She took it only because it seemed to be all she had, but she knew it was almost useless. Then she tried the back door. It was not locked and swung open without any creaks. She crouched in the kitchen. A refrigerator hummed to life.

Suddenly, Kildeere heard music coming from the front of the house. It played for a few seconds and then stopped. Different music started and continued. Directly in front of her, an open door revealed a descending staircase. She heard muffled footsteps going upward and she realized the kitchen stairs were underneath the stairs up to the second floor.

If that was him…

Kildeere stood and walked as quickly as she could while remaining silent to the open stairs. She did not pause but walked down them, trying to keep her work boots from clopping on the wooden stairs. It sounded like she was jumping from stair to stair.

At the bottom, she looked to her left as if forced to do so. Jackie Flinthill lay on the floor on his side. He was unconscious with his hands bound behind him and his ankles restrained by large zip ties. To one side was a stack of rolls of clear polyethylene plastic whose purpose she did not know.

"Shit," Kildeere whispered as she stepped to the boy. Jackie was breathing and that was enough. She shook him lightly but he did not respond. She picked the boy up and slung him over her left shoulder. Holding his dangling legs with her arm, the narrow stairs force her to press her right hand and the hammer it held slightly behind her leg. Even so, her shoulder rubbed against the wall as she tried to keep Jackie from striking the other wall. She took the stairs two at a time, expecting to hear a shout or maybe a shot with each step.

Finding a man standing in front of the kitchen door almost seemed anticlimactic.

Chapter 29: Raven talked to a woman

He was White, heavy-set, dressed like he was some kind of professional with a white shirt and a bright blue tie. His slacks, held up by a thin leather belt, were sharply pressed and his black shoes reflected the overhead light like mirrors.

He had thinning blonde hair losing its battle to halt his receding hair line. His eyes were squinting a little, as if he needed glasses but didn't like to wear them. His nose was strong as if designed to emphasize his forward advance. But his mouth was fleshy, soft, and made his whole face appear weak.

He smiled as if entertained, like he had just heard a series of very funny jokes and now was waiting for the topper, the comedian's perfect closer guaranteed to bring the house down.

Or kill everyone. He had a gun, some kind of black automatic pistol with a short barrel. He held it with one hand and waved it back and forth in small circles maybe just to have something to do.

"Turn around," he said, in a soft, amused voice. "Take him back where you found him."

He was overjoyed. The Black woman was not a problem, but an opportunity. That cliché of the meme era was magnificently true. He saw her eyes look at his gun and she seemed so helpless as she lowered her head in defeat.

"You followed me all this way. All for nothing." It was petty to bait her, he knew, but he liked doing it, something he learned from the women he had taken in New Jersey. It just added to it all. "Turn around and back down the stairs."

Head down, she turned slowly, obviously afraid of his pistol. She would be even more afraid if she knew he never had to fire it. Suffocation by wrapped, plastic sheeting drew everything out.

As she slowly turned, he got a good look at the boy. The little bastard was still out and still breathing. Good. He had questions that his mission required answering.

She was moving too slow. Obviously reluctant to go into the basement. He stepped forward and reached out and pushed her shoulder.

Kildeere spun, pivoting in the direction of the push, and her right hand, still gripping the ridiculous hammer, whipped out in a savage backhand. She missed.

He jerked his head back and something almost whistled under his chin. He stepped back too quickly and lost his balance. He threw his hands out to steady himself and saw she was stepping towards him.

Kildeere almost closed her eyes as she missed the killer; she knew her failure meant death to her and Jackie. The worst emotions she had ever had, worse than the bridge, worse than all her years of fear, exploded within her even as her failed blow forced her to take a staggering step for balance towards him. She saw triumph flash onto his face and she swung again, part of her knowing her second try would be too late, even if she whipped the hammer at his smiling face with more force than she had ever struck a stone, even as she swung with her entire body behind it.

"Fuck!" he yelled and swung his pistol at her. He saw, for the second time that day, his pistol hit the side of her head but before he could feel the joy, his face exploded in pain he had never known before.

She knew why her face was on the linoleum floor of the kitchen. It was like someone was explaining it to her as her awareness came back. Now both sides of her head hurt, especially the side that hadn't before.

A great weight pressed her down and she couldn't seem to raise her head to look around.

"It's important that you do."

Someone was still explaining things to her, which was very strange, as she was certain the man she had faced was not going to explain anything at all to her and Jackie; killing was for him its own explanation. And Jackie, well…

Jackie was laying on top of her. How that had happened seemed to be a puzzle she was incapable of solving.

Kildeere heard a groan as she opened her eyes. The groan came from the White man. He was on the floor, on his back, both hands covering his face. Everything about him seemed covered in blood. She looked to one side and saw, just beyond Raven's black talons, her hammer.

Raven?

Impossible.

A series of short calls, high pitched but raspy, seemed to argue otherwise.

"Get up."

"Stop talking to me," she said to Raven as she slowly rolled to one side, easing Jackie off her. "You're freaking me out."

She lowered her head, resting on the side of least pain. Kildeere still saw the hammer but no longer could see talons.

Kildeere pushed herself up. Everything that wasn't her head hurt. Her head felt something beyond hurt. Her breath came out in gasps, once almost a sob, but she cut it off and forced herself up.

She managed to get to her hands and knees. Then she moved to the hammer. Each limb had to be ordered separately. The killer was still moaning and Kildeere really wished he would stop it. The distraction was making it hard to move. Even remember why she was moving.

Her hand came down on the hammer and suddenly everything became clear. She looked around. For a moment, the movement accomplished nothing more than getting blood to slowly run into an eye. She looked down. The floor was covered in blood; smears and spattered drops were everywhere.

She looked back at the killer. He still groaned, still covering his face with his hands. Then he opened one eye which rolled toward her. It widened and a hand left his face and smacked the floor, reaching for something.

Kildeere saw what it was; his pistol. His leg laid on it, covering all but the grip. She crawled to him and his eye went wider while his breathing, bubbling up through his remaining hand, forced droplets of blood into the air. His hand moved clumsily as he tried to grasp the pistol and pull it free of his bulk. She shoved her hand past his and jerked the pistol free.

"Excuse me," she said, and then wondered why.

She raised herself to her knees and sat on her heels. In one hand, she held the pistol. In the other was her hammer. Kildeere looked at the killer. Blood masked the lower part of his face and seeped through his fingers. He raised one hand in the waving motion it had made when it held the gun and she saw what the hammer had done when she had swung it the second time. It was hard to be sure what remained. Maybe his nose and upper mouth were gone, maybe more, maybe less. It was all bloody and broken, like the remains of a shattered battlefield just evacuated by a defeated army.

"Maybe he has another gun."

"Kind of an obvious observation," she said and began patting the man down. His hand tried to grab her arm. She bent one of its fingers back until he released her. She found nothing else in her search except, in a bulging back pocket, an opened plastic bag of long zip ties. What the hell?

Kildeere looked at the pistol. A little lever on the side was down, sort of aiming at the trigger, and had revealed a red dot. The safety was off. She looked at the man, now with both hands pressed against his face. If that was what a little hammer could do, she wondered what would happen if she put the muzzle against his forehead and pulled the trigger.

"Enough."

"I told you," she said to Raven, still looking at the man who wanted to kill her, "you're freaking me out." Kildeere looked around but there were no birds in the kitchen. She took another look at the killer and then slapped his hand.

"Pay attention," she said and leaned over him. His eyes followed her and they were wide with terror. Fine. "I'm going to roll you over. Then I'm going to tie your ankles and hands together, then I'm leaving with the boy because I think you gave him something and he needs a hospital. If you fuck with me, I will burn your house down." Kildeere let the words sink in. "With you in it. Look at me, child-killer. Do you see any reason to doubt what I am saying?"

It seemed like several days passed before, with his eyes locked on hers, he slowly moved his head back and forth.

He didn't resist when she rolled him over, though he groaned. The ties were about two feet long and she used multiple ties to secure his crossed ankles, tightening them as much as she could. When he stirred, she put the muzzle of the pistol about where she thought his anus might be and pushed. He stopped moving.

His fat wrists could not be brought together, so she used a pair of ties on each wrist. Then she connected them with another pair.

She stood up and looked around the kitchen. She saw what she wanted and went over to a block of wood holding several knives and took one, pausing to grab a dish towel. She folded it over and lifted the man's head by its hair.

"A weave?" She shook her head. "Vanity." She put the towel under his face and let go of his hair. No sense letting him die by drowning in his own blood.

Kildeere went to Jackie and freed his hands and feet. Then she pushed the little lever on the pistol up until the red dot was covered and shoved it into her pocket.

She stuck the handle of the hammer in another pocket, wiped at some blood getting into her eye, and then reached down and picked up Jackie Flinthill. Cradling him in her arms, Kildeere carried him through the house, across the porch, and down the driveway to her car, getting there as Ellen Parker and her friends arrived. She carried him all that way, in spite of everything, and did it easily.

Morrigan Kildeere had always been a strong person.

Chapter 30: Boiled eggs and a witch's raven

Chernov and Janowski arrived a moment after Ellen Parker. Janowski stayed to keep an eye on the bound man while Chernov took Kildeere and Jackie to the emergency room of Brandywine Hospital.

The cards, now shuffled, were dealt out in a pattern that might be mistaken for random.

An ambulance took the killer away and task force forensics people went over the house in detail, especially the basement. Janowski, sitting on the front porch of a house belonging to a killer of children and women, not thinking of much except that things appeared to have worked themselves out. He hoped he'd be able to tell his son all about it when he came home to visit from the Army, maybe over Christmas… Then he figured something out, a flash of understanding, a hunch, that what had happened on a Philadelphia bridge six years ago was more than someone having too much to drink. He stood up and brushed his hands off. Michael Janowski, Corporal, New Joyton Police Department, decided to do a little follow-up on his hunch because that is what good officers of the law do.

Bobby Flynn was interviewed by every police department and prosecutor within a hundred miles and a few even further away, or so it seemed. It took him a while to realize that he was being checked out as a potential target for prosecution as well as an information source. A friend told him to get a lawyer but, oddly in these times, he trusted the judicial system. Even more oddly, nothing bad happened. While Saint Barnabas went through a convulsion that seemed to never end as all of the story came out, he looked for another job and wrote a book. Of the several books about the red ribbon murders, his made the most money, enough that he left his job. He wrote two books about the immigrant experience, interviewing many families, including his own. Both did well among sociology academics. He took an administrative job in one of the many colleges around Philadelphia and continued to write.

His supervisor approached James Hardy by phone and tried to get him to return to work as a consultant. James said he'd think about, waited two days, and called the supervisor back. He said he didn't think he'd fit in any more, thanked him for the offer, and hung up. Terry Ridgway, his friend from work, suggested he contact Bill Monahue, who was still trying to send him email. James thanked him and did. Three weeks later, James moved to the suburbs of Baltimore. Three months after that, he was designing "doc in the box" community care clinics in South Asia.

It was there that Terrence, now working for a hospital in Philadelphia, told him via Skype Mrs. Alice North, who everyone knew, but not really, had accumulated shares in the company and organized other shareholders, using some documents she had obtained from an anonymous source, to expose phony accounting practices. The storm that followed caused company stock to plummet – Mrs. North and her friends bought up every share they could and the old company board vanished over a busy weekend.

James was surprised by the news and, after thinking about it, sent Ellen Parker an email – he was a regular correspondent with her; she seemed fascinated by his adventures – that just said, "Thank you."

Ellen knew the rainy night it referred to.

The task force wound down, releasing all the officers who had participated in investigating the killings in Pennsylvania. At the last staff briefing, all the non-FBI people came in their various uniforms. Special Agent Karen Deevers walked to the front of the room and briefly summarized what was going to happen with all the various prosecutors in at least two states. Then she held up a cell phone in an evidence bag.

"It is his," she said, and no one needed telling who "he" was. "We knew where the boys were because we found them or he told us. But he kept a record, the GPS coordinates, of every woman in New Jersey he killed and buried. He has nothing left to bargain with. We have it all, his DNA, his finger prints, the drugs, the plastic sheeting, all of it. He's done."

There was tentative applause that grew larger and sustained. When it stopped, Deevers put the phone down on the podium and picked up another evidence bag.

"He was on a mission from God to gain a clean slate, to bring back this." She raised the bag a little higher. A small red thumb drive was in it. "I know most of you haven't seen this but you all have heard about it. We've sent copies to every prosecutor, state and federal, working on this issue." She paused. "I don't think God makes those kinds of deals. I hope someday he gets that explained to him."

Agent Brown stood in front of them, looking from face to face. As he did, the women and men stood. When they were all on their feet, he came to the FBI equivalent of a military stance and said, "Thank you."

The family of Marc Gramm, the other surviving Sneaky Snake from the raid on Saint Barnabas, was briefed by Sergeant Elizabeth Chernov, New Joyton Police Department, as one of her last activities in the task force. Between the tears and confusion in understanding what had happened, the parents decided not telling their son would be the best thing to do. Naturally, he learned all about it with the news media chatter about the "red ribbon killer" and was a little freaked by it. His parents also misunderstood what Chernov told them about Jackie and thought he hadn't told the killer Marc's name despite some unspecified torture. They drove to his house to thank him and brought Marc along. While they were talking with Virginia Flinthill, Marc and Jackie went to Jackie's room and played video games because that's what boys do when the world seems suddenly too large to comprehend. They played online games together later on, but both dropped out of the Sneaky Snakes.

Ellen Parker walked into her living room one morning and realized that Robert Blasingame wasn't in it. After a moment, she realized what she was feeling was loss. After another moment, after another day, she called him.

There were things about Robert's past she would probably never know. And that was all right, after all. Maybe all that counted was what she knew now. When she called, he answered immediately, almost as if he was waiting for her.

She never thought that strange.

For her stitches, the ER staff shaved Morrigan Kildeere's temples. She saw the patches in a mirror a nurse held and asked the nurse to "even them up, please." The nurse understood and the doctor who was going to do the stitching smiled and stood back.

She didn't let them throw her sodden, black bandana into the Contaminated can. She would have to wash it twice to get all the stains out but, for a reason could not say, she did not want it discarded.

When Kildeere was released, Ellen Parker was there and drove her home – there was some confusion about her car but a few days later the police would take her to it.

"Welcome home," Ellen said and grinned. Kildeere looked at her house and studio and, for a moment, said nothing.

"I don't know why," she said, "but I am scared to death." She turned and looked at Ellen with eyes tear-filled. "Do you have to go someplace?" Ellen shook her head.

Kildeere walked through her studio; Ellen walked with her. The Black woman touched the stone and metal and tools as if they were fragile or belonged to someone else. She stepped outside and looked at her house. There was nothing to be seen.

She took Ellen inside and fixed tea.

"I'm out of coffee," she explained.

"No time for shopping?" Ellen asked innocently and Kildeere laughed for a moment. Then she cried and Ellen held her.

After they sat down, there was silence and Morrigan did not look at Ellen. Finally, she sighed.

"I read your articles," she said. "The ones about the women in the military. And about Doctor John." She took a sip, still not looking at Ellen. "They, you, were in bad shape afterwards."

"I was a mess," Ellen said.

"You got through it."

"Not alone. Friends, a really good counselor, my job."

"I don't think I have many friends."

"You've got one I know of."

Morrigan looked at Ellen from the corner of her eye and almost imperceptibly nodded.

"May need a shrink. I've been messed up for a while."

"I'll leave you her name and number. She's pretty good."

"Is she one of the therapists you interviewed for the military women article?"

"Yes."

"Those shrinks seemed like they weren't idiots."

"They weren't."

"Good, because I'm idiot enough for two."

"Isn't that a requirement when you become an artist?" Ellen asked tentatively, saying the kind of thing one might to a new friend.

"It's in the fine print on our guild cards."

Later, Morrigan walked Ellen out to her car.

"You didn't ask me for an interview. What kind of reporter are you?"

"I usually just make everything up anyway, so it doesn't matter." Ellen opened her car door. "I'm not writing this one up. Not part of it, anyway. Too close to some of the participants. Just covering the investigation and the prosecutorial work, the stuff on the network. Is that what you want, to be interviewed?"

"God, no."

Both women laughed but Ellen suddenly stopped, her expression serious as she looked over Morrigan's shoulder.

"Well…"

Morrigan turned. Raven stood on the side porch roof, watching the two women for a moment before throwing its chest out.

"I wondered where he went," Morrigan said.

Raven made kind of a loud cluck, several close together, sounding like hollow bamboo staves struck together.

"What does that mean?"

"I think it means Raven's a she," Morrigan said. "I think that's a sound a female raven might make. But she might just be jerking our chains and Raven's a he. I'm not sure."

"It's that kind of world," Ellen said. She got into her car and drove away, waving.

After the return of her car, Morrigan went to a hair dresser and had the shaven parts of her head extended, turning the rest of her hair into a limp Mohawk. Then she had that hair turned into cornrows with gold beads, making no effort to hide the stitches. It was a kind of celebration, she would have answered if anyone asked about it, but no one did.

Janowski drove down the road to Morrigan Kildeere's home and felt a little tired – Philadelphia traffic could do that to you. He never understood how people could put up with it for an hour each way commuting to and from work. Once in a blue moon was enough for him. He drove his personal vehicle, the green Ford F-150 with the bumper stickers saying he was a proud parent of a Soldier and commenting that his dog was smarter than your honor student, and wore civilian attire. He had his pistol but it was key locked in a steel box bolted to the truck deck under the passenger seat.

He did not know if Morrigan Kildeere would be at home but he guessed right; as he turned into her driveway, she stuck her head out through the sliding doors. Janowski raised a hand in greeting but she did nothing in reply.

Maybe she thinks I'm a reporter – bet she's had to talk to a crowd of them. Then he smiled.

Maybe she thinks I'm a cop – bet she's had to talk to a crowd of them, too.

He stopped the truck and then got out a little slowly, trying not to appear aggressive.

"Afternoon, Ms. Kildeere," he called. "You remember me. Michael Janowski."

"Good afternoon, Officer Janowski," she said. He saw she looked a lot better than when he had helped load her and the Flinthill boy into an ambulance. As he walked up to her, she took off gloves and lifted a red bandana from her head.

"Not official, ma'am. Not at all. You can call me whatever you want."

"What can I do for you, Officer Janowski?" She was guarded and looked tense. Well, no one could blame her for that.

"Wanted to talk about something with you," he said. "Just some things I was thinking about, things I looked at." He looked to his right, smiled, and shook his head. "I remember the first time I saw your tower. I thought that would be something I'd see in a nightmare or something. Have to say, I still haven't figured it out, but it does seem to be in touch with the times."

"Officer Janowski," Kildeere said slowly, "Michael, would you like some local root beer?"

"I would, ma'am. That sounds great."

He followed her to the side porch. Her pet raven was gone. She gestured and he took a seat on an old, wooden chair. In a moment, she returned with a cold bottle and handed it to him.

"Thank you, ma'am."

"Michael, you can call me anything but 'ma'am.'"

"That's right, that's what you told us, and I forgot. I apologize."

Kildeere just waved a hand and took a sip from her bottle.

"What brought you all the way from New Joyton, Michael?"

"Philadelphia. I was in Philadelphia. Had to check a couple of things. I've had this hunch for a while, mostly right after we got to you and Jackie. By the way, you did some great work with all that. Fantastic work." He held up his bottle as if offering a toast and took a sip. Kildeere did the same.

"You were working on your day off, chasing down a hunch?"

"It was, it is, all hypothetical. Nothing solid. But I had to figure it out. Gnawed at me." He took a sip. "Let me tell you about it. I think it might be, I don't know, important to hear about."

"Really?"

"Hypothetical." He took another sip and carefully put the bottle on the porch floor. Then he looked at Kildeere.

"Once upon a time," he said, "there was this very talented woman who everyone said was going to be a superstar. The man supposedly helping her, well, he had a very large reputation as a bully, maybe even a rapist. One night he got drunk and fell into the river and was found dead downstream from the bridge he had been on. What was weird was the talented woman, who had to know, sooner or later, that this jerk was someone she ought to get the hell away from, that woman kept like a monument to the dead man. Newspaper clippings, stuff printed from the internet. Almost like a shrine." He reached down and picked up his bottle. He took a sip and studied Kildeere's expression. She showed nothing.

"Another weird thing was the woman almost dropped out of sight even though she'd was just on the edge of being a superstar. She took herself out of contention. Boom, just like that, overnight. She's free of the bully, why doesn't she grab the brass ring and ride off into the sunset or whatever it is you do with brass rings?" He shook his head. "Didn't make any sense to a middle-aged cop who bumped into these jigsaw pieces. He tried to make it fit but couldn't, except one way."

"Maybe the jerk had some help going over the bridge. Maybe he did something a jerk would do, like get drunk and put some demands on our talented woman. And when she said no, that wasn't good enough, and in the middle of the night on a very dark bridge, he went after her. But she, maybe she wasn't the push-over he thought. Maybe life made her as hard as she needed to be, kind of like that iron and stone she beat up." He shrugged.

"Self-defense; it would be ugly, but she'd probably have bruises or something. Bolster her case if the law got involved. But what if it started as self-defense but then she, maybe at least in her own mind, went too far.

Maybe she didn't just knock him down. Maybe she threw his ass in the river. Or maybe the coroner's report that he had a shattered forearm was because she was strong enough to do that to keep him from staying on the bridge. In he goes."

Kildeere felt her stomach twist but still she showed nothing, her control freezing her in place.

There was a rustle above them and then a shadow swooped down and the raven landed on the edge of the porch, pretending the two humans weren't there. Janowski smiled at it and then turned back to Kildeere.

"Philly P.D., they do their measurements. They know all about the currents in the Schuylkill River, they calculate from where he was found to the bridge they knew he would take and decided he went over at such and such a spot." He finished his soda and put the bottle down.

"They got it wrong, as it happens. If you use the current averages, they were dead on. But the river was running a little high that night from rain 'way upstream. Someone goofed at a thing they usually don't goof and didn't factor that in. If you do, then the bully went over the bridge a lot closer to its end."

"That might explain why our almost a superstar dropped out of sight. She didn't want any police to notice her and wonder what really happened that night, find their error, and look for evidence in the right spot. So low, low profile. But then some child killer shows up and she has to choose between, well, you know." He shook his head.

"Yep, hypothetically, I think keeping out of sight of the law was a part of it, but only a part of it. I think the biggest thing was, she killed someone. Accident, self-defense, deliberate, whatever. In the movies, the scales are cardboard simple. But in real life, that's not the way it is. Some people, they take a life, they bury their own, maybe thinking they don't really deserve one." He paused.

Kildeere's tension eased a little, though she did not know why. Was it because someone knew?

"Maybe all of this is a part of files and pictures and papers stored in a basement. Maybe some dumb, old cop stumbled into some of this, thinking about some of this, because his son, his boy, got back from his third tour in the sandbox and is dealing with, is trying to deal with, taking someone's life. The dumb cop, a guy whose son is hurting, has tried to think really hard about these things and justice and right and wrong and what you do with it all. Just a dumb cop who was primed to pay attention to some things."

"This cop had to go look, of course, at stuff he didn't have a warrant for. Saw things that he didn't really understand. And then, when he thought he put it all together, thought maybe the superstar had done something on that bridge I was telling you about, he had to go and look at it. All of it. All the railings, east and west. He's dumb, but thorough." He smiled, almost to himself.

"The superstar might have thought she left some kind of trace on the bridge. Six years after, she was still trying to duck out of sight. What could possibly be left after six years? Not blood or fabric. He remembered a circle the superstar had drawn on an old newspaper picture and looked there really hard. Superstar spent six years hiding from something. So much fear, so much punishment." The smile was gone.

"But when a boy got in trouble, about the worst trouble there was, without even looking at the bridge, just because it was the right thing to do, she went after him." Janowski slowly shook his head. "There is something in the water of this county. My sergeant keeps telling me that."

Janowski looked at the raven who looked back and stood very still. Janowski slowly stood and lightly held up the fingers of one hand as Kildeere started to her feet.

"All hypothetical. My opinion, this business of trying to balance scales by hiding wouldn't ever be enough. Person would have to do something significant, something with meaning outside of herself, for someone other than herself. I don't know, maybe risk her own life to save the life of a little boy and to hell with the low profile. Something like that might do it." He paused and took his sunglasses ought of his shirt pocket. As he put them on, he said, "I really hope it does." He looked at the raven again and smiled.

"That is one damned big bird," he said. Janowski looked at Kildeere, his eyes hidden. "I thank you all for the root beer. It was great. You take care, now." He threw a half salute toward Kildeere and waved at Raven.

Then Janowski was in his truck and gone. Whenever he thought about it afterwards, he would nod to himself and think that things were all right. The best cops have a sense of justice at least as large as their sense of order.

Morrigan Kildeere sat on the porch and watched a damned big bird prance around and amuse itself. After a few minutes, she talked to the raven, explaining things, putting pieces together. Raven listened, or didn't, but hung around when she went into the kitchen and brought back hardboiled eggs. While she talked, Raven finished the eggs and then tried to reduce the shells to dust.

They both got something done.

A few days later, a broad-shouldered Black woman with beaded cornrows got off a commuter train arriving at 30th Street Station. She wore serious work boots and a Honda motorcycle t-shirt under a flannel shirt with its sleeves rolled up. Her temples were shaved, revealing stitches on both. She walked with strong strides out the east doors of the station and crossed the street to the bridge over the Schuylkill River. She went to a place on the south side of the bridge and looked at the box-steel railing. She walked the length of it, from support pillar to support pillar, running her hand along it, feeling how smooth it was, without a dent or even a paint chip anywhere on it. Perhaps she was some sort of architectural engineer or a safety inspector. Whatever she was, she calmly evaluated everything and then spent some time leaning against the railing and just watched the river go by as if it was something she enjoyed. Then she turned and walked back into the station and then rode the train home.

Virginia Flinthill called her several times, but it was a few days before Morrigan had a new phone. Once she did, Ginny called daily thanking her for saving her son, asking about her health, thanking her, and talking about Jackie. She spent a lot of time crying and it occurred to Morrigan that the single mother might not have a lot of people to talk to, something Morrigan had no trouble understanding.

"He doesn't go out of the house," Ginny said. "Not even to fly his drone."

"Do you think he would be up for visiting me?"

"I suggested it. I should have asked you but I suggested it without thinking. He didn't."

"What if I suggest it? Or you bring him over?"

"Like when you found his drone?"

"Right."

"I... He's thinking he's helpless. You know?"

"I hear you."

"I'd like to see him take his own steps."

"That makes sense. He doesn't have a drone to go find. Something like that, though?"

"Yes, something like that." Ginny was silent for a moment. "After his father died, he retreated just like he's doing now. His online friends, some of whom were local boys, you know. Their absence... It helped him to have them. He's got a friend, Marc, but he's not really doing anything with him.

"Would he help Raven?"

"That big bird of yours? I don't know. He talked about him a lot but I haven't heard him say anything about it since everything."

"Maybe tell him you talked with me and I mentioned Raven seemed to be looking for someone. See what he does with that."

"Well, maybe it will get him out of the house," she said but the doubt was obvious.

"If it works, give me a yell. I'll try to be here."

"OK."

When the call came, Morrigan was in her studio, black bandana tied around her head and bunching the beaded cornrows on her neck.

"Good news," she said. "But the bird's not here."

"That's all right," Ginny said. "He's doing something. On his bike, be there in a few."

Morrigan walked across her front yard and stood at the corner of the fence. In a few minutes, she could just make out the boy on his bicycle. She went to the kitchen and got two bottles of local root beer out and a small bowl of shelled hard-boiled eggs. She took them out to the side porch and sat in a wooden chair and waited.

Jackie pedaled into the driveway and leaned his bike against the fence. He looked around before he saw Morrigan. He smiled as if embarrassed.

He came through the gate and walked over to Morrigan. He did not sit down and she thought he was trying to say something. She stood when he held out his hand.

"Thank you," he said. He shook her hand, his expression serious, and Morrigan glimpsed what he would look like as a man and it was heart breaking.

"You are most welcome," she said. "Did your mother tell you to say that?"

"No. I wanted to say it." He said it as naturally as saying the sky was blue.

Morrigan sat down, fighting down an urge to cry, and motioned at a chair. Jackie sat in it. She handed him a root beer.

"I recall you like these."

"I do," he said and took a big gulp that almost caused the bottle to overflow. "Where's Raven?"

"Don't know. She was here yesterday but she hasn't come by this morning."

"He's a 'she'?"

"Made a sound that female ravens make, I think. I listened to a sound online, you know?" Jackie nodded and took a conservative sip. "It's a kind of call, maybe like advertising."

"I like your hair. Are those bells?"

"No, they're beads. But they do clink together when I don't have the bandana on."

"You have it on now," he said. "Could you take it off?"

"Well," Morrigan said, drawing it out, "it will show my stitches. I don't want to freak you out."

"You have stitches? Can I see?"

Morrigan untied the black bandana and lowered it as the beads clicked together and her hair came down in thin streams around her neck.

"Did he do that?" Jackie looked like he had stopped breathing.

"He did, twice. See?" She turned her head and pointed at them. Then she turned and looked into his eyes. "But it is all right. I am fine, and so are you, Jackie."

"I thought I was coming to help you, that's what he said, he said you were hurt, and I ran to you." There were tears in the boy's eyes.

"That's what friends do, they come for each other. When he took you away, I came for you, when you were hurt, I ran to you as fast as my car would go. Just like you."

"You could do that. You could. He fooled me. He made me sick. He was going to hurt me, kill me, they said." He shook his head. "You're stronger. Stronger than me. You're the strongest person I know."

Tears came from Morrigan's eyes and she did nothing to stop them.

"He was afraid of us," she said. "He had to fool you. If you'd known what he was doing you would have gone for help and that would have been it for him. He made you sick, tied you up, to keep you helpless. No one does all that to someone they're not afraid of. Does that make sense?"

"Kind of," he said. He wiped at his eyes. "Is that why he hit you?"

"Kind of."

"Mom said you fought him to protect me."

"To protect both of us, because I really didn't like him, I didn't like what he did to my friend, and I didn't like what he wanted to do to me."

"She said you hurt him pretty bad."

"I tried really hard."

"What did you do?"

"I broke his nose and knocked out some of his teeth." That was enough detail, she thought.

"Wow. That's pretty cool."

"I was pretty angry."

"I'm sorry I didn't save you."

"Listen, Jackie. Friends don't keep score like that. When a friend needs you, you come. You came to help me, right?" The boy nodded. She nodded back. "That's what a friend does. Then it was my turn." She smiled. "I still managed to get hit in the head again."

"Does it hurt?"

"No. Not now. How are you feeling?"

"I'm all right." He paused. "I've been afraid to go outside."

"I know what you mean. I couldn't go into my studio by myself for a while. It was like I needed to learn things were all right."

Jackie nodded. Then he looked at the woman.

"You said we were friends."

"We are, aren't we?"

"Yes, ma'am." He grinned and took a drink.

"What's so funny?"

"Raven snuck up on a witch."

Morrigan turned and looked at Raven. She, or he, looked into her eyes with her, or his, right eye, then the left, and then, over a beak black as all the thoughts of midnight, with both eyes.

"I wondered where you were," she said. Morrigan looked at Jackie. "Did you just call me a witch?"

"It's all right," the boy said as he fragmented a boiled egg to throw to Raven. "All my best friends are witches."

Also by Steven M. Silver

With Susan Rogers, Ph.D. *Light in the heart of darkness: EMDR and the treatment of war and terrorism survivors.* Norton.

Poetry

American Travelers
Hot Chrome, Smooth Leather, and a Red Bandanna
Victor Echo Zero Five

Fiction

The Wild Geese Saga
Mercenary's Heart
Mercenary's Honor
Mercenary's Code
Mercenary's Logic
Mercenary's Destiny
Mercenary's Soldiers
Mercenary's Redemption
Mercenary's Courage
Mercenary's Peace
Mercenary's Justice
Mercenary's Humanity
Mercenary's Promise

The Ellen Parker Series
A Dangerous Man
Killers
Woman on the Wire
Hidden Things

Steven M. Silver

Child in the Dark
The Boy Killer and the Woman Who Talked to a Raven

www.ingramcontent.com/pod-product-compliance
Lightning Source LLC
Chambersburg PA
CBHW070634260626
47161CB00007B/2702